TO M
BE

DEAD END

By

Jon Schafer

Book Four of The Dead Series

For Denise Paz

Cover Design by: Victor L. Castro Jr
You can contact him at originalgilgamesh@yahoo.com

Special Thanks to:
Susan Herkness for her mad editing skills.
https://www.facebook.com/susan.herkness and
all those that donated $$$ to their favorite charity in exchange for being in this book: Z-Girl Lisa and Z-Girl's Everything Zombie Apocalypse, Jennifer Bosquez-Morales, Lena Begnaud, Megan Begnaud, Ethan Begnaud, and Rick Rife (AKA Commander Rick Styles)
And a big shout out to Pepper Akerfelds who gave her owner, Džūlija Akerfelds so much crap that she finally coughed up the money. Go Pep...

Visit Jon Schafer's website at http://www.jonscatbooks.com
Friend him on Facebook at http://www.facebook.com/jon.schafer.94
Watch the promo video for The Dead Series on YouTube at http://www.youtube.com/watch?v=e0i5CF9QbWY

Dead End: A point beyond which no movement or progress can be made; an impasse.

CHAPTER ONE

The Happy Hallow Insane Asylum:

The fingernails of the dead made a screeching noise as they were raked down the aluminum storm panels covering the first floor windows. The constant, nerve racking din echoed through the first floor, making the same sound as if they were being dragged across a chalkboard. This interminable noise was intermixed with thumping and banging as hundreds of animated corpses tried to pound their way through the barricades on the windows and doors. Above it all, the whine of over a thousand dead voices cried out as they fought to bust inside to tear apart and devour the flesh of the living.

Steve Wendell heard none of it as he looked down at the covered body of Mary lying on the couch. A large stain had soaked through the afghan he'd used to cover her, making a brownish-red blotch at her midsection. Leading down from this, a red trail traced where her blood had run to drip onto the floor and slowly congeal and form a tacky looking puddle. This was a dark reminder that in a world where the dead had come back to life to feed on the living, she had died from a gunshot wound rather than at the teeth and nails of the walking corpses that populated the earth. Shaking his head in regret as a single tear emerged from his eye and flowed down his cheek, he knew that the scene in front of him would be burned into his memory forever.

Anger flowed through him at the thought of Sean, the person who had murdered Mary. The weasel had panicked at the sight of the dead mobbing the fence surrounding the insane asylum and had attempted to flee in one of the minivans they were going to use to escape. When Mary tried to stop him, he shot her and rammed the gate, letting the dead flood into their compound and ruining their plans to take a majority of the dead out with dynamite and then make a break for it. After what was left of the group retreated into the mansion, Steve had tried to save Mary, but it was hopeless. She ended up being one more casualty in their fight to survive. They had lost so many people that their faces and names should only be a blur to him, but he remembered every one of them.

Shaking off his anger and sorrow, Steve turned and headed for the roof, his mind working overtime on how to escape. They were surrounded by over a thousand dead, with tens of thousands more heading directly toward them, so it wasn't looking good for the home team. This would be his third trip to assess the situation.

His first plan was to for them to use their rifles and pistols to thin out as many of the dead as possible before making a break for the remaining vehicles still parked in front of the mansion. After lining everyone up along the south side of the mansion roof, they fired into the mass of Zs pushing up against the side of the building. With seven rifles pouring fire down into the mass of dead, it was a turkey shoot. The animated corpses fell like tenpins under the onslaught of lead. At first elated by his success, Steve saw something that caused him make everyone cease fire.

They were creating a ramp of flesh for the Zs to get into the second floor windows.

As the dead fell, the ones behind them stepped onto their bodies to get as close to the food as possible. When these were shot in the head, others climbed on top of them. In just a few minutes, the morbid pile had reached three feet in height. Judging by the amount of dead they would have to kill to clear the area, Steve realized that they would only dispose of half of them before the rest could get in through the second floor windows.

Next, they tried to attract as many of the dead as possible to the north side of the mansion. With less Zs to deal with, they could get rid of the remaining ones and make a run for it. They were successful in getting most of them away from the front of the building, but as soon as they went back to the south side and opened fire, the dead returned. Whether they were attracted to the gunfire or the presence of food, no one knew. In the past, they seemed to avoid weapons, but with the huge number in this group, and more swarming into the compound by the minute, this seemed to make their urge to feed overcome their instinct for self-preservation.

The dead were getting aggravated at their presence, so everyone left the roof until they could come up with a new plan. While some of them went to find something to eat and others to rest, Steve went down to pay his last respects to Mary and to try to figure out where he had failed and caused her death.

He came up blank.

He knew there was something he could have done, or not done, to save Mary, but he couldn't figure out what it was. Shaking his feelings of failure off, his thoughts turned to the problem facing the living as he headed up the stairs to the second floor. Mulling over what would happen when the huge herd of the dead hit them from the east, he knew that the tens of thousands of bodies pushing up against the walls of the building would eventually burst them and the dead would flood in. There had to be a way out, he just needed to figure out what it was. He was so wrapped up in coming up with an escape plan that he almost ran into the group of people standing at the top of the stairs.

Startled at their sudden presence, he raised his rifle to fire. Recognizing who it was, his finger tightened on the trigger for a brief second before relaxing. Unable to hide the disgust in his voice, he asked, "What the fuck do you all want now?"

Physically taken aback by this, it took a moment for the spokeswoman for the others to recover and say, "We want to help." She hesitated, and then added, "We want to fight."

Now it was Steve's turn to take a step back.

Slowly, he appraised the group. He could see they looked scared, but who didn't? If there was a mirror around, he knew he'd look like a long-tailed cat in a room full of rocking chairs. Dwelling on this, he realized that out of his whole group, only Tick-Tock never seemed to show fear. Whether he was facing a horde of the dead or sitting down to dinner, the ex disc-jockey always appeared to have a half smile on his face, as if this were something he'd been looking forward to all day.

Wondering if his friend might be a sociopath, Steve made a mental note to ask him.

Turning his attention back to the others, he asked, "How many of you are willing to use a weapon?"

All hands were raised followed by numerous calls of, "I will," "I want to learn," and "I'm in."

Not really shocked that this was happening, but regretting that it hadn't happened earlier, Steve had known all along that sooner or later the survival instinct would kick in with these people. It was only a matter of time until they saw that they would have to fight to save their own lives. When he'd first boarded The Battleship Texas, he'd seen how Denise had treated the others so poorly but had said nothing. The others needed to learn that there was no one out there to save them and that they needed to take personal responsibility for themselves. Some people caught on to this quickly, but others needed to go through a really life threatening event to understand this.

Being surrounded by thousands of the living dead with no way out seemed to be the catalyst they needed, Steve thought to himself.

Instead of berating the group for taking so long to come around, he asked, "Is this everyone from your group?"

A voice from in back replied quietly, "All ten of us. Everyone who's left." Steve started to say something, but was cut off by the same voice saying slightly louder and stronger, "We didn't really realize how bad things were. We were scared. It was confusing at first, but now we realize we were following Sean and he was..." The voice trailed off before regaining strength to continue, "Things are different now. The old way we did things are gone. I want to apologize for being a burden, but I'm ready to do my part now."

More voices chimed in agreement to this.

"The past is the past," Steve told them. "If you're really going to step up, then you need to do a few things."

He was cut off by the spokeswoman interjecting, "Like if you tell us to do something, we do it. Just like you told us after we froze up at the railroad bridge. Only now, we're ready to do it."

The voice from the back added, "And we're also going to keep up. No more letting you carry our weight. We know that if we fall behind or run off that we're on our own."

Steve nodded as the spokeswoman said with a half-laugh, "And just to let you know, we got together in a committee and decided that there are no more committees except on how to survive."

Slightly elated by the turn around in the others, but knowing that even with the added firepower their chances were still slim, Steve said, "I've got to get you organized and armed, but I've got a lot going on right now so that's going to take a while." Stopping for a moment to gather his thoughts, he continued, "For right now, I want you all to stay here."

Seeing the crestfallen look on their faces, he added, "Don't worry, you'll get your chance to prove yourselves soon enough."

As he made his way through the group in front of him, Steve's mind spun with everything he needed to deal with, but the most important was finding a way to get through the dead. Unless he could do this, they were screwed.

Entering the radio room, he found Brain and Connie talking quietly in the corner. When he entered, they both fell silent and looked up at him with huge question marks on their face.

Steve stopped in his tracks at this.

After the dead started coming to life, he had led his group through their time barricaded in the radio station, through a cruise ship adrift in the Gulf of Mexico filled with religious nuts and the dead, and through a shattered landscape full of even more dead when they reached shore. Through all of this, whether he liked it or not, he was their leader and they counted on him to keep them alive. But standing here looking at the searching, hopeful look on the faces of two of his people dragged him down. Knowing that they were waiting for him to tell them that everything would be fine and that he had a plan filled him with exhaustion and made his heart sank. Where before he'd always seen a way out of whatever situation they'd found themselves in, this time, he was drawing a blank. Everything he came up with so far seemed to fall apart before they could even start. It was like everywhere he turned, he was met by a wall of the dead.

Almost laughing aloud at the pun that came to mind, he thought, this time we ran into a dead end.

He sobered immediately as the reality of the situation came back to the forefront of his thoughts. With everything they were facing weighing on him, he knew he had to try something different before he let the situation overwhelm him. Realizing that in the past, while he had never outright lied about how bad things were, he had withheld the truth from most of his group to keep panic from spreading, he decided to change that. He had only relied on Heather, Tick-Tock and himself to steer their course while using the rest of the group for only whatever specific knowledge they had that fit in with their overall plan. They did what they were told and that was that. But now, with sudden insight and a spark of hope, he thought that maybe it was time to try something new. With so many of his group gone and with the others finally stepping up, it was time to be blunt. After all they'd gone through, the remains of his core group were experienced in the ways of the dead, so why not use that? In a crazy world where they needed to think outside the box, it was time to stop just utilizing a few resources and see what was outside everyone else's box.

"Things are sucking swamp water," Steve told them in an even tone. "You're not deaf, dumb, blind or stupid so you know how bad things are. I'm basically out of ideas. What have you got?"

Seeing fear spread across Connie's face at his statement, he thought for a second that he had made the wrong decision. His eyes switched to Brain, and he could see the tech's brow furrowed as his friend thought through the problem. Brain was an engineer, so Steve expected mostly linear thinking from him, but the man knew what they were up against and might come up with an idea. Maybe not an entire plan, but something they could use as a basis of a plan.

Although Brain was deep in thought, he was still aware enough of his surroundings to put a reassuring hand on Connie's shoulder when he sensed her starting to panic. He murmured, "Don't worry, babe," before turning his full concentration onto task.

A full minute passed as Brain tilted his head from one side to the other as he mouthed words that Steve couldn't hear.

Suddenly, he looked up and said in a clear voice, "I think I have something but we need to talk it through. We had a good plan before but it got shot to shit. First off, do you think that the explosives would have done the trick in clearing a path to escape?"

"Yeah," Steve said, "that blast you set off damn near did the trick all by itself. If we could have set off the other mines, we would have been home free. But between us and the detonator are a lot of Zs, so setting the rest of the dynamite off is pretty much a dead subject. Besides, from what you told me earlier, there's no way we'll find the wires, so there's no way we can use them."

"But if we had more explosives," Brain asked, "do you think that might do the trick?"

Steve brought up a mental picture of the dead pressed up against the house as they tried to find a way in. It would be hairy, but it might work. Keying his speech to Brain's, he said, "It would be dangerous since the Zs are so close to the walls, but if we keep the blast radius far enough away to take out the dead without compromising the mansion's integrity, more explosives might work. We could exterminate as many of them as we can and then use firearms on the rest. The main problem is, we don't have any more explosives."

A wicked smile crossed Brain's face as he said, "But we can make some if I have the right materials."

This almost floored Steve. He'd heard of the anarchist's cookbook and websites that taught you how to make plastic explosives from common household materials, but he'd never thought to ask if anyone in the group knew how to do it. What with the dynamite that Delightfully Grimm had supplied, there had been no need to.

Until now.

Wanting to grab Brain in a bear hug, but holding off on any premature celebration since the tech had said 'if' he had the right materials, Steve kept the excitement out of his voice as he asked, "What do you need?"

"I need Grimm," Brain replied. "She'll know if we have all the ingredients."

The sound of Grimm's voice asking, "Ingredients? Are we baking a cake," made them all spin to where she was standing in the doorway. "A soufflé would be nice," she said with a thoughtful tilt of her head, "but I fear with all the banging going on that it would fall in the oven."

With the cowl from her cloak covering her face and scythe in hand, she made an imposing figure.

Not intimidated by her look anymore, Brain took two steps toward her and said, "I need Styrofoam. Lots of it. And gas and oil. And I also need nails, nuts and bolts. Anything I can use for shrapnel."

She thought for a moment before saying, "Gas and oil we have, and I know we have a bunch of nails in the maintenance closet, but I'm not sure on the Styrofoam." Turning, she called down the hall, "Come here Thing two and Thing one."

Grimm entered the radio room to be followed by the former Raggedy Anne and Andy. Now wearing orange body suits with Thing one and Thing two stenciled on their chest and with blue fright wigs framing their white painted faces, they had transformed themselves into the Dr. Seuss characters from The Cat in the hat. They had even gone as far as to don orange mittens and slippers to complete their costumes.

Grimm smiled at Brain and said in introduction, "This is Thing one and Thing two, Thing two and Thing one, they can find anything, anything, anything under the sun."

Steve let out a short bark of laughter as Brain asked Thing one, "Do you know where I can find some Styrofoam?"

Thing one snapped to attention before spinning on his heel. Followed by Thing two, he marched out the door.

Perplexed, Brain stood for a moment until Grimm said, "They are Thing one and Thing two, so they do not speak, you might want to follow them though, for they will show you what you seek."

Taking Connie's hand, Brain hurried out the door.

When they were gone, Grimm turned to Steve and said, "By what you search for, I can only assume that you are making explosives."

Steve nodded and said, "If we can, we're going to use them to blow a hole in the dead and try to make for the vehicles."

Grimm looked thoughtful for moment before saying, "You might find that a little difficult."

"You saw what the dynamite did to the Zs before when we set it off," Steve said. "A few good blasts and we can take out what's left of them with rifle fire."

"When was the last time you were on the roof?" Grimm asked.

Not liking the sound of her question, Steve headed for the ladder as he asked, "Why, what's happening?"

"Hundreds more of my children have arrived," Grimm told him as he started to climb. "They are now clustered deep around the vehicles you want to use. If you use your explosives too close to them when you reap, you will destroy your transport."

As Steve emerged onto the roof, the high pitched keening sound of the dead seemed to drill into the center of his brain. Trying to ignore it, he climbed over the peak and saw Heather and Tick-Tock standing at the edge of the roof as they looked down at something. He called out to them, but the noise of the Zs drowned out his voice. Making his way cautiously down to them in a backward crabwalk, since if he lost his footing, slid, and went over the edge, the fall would be the least of his worries. He finally stood up when he was next to Heather, but found himself tilting his body backwards to keep his balance. He didn't have vertigo, but it still took him a few seconds before he felt comfortable enough to lean out carefully and follow her gaze.

Dead, snarling faces looked up at him as the Zs tried to push each other out of the way to get near the building. At first glance, Steve could see that at least five to six hundred more of the dead had entered the compound since he'd last looked only twenty minutes ago. The flood of walking corpses coming through the smashed gate had slowed somewhat, but he knew this was only temporary. Leaning further over the edge, he looked down. What Grimm told him was readily apparent; the dead were now so deep around the house that they completely enveloped the trucks and remaining minivan. Speech was impossible with all the noise, so he waved to get Heather and Tick-Tock's attention before pointing toward the other side of the roof. When they reached the peak, he let them go ahead and took a few minutes to study his surroundings.

The dust cloud was still there to the east, hanging ominously in the sky. He could see that it had moved closer, but this wasn't the reason for stopping. Turning to the north, he considered the fence and woods beyond. When he was satisfied, he made his way to the hatch and climbed through it.

Once all three of them were back in the radio room, where they found Grimm laid out on the bed while she lazily poked holes in the wall beside her with the point of her scythe, Steve asked Heather, "How long ago did this happen?"

"A huge surge of them came in about ten or fifteen minutes ago," she explained. "There were so many trying to get through the gate at one time that we thought they were going to bust down the fence on both sides of it."

"And these uglies didn't come down the road either," Tick-Tock said. "They came from the west. I think we're attracting Zs like an all night Dunkin' Donuts attract cops. As soon as we saw them, we sent Denise to find you."

Just then, Denise came through the door. Slightly out of breath, she said to Steve, "There you are. I've been all over the place looking for you. I ran into Brain, Connie and the thing twins and they said you were up here." Looking at Tick-Tock, she asked, "You told him?"

"He saw," Tick-Tock replied. "We were just filling him in on the details."

"Not a lot to fill in," Denise said. "We're screwed unless we can grow wings."

"We still might have a chance," Steve told them. This got their attention, and they listened intently as he continued, "If Brain can find the right materials, he told me that he can make explosives. My first thought was to clear the front of the mansion and drive out of here, but there's no way we can do that now. There's too many of them around the vehicles and we can't throw the bombs too close to them or we wreck our ride. And even with all of us and the others shooting, we'd never be able to clear enough Zs to get into the vehicles, get them started and haul ass."

"What do you mean by the others shooting?" Tick-Tock asked.

"Yeah," Denise chimed in. "I ran into them and they were all standing around at the top of the stairs. They were all quiet for once too. It was kind of creepy."

"They offered to help, so I told them to wait there for me," Steve said. "I don't know how much help they'll be until we teach them to shoot, but they're with us now for better or worse."

Denise nodded and said, "I knew they weren't all completely worthless. When Linda came over to our group, I could see a lot of them wanting to do the same. Sean was the only reason they didn't all step forward that day. He was a strong man to them. Their leader. The problem was, he kept them living and thinking in the past so they didn't take a good look at the present."

"Can we really trust the others?" Heather asked her.

"They're not the kind of people to shoot us in the back if that's what you mean," Denise said. "They might shoot themselves in the foot though."

"And that's where you come in," Steve said to Heather.

"You want me to shoot them in the foot?" She asked.

They all burst into laughter.

With the tension eased somewhat, Steve said, "No, honey, I want you to give them a crash course in firearms. You and Tick-Tock team up and get them all up to speed. We've got to move out of here soon and we'll need them to be ready. Denise can help you get their packs together."

"I thought you said it was useless to try and get to the trucks?" Tick-Tock asked.

"We're not heading for the trucks," Steve told them. "We're going north through the woods."

From where she was stretched out on the bed with her scythe laying along her body and the blade pointing straight up toward the ceiling, Grimm said, "If you go through the woods, make sure you stay off the psycho path."

***

Brain looked at the bags of packing peanuts with undisguised glee. He counted five on the first shelf with even more stacked against a wall at the far side of the room. A thought occurred to him, so he asked, "Why do you have all these?"

Thing one and Thing two looked at him for a minute before having a quick whispered conversation. Thing one then said, "We are Thing one and Thing two. We can't talk to them or you."

Connie laughed and said, "But you just did."

This confused Thing one for a second. He thought about and finally said, "Okay, this time I'll tell you, but no more questions from here on out. We are Thing one and Thing two and we don't talk or shout."

"Agreed," Brain said.

Thing one took a deep breath and said in a somber voice, "Sometimes, the people who stayed here didn't go home when they got better. They got worse and went to the State mental institution. When that happened, the staff packed up their belongings and sent them to their family. That's why we have all of these."

Brain nodded at this as he said, "Must have been pretty rough living here with the possibility of that hanging over your head." Getting no answer, he turned his attention to the peanuts and added, "If we each grab two bags, we should have plenty. I already know that you keep the gas in the room next to the generator, but what about oil?"

Thing one and thing two ignored his question by grabbing two bags and starting out of the storeroom. Brain looked at Connie, shrugged and slung his own bags over his shoulders before following them.

***

Linda was startled out of her thoughts at their predicament when Cindy asked, "Are we going to die?"

Forcing a smile, she replied in a reassuring voice, "No, pumpkin, we're going to be just fine."

"Mary and Sheila died," Cindy said as tears started to roll down her cheeks. "And so did Susan. And I know that so did Jonny-G and Marcia and a whole lot of other people too. I didn't know Marcia for long, but I liked her."

Pep had been lying next to Cindy, and she lifted her head and laid it on the young girl's leg when she saw one of her human's was in pain. Crossing the small room to sit next to the little girl on her bed, Linda took her in her arms. She stroked her hair and murmured reassurances until she heard her say, "And it's all because of me." Looking up suddenly at Linda, Cindy added in a small voice, "Don't you die too. Everyone who helps me ends up dead and I can't stand it anymore."

Linda took a deep breath and said, "No has one died because of you, Cindy."

"They did so," she said defiantly. "They're trying to get me to some G.I. Joe base or something. They all think I'm special because I didn't turn into one of those things after I got bit."

"And you are special," Linda said. "You might hold the cure for all of this crazy stuff that's going on. And on top of that, we all need to get somewhere that's safe. I was talking to -" at this, Linda stopped before saying Mary and Sheila's names. This was a raw, open wound that needed time to heal. "- some of the people in your group," she continued, "and they told me a lot of what you've been through."

Cindy nodded and said, "It feels like we've been around the world twice. I try to forget most of it, but I can't."

Raising one eyebrow, Linda said, "Then do you blame yourself for when the building in Clearwater got overrun by those things?"

In a small voice, Cindy replied, "No, but-."

"Well then, when the building was lost, you would have had to leave anyway," Linda interrupted her before asking. "And do you blame yourself for the crazy people you ran into on the cruise ship?"

Cindy shook her head.

"Or the sailboat getting that hole in it?"

"But that's different," Cindy almost whined.

"Different how?" Linda asked.

At a loss for words, Cindy was quiet for a few seconds before saying in a low voice, "But I still feel like they died because of me. Trying to protect me." At this, she started to cry silently, her small body shivering.

Linda pulled her close and said, "I think I know enough about people like Heather, Steve and Tick-Tock to say that any one of them would give their lives to save anyone else in the group."

Her voice muffled from having her face pressed into Linda's shoulder, Cindy said, "Then I want to at least be able to protect myself. I don't want anyone else dying because of me."

Looking down at the little girl, Linda wavered on what to do next. Cindy was so young, but after considering the world they now lived in, the decision was automatic. Extracting herself, she got up and pulled the end table in front of them before extracting her pistol and ejecting the clip. She cleared the round in the chamber and laid the weapon in front of them.

Igor looked on in silent approval from where he stood guard at the door, as Linda took on a serious tone and repeated the words that Heather had used to begin her firearms training, "This is not a toy. It's a tool, but it's a tool that can kill..."

***

Brain looked at the pots sitting on the stove as he ran the formula for plastic explosives through his mind again. There were only a few dos and don'ts and he wanted to make sure he had them all down before he started. The last thing they needed was for him to blow a hole in the back of the mansion or set it on fire.

When he was sure he had it right, he twisted the knobs of the burners to high and turned his attention to his helpers.

Looking to where Thing one and Thing two were plugging the last of the two way radios into a base charger, he asked, "Is that all of them?"

Thing one pointed to the seven radios and nodded his head vigorously.

The radios had been an unexpected bonus. The plastic explosives he was making were supposed to detonate if they was thrown against something, but it wasn't a sure thing. An electrical charge was the only certain way to set them off. Brain's only regret about the radios was that he hadn't known about them when he was wiring the dynamite. With the way things turned out in front of the mansion when Sean freaked out, it might not have made much difference, but at the very least, he would have been able to take a hell of a lot more Zs out with command detonated mines.

Turning to Connie, who was standing in front of the eighth radio lying on the center island with its back cover off and its wiring exposed, he asked, "You think you can remember what I showed you."

"I've got the example right here," she replied. "It should be simple enough."

"I'll be able to help you while I'm waiting for my stuff to cool down," Brain told her, "so if you get stuck, just wait."

Turning once again to the stove, he took a deep breath and let it out before scooping the first double handful of Styrofoam peanuts into the biggest of the pots.

***

Linda joined the others as they followed Steve, Heather and Tick-Tock into the makeshift armory. At first she was uncertain if she should say anything about giving Cindy her pistol, but decided in the end not to. While the group cared about the little girl, Linda could see that they didn't know much about how she was feeling or what she was going through. While she didn't doubt that they would kill and die to protect her, they so were busy keeping them all alive that they might decide she was too young to have a gun before thinking it through.

Steve saw her and raised a questioning eyebrow. With a sheepish grin, she said, "I hate to tell you, but I lost my pistol when we were running for the house."

"You still have your rifle though," Steve said.

"Still got it," Linda assured him as she hefted the weapon. "It was on a strap over my shoulder. The pistol was in my pocket though and must have fallen out."

After thinking about it a moment, Steve asked, "I know you shot your pistol a few times when the shit hit the fan out front, but did you ever get a chance to fire your rifle?"

Shaking her head, Linda replied, "I didn't get it until yesterday, and we didn't want to make noise and telegraph our position so I never got a chance to shoot."

"Then you can join the othe-," Steve stopped in mid-word and continued, "the rest of the group. They're going up on the roof for some weapons training and target practice after Tick-Tock gets them squared away."

Eying the assortment of rifles and pistols stacked in the closet, Tick-Tock added, "And there won't be any shortage of targets."

CHAPTER TWO

Jasper, Texas:

In October of the previous year, many small towns and cities were spared the initial impact of the infectious dead rampaging across the United States due to their relative isolation and the steps its people took to protect themselves. For all of them, survival was a near thing in the beginning, but in the end, as the H1N1 virus took the world by storm, it didn't matter...

When the dead started to replace the living population of the major cities in Texas, the first of many emergency town council meetings was held in the town of Jasper, Texas. Although there was a lot of shouting about action, and even more fist banging on the podium where the townspeople stood to be heard, it was decided to adopt a wait and see attitude. It was pointed out by the council that almost all the citizens owned at least one firearm, and the average was four per household, so it was taken for granted that they could protect themselves. Hell, one of the councilmen told the crowd, even Fox news was reporting that the situation was under control.

This, combined with a small National Guard unit deployed at the center of town served to assuage most people's fears. As the meeting was winding down, the head of the city council also pointed out with pride that they were all Texans and could deal with anything that was thrown at them.

As he was about to bang his gavel to close the meeting, a young girl named Megan bravely stood up and approached the podium. Resting her hands on its top, she stood with a slight tilt to her head, waiting silently until she was recognized by the chair. A few of the city council members groaned and shook their heads when they saw her, regretting a decision they had made a few months ago to let everyone have their say regardless of age. Ever since doing this, fourteen year-old Megan had gotten up at each and every meeting to lecture them on everything from Monsanto's use of illegal substances in their products to mandatory firearm safety for everyone over the age of ten.

Reluctantly, the chairman said, "The council recognizes the next - and last - speaker."

Not holding back, Megan told them in a loud, clear voice, "Your 'wait and see attitude' is going to get you all killed."

This brought gasps and excited chatter from the crowd, loud enough that the chairman had to bang his gavel to restore order. When it was quiet once again, he started to say, "Now Megan -." But she cut him off before he could finish.

"Have any of you seen or heard about how bad it's gotten?" She asked. "The internet is full of stories about the dead coming back to life and feeding on the living. It's a very virulent disease and it's spreading like wildfire. It's worse than the Black Death, and sooner or later it's going to come here."

This caused another outbreak from those gathered, and when it was again subdued by the pounding gavel, the chairman said, "We've all heard the rumors, Megan. But they are nothing but that – rumors. The situation is being taken care of by the authorities."

"What if I could show you how what the disease is really like and how well these so called authorities are taking care of the problem?" She asked. Without giving them time to say no, she pointed to the case hanging from a strap on her shoulder, and said, "I brought my laptop with me and I can -."

She was interrupted by one of the councilwomen laughing and saying, "And what are we all going to do, crowd around its little screen?"

With a self-satisfied smirk, Megan said, "Not to worry, I also brought a projector. Waving her brother Ethan forward, he reluctantly started setting up the equipment while trying to keep a low profile. While he shared his sister's love of technology, he hated her bringing so much attention to them.

This is so uncool, he thought.

After calling for the lights to be dimmed, Megan said, "I was going to do a Power Point presentation but I ran out of time. What you are about to see is raw video footage taken from across the United States. Some of it's from news crews that managed to upload their material before the government could confiscate it, but most is from people just like you and me."

"Where did you get this footage?" One of the councilmember's asked.

Knowing that if she told the truth - how she had hacked into a number of websites –she would get in trouble, Megan replied with a shrug, "I surf the web a lot and came across them. The first video is of particular interest since it came from a researcher."

For the next half-hour, the crowd sat in mortified silence as dozens of scenes of blood and gore were projected onto the wall behind where the council sat. Starting with the video shot by Professor Hawkins, the same video that Steve had watched in his apartment on Indian Rocks Beach, and followed by numerous lengths of footage showing the dead coming back to life to feed on the living, it ended with an overhead shot of the streets of Little Rock teeming with thousands of the dead. When the screen faded to black and the lights were turned back up, not a sound could be heard.

Finally, a man in the crowd asked, "Is this for real or is this some kind of prank you and your friends cooked up to try and scare everyone half to death? Because if it is a joke, it's not funny in the least."

"It's real as it gets," Megan answered. "I downloaded all of this from reliable sources."

The council looked at each other in shock. The reports from Austin kept saying that these were isolated incidents and that were being taken care of, but what if this video proved that to be a lie. A catastrophe of this magnitude was nothing they'd ever had to deal with before and they had no idea on how to proceed. Most of them had grown up with the threat of nuclear war hanging over them and knew how best to survive it, but these precautions didn't seem practical in dealing with an invasion of the dead. In event of a thermonuclear war, you got a store of food and water and went into your basement or storm shelter until the radiation levels fell, but these safeguards didn't look like they would help in this situation.

Radiation didn't chase you in groups of hundreds - or thousands - until you were pulled down and torn apart to be eaten alive. Radiation didn't infect you so that you died and came back to life to eat the living. Radiation didn't mutate your loved ones into flesh eating zombies that turned on you and tried to eat you. Radiation didn't come at you in numbers so large that they overwhelmed any structure they came across.

The dead coming back to eat the living was something totally new and terrifying.

Finally, they chairman cleared his throat and said, "I suggest a fifteen minute recess before we discuss this enhanced threat." He banged his gavel and added in a lower voice, "Megan, would you come up here and talk to us please? And bring your laptop."

The recess ended up lasting more than an hour while the council sought more information. They viewed numerous official sites that assured them that everything was alright, and the same amount of independent ones reporting the end of the world by the flesh eating dead. With so much contradictory information, the council ended up splitting into two factions. The smaller one believed it was a hoax perpetrated by the commies, the Arabs or the Chinese while the larger group was quickly becoming believers in a zombie apocalypse. Coming across a recently updated map from the CDC that showed the extent of the spread of the virus across the United States, one of the naysayers pointed out that only a small part of the country was infected. Gesturing at the black blur that covered most of the country, he then zeroed in on the outlying areas in white.

"Here's you proof," he said pompously. "An official government map that shows only a small percentage of our country is infected. All those other videos are staged to try and panic us."

When Megan scrolled down to the map key, his triumph was short lived. Black referred to the areas with outbreaks of the HWNW virus while white showed the areas that had been spared.

So far.

Realizing that evacuation was futile, the council decided unanimously that isolation would be their best defense. When they finally reconvened, a number of recommendations were brought up and passed.

It was decided to mine the bridge that crossed BA Steinhagen Lake to their west. A majority of the span was built on a causeway, but they could set dynamite under the bridge near the western shore and blow it up if they needed to. This would force any of the dead coming from the west to make a huge detour and also give them time to marshal their forces against them. Observation posts would be set on the eastern shore of the lake to watch for any threat and to keep track of it.

Checkpoints would be erected on all of the roads leading in and out of town, and anyone wanting to come into town would have to undergo an examination to make sure they hadn't been bitten or infected. If they refused, they would be barred entrance. This would be enforced by the local police.

Roving patrols of well armed citizens would crisscross the fields and back roads that surrounded the city to catch anyone trying to sneak in on foot, and the small airfield to the west of town would be shut down to any incoming traffic. Volunteers would be needed for this duty.

Rick Styles, the leader of one of the local Militias, stood up and told the council that he and his men would secure the airstrip to the west of town. The chairman hesitated for a long moment before giving a nod of approval. He knew that even with the townspeople helping, their manpower was pretty slim and they would need whatever resources they could get. Even if it meant recruiting the militia.

Prior to the dead coming back to life to feed on the living, most of these militia groups of 'Preppers' as they were called, were looked on with slight amusement since they were always getting ready for the end of the world. While it hadn't come as they thought it would in a collapse of the monetary system or a Civil war, a zombie apocalypse was the next best thing. This was one of the reasons for the chairman's hesitation. Rick Styles, and the small group of camouflage clothed men and women sitting with him, seemed almost happy at the thought of finally being proven right. A few other groups like his volunteered, so the chief of police told everyone who wanted to commit to being in the Jasper Defense Force to meet in front of Sunshine Groceries at seven AM.

Satisfied that they were doing everything they could, the crowd unanimously agreed to implement the board's precautions starting the following day. Megan was one of the few dissenters, but her cries that it wouldn't be enough were lost in the roar of 'ayes' and the noise of hundreds of chairs scrapping across the floor as people stood up.

The meeting was adjourned.

The townspeople patted each other on the back as they filed out, feeling good about taking action. They discussed other ways of protecting the town and came up with a few useful ideas. Their talk then turned to home defense, but no one thought it would come to that. They knew they would persevere as long as they kept the infection from entering their town.

Although they seemed to have thought of everything, the end didn't come from the outside as they believed it would, but rather from within. The barricades and patrols did an excellent job of keeping anyone who was infected out, but no one thought to check on the several thousand residents already living in town.

Days later, Jasper Texas was nothing but a wasteland populated by the dead.

***

Lena let out a sigh mixed with grief and regret as she looked at the barn that she and her husband had almost finished converting into their home. Leaning on the shovel stuck into the loose dirt covering the body of her best friend, she wiped sweat from her forehead with a blood soaked bandana tied around the bite on her wrist. Cursing silently as she pushed down on the handle, she chided herself at knowing better than to let Shawna into her house. She had heard about everything that was going on, but her kindness had overridden her common sense.

As she looked over at a similar mound of dirt that covered the body of her husband, the grief she felt, really a deep feeling of loss, mixed with the regret of making her first, and last, mistake in a time when the dead had come back to life.

She and her husband weren't 'Preppers' like their friend Rick, she told herself. Even if we were, we just weren't prepared for what came into our house and their lives today. We aren't end of the world enthusiasts who's every waking moment was filled with what to do if a race war started or the government declared martial law, we only wanted a more simple life for ourselves and their children. That was why we bought the property at the edge of Jasper. I learned to can fruits and vegetables while my love worked in the fields and tended to the two-dozen head of cattle we bought. The kids joined 4H and everything seemed honky-dory until two days ago when the reports of a new disease started to appear on the news.

The talking heads said that a virus had broken out in a few major cities. Nothing to worry about folks, they told everyone. Everything was being dealt with and you should keep on with your day-to-day lives, they kept repeating. The chances of being infected with this strain of flu were 2,000,000 to 1, they promised.

And at first, I believed them, but not anymore. Not after what had happened in my very own living room in my own house that morning

Rage replaced her sorrow as she pushed down into the soft dirt of the grave with her shovel.

"Liars," she said vehemently as she ground the blade into the dirt, hoping to again cut into the thing that had destroyed her life in only a matter of minutes.

Looking over to where Megan and Ethan stood wide-eyed as they tried to discern this outburst from their mother, her heart melted. She knew that no matter what happened, she had to protect them. She had to get them away from the madness that was taking over the world.

After a few seconds, she steadied her emotions. Once her mind was at somewhat of a more even keel, she realized that she had no way of knowing that Shawna was infected with the H1N1 virus. Despite this, guilt kept creeping in to cloud her thoughts. Trying to shake it off since she knew she had to think clearly now to protect her children, but images from that morning kept blasting into her mind to cloud it. Mental pictures of her friend coming to the door and telling of how her car had broken down outside of town, her friend being invited in by her husband to use the phone since only landlines seemed to be working, and only a few minutes later, watching as Shawna went into convulsions and died before rising up to attack her husband.

Looking down at the shovel, Lena thought disjointedly, you did double duty today.

When Shawna started going into seizures, the first thing that flashed through Lena's mind was what her daughter had been telling her was happening across the United States. Up until then, she hadn't really believed her or the news reports, but seeing was believing. While her husband rushed forward to give aide, Lena instead looked around wildly for a weapon. Spying the shovel leaning against the wall in the mud room, she yelled at her husband to get away as she ran to grab it.

But she was too late.

Shawna died, came back to life and sank her teeth into the chest of her rescuer as he tried to give her CPR. In a spray of blood, she tore out a huge chunk of muscle from below his left pec before digging both hands into the wound to open it wide. More blood sprayed across the two combatants as she flipped her victim over and straddled him, alternating her hands between stuffing pieces of flesh into its mouth while digging deeper for more. The thing that had been Shawna ignored the weakening blows from her prey as they bounced harmlessly off its face and body.

With her husband's screams turning to a gurgling noise when dead fingers punched into his lung, Lena rushed forward and hit Shawna on the side of the head with the flat end of the spade. Black puss mixed with a small amount of blood sprayed across the carpet and wall as the blade connected, sending the zombie rolling across the floor. Stepping between her husband and his attacker, fear ripped through Lena at the thought of going to prison for assault. This was only a fleeting thought though as she watched the dead thing shake off the blow and roll into a crouch to attack.

The shovel hadn't even fazed it.

The dead and the living stared at each other for a second before Shawna let out a high-pitched whining noise.

Raising the shovel again, Lena swung it back and forth in warning as a string of curses flowed from her mouth. Shawna seemed to back away a step and hesitate, and thinking it was over, Lena hesitated too as she thought to talk to her lifelong friend, to try to make some sense out of this madness. She started to ask what was happening, but the words fell on dead ears and only encouraged the thing to attack.

Shawna flailed her arms and charged, leaping forward in a crouch to get inside the swing of the shovel. With a squeal, the dead thing sank its teeth into the bony part of Lena's wrist.

Shaking off the bite by thrusting forward, Lena pushed her friend back before lifting the shovel over her right shoulder and coming across in a round-house swing. The blow connected with her attacker just below the ribcage, the blade sinking half-way into dead flesh as black puss sprayed out from the impact.

The dead and the living stopped, connected only by the shovel buried into the zombie's side.

In shock, Lena saw that even this didn't slow Shawna in the least.

Reaching down, the dead woman grabbed the edge of the shovel and wrenched it loose, pulling a length of severed intestine with it. Lunging forward, she gnashed her teeth as she tried to get at the thing that was denying her food. Hearing her daughter call out that she needed to destroy the brain, Lena brought the handle of the shovel across her chest and used it to push Shawna down. Raising her weapon like she was splitting firewood with an axe, she came down with all her might and buried the blade into the top of her friend's head with a wet thud. The shovel was wrenched from her hands as the thing that had once been living spasmed wildly, shuddered violently as it died its final death.

After watching for a second to make sure Shawna stayed down, Lena then turned her attention to her husband. She saw that he had pulled himself across the floor and propped himself against the side of the couch. What was left of his tattered shirt was covered in blood, but none was coming from the ragged wound in his chest anymore. Megan and Ethan were standing over him, shifting their weight from one foot to the other as they tried to decide how to help him. Suddenly, they both jumped backwards with uttered cries of revulsion.

Lena could see immediately what had startled them.

What had once been her husband had died and come back to life.

Dead eyes set in bluish skin stared out at the world, and when they locked on her two children, Lena could see they looked at the youngsters the same way a starving man would look at Thanksgiving dinner. With a squeal, one of its hands reached out to try and grab at the food in front of it while the other tried to lever it onto its feet.

The instinct to protect her young took over, and Lena didn't hesitate in the least as she twisted the shovel free from Shawna's head and used it on her husband's.

Clearing her mind of the horror as she used the bloody bandana to wipe the sweat away again, Lena studied the two graves again before turning her attention to her children. Megan and Ethan stood a short distance away, unsure of what to do next.

They might not know what to do, Lena thought to herself, but I do.

She told them to go to their rooms and pack some clothes. Not in a suitcase, she warned them, but in one of the backpacks they used to go camping. Once they were gone, she went inside and called the only person that could help them.

An hour later, Rick Styles pulled up in front of the house in his truck. Before his combat-booted feet could hit the dust of the driveway, he stopped. Taking in the two fresh graves, he knew it was as worse than Lena had described on the phone. Seeing her and the two kids standing in front of the mounds of fresh earth with heads bowed in prayer made him choke up a little, but he pushed it down.

Wanting to give them a few moments, and to distract his mind at the thought of having lost a good friend, he played with the radio, spinning the dial to see if he could pick up anything except the lame-ass reports from the EBS telling everyone that all was well, to boil any water before you drank it and to avoid large crowds.

Yeah, he thought to himself, avoid large crowds of the dead, but that looked like it might be getting harder and harder to do these days.

Movement caught his eye, and he looked up to find Lena and her kids walking toward him. Getting out of his truck, he forced a smile and said, "The cab only seats three, so one of you is going to have to ride in the back."

"I'm not going," Lena said.

"But I thought I was picking you all up?" Rick asked.

Holding up her bloody wrist in explanation, Lena said, "I need to talk to you for a minute, Rick." Turning to her oldest, she said, "Take Ethan and go over by the truck."

Megan hesitated, but a stern look from her mother got her moving. They had already gone over what needed to be done, but it didn't make it any easier.

When they were gone, Lena led Rick a short distance away before saying bluntly, "I got bit by Shawna after she died and came back. She killed..." Choking up at the very mention of her dead husband's name, she shook it off and continued, "I didn't tell you when I called because I didn't think you'd come if you knew what really happened. I didn't believe it before when Megan was going on and on about what she'd been seeing on the web, but I believe it now. From what we've been able to gather from the reports, it means I'm infected."

"It does," Rick told her. "We've been finding out the same thing in town. If you get bit or get any fluids from one of them on you, you get the disease. You die and then you come back. I heard from the sheriff that they've had quite a few cases today inside the city limits. Seems like people are dying and getting back up and then attacking and eating each other. It's gotten so bad that the council got together and decided to isolate us as much as possible. They're planning on blowing up the bridge later this afternoon. I don't know what good it will do though, seems like we've got quite a few infected people that already snuck in. They might have been away on vacation or whatever and got bit, and came home because that's where you want to be when you're hurt."

"I know Shawna was out of town visiting her family," Lena said. "She must have caught it there."

Rick shrugged and said, "Nobody knows much about this thing, and the news media isn't telling it straight. Who knows, some of the dead might have been here the whole time." After thinking about it for a few seconds, he gave Lena a sideways glance before adding in a quiet voice, "I've had to kill two today, do you want me to end it for you too?"

Lena thought about it for a moment before saying, "I've gone over that in my mind a million times since it happened, and I have to say no. Like you said, nobody knows shit about this disease, so I'm going to sit here for a day or two and see what happens. If I don't turn into one of those things, I'll come get my kids. But if I do die and come back..." Her voice trailed off.

"What about your kids," Rick asked, "did they get bit or scratched or anything?"

Lena sighed and shook her head before saying, "No, it was only me."

Rick shrugged again and said, "Well, I'll take care of your kids, but if I don't see you in forty-eight hours, I'll come back and do what has to be done."

"Thank you," she said. "I've always had a good immune system, so maybe I'll work through it." Turning to the truck, she called out, "Megan, Ethan, come here and say goodbye to your mother."

After a tearful parting, Lena watched as the truck drove away. With a heavy heart, she walked over to the fresh graves and sat in the shade of a nearby tree.

Forty-five minutes later, the first convulsion struck. A minute later, Lena died. Two minutes later, it rose. It was hungry.

Wandering down the drive to the main road, it would stop occasionally to sniff the air for prey. Its brain was almost gone except for its base functions, but its senses were still keen. Even with its extremely diminished mental capacity, it knew that if it kept to the cleared areas, its chances of finding flesh were better than being in the woods. Not smelling any food, it started on and then stopped, suddenly overcome by the urge to hide, to wait. It had to stay safe, feeding would come later. Its deep-rooted instinct told it to suppress its hunger until it could join others like itself. It knew that in a pack, the hunting would be good.

With saliva running down its chin, it gave in to this urge and headed into the woods. It had no particular place in mind to go, but nonetheless, its feet carried it with a purpose. Before long, it came across three more like itself, standing in a clump of trees and moaning with hunger pains. Within a few hours, their group had grown to over twenty.

Then, as if by some unheard signal, they all started off in the same direction. Along the way, they picked up more stragglers until their number had grown to thirty. Within half an hour, they came to a clearing with a small house set in the middle. Night was upon them, so the lighted windows threw long beams of illumination across the well tended lawn. The dead grew still for a moment, taking in the scene as their senses tried to discern if there was food inside. When a figure passed by the glass of a large picture window, it was all they needed.

With what had once been a woman named Lena in the lead, the dead lurched forward as a group. While Lena might have forgotten her past life and everyone in it, she did know that the flimsy glass was no barrier against their numbers.

***

The small groups like Lena's that formed in and around Jasper eventually merged into one larger herd of dead. Now a thousand strong, they swarmed over the town, easily overwhelming its defenses by sheer weight of numbers. Doors were busted down, not with axes and battering rams but with the pressure of hundreds of bodies pushing against them. In this initial onslaught, thousands of the living fell to the dead.

First the humans and their domesticated pets were killed and eaten, and after they were gone, the cattle were set upon and devoured to the bone. Woodchucks, rabbits, gophers and anything that burrowed into the ground were then dug up, torn apart and stuffed into the mouths of the dead in a quest to assuage their never-ending hunger. Some animals like the coyote and the bear fled before this onslaught, and this proved to be the wisest course of action. It was the same for man and animal alike; if you barricaded yourself inside their home or den, you eventually starved to death or were forced to venture out in search of food and water. Once away from shelter, anything living was easily outnumbered by the lingering zombies and was torn apart. Then, the ones that didn't have their brain destroyed in this carnage got up to join their brethren. The only thing that didn't get up were the animals since the disease wasn't able to jump the biological barrier between man and animal.

After the entire population of the city was dead, in one form or another, the group moved on to the nearest population centers. With the bridge to the west gone, they headed east.

Burkville and Newton, Texas had had their own outbreak, so the dead from Jasper found little to eat. The groups of dead from these three towns merged into one and moved south and then further east. After ravaging this region, they went back and forth through the area in a constant search for food; wiping hundreds of square miles clean of anything living. Now on their way back west to scour the bleak terrain once again, they would let no barrier made by man or nature stop them until they found flesh. The downed bridge had been a deterrent so far, but not anymore. The urge to feed was so strong that they would go over, under, or through anything that stood in their way.

Located between the lake and the outskirts of Jasper as they trudged westward, the herd stayed on Highway 190 since it gave them an easier path than cutting through the forests and fields on both sides of the road. Coming to the edge of the lake, the road narrowed as it funneled them into a single column of tightly packed dead flesh that stretched from shore to shore as they spilled onto the causeway. Coming across the downed section of the bridge, without hesitation, those in the lead stepped off to drop into the water.

The rest of the dead followed, looking like collection of gruesome lemmings following the leader over a cliff. After hitting the water and sinking to the bottom, they slogged through the mud and silt that made up the floor of the lake, endlessly moving forward in a search for food.

With their number at over twenty-thousand, the dead in the lead were well ashore and moving off the causeway before the final zombie dropped over the ragged concrete and exposed rebar that made up the edge of the blown bridge. It took hours, but finally, the last of the stragglers made it across. These at the rear were not the walking dead, but rather the legless that had to crawl and the blind that made their way on all fours as they felt their way along. Dripping wet, they made their way on shore and moved forward, closer now than anyone at the mansion realized.

CHAPTER THREE

The Happy Hallow Insane Asylum:

Sitting on the bed of an unused room, with his back against the wall and a map laid on his lap, Steve studied the unlit cigarette in his hand. His mouth already tasted like he'd scoured it out with oily steel wool from smoking too much, but the habit and the stress kept him wanting another one. It gave him something to focus on, something to think about other than the mess they were in. Instead of lighting it, he took a drink from the water bottle lying next to him. After screwing the cap back on, he said, "Fuck it," and fished around in his pants pocket for his Zippo lighter. As soon as he took the first drag off the stale Marlboro though, his body said 'No' and he started dry heaving. Grinding the butt into the tile floor, he coughed and gagged a few times as he fought not to throw up.

"Those things are going to kill you," Heather told him from where she stood at the door.

Half-way regaining control, Steve choked out, "I hope I live that long."

"We're all going to live a long time," Heather reassured him. "I just checked on Brain and he said that he's almost finished with the explosives."

Looking up in interest, Steve said, "I didn't hear a loud boom followed by us getting eaten, so I guess everything went well."

"I was down in the kitchen watching him for a while before I went up to help Tick-Tock," Heather told him. "It was scary for a second when he was moving the pot off the stove some of the Styrofoam dripped onto it. I thought Brain was going to shit one big brick when it happened, but luckily, none of it hit the open flame." Laughing, she added, "When he said, 'Got to remember to turn that flame off next time,' it sounded like his balls were in his throat "

"They would have been if it went off," Steve commented with a laugh, "or more likely in New Jersey. How long until he's ready?"

Walking over to the bed, Heather held out her hand and said, "He's molded them all and set the detonators in them, but he told me they still have to cool and harden for a little bit. He said it would be another hour or so, which means it's time for you to get up and get to work. Tick-Tock and Denise are almost done getting everyone organized, so the next step is to take them on the roof for target practice. We could use your help."

Steve grimaced as he grabbed her hand and let her pull him to his feet. After steadying himself, he stopped for a moment, thinking about something that had been weighing on his mind. Quietly, he asked, "What do you think our chances are?"

Heather's stopped to think about this. After a moment, she said, "Overall, I have no idea. I learned a long time ago that when I'm facing something that seems overwhelming, to break it down into steps. First, when you consider that we have to travel over forty miles -."

"Double that," Steve interrupted. "It's over forty miles to Fort Polk as the crow flies, and since we're driving it will be more than that. Then you have to consider that we're going to have to make a huge detour to the north to get around the mob coming at us from Jasper -."

"So call it seventy miles to get to Polk," Heather interrupted him this time, "but once we get into radio range, we should be able to get someone to come pick us up, so I'm going to go back to my estimate of forty."

Steve opened his mouth to say something else, but Heather cut him off with a warning look not to interrupt her again. He saw this and chose to remain silent, so she continued, "The best way to complete a journey is in stages. First stage, we have to get away from the mansion. I think that once we do that and get into the woods, we should be in pretty good shape."

"Why's that?" Steve asked. "We've probably got thousands of Zs around us, not counting the ones bunched up around the mansion, and they're not going to just let us leave without following."

"Well, from everything we've seen and heard lately, it seems like the dead are mobbing up into big groups," Heather told him. "We've got these big herds -."

Steve laughed and said, "Herds?"

Heather shrugged and said, "It's as good a name as any, now back to what I was saying, we have these big herds wandering all around us, but I think that since they're all bunched together, they'll be easier to spot and avoid. If we stay on the move and send scouts ahead our main group, we should be able to avoid them. Think about it, most of the people we've lost have been to one or two Zs that were hidden somewhere and came at us from nowhere. From here on out though, we'll be in a position to keep track of them. As for the dead that follow us, we'll just have to figure out a way to lose them. When we were looking at the map earlier with Tick-Tock and Denise, I saw a couple of choke points that we can use to slow them down."

"I was just going over the topographic map before you came in and I saw the same thing," Steve told her. "It's a good plan, and while it sounds good saying it here, who's going to be the person that stays at these choke points and keeps the Zs from following?"

"No one," Heather replied. "I promised Brain not to steal his thunder, so he'll tell you what he has in mind. It should slow the dead up long enough for us to get away."

Steve thought for a moment before saying, "If Brain's got something up his sleeve, then we might have the beginnings of a plan beyond blowing a hole in the dead and running. Our first objective is to get as far away as possible, but there's still a lot of unknowns in front of us so we'll just have to adapt to whatever situation comes our way. The main thing I'm worried about is how to lose any of the dead that come after us. But, if Brain has something we can use, we'll just have to do like Tick-Tock always says and -," They both finished in unison, "Improvise, adapt and overcome."

"Now you need to quit feeling sorry for yourself and get your ass moving," Heather added. "You're sitting in here doing nothing when there's too much to do."

Dropping his head, Steve said in a quiet voice, "I was mapping a couple of escape routes, but I had to stop because I couldn't concentrate. I keep thinking about Mary, I should have been able to prevent her getting killed."

Heather stopped and studied Steve for a few second while she tried to decide which way to go with this. Knowing they didn't have a lot of time, she opted for hardcore to pull him out of his depression and get him motivated.

Before he could say another word, in a loud sarcastic voice, she asked, "And who the fuck died and made you god?" She could see this startled him, and at least he was looking at her now, so she continued, "There's nothing you could have done to prevent what happened to Mary. Sean was nothing but a coward and they're the most unpredictable. His actions killed her, not yours. But I'll tell you one thing right now, you better get your head screwed on straight or you *are* going to be the one to get people killed. Everything bad that's happened to us so far has just gotten ten times worse. We need to have you on the ball if we're going to make it to Polk. Now pull your head out of your ass, get off your pity-pot, and go down and see Brain. When you're done with that, you need to get your ass up on the roof and help us teach the others how to shoot."

Steve felt anger flash through as he said, "Bullshit, I should have seen what Sean did coming."

"How?" Heather asked as she threw her hands up in exasperation. "Do you have a crystal ball that you've been hiding from the rest of us? Sean acted like the little worm he'd always been up until the second he snapped. If anything, I would have guessed he'd hide on the floorboards instead of trying to drive through a herd of the dead but panic and fear do strange things to people. You can never tell how they're going to react until they do. Look at the rest of the people in his group for example. They're all stepping up now."

Distracted from his thoughts of Mary, he knew Heather was right, but a small tug in his gut told him different. He might be able to rationalize it in his mind, but his emotions didn't listen to common sense. Instead of arguing the point further, he let go of his pride and asked, "How do you think the others will do?"

Picking up his M-4 from where it leaned against the wall and holding it out to him, Heather said, "There's only one way to find out. You need to get that cute little ass in gear and get to work."

***

Tick-Tock stood by patiently as the last of his trainees reassembled their weapons. It would have been easier if they all carried the same model of rifle and pistol, but that was not to be. He'd had a rough time in the beginning as he, Heather and Denise had them all break down their rifles to make sure they were clean enough to fire without blowing up in their hands, and with the mish-mash of bolt action and semi-automatic weapons he'd had to deal with, he was amazed that they'd eventually figured out how to take them all apart to make sure the barrels, gas chambers and bolts weren't jammed up or plugged and that the firing pins were intact. The pistols came next, but they had worked out a system by this time so it went slightly faster.

When the last piece was finally snapped into place, as the man fumbling around with it finally figured out how to get the cylinder back on his revolver, Tick-Tock gave a silent sigh of relief. The trainee looked up at him as if expecting praise that he'd finally gotten it right, and Tick-Tock had to bite back an acid comment at this. He knew that if he had more time, he would break these people down before he built them back up, but he didn't have time. Time was their enemy. He didn't have the time to give them a thorough training, so he needed to use a combination of praise and a boot in the ass to get everyone ready to move. He wanted nothing more than to get down in this guy's face like a drill instructor and scream that if he ever finished last again that he would be doing bends and motherfuckers until he puked, but this was not to be.

Forcing a smile, Tick-Tock gave the man a strained, "Good job," before saying in a louder voice to everyone, "now we need to go through your packs and make sure you have everything you need and that you're not carrying a bunch of crap that you don't. I want everyone up on their feet with their weapons in front of them. If you still have a pack, put it at your right foot and your sleeping bag at their left."

They all rose from the blankets and sheets they had laid out on the floor of the recreation room to break their weapons down on and stood at a semi-posture of attention. Two of them picked up their packs and started to rummage through them until Tick-Tock stopped them with a barked, "Did I tell you to do that?"

The packs were immediately dropped and the whole group went rigid.

Lowering and shaking his head in mock disgust, Tick-Tock said, "We went over this before. We need to act and think as one. If you want to be an individual, you're going to die like an individual." Pointing at the first woman that had picked up her pack, he asked, "Why?"

Stammering slightly, she said, "I knew we were going to go through them, so I figured I'd pick it up and get started."

"I'm only going to tell you this one last time," Tick-Tock said in a stern voice. "You only do what I say to do when I say to do it. Nothing more and nothing less. I don't expect you all to become some kind of Rambo, zombie killer ninja assassins, nor do I want you to be. That's not what I'm trying to do here. All I'm trying to do is teach you how to survive. Your greatest asset is staying in a group, moving as a group, and thinking and acting like a group. To do this, you need to follow some simple instructions. If you learn do that, we'll all make it through this to safety. Are we clear on this?"

The, "Yes, sir," came almost as one voice, giving Tick-Tock hope.

Looking at Denise standing behind them, he raised one eyebrow. She smiled and blew a kiss at him before taking over. With a list in her hands, she said, "We told you all before to make up a new pack if you lost yours in the minivan, so I want everyone to pick up their backpack and dump it out in front of them. Get everything out of the side pockets too. You might have been ready to go before, but that was in a vehicle. Now we're going on foot so you'll need to carry only the essentials."

When the contents of the assortment of book bags, packs and even a few pillowcases they had scrounged were scattered in front of them, she continued, "I want everyone to place their bag in their left hand and pick up each item with their right and hold it up as I call it off. If you don't have that item, raise your right hand."

When they were ready, she called out loudly, "One pair of pants".

When everyone had them in their hand, she said, "Roll them up tight and stuff them in."

When they were done, she called out, "One shirt."

Going down the list, she called out two pair of socks, one pair of underwear, two full water bottles and one knife. When she came to the knife, a half-dozen people raised their hands that they didn't have one. Now it was Tick-Tock's turn. Going up and down the three rows, he handed out the few hunting knives they had and gave the rest of his trainees whatever decent blades he had found in the kitchen. In addition to this, he also handed every third person a pencil sharpener

When he was done, he said, "I don't have time to teach you knife fighting for a couple reasons, the first being that I never learned how to do it since I prefer to stand well back and shoot my attacker." The group laughed, so he added, "And the greater the distance the better."

After the laughter at this died off, he said, "Your knife is a tool for making kindling to start a fire and any number of other things that I'll go over later, and it's only to be used as a weapon as a last resort. Don't start thinking you're Bizarro the magnificent knife throwing god and do an overhand toss at an attacking Z because you'll only be throwing a perfectly good knife away. The pencil sharpener is also to be used for making kindling. Find a stick the size of a pencil and use the shavings."

When Denise was done with her list, the remains of the group's belongings lay on the floor in front of them. Tick-Tock watched as they looked down at their property and then back up at him, waiting for him to tell them they could put the rest of their personal items in their backpacks. Instead, he picked up a phone book from a pile stacked on the ping-pong table and tore off two inches from it. Walking up to the first person in the front row, he handed it over to him and said, "Put this in your pack." When the man looked at him oddly, he explained, "That's your toilet paper. Use it sparingly since we might be on the road for a couple days."

Hearing one of his trainees say in a questioning voice, "Phone books," without missing a beat, Tick-Tock said, "We're using phone books because I couldn't find any copies of Hard Choices by Hillary Clinton in the library."

There were a few chuckles, and feeling that their training was winding down, a man in the back row raised his hand to ask a question. Tick-Tock had told the group at the beginning that they needed save their questions for the end. He wanted them to just learn to do what they were told, but he reminded himself that these were not Marine Corps recruits.

Although they still had to learn how to hold and fire their weapons in a safe manner, Tick-Tock decided to relax the mood a little, so he said, "Training's not over yet, but go ahead."

"How long will we be walking?" He asked.

Without breaking stride as he moved to the next person and ripped off another section of the yellow pages, Tick-Tock replied, "When I was in the Corps, on my last day of jungle warfare training, we got back from a three mile run followed by a forced march of ten miles through what was mostly swamp. We came back to camp and unassed all our equipment. All we were looking forward to was a shower and graduation the next day, but then our instructors came in screaming that we had to get our shit together and get ready for another ten mile hike through the beautiful jungles of Panama.

"Most of us grabbed our gear and got ready, but a couple guys quit. They were bitching and whining about how unfair it was. They were saying it was bullshit since we were all done with training. The one's that didn't quit lined up outside and started off at a quick march. That's one-hundred twenty steps per minute. We'd barely gone half a mile though when we came across a couple trucks parked to the side of the road with a bunch of guys hanging around a bonfire drinking beer and having a good old time. Our instructor stopped us just short of them, and that was when we recognized these guys as the men that had been training us in everything from ambush to improvised explosives over the past six weeks. That was when they came forward handing out beer and telling us we'd made it."

Clearing his throat, Tick-Tock said, "You won't quit. You will walk as long as you need to, to get to where you're going. Don't project on the time or the distance. Set yourself a goal. Pick out a tree or a rock in the far distance, and say to yourself, 'That's my spot. That's where I'm going.' When you get there, pick out another spot and head for that. Always remember, mental projection is just like mental masturbation. You're only fucking yourself."

When he had finished handing out their impromptu toilet paper, Tick-Tock stood in front of the group and said, "Now I want everyone to put your pack down and pick up your sleeping bag or blanket and shake it out. I'm going to teach you how to roll everything up nice and tight."

***

Looking down at the white clumps studded with finishing nails sitting on the kitchen counter, Brain reached down and laid three fingers on one of them. Feeling no heat coming from it, he checked the wires to the radio duct taped to the formless wad. Satisfied, he said to Connie, "They're ready."

"But will they work," Steve asked from the other side of the kitchen.

Startled at his sudden appearance, Brain jumped slightly. Regaining his composure, he said, "There's no reason they shouldn't."

"What kind of blast can we expect from them?" Steve asked.

"About a third as much as the dynamite I set off," Brain told him. "The big difference in these though, is that the shrapnel from the nails is going to do a lot more damage. We're going to get a lot more Zs staying down after the blast."

Thing one and Thing two took this as a sign to dance around as Steve asked, "You're sure they're going to work though."

Annoyed at being asked the same question twice, and feeling like Steve was questioning his abilities, Brain asked defiantly. "Have I ever been wrong?"

Steve laughed and made a placating gesture with his hands as he said, "Just making sure. Everything hinges on blowing a hole through the Zs so we can make it to the woods." Looking at the bombs lined up on the counter, he asked, "Can you set them to go off one by one?"

Brain shook his head and replied, "We've only got one transmitter to detonate them, so they'll all go off at the same time."

Steve thought about this for a second before saying, "Then we can only use six of them on the dead since we need the last one to blow a hole in the fence. Is there any way you can set one of them to go off separately?"

"No, but they also go off if you throw them against something," Brain told him, "The impact will do it. I used the left over Styrofoam to make a dozen extra that we can bring with us. I figured they might come in handy. I can use one of those to blow the fence and the rest to slow down the Zs that will be following us."

Steve nodded as he brought up a mental image of the map and considered the most effective places to use these as he asked, "Who's going to be carrying the bombs?"

Puffing out his chest a little, Brain replied with a touch of bravado in his voice, "I am."

With a smile, Steve said, "Then if you trip and fall, make sure I'm not around."

***

Climbing up through the hatch in the roof, Steve could hear the muted sound of firing pins falling on empty chambers above the low whining of the dead. Surprised that he could hear anything above the voices of the Zs, when he was completely on the roof, he noticed a marked drop in the volume coming from below.

Seeing Heather helping a slightly overweight man adjust the sling on his rifle, he waved to her but ignored the glances he received from the group standing a few feet away with their rifles held at a semi-resemblance of port arms. Edging to the side of the roof, he cautiously looked down.

Disgust welled up in his throat at the sight of the nude and semi-nude dead bodies pushing up against the side of the building. Disfigured and torn in ways that would gag a maggot, they were strangely silent. Pushing away his revulsion, he studied the dead for a moment as he tried to figure out why they were being so quiet. Nothing had changed in their demeanor, as they were still desperately trying to get into the mansion, but most of them weren't making the high-pitched keening sound anymore.

Realizing Tick-Tock had joined him, he asked, "What gives, not even a couple hours ago, you couldn't hear yourself if you screamed up here."

Tick-Tock shrugged and said, "They were like this when we came up. I thought they'd start back with all the noise when they saw us, but it's been like this ever since. Maybe they know we're trapped or some other shit and they're saving their breath."

"They don't breathe," Steve said absently as he focused on a Z with the left portion of its skull missing and its brain exposed. Dark fluid covered the wound and he could see that underlying grey matter was actually a dark red.

"No shit, Sherlock," Tick-Tock said with a laugh. "What was your first clue they don't breathe?"

Shaking off the sight below him, Steve turned to his friend and laughed. "Sorry, just talking. The sight of these things makes me want to blow chunks, but it also makes me want to know what makes them tick."

"You should have been a scientist," Tick-Tock said wryly.

"And you should have been Proctologist," Steve shot back with a laugh.

"Then you'd only have to worry when you felt both my hands on your shoulders," Tick-Tock replied.

They both laughed at this old joke before Steve asked, "How are your trainees doing?"

Tick-Tock shrugged and said in a low voice, "A couple of them show promise, but..."

"But what?" Steve asked.

"I need at least two days with them to be able get them to shoot straight," Tick-Tock answered.

"You've got until tomorrow morning at dawn," Steve told him.

Already having guessed this, Tick-Tock was nonetheless excited at hearing they would be going soon. With a slight grin, he said, "I figured as much, that's why I've been busting ass to get these people ready." Pointing to the dust cloud to the east that had dissipated for a short while only to reappear closer to the mansion, he added, "Looks like the Zs crossed the lake. Even tomorrow morning might be cutting it close, but we should be able to get out of here before they hit us."

Steve nodded and said, "If I had it my way, we'd go today, but we don't have enough light left. We need to keep an eye on that herd though so they don't surprise us. I want two people on watch at all times through the night. Even if they can't see shit, I still want them up here."

Tick-Tock nodded and said, "Done deal, Denise and I will take the first watch and then you and Heather -."

"The trainees take their turn too," Steve cut him off. "Split them up and get them organized. They stepped up, so they'll help in everything we do from here on out. I want one of us and two of them to take each watch. I hate to be still making the distinction between us and them, but until they get up to speed, that's the way it is. I want everyone well rested for tomorrow, so that means they pull their weight too."

Tick-Tock nodded and said, "Consider it done, and it's about time." Turning to where his people were standing along the edge of the roof, he said in a loud voice, "We're done snapping in, so now it's time to use live ammunition. For those of you with a magazine fed weapon, I want you to extract the clip from your pocket and insert it into your rifle like we showed you. For those of you that have a top-fed, bolt action rifle, I want you to load your bullets into your rifle like we showed you." Pointing to two men holding lever action rifles, he added, "And I showed you both how to load your weapons, so go ahead and do it."

Steve noticed that no one made a move to do as they were told. He was about to comment on this when Tick-Tock barked out, "Ready... load." In a flurry of motion, the trainees inserted magazines and loose rounds into their rifles. When they were done, they stood waiting.

Impressed at the discipline that Tick-Tock had instilled in these people in such a short time, Steve said, "Looks like you have everything well in hand."

"Not even close," his friend replied. "I can still use some help since none of them have ever fired a gun before."

Without hesitation, Steve asked, "What do you want me to do?"

Moving back over to the trainees, Tick-Tock said, "We've got plenty of targets, but I want to make sure they're hitting – or at least hitting near – what they're aiming at. With all the Zs down there, it will be like lining these guys up along the side of a boat and telling them to shoot over the side and hit the ocean."

"So what's the plan?" Steve asked as he followed.

They reached were Denise and Heather were standing as they waited on them, and after exchanging greetings, Tick-Tock said to Denise, "Steve's going to help us by marking our targets, so give him the splat gun. That frees you up, so I want you helping me and Heather on the firing line in case anyone gets a jam or does something stupid."

Denise extracted a paintball gun from the pack at her feet and said to Steve, "We took the big feeder off the top so you have to load it one shot at a time."

Hefting the weapon, Steve asked, "Why?"

"So you can load different colors," she explained. "We want to make sure they're hitting what they're aiming for, and we want to be able to tell different trainees to aim for different colors when we teach them snap shooting."

Turning to Tick-Tock, Steve asked, "Are you sure they're ready for snap shooting?"

"I'd rather teach them how to do everything right from the get go," he answered. "I know it takes a lot of practice to be able to raise your rifle or pistol in a flash and snap off a shot that hits your target, but I want them to at least know the basics and how to do it safely." In a lower voice, he added, "I doubt any of them will remember half of what I teach them, but I have to go through the motions. Maybe enough of what I tell them will sink in so they don't accidentally shot each other or one of us."

Steve nodded and said, "You're the instructor."

"Damn right I am," he said with a smile before raising his voice and saying to the line of trainees, "Remember your sight picture and remember that the only person shooting will be the one Heather, Denise or myself is standing behind and telling to shoot." Turning to Steve, he said, "I need about twenty targets spread out across the back of the house. Try to find the ones on the outer edge of the mob that aren't moving around too much. I don't want to make it too hard at first, and we'll get to the part about how to hit a moving targets later."

Steve complied, and within a few minutes, twenty of the dead had splatters of red, green, and yellow paint marking their heads and chests. Tick-Tock moved behind the first person in line, a woman who looked extremely nervous but determined, and said, "Pick one target and tell me which one it is."

The woman looked for a moment before pointing directly out in front of her and saying, "The one with the red paint dripping down its neck. It's got what's left of a flannel shirt hanging off its back."

"Then raise your rifle, get your sight picture and squeeze the trigger like I taught you," Tick-Tock told her. "I'm going to be right here, so don't be afraid."

Hesitantly, the woman raised her .22 rifle and put it against her shoulder, the barrel moving around a bit as she looked down the sights and searched for her target. Finding it, she steadied herself and then squeezed her eyes shut.

Seeing this, Tick-Tock said, "You're pulling a Brain."

She laughed nervously as she thought of the story he had told her of how Brain thought shooting was aiming in the general direction of a Z, closing his eyes and pulling the trigger until he was out of ammunition.

Resettling the weapon, she aimed again and jerked the trigger. The shot went high and struck a dead thing standing behind her target in the arm.

"Damn it," she said out loud, "I missed."

"Squeeze the trigger," Tick-Tock said gently.

"I was worried about the kick when I shot, but there's hardly any," she commented as she looked down the sights again.

It took her three more tries, but the Z finally went down in small spray of black pus.

She let out a little squeal of delight and said excitedly, "I did it."

"That you did," Tick-Tock told her. Turning to Steve, he said, "Mark another target for her let her go at it. She's got six more rounds, so let's see if she can get six more."

"I know I can," she said confidently. "This is easier than I thought."

"Then get to it," Tick-Tock told her before moving on to the man standing beside her with his rifle at the ready.

For the next two hours, the air around the mansion was filled with the sounds of gunfire.

***

Steve entered his room and fell into bed with his boots still on. Coming through the door behind him, Heather said, "I don't think so, buddy. Get those things off. We're not barbarians."

Reluctantly, he sat at the edge of the bed and started untying them, but stopped suddenly as a thought hit him. Looking at Heather, he asked, "Have you seen Grimm lately?"

"Not since you went up on the roof to help Tick-Tock," she replied. After a second, she said, "Come to think about it, I haven't seen Thing one and Thing two for a while either."

"They were with Brain in the kitchen when I went down there earlier, but I haven't seen them since. We still need to find out what Grimm's going to do," Steve said. "It looks like Igor is along for the ride, and she knows she can come with us too, but the last time we brought the subject up, she said she was going to stay."

"We can't let her stay," Heather said. "When that herd coming from the east hits this place, they'll overwhelm it."

"We can't force her to come," Steve said. After a second, he added, "And I don't want to be the one to try it and end up with the pointy end of that scythe up my ass for my efforts."

"I'll try to find her and talk some sense into her before I go on watch," Heather said as she plopped down in a chair and removed her boots.

"I'd like to get her input on the escape route we picked too," Steve said.

Heather sighed and said, "We just spent an hour going over those maps and I swear I'm seeing double."

Lying back on the bed, Steve asked, “How many of me do you see.”
With a familiar half smile, Heather said, “One, and that’s more than enough.”

CHAPTER FOUR

Russellville, Arkansas:

Doctor Hawkins led Sergeant Cain into the basement of the farmhouse as he briefed him on his latest orders from Washington. "The Joint Chief's are pleased with the latest report of the Malecton's effectiveness and want to start mass producing it as soon as possible."

Cain nodded and said, "Might get a little tight in camp with all the extra people coming in to work on it. We don't have a lot of extra space."

Hawkins snorted and said, "No, we won't be staying here. In fact we're almost rid of this wretched place. An instrument of this importance needs to be treated in a manner befitting it, so I sent a request to Washington to have my lab moved to Virginia. I received the approval only a few minutes ago. They tell me that there's an unused facility along the Potomac that suites my needs, so as soon as the military cleans it out, I move in. Once I'm set up, I will be furnished with everything I need to produce hundreds of Malectrons. I've been told that the Chairman of the Joint Chiefs sees the true impact that my device has and is pulling out all the stops."

"I'm sure the idea of world domination through controlling an army dead had a lot to do with that decision," Cain said thoughtfully.

Hawkins chuckled and said, "I'm sure it did, but regardless of that, I'm happy to finally be leaving Arkansas. This base and the people here served their purpose, but now that's done."

"They won't be coming with us?" Cain asked.

Hawkins shook his head and replied, "The Chairman will provide us with a top notch security detail to protect the new facility. I will oversee production of course, and I've asked that you be brought along to command the troops that will be protecting us."

Cain stopped in the middle of the hallway and said, "I'm honored, sir."

"You deserve it," Hawkins told him. "You see the need for this device and are willing to remove anything that stands in the way of its development."

"Like Randal," Cain said.

"Some people, like Lieutenant Randal, are misguided in what is right and wrong," Hawkins told him. "They don't see the big picture like we do. They talk and talk about a cure for the NWHW virus, but they don't see that controlling the dead is in our best interests rather than eradicating them."

Standing up straight, Cain said, "I'm willing to do whatever it takes to see this project through to the end."

Putting his hand on the man's shoulder, Hawkins said, "And you proved that already. My only concern now is Major Cage and that Sergeant he's always with. What's his name again?"

"Staff Sergeant Fagan," Cain said.

"I don't trust them," Hawkins said wistfully. "Even though we never proved that they were trying to undermine my research, I get the suspicion that they're up to something."

Knowing where the conversation was heading, Cain thought for a moment before saying, "It would be too risky to take care of them the same way we did Randal, but there are other ways. I know someone who will help."

Smiling, Hawkins said, "Then I'll leave that in your capable hands."

***

Major Jedidiah Cage motioned for the two men behind him to stop and crouch down before moving off into the brush. Staff Sergeant Fagan and Private First Class Jimmy McPherson instantly obeyed, facing outward to cover their flanks. Looking into the winter thinned woods on both sides, neither man could see any dead approaching, but from the front, they could definitely hear them.

After a few minutes, Cage duck walked back to them and said in a quiet voice, "I can see the observation post and it was overrun by Zs just like we thought. Looks like they knocked it to the ground and then they swarmed it. Can't tell how big of a group it was originally, but there's still over one-hundred of them moving around. There's about forty of fifty more with headshots lying on the ground so it looks like the guys in the OP put up a good fight before they were taken down."

Jimmy shuddered at the thought of what had happened here. Off the beaten path near the top of Mount Nebo, the observation post was manned 24/7 by two people on a rotating basis. They kept an eye on the surrounding area and warned the camp if they saw any big groups of Zs heading their way. He'd never been here, but from the stories told in the mess tent, it was one of the more dangerous duties in the camp. As isolated as the post was, if the dead spotted you before you spotted them, it would take hours for a relief force to come rescue you.

"No survivors?" Fagan asked.

Cage shook his head and replied, "Only two big smears of blood."

"So what's the plan, sir?" The Staff Sergeant asked.

"The platform is trashed so we won't be leaving anyone here to man it, but we still need to clear the dead out and retrieve whatever equipment we can," Cage answered. "Both the people up here had noise suppressors, night vision gear and a shitload of ammo. We're going to need those things."

This wasn't the reply that Jimmy wanted to hear. He'd only gone on this mission because he wanted to scope out the area for when he made a break for it, not get into some kind of half-assed firefight with a bunch of Zs. He knew that when he eventually went AWOL that he'd have to go on foot, so he'd volunteered when he heard Fagan talking about losing contact with the OP. Going on this relief mission be the perfect way to plan his route. Looking at a map of the area, he had decided that when he left, he would cut across Nebo before heading south to Louisiana where he hoped to reunite what was left of his family. He'd been pleased so far since from what he'd seen. The area was pretty clear because most of the dead seemed to congregate around the camp. Once he made his break, it would only be a matter of days if he could find a vehicle, or weeks if he had to go on foot, until he was home.

Daydreaming about the joyous reunion he would have with his brothers and sisters, Fagan interrupted his thoughts by telling him, "McPherson, go back to the squad and tell them to hold in place, and then I want you to come back here. We're going to need your rifle when we do this."

Jimmy nodded and went to do as he was ordered. When he returned, he found that both men had already secured noise suppressors to the barrels of their rifles. Crouching down next to them, he pulled his out of his pack and fumbled it for second. Regaining his grip, he started to attach it but couldn't seem to get it to slide onto the barrel of his M16.

After a few moments of trying, he heard Fagan say in an amused voice, "Nine out ten rhesus test monkeys can attach a noise suppressor to their rifle on the first try."

Jimmy heard Major Cage give a quiet laugh at this.

His face turning red, Jimmy said softly, "Screw you, Sarge." To which, both Cage and Fagan laughed.

Finally getting squared away, he sat on his haunches and listened to the Major lay out their plan of attack.

"We keep it simple," Cage said in a whisper. "Our closest targets are only fifteen to twenty feet away from the edge of the clearing so we'll take them out first. We'll form up abreast in the tree line and start with the nearest one's that are facing away from us. I want to get as many as we can before they know we're here. These things are brain dead, but I've seen how they act when they realize they're under attack. They'll turn as a group and rush us, and I don't want all of them coming at us at once. I really don't feel like running all the way back to the pickup point with a bunch of Zs on my ass. Are we clear?"

Both men nodded, so Cage said, "Follow me."

As they moved into position, Jimmy got his first good look at the carnage the dead had wrought on the observation post. He knew from the stories he'd heard that it was an eight foot square covered platform standing twelve feet off the ground, but to look at what was left, he never would have known it.

Splintered six-by-six posts jutted up from the ground, broken off by some unimaginable force. The platform itself was nothing but mangled triangles of broken plywood scattered across the small clearing where it had been erected, and like Major Cage had said, of its two occupants, there was nothing but large smears of blood and small pieces of gore in two spots. A tarp was draped across some brush, torn and tattered from being dragged there by countless feet.

Shuddering slightly at the destruction, Jimmy moved behind the tree Fagan pointed him to and raised his rifle as he focused on the dead that swarmed the area. They milled around the clearing with their heads down as they searched the dirt and weeds, looking for something to eat. As he watched, one bent down to pick up what looked like a dirt and bug covered piece of intestine and shoved it into its mouth. Most of them were whining, but a few had been silenced due to the fact that they'd had their throats ripped out or their mouths and tongues were so torn up by the gnashing teeth that had originally attacked them that they could make no sound. The sight of half clothed and fully nude, bluish grey bodies brought up Jimmy's gag reflex, but he forced it down.

In his short tour of duty in New Orleans, he had seen many of the dead, but these had been living in buildings so their clothing was mostly intact. The ones out in the countryside had worn their attire away to little or nothing at all. A few still had boots or shoes on, but their pants, shirts and dresses had been reduced to rags or were completely gone.

A small stone hit him in the leg, so he turned to his left to find out what Sergeant Fagan wanted. Seeing he was holding up his forefinger, middle finger and ring finger, Jimmy knew that the countdown to the slaughter was about to begin.

First, Fagan's forefinger dropped, then his ring finger. With a smile, the Staff Sergeant flipped him the bird before dropping it and turning to sight down his rifle.

Jimmy did the same and found his first target, a young girl with the vestiges of a yellow scarf still hanging around her neck. Squeezing the trigger on his silenced rifle, he heard a click of the firing pin striking the bullet followed immediately by what sounded like a muffled cough.

The girl's head erupted in a blossom of black puss, bone and hair as the bullet hit home. Knowing it was a kill without having to watch the body hit the forest floor, he turned and sighted in on the next, closest Z that was facing away from him. Out of the corner of his eye, he could see dead bodies drop from Cage and Fagan's fire as countless times, he switched his aim, stroked the trigger and watched a head explode before moving on to his next target. Expecting to be discovered quickly and rushed by the dead, Jimmy was surprised when he stopped to reload and saw that they had decimated at least half the Zs in the clearing without their knowing what was going on.

Sighting in, he started firing again. With each shot, his excitement rose at the thought of discovery. Just when he felt like the turkey shoot would go on like this for eternity, he heard Major Cage break the stillness of the forest by calling out, "Fresh magazines, line abreast. Advance through the clearing."

Ejecting his almost full clip, Jimmy slipped in a fully loaded one, let the bolt slam forward, and rose from his firing position to line up ten feet to the left of Staff Sergeant Fagan. He could see that the dead were well aware of their presence now and were heading toward them in a loping run.

Cage called out, "Advance." So Jimmy stepped off as he sighted in on the head the first Z rushing toward them. Without thinking, he walked forward as he pulled the trigger repeatedly, watching as heads snapped back from the impact of his bullets. He could see that there was only twenty or more Zs charging them, and the three of them made quick work of sending them back to hell. When the last of the dead fell, there was no need for the order to cease fire. All three men could see that they were the only thing, living or dead, still standing in the clearing.

"Go back and get the rest of the squad," Fagan ordered as he pulled a noise suppressed Hi-standard pistol from its holster and joined Major Cage in finishing off any of the dead that were still moving. They had gotten the ones that were on their feet, but some of them that were missing legs or were too torn up to stand upright were still crawling across the forest floor toward them.

Excited by the slaughter of the dead, Jimmy almost ran back to where the other men were waiting. When he returned to the clearing, he found that Cage and Fagan had finished off the last of the Zs and had already scrounged a small pile of equipment. After motioning for the Jimmy and the men in the squad to take over, Cage and Fagan walked a short distance away where they could talk without being overheard.

This being the first time that they could speak freely since receiving their orders to relieve the people manning the observation post, both men started to talk at once. While Cage asked out loud why the Staff Sergeant thought he had been specifically ordered to lead the squad on a simple rescue and recovery mission, Fagan was asking the same thing.

Fagan motioned for his superior to talk first, and Cage said, "So what gives? I was shocked as shit when Hawkins's little do-boy, Sergeant Cain, came and told me that I had been ordered to lead this little soiree."

Fagan shook his head and replied, "I was as shocked as you, sir. My only guess is they want you out of the way today."

"That's what I was thinking too," Cage said before asking, "but for what? And they even got a full-bird Colonel out of Hood to sign the order. It doesn't make sense because if they really wanted me out of the way; all they'd have to do is get one of the higher-ups to cut my orders to one of the Dead Cities and be done with it."

"But it's different for higher ranking officers, sir," Fagan told him. "If you're enlisted, they say go and you go, but for anyone over a Captain in rank to be sent into the shit, they would have to be a real fuck up. Word would get around as soon as you reported in and questions would be asked. You have to remember, the officer's corps has been chewed up pretty badly, but the good old boy network is still intact. If they just up and sent you to Orleans or Minneapolis without a good reason, it would stir up a lot of shit."

Looking down at the oak leaf cluster on his collar, Major Cage said, "You're right, I forget sometimes that I'm not just a Lieutenant that can be shuffled around like so much meat."

Fagan nodded and said, "My guess is that they don't want you out of the camp for just today, sir. There was nothing going on at the farmhouse, and the only incoming air traffic was the resupply chopper, and they came and went before Cain even showed up with your orders. I think it all goes back to us interfering with Hawkins tests."

"So what gives then?" Cage asked.

Pointing to the carnage around them, Fagan replied, "Maybe since they can't openly get rid of you, they're sending you out to try and get you killed."

CHAPTER FIVE

The Happy Hallow Insane Asylum:

Steve Wendell cocked his head to one side. He was sure that he heard music, but the sound was so distant that he wasn't sure if he was imagining it. Wondering if he was hallucinating, he dug his finger in his ear and wiggled it around vigorously. It took him a few seconds to figure out what he was hearing, but then he realized that he hadn't lost his mind, but was hearing Anna Nalick singing "Breathe."

Walking down the second floor hallway, he followed the music until he came to a door near the radio room. A capital 'A' inside a circle with a line through it had been spray painted across its face. He paused for a moment before knocking softly.

The music cut off abruptly before a voice called out roughly, "Who is it?"

"It's Steve."

After a moment, the voice said, "Advance and be recognized."

Smiling at the familiar sound of Grimm's voice, he pushed down on the lever and let the door swing open on its hinges. Expecting to see the imposing figure of death greeting him, he stopped at the threshold at what he saw. Instead of finding Grimm in full regalia, he found her naked from the waist up.

Grimm saw him hesitate and avert his eyes, which caused her to laugh and say, "I was just getting dressed, but I'm sure it's nothing you haven't seen before."

Steve laughed nervously and glanced down the hall. No matter how innocent the encounter was, if Heather walked up on them right now, he'd be screwed. Sneaking a peek back into the room to see if Grimm had put something on, and, after all, he was a guy, his attention wasn't drawn to Grimm's breasts, but rather to her arms. He had seen her in action swinging her scythe and was amazed at how thin and delicate they appeared. Not wanting to look like a dirty old man, he averted his gaze back into the hallway.

After picking up a tee-shirt from the bed, Grimm slipped it over her head and added, "Its safe now. So what do I owe the pleasure of this visit?"

Turning around and seeing that she was dressed, Steve said, "I heard the music and was wondering where it was coming from. I'm glad I found you though, since we need to talk."

Glancing down at her radio, Grimm said, "Just getting my mind right before the shit storm of epic proportions you're about to stir up hits the fan and sprays across the countryside. I'm going to have my hands full after you leave."

"That's what I wanted to talk to you about. You need to go with us," he told her.

Smiling, Grim shook her head and replied, "We've talked about this before and you just don't get it, my work is here."

"Work?" Steve asked.

"I have much reaping to do," Grimm told him. "Before you came, I only took the ones that crossed my path. Now, I have thousands of my children to take. I am going to by busy, busy, busy for the next few weeks."

"But what about the huge group coming from the east?" Steve asked her. "There's no way this house is going to stand against them and there's no way you can stand against them."

With a dramatic sigh, Grimm said, "But I will not stand against them, silly rabbit. In the immortal words of Muhammad Ali, I'll move like a butterfly and sting like a bee."

Steve started to protest, but Grimm cut him off by saying, "And now you need to go and make sure your group is ready, and I must finish my preparations. It is going to be a busy morning." Seeing Steve open his mouth to argue that she needed to go with them, Grimm said in a reassuring voice, "Don't worry, I'll be fine. If it makes you feel better, my plan is that when you make your grand exit, I am going to use that as a distraction to do the same since you will be drawing my children off. Thing one and Thing two are coming with me, but I believe that Igor is going with you. He sees the little girl as some kind of savior and himself as her protector."

Still hesitant, Steve said, "You and the Thing twins would be safer with us."

"Safer, maybe," Grimm agreed, "But like I said, I have my job to do, and like I also said, I still have a lot of other things to do, so you need to go."

"Do you need any help?" Steve asked.

With a slight grin she replied, "I may have showed you my tits, Steve, but a woman has to have some secrets."

***

The sun was barely peeking over the horizon and false dawn had come and gone. Shapes were taking form from the shadows as Tick-Tock stood with Denise and Brain looking down at the mob of dead pushing against the rear of the mansion. After a moment, he asked, "So who's got the best throwing arm?"

Denise spoke up, saying, "I pitched on my college softball team."

Raising an eyebrow, he asked, "Fast or slow?"

With a smirk, she replied, "I like it slow, but I can do it fast when the mood strikes me."

From behind them, Brain muttered, "Jesus, you two need to get a room."

Tick-Tock laughed and said, "We'll stop at the first Super 8 we come to," Nodding to Denise, he added, "You're it then. There isn't a bull pen to warm up in so you'll have to wing it."

Setting the book bag filled with explosives at Denise's feet, Brain said, "The bombs are fairly stable but you still need to be careful. A sudden shock can set them off, so throw them gently if you can."

Pointing to a spot on the fence that he had marked with the paint gun earlier, Tick-Tock said, "That's where we need to get to. Grimm told us that there's a trail through the woods just beyond. I want you to throw each bomb about twenty feet apart in a straight line away from the building heading directly to that spot. You should have a couple left over, so toss them about forty feet to both sides of the Zs to widen the corridor." Turning to Brain, he asked, "And you've got the rest of the bombs?"

Patting another book bag slung over his shoulder, he replied, "Right here. I'll use one or two for the fence and the rest for any of the Zs that follow us. Steve already showed me on the map where he wants me to use them."

Tick-Tock nodded and said, "Then get down to the first floor with everyone else and get ready to go. Tell Steve -."

He was interrupted by his friend asking, "Tell me what?"

Turning, they saw him climbing through the hatch in the roof.

"That we're almost ready to go," Tick-Tock finished.

Making his way carefully to the edge of the roof, Steve looked down and surveyed the gruesome scene below him before asking, "Who's the designated pitcher?"

"I am," Denise said.

Looking her straight in the eye, Steve said tersely, "Make every one count," before waving for Brain to follow him as he turned sharply and headed for the hatch.

When they were a short ways off, Denise said, "That was kind of abrupt."

Tick-Tock shrugged off his own feeling of anxiety at the way Steve was acting and reasoned out loud, "I guess he's under a lot of pressure. Sometimes I think he takes too much on. I don't think I've ever seen him so serious about anything though."

Just then, Steve poked his head up through the opening in the roof and said loudly, "Hey, Tick-Tock."

"What's up?"

"There's something I've been meaning to talk to you about," Steve said in a serious tone.

After a moment he smiled and asked, "Are you a sociopath?"

Tick-Tock gave a half-laugh and said, "Probably, but why do you ask?"

"You seem to be enjoying yourself too much with a zombie apocalypse going on and everything," Steve told him.

Tick-Tock didn't hesitate as he said, "It's the most fun I've ever had in my life."

Steve laughed and said, "That's what I thought." Before disappearing into the mansion.

Motioning out toward the field of dead, Tick-Tock said to Denise, "Time to do your Catfish Hunter imitation. Make it count, babe."

***

Heather looked at the grim faces surrounding her in the first floor bedroom and said, "I need the guys with the crow bars to come up front."

Two men made their way around Linda and Cindy to stand in front of Heather. Nervously, they shifted from one foot to the other as they waited to be called into action.

Seeing their discomfort, Heather said, "Take it easy. All you have to do is pry the storm panels off and then get out of the way." Trying to ease their nerves, she pointed to where the window and part of its frame had already been ripped off to enlarge the opening and added, "You did a great job so far, just calm down and focus on what you have to do."

Movement out in the hallway drew their attention as three of the people that had been standing in the doorway moved aside to let Steve and Brain through.

Raising his voice to be heard above the sound of dead hands pounding and scratching at the storm panels, Steve said, "They're ready up top, so I want to go over everything one more time. We can't afford any screw ups." Looking around to make sure he had everyone's attention, he said, "After the bombs finish going off, I want those panels down as quick as possible." Pointing to Brain, Connie, Igor and Linda, he said, "You three will be backup and Denise will back you up. You'll all be covering Cindy too. I want her in the center of you at all times. Make sure that one of you has Pep on a short leash. You know how she gets when she sees the Zs and I don't want her running off. When the panels are down, Heather, Tick-Tock and myself will use our rifles to clear away any of the Zs that might be left standing near the opening. After that, we'll move out the window first and cover everyone as they follow. Once we're all clear of the building, we move to the fence as a group."

Turning to Brain, he said, "Once we get out of the building, I want you with me. I want you so close that if I stop fast, your nose goes up my ass."

There were some nervous laughter at this.

Steve waited for it to die off before continuing, "We'll stop about forty feet from the fence and Brain will do his thing. Once the fence is down, we head into the woods. At this point, we're going to start moving fast and I can't stress again how important it is that everyone stay together. From what Grimm told us, the path is wide enough for two or three people at first but then it narrows down so we'll have to go single file. Just follow the person in front of you, and once again, stay together. If someone goes down because they're bitten, shoot them in the head. If they go down for any other reason, get them up and moving. If they can't move or we can't carry them, we have to leave them."

Looking at the faces staring at Steve as they digested this, Heather added, "And be ready to adjust to any situation. Make sure that if you have to shoot that you only shoot at the Zs that are an immediate threat. You may think that you're all carrying a shitload of ammunition, but it will go fast if you start popping away at everything."

"And also make sure of your target before you pull the trigger," Tick-Tock added as he entered the room with Denise behind him. "Fire control isn't just for Smokey the bear."

The ten remaining people from The Battleship Texas nodded at this. To Steve, they all looked scared, but behind this readily apparent fear was a posture of determination. This pleased him. They had a long way to go, with numerous unknowns in front of them, and he needed everyone to pull their weight.

Heather said loudly, "Everyone get into position."

As they moved around to find the places in the hall that they had been assigned earlier by Tick-Tock, she said softly to Steve, "I'm still worried that we don't have anyone spotting to make sure the area is clear before we pop those panels off."

Steve shook his head and replied, "We've been over it a dozen times and keep coming to the same conclusion. If we leave a spotter on the roof, or even on the second floor, we'd have to wait for them to catch up and it will leave everyone too exposed. We saw before how quick those things recovered from the blast from the dynamite, so we know we'll have to move fast. On top of that, the dead from the sides and the front of the mansion are going to come quick. If we wait for a spotter before popping the panels, we all might not get through. Anyone that's even a minute behind us will probably get cut off if we wait outside for them. We only have one shot at this, so it's win or lose."

With a sigh, Heather said, "I know, but it's still a big risk."

With a laugh, Steve said, "And so is everything else we've done so far." Seeing her uneasy look, he gave her a hug and said, "I'm not going to say that everything is going to be okay, but it will be what it's going to be."

Hugging him back, Heather said softly, "That's fucking reassuring."

Steve laughed.

***

With a half bow, Brain pulled the detonator from his pack and handed it to Connie as he said, "Would you do the honors, my lady?"

With a strained smile, she took the radio as Tick-Tock called out to his trainees, "I want everyone to squat down and put their palms against their ears and open their mouths just like we practiced. I don't know how bad it will be, but I don't want anyone going deaf from the concussion."

Hands rose to do as they were told as Connie looked unsure at the detonator in her hands. She didn't know when to press the transmit button, so she looked questioningly at Brain.

"I'm going to say 'fire in the hole' three times and then you press the button," he told her. Looking to Steve, who nodded, he said loudly, "Fire in the hole, fire in the hole, fire in the hole."

***

The dead thing looked at the lump lying beneath the shuffling feet of its brethren before dropping to its knees and picking it up. The object had seemed to fall from the sky just seconds ago to bounce off the head of what had once been a shopkeeper to land in front of it.

When it had been alive, its name had been Ethan, but it had no recollection of this or how it had died or where it had come from. It would be impossible to explain to the raggedy dead thing that it once had a mother named Lena and a sister named Megan, or that it had been infected and died when it had gone on a foraging trip with his sister, and that she couldn't bring herself to put a bullet into its brain. It didn't know that after it had died and come back that it had wandered westward for days before coming across a group of things just like it.

Instinct told it to join them.

Since then, they had come across three separate bands of travelers that they had fallen upon and eaten, but now, humans had become elusive. It had dug for grubs and termites to try and feed its insatiable appetite, but even those had become rare. The lure of food had brought it and its herd across this area four times before they ended up outside the mansion.

The thing that had been Ethan might not have known any of this, but when it saw the thing lying on the trampled grass at the back of the mansion, the faint memory of a word passed briefly through its shattered mind.

'Ball'.

Holding the white blob of plastic explosives against its chest, it made its way through the tightly packed mass of dead. Being only eleven years old helped as it occasionally dropped down to weave its way between the legs of the mob and finally into the open.

After reaching the outer edge of the mass of dead pressed against the building that held the food, it suddenly stopped. Looking at the open area leading to the fence, it turned its head and looked back at the mansion. It had completely forgotten about the object in its hands or that it had wanted to get away from the rest of its kin so it could play. Reasoning was gone forever from its brain, so instead of asking itself what it was doing out here, when only moments before it had been less than twenty feet away from the food that was very reason for its existence, it turned and started moving back the way it had come.

The blast came before it took its first step, disintegrating what had been Ethan and shredding all those close by with shrapnel as it knocked them down.

***

The explosions came so close that they sounded like one. Dust dropped from the ceiling from the concussion and the walls shook so hard that a picture of Jesus holding a lamb in his arms fell with a resounding crash. The noise from the blast was barely a memory when the two men with crowbars jumped up and ran into the room to frantically pry at the storm panels covering the window.

Steve, Heather and Tick-Tock followed, stopping to stand a few feet behind them with their rifles at the ready. The lights flickered for a moment and then died as the generator gave out, leaving them with nothing but a few rays of dust-filled sunlight shining in through the cracks around the panels. One of these widened as the panel on the right pushed outward, but then it stopped after only a few inches to be pushed back.

The man that had been working on it stepped back and raised his foot to kick it, even as Steve yelled at him to stop. He had seen that the storm panel had been pushed back by something on the outside and that could only mean one thing.

In his quest to be free of the dust and confinement of the small room, the man didn't listen and lunged out with his foot. The panel flew off, but instead of the opening being filled with sunlight streaming in, it was filled with the faces and clawing hands of the dead as they grabbed on to the extended leg and dragged the screaming man into their midst. Vicious teeth and nails dug into him from all sides as he was literally torn apart before his body disappeared into the throng of dead outside the window.

Gunfire and shouts erupted as the group reacted. The dead that showed themselves in the opening were quickly shot down, only to be replaced by more. These too were quickly dispatched by the accurate, almost point blank fire from Heather, Tick-Tock and Steve, but a never ending stream of dirt covered snarling faces and clawing hands replaced them. The noise was tremendous and soon the stink of burnt gunpowder filled the air to mix with the dust and create a haze in the small bedroom.

Knowing that it was taking too long, Steve yelled, "Cover me," as he approach the window from an angle for a better look, moving moved side-ways to stay out of the line of fire. They had been killing the dead at a steady pace for almost half a minute, with what seemed like little effect on the continuing stream of Zs trying to get in, and he needed to see exactly what they were facing. It was hard for him to imagine that there were this many of the dead left after the tremendous blast from the explosives, and he had to see how many they were facing. He knew they had to get rid of them fast since they only had a short time before the ones from the front and sides of the house came around back and cut them off completely. His first thought was to use another of Brain's bombs.

Finding it hard to see with all the bodies climbing over each other to get at them, he yelled, "Pour it on," to Heather and Tick-Tock to see if they could shoot an opening through the Zs. The dead fell away momentarily from the onslaught of lead, but he still had to jump up get a better look over the crowding heads of the dead.

On his second leap into the air, he finally had a clear view of the back of the mansion, and what he saw filled him with dread.

The dead were massed twenty or thirty deep around the window with more coming to join them by the second. He could see the carnage inflicted by the explosives, but it all appeared to be further away from the building. The first bomb should have taken out most, if not all, of the dead they were now having to shoot, but it looked like it hadn't gone off.

Bouncing up again for one last look, he rejoined his friends and said loud enough to be heard over the gunfire, "The first bomb didn't go off. There's too many of them back there and we're out of time. It looks like there's already a shit-load of them coming around from the front of the house too."

Heather shot into the forehead of what had once been a house-wife from Dallas and then pointed her CAR-15 at the motionless bodies of the dead that were starting to clog the opening as she said, "Looks like we're plugging the hole though."

Steve considered this for a few seconds. Even with the volume of outgoing rifle fire, a few of the dead had managed to get close enough to start climbing in. As they were shot down, their bodies dropped to lay like broken sacks of meat across the window sill. As the ones behind them tried to climb over them, they too were shot down and added their bodies to the mass that was starting to block up the opening.

At first elated that this immediate threat was being solved, Steve's spirits dropped at the thought that in the long run, it wouldn't matter. With the huge mob of dead coming at them from the East, and with the weak spot the window now presented, they would be overrun that much quicker when the herd arrived.

Trying to find a way to somehow turn this disaster to their advantage, a thought struck him. To have planned their escape in the way he was thinking would have been insanity, but since it was happening, he knew he had to go with it.

"We've got to keep them back away from the window," he yelled. "If we block it up it might not attract enough of them." As the three of them moved forward, firing as they went, he said, "We can still turn this in our favor. With all the noise and the shooting, we'll draw the ones away from the front of the mansion. Once we've got them clustered up back here, we head out the front."

"We'll be able to get to the trucks that way and -," Heather said with excitement before stopping abruptly when a thought came to her. With trepidation, she asked, "And who's going stay back here and keep drawing them in? No matter how many Zs we get to come to the back of the house, there's still going to be a bunch clustered around the front. Even more if we all cut and run at the same time. We've seen too many times how fast they moved back to where they were when we tried to draw them off. Once everyone makes a break for it, whoever's left behind will be cut off."

Distracted by some of the dead that had gotten too close, she turned her attention to firing into the heads of the Zs. In the pit of her stomach though, she had a sinking feeling she knew who would volunteer. Shaking it off, she focused on her targets and didn't repeat the question lest she get an answer she didn't want to hear.

Steve considered the wall of dead flesh only feet away, knowing he had already made his mind up on who would stay. Glad Heather's attention was taken by the dead, he considered his own demise. He knew his plan had one fatal flaw, and that was while everyone was going out the front, one person needed to stay and keep the Zs interested in the back of the mansion. His thoughts turned to when he had sat at his desk at the radio station only days after this had all started while contemplating ending his own life. Instead of putting his pistol under his chin and pulling the trigger though, he had resolved that if it ever came to it, he would take as many of the dead things with him as he could when he went. He considered that decision every day in a world ruled by the living dead, and felt that this would be the time.

Ignoring Heather's question, he turned his head and yelled, "Brain, get everyone to the front of the house and get one of your grenades ready. We're changing the plan. I want everyone at the top of the stairs and ready to go out the front."

"Out the front?" He questioned. "A grenade?

Steve said tersely, "We're going out the front, the grenade is for the doors since we don't have time to fuck around with pulling the boards off. Now move your ass."

As Brain turned to go, a sudden thought struck him and he yelled for him to wait. Turning to Tick-Tock, as his friend fired into the mass of dead that they had forced back a little more than ten feet from the window, he asked, "How much ammo do you have?"

Without taking his eyes off the Zs as he clenched the pistol grip of his rifle with one hand and continued to fire, Tick-Tock felt his ammunition pouches strapped to the harness he had taken from the National Guard MRAP and the cargo pockets on his pants before saying, "I've got about four clips left plus the one in my rifle."

Without having to be asked, Heather said, "I've got five plus what I have in my rifle." She fired three rounds into the massed dead and the bolt of her rifle locked back. After switching out her empty magazine for a full one, she let the bolt slam forward before adding, "Make that four."

"Not enough, you're going to need all that," Steve said. Turning to Brain, he said, "Give me all your spare magazines. Only keep two or three for yourself."

Hearing this, and knowing from her fears had become real and that Steve had decided he would be the one staying behind, Heather said, "It's not going to be you." She could feel the tension build in her at the thought of losing him.

Playing dumb, Steve asked, "Me what?"

"The one who stays behind," she said abruptly before firing out the window. "The group needs you too much. I'll stay."

"You're not staying behind," Steve said. "If it's anyone, it's going to be me."

Turning to glare at him with a combination of ice and love in her eyes, Heather said firmly, "No way, I'm staying."

Next to her, Tick-Tock said with a laugh, "Well I'm not fucking staying, so you two need to figure this shit out."

His wise crack broke the tension and caused Heather and Steve to break out in a burst of nervous laughter. Despite this, they both knew that a decision had to be made. As Steve opened his mouth to say they would ask for a volunteer to keep the dead's attention at the back of the mansion while the other fled, a voice from the behind him said loudly, "Do not be afraid, I will be the one to keep the savage hordes at bay while you all escape."

Turning, they found their host standing just inside the doorway with Thing one and Thing Two on either side of her, both of them armed with Uzi machine guns. With her MP5 machinegun in her hands and her scythe slung over her shoulder, she made a deadly figure.

"Never fear," she said, "Delightfully Grimm is here."

CHAPTER SIX

The Happy Hallow Insane Asylum:

With the faint noise of gunfire reached his ears, Steve faced the group gathered at the top of the stairs and said, "We're going to try for the truck and the vans, but that doesn't mean we're going to make it. I need all of you to be ready for anything. Once those doors blow, Tick-Tock and I will be the first ones through. We're going to clear any immediate threats." Pointing to Heather, he said, "You're going to be right behind us or on my right depending on how big of a hole the bomb makes. Once we get through the door, I want you to clear the porch to the right while Tick-Tock gets the area to the left. I'll deal with anything coming at us from the front. We'll try for the trucks first, but if that's a wash, then we head for the gate. If there's too many of them there, we find the clearest route and head for the fence."

Looking at the grim faces in front of him, Steve continued, "And if they're too bunched up and everything goes to hell, Brain is going to start throwing his grenades to clear them out. Only as a last resort should we split up. If that happens, head for whatever gaps you can find in the Zs. Get over the fence and head for the woods. If you make it that far and clear the area, head east until you hit a creek. It's in a really deep wash so stay up on the bank. Follow it north until you come to an old wooden bridge, but make sure you don't have a bunch of them following you. This is where we're going to meet back up and I don't want anyone leading a shitload of Zs right to us. Don't wait any longer than three hours. If anyone's coming, they'll be there by then."

"And then what?" One of the women in the group asked. "What do we do?"

"We all continue on to Polk like we planned," Steve told her, leaving out that it would be whoever was left alive, and if they had to scatter, it wouldn't be many.

Denise appeared at the bottom of the stairs and called up to them in a slightly winded voice, "From the roof, it only looked like there was a few hundred biters left out in front of the house. I checked in with Grimm and she said that she thinks she's got as many as she's going to get at the back. She's having a hard time holding them off, and a few of the Zs even made it into the room before her and the Things cut them down. She said that if you're going to go, then you need to go now."

Despite her reassurances that she would be fine, Steve felt a twinge of regret at leaving Grimm behind. What finally swayed him to let her keep the dead occupied while they escaped, was when she said in her eloquent voice, "You have your plans and I have mine, and my plan doesn't include dying in this exclusive retreat for wayward oddballs. The whole time I was here, all I could think of was escape, and while the minions that run this fine establishment caught me twice when I tried, I finally figured it all out. I was just about to unroll my master plan when my children came back to life and set me on my new course. Now, I will combine my plan with your plan and give you the time to get clear."

Steve waved for Denise to join them before turning to Tick-Tock and Heather to ask if they were ready.

Heather simply nodded.

Tick-Tock hefted his M4 assault rifle and said, "We've got the guns but they've got the numbers."

Steve thought about this for a second, and not knowing if this was a good or a bad thing, turned to Brain and said, "Get ready to throw your bomb as soon as everyone's down."

Brain hefted the misshapen, off-white mass in his hand and said, "Don't worry, when this baby goes off, it'll leave a hole big enough for all of us to go through shoulder to shoulder."

Steve smiled at the exaggeration as the group took cover in the halls leading off the landing at the top of the stairs. Denise was last and found a spot between him and Tick-Tock.

When they were clear, they covered their ears and opened their mouths to lessen the concussion. Every eye was on Brain as he judged the distance like a major league pitcher before going into a wind up and throwing the bomb with all his might and then dropping down flat.

Everyone scrunched their heads down and closed their eyes as they waited for the expected blast...that never came.

After a few seconds, Steve called out, "What the hell happened? Is that thing going to go off or what."

Brain rose from the floor and looked down in question to where his grenade lay a few feet from the door. He knew he had thrown it hard enough and far enough to hit what he was aiming for, but it hadn't gone off. After a second of thought, the answer came to him and he said, "It didn't impact with enough force. I'll try again."

After retrieving the bomb, Brain stood at the top of stairs and tried again. This time, he waited long enough to make sure the bomb hit its target before dropping down.

Again, nothing.

Steve watched as Brain rose to get the grenade while Denise said from behind him, "Jesus, next time just hit it with your purse."

His laughter turned to concern though, when she jumped up and ran down the stairs while saying to Brain in passing, "Get behind something and watch how to throw."

Steve started to object, but stopped when Tick-Tock said, "Kick back and enjoy the show. She's got this."

Steve did just that as he watched Denise pick up the grenade and back up to a spot near the bottom of the stairs.

***

Denise turned the bomb in her hands over a few times before tossing it in the air to get a feel for it. Judging the distance, she didn't even consider if she was too close. She knew how far the mound was from home plate, and this was the optimum distance to get the most impact out of her pitch. All she had to do was adjust to the size of the bomb and keep her hand a little further away from her thigh when she threw it. When she felt that she was ready, she went into the windup and underhand throw that was so familiar from college, and watched as the bomb hit its target at sixty miles an hour.

Overjoyed at what she knew would have a perfect strike, the blast enveloped her so fast that she didn't have time to feel fear before her world turned red, white, and then faded to nothing.

***

Grimm was swinging the point of the scythe down into the top of the head of an animated corpse still dressed in the remains of a pair of bib overalls when she felt and heard the blast. From either side of her, Thing one and Thing two fired short bursts of bullets into the heads of her children that got too close.

Just seconds earlier, they had been forced to abandon the room and were now holding the dead back from the doorway. While it should have been easy to keep them away from the bottleneck that the window made, they walking corpses had come at them from along the outside wall to continually claw at the edges of the window before being dispatched. In this way, they had slowly made the opening bigger as they picked away at the hole the men with the crowbars had originally made. The final decision to fall back came when numerous dead hands had pulled a large chunk of the wall to the right and below the window away before being shot down by the Thing twin's Uzis.

As she swung her blade and beheaded one of hell's returnees, she turned to her two minions and said, "We hold for one more minute to give Steve and his people time and then we start backing up."

***

Tick-Tock was the first to the bottom of the stairs when he saw Denise go down. As his boots pounded on the wooden treads, his mind screamed over and over, 'Not again.'

Reaching her, he heaved a broken clump of plaster and lathe from her body and knelt down by her side. Putting a hand to her chest to check for breathing, he was relieved to hear her say in a faint voice, "You horny bastard. Trying to feel me up at a time like this."

Smiling so hard that he thought the corners of his mouth would split, Tick-Tock ignored this as he ran his hands over her body while he checked for broken bones. Finding none, he asked, "Can you get up?"

Lifting her hand for help, she said, "Give me a boost."

Seeing how shaky she was, he was gently putting one hand under her head and the other behind her back to lift her when a woman from the group appeared on Denise's other side to help get her into a sitting position and then onto her feet.

Turning to where Steve and Heather were shooting through the gaping hole left by the bomb, Tick-Tock said, "I've got to go, babe. Are you going to be alright?"

"I'll be fine, she said as she swayed slightly. "Go help Steve. I'll be right behind you as soon as the room stops spinning."

Looking into the eyes of the woman who had helped them, Tick-Tock said, "Stay with her no matter what. You're responsible for her."

Turning to leave, he took one last look to make sure Denise was alive and that he wasn't dreaming. He had been looking around the corner of the hall with Steve and had seen the blast from the bomb lift her off her feet and slam her into the stairs. Her body had bounced off them been propelled forward to land in a heap at their base. He'd thought for sure that she was dead before she hit the ground by the way she'd been thrown like a ragdoll to lay motionless. Recalling the sight now, he thought that this might have been what saved her from serious injury. The concussion from the blast had knocked her unconscious before she hit, so her body wasn't tensed up as her mind told it to prepare for impact.

Hearing Steve call out for him, he ran across the debris littering the floor.

***

The mass of dead had enlarged the window in their frantic effort to get to the food that had finally appeared after so long of a wait and crowded into the room, pushing Grimm and the Thing twins into hall. From the doorway, they had done her best to hold the dead back, but their numbers were too many. The final straw was when they started busting through the wall to their right when the weight of their numbers made the old plaster and lathe collapse.

Calling out to the Things, Grimm ordered them to fall back. It hadn't been a full minute like she'd planned to give Steve, but if they tried to hold in place, they'd be overwhelmed.

***

As he stepped into the sunlight, Steve shot into the contorted face of one of the dead, not even seeing the spray of black ochre, bone and brains that flew out from the back of its head as he searched for a new target. With Heather beside him, they quickly took down ten more of the dead that were close enough to be considered an immediate threat. Dozens of bodies that had been caught in the explosion when the front doors had been blown either lay writhing or still on what was left of the porch and the lawn that grew on either side of the walkway leading up to it.

Looking around quickly, Steve could see that most of the remaining dead that were still on their feet were clustered to the front of them. Regrettably, this meant that they were also around the vans and the truck they wanted to use in their escape. Taking in the situation at a glance, he knew it would be impossible to make it to the vehicles, start them and get away before they were overrun. Making a snap decision, he called out to Heather, "We head for the fence to the right."

Instead of hearing Heather's voice, Tick-Tock replied, "There's just as many Zs to left. If we go that way though, we'll be closer to the path that leads to the creek and the bridge."

Surprised to hear his friend's voice, Steve asked, "How's Denise?"

"Definite concussion," he answered. "I just hope it's not a fractured skull."

At first, Steve had been angry when he saw Tick-Tock abandon their plan and head directly toward his girlfriend, but had gotten over it quickly. With his anger had come the realization of how he would react if it had been Heather in a similar situation.

"To the left then," Steve said. Turning to Heather, he told her, "Get everyone out here, it's time to haul ass."

Within seconds, the entire group was clustered in the area that had once held the front doors. Steve waved Heather and Tick-Tock to either side of him and they made short work of the few dead between the end of the porch and the fence as they moved forward at a steady pace. A few shots rang out from behind them as some of the Zs on their flank got too close and were taken out, but on the whole, it seemed to Steve that they were going to make their escape unscathed.

That was until they reached the end of the porch and he looked down the side of the building.

The dead were coming toward them in a mob as they emitted a high pitched whine that sent shivers up his spine. He had expected quite a few of the dead to be attracted by the explosion, but he wasn't prepared for the gruesome sight of hundreds of them coming at them from around from the back of the house so quickly. Gauging the distance to the fence and the distance to the main body of Zs, he saw that they were a lot closer than he would have liked.

Knowing that retreat was not an option, he yelled out, "Move, move, move," as he leapt over the railing and fired a few shots at the closest targets.

Heather and Tick-Tock joined him in laying down covering fire as the rest of the group jumped from the porch and onto grass that had been trampled and torn up by thousands of dead feet. One man landed awkwardly, but was helped up by Linda and Cindy.

Heather called out that they were all clear, so Steve yelled for Brain, jumping slightly at the sound of the tech's voice saying, "Here," only inches from his ear. Spinning, he found his friend almost nose to nose with him.

"You said to stay close," Brain said when he saw the look on Steve's face.

"Not that close," he replied as he leaned back. "Now use one of your bombs and blow a hole in the fence."

Taking a quick look down the porch, Steve could see that the dead from the front of the house were mostly ignoring them. A few started in their direction, where they were promptly shot down by various members of the group, but most of them seemed to be heading into the mansion. At first delighted by this break, his thoughts turned to Grimm and the Thing twins. Hoping they would be alright, he turned his attention to the mob that was coming closer with every second.

Brain reached into his backpack and brought out one of his grenades. Looking around for Denise, he saw her being supported by a woman from the group. Her face was pale, and as he watched, his best friend's girl reeled unsteadily as she tried to keep her feet. Realizing that she wouldn't be any help this time, he turned to the fence as he tried to decide the best way to make sure his bomb exploded when he threw it, but not blow himself up like she almost had.

Wondering if he could mimic Denise's underhand throw, he felt he would probably end up tossing the grenade over the fence if he tried. He already knew his overhand throw was too weak to set the bomb off from any distance, so that was out. This left him only one option.

An image from his childhood flashed through his mind. It was of a poster hanging on his closet door depicting Snoopy on a surfboard hanging ten on a huge wave. Remembering what the Peanut's character was screaming, Brain let out a piercing, "Cowabungaaaaa," as he ran for the fence.

Delightfully Grimm ejected the magazine from her machine gun and reached inside her cloak for another. Finding nothing, she let the weapon fell to the floor as she unslung her scythe from where it hung over her shoulder. As soon as she had it in her hands though, she knew that in the confines of the hallway it would do no good. The walls were too close to get any kind of strength behind a swing. Eyeing the approaching dead that climbed over each other to get at them, she called out to the twins to follow her. Turning, she raced for the front of the house.

Reaching the entry, she was pleased by the destruction that Steve and his people had wrought, but not by the sight of her children spotting her as they flooded through a hole where the doors had been. She knew there too many of them to fight their way through to safety, so she motioned for the twins to follow her to the base of the stairs. They had to keep the high ground if there was any chance for their survival.

Grimm had known all along that staying behind had been a suicide move, but Steve and his people were on a quest greater than hers. She would have loved nothing more than to join them and see how it all played out, but she had her work here. Taking a deep breath, she called out loudly, "Come, my little ones. Come to me. I will send you to peace everlasting."

The first of her children rushed at them and was decapitated for its efforts. More followed and were cut down by the scythe and the accurate fire of the Thing twins as the trio backed up the stairs.

***

Brain could feel his pulse pounding in his head as he ran toward the fence. The sound of the dead whining, rifles firing, and Pep barking at the dead was lost in the thundering beat of his heart. Judging the distance, he knew he had to get close enough to make sure the bomb exploded.

Anxiety rose in him as he neared his objective. Alternately thinking that he was too close and then not close enough, he started to throw and then stopped himself. Knowing he only had one shot at this, he ran to within twenty feet of the fence before lifting his arm over his shoulder and whipping it forward as he fell flat onto the grass.

***

Grimm heard the explosion and smiled as she hooked the point of her scythe under the chin of one of her children and jerked upwards. The sound of the blast meant that Steve and his people were still alive and had blown a hole in the fence. Her grin widened at the thought that she had bought them enough time, and that now she and the Twins could start the next leg in the everlasting journey called life.

And death.

Deep in her heart, she knew that all was said and done, everyone ended up exactly where they needed to be.

Considering her own position, she could fell a burning ache in her shoulders from swinging her scythe, she had a pounding headache and all she could think about was endless sleep. She had been up all night making preparations for her final exit, and her body was worn from the drawn out battle she had just been through and was still fighting. Her children were still coming in droves up the stairs and onto the landing where they were being reaped, but her legs started to sag with the knowledge that she had done all she could in her duty to mankind. Now it was time to rest.

She was in the exact spot she needed to be to put an end to this chapter.

Yelling to be heard over the screeching of the dead and the firing of the Uzis wielded by her minions, she called out, "It is time."

Instantly, the Thing twins ceased fire and closed in on either side of her.

Wrapping her cloak around them, Grimm watched as her children drew near. With nothing holding them back, they closed in with a rush, squealing at the sight of food.

Thinking to herself that this wasn't the end, but just a new beginning, Delightfully Grimm laughed as she and Thing one and Thing two disappeared under the mob of dead that fell on them.

Steve and Tick-Tock scooped Brain up from where he was kneeling on the grass and helped him over a section of twisted wrought iron that had once been part the fence. Connie was right on their heels and took charge of him so they would be free to deal with the threat of the Zs close on their heels. Once unburdened, the two men stood on either side of the hole as they fired into the heads of the closest of the mass of dead heading toward them.

The fence and its brick posts were scattered across the grass inside and outside of the compound, so the group had to pick their way through the rubble into the deep grass beyond. Once they were clear, some of them started to run for the woods, but Heather stopped them before they could go too far. When everyone was assembled, she called out to Steve and Tick-Tock.

After firing a last shot into the forehead of one of the advancing Zs, Steve ignored the spray of black blood and brains that flew out to take a last look at where the dead had swarmed around from the back of the mansion and were now heading towards them in one huge horde. This gave him cause for concern that they would have to lose them, but it also gave him a brief surge of hope that they were drawing enough of them off to let Grimm get away. This feeling of accomplishment only lasted a second though when he took in the hundreds of walking corpses flooding onto the porch and into the building through the shattered front doors.

Hoping against hope that Grimm and the Thing twins had somehow made it out through one of the windows on the far side of the building before they were cut off, he turned to Tick-Tock and said, "Let's go."

The group followed Steve at an easy jog as he led the way through the waist high grass toward the path. Their initial hope was that most of the dead would make a straight line toward them as they moved, thus putting the fence between them, but this was not to be. A few of the stragglers at the rear and side of the mansion, the slower dead that had been incapacitated by their wounds and those without legs did this, but a majority followed them through the hole in the fence.

Thousands of them.

With terror at the thought of what faced them at the teeth and digging claws of the undead, the group went from a jog to a full out sprint, running to put as much distance as they could between themselves and the horrors that trailed them. The grass tangled in their feet and many fell, but were quickly picked up, dusted off, and given an encouraging word or a boot in the butt to get moving.

Finally reaching the path, Steve had to yell at them three times to stop when they bunched up as they all tried to push onto the trail at once. When his shouts finally got through to them, he called for a break while they waited for a few of the slower people to catch up. When everyone had made it, he got them organized. He sorted them into a rough line with Cindy, Linda and Igor at its center, and the faster people in the front and the slower ones to the rear since he didn't want them jamming up the trail. With the dead quickly approaching, they started out two abreast along the shady corridor of the trail at a steady walk that soon turned into slow jog.

Everyone was on edge, expecting an animated corpse to jump out at them any second, but none did. The path narrowed, and soon they found they could only move single file at a faltering pace. After fifteen minutes of tripping over tree roots and having branches whipped back into their face by the people in front of them, pleas to slow down and take a break rang out, but it wasn't until huge gaps began to appear in the line of survivors did Steve stop so they could regroup. Knowing that even he couldn't keep up the grueling pace he had set, he let them rest for a few minutes as he tried to gauge how near the Zs were by the sound of their high-pitched whines. Between doing this, and gasping for breath, he explained that from here on out, they would fast-walk for three minutes, jog for three, run for three, and then rest for two.

A veteran of many forced runs in the Marine Corps, Tick-Tock kept everyone on their feet to prevent them from cramping up. When they started out again, Heather led the group while Steve made his way up and down the line to ensure that everyone stayed together.

Soon, the whining noise of the dead was barely audible to anyone.

Except for two of the group.

Tick-Tock stayed with Denise when they started off at the start of the trail, urging her on and half carrying her. When she began throwing up so badly from her concussion that they had to stop, he put her in a fireman's carry and kept moving. He knew he wouldn't last long doing this, but there was no way he would leave her.

Slowly, they fell behind even the slowest of the group.

The world became a blur as he trudged along. His shoulders and legs shook with the strain, but he knew he had to make it only a little bit more. He would pick out a spot a as far as he could see down the trail and head for that, and when he reached it, he picked out another and did it again.

As his boots pounded on the loose dirt of the path, he kept urging himself on by saying, "Just one more step, just one more step."

He knew that he was faltering as the spots he picked grew closer together. His thighs burned and it felt like someone had poured ground glass into his spine, slowing his pace in direct proportion to the rising sound of the dead.

Falling to one knee when the strain finally took its toll, he knew it was over. Despite this, he shrugged his shoulders to get Denise further up and to ease her weight so he could keep moving. Trying to stand, he fell forward onto his side, watching Denise roll off him onto the grass to lay motionless. Reeling, he started to crawl forward to pick her up again, but knew that it was no good. He might be able to make it to safety if it was just him, but there was no way he could carry his love another step. Fear and anger rose up in him at his inadequacies, but looking at the unconscious body lying spread eagle in the dirt, he was suddenly grateful that she wouldn't see the end.

With her weight off him, Tick-Tock rose shakily to his feet and unslung his M4. A burst of adrenalin surged through him, but his already saturated system barely felt it as he checked that he had a full magazine in his rifle.

His last magazine, he realized.

So this is how I die, he said to himself as he rammed the clip home and drew back on the charging handle to chamber a round. Looking down at the bullet he had ejected, he bent down and picked it up, twisting it in his fingers before extracting an empty clip and loading it. Methodically ejecting another round from his rifle, it followed the first one.

This one is for Denise and last one is for me, he decided. I'll fire the last of the rounds in the rifle, fire my pistol until it's empty, and then load this magazine for her and me.

A squealing noise seemed to come from close by, causing him to jerk his head up and try to see around a long curve in the path. With his arms and legs shaking, he knelt down next to Denise and sighted back the way they had come.

He didn't have long to wait for the first of the dead to appear.

Sighting in on its head, Tick-Tock slowly let out his breath as he started to squeeze the trigger. Knowing he only had a fraction of an ounce of pressure left before the rifle went off and the fight was on, he was startled by the voice that called out from behind him, "Are you okay, sir?"

Spinning around, he found five of his trainees standing only a few feet behind him.

Turning his attention back to the trail, he saw three more of the dead appear behind the first. Without hesitation, he shot them each in the head and then pointed to Denise saying, "Pick her up and get moving." Motioning to the lady he had first taught to shoot, he said, "You're with me. We hold them long enough for everyone to get away." As they all reacted to his orders, he added, "And someone give me their rifle and ammo."

***

Steve looked anxiously down the trail as he waited for Tick-Tock and his people to show. After what they had just been through, he had hoped to call the others part of the group now, but he knew that from here on out, they were Tick-Tock's people.

Upon reaching the bridge, and finding that his second in command and his girlfriend were missing, Steve immediately started back to look for them. He had barely taken a step though, when he was halted by an older man named Brent, defiantly standing in front of him and blocking the way.

About to curse him and push him aside, Steve was surprised into silence when Brent said firmly, "You've done enough. We'll go look for Tick-Tock. He's our leader and we'll go get him."

Steve opened his mouth to protest, but Brent shut him up by saying loudly, "It's not up for discussion." Turning, he picked out four others and started down the trail at a run.

That had been fifteen minutes ago, and since then, Steve had heard a lot of gunfire. At the sound of the first shot, he had wanted to drop his pack and run to help, but Heather held him back by telling him he would do more good here covering the retreat of the rescue team when they showed up.

Looking at the fifty feet of open space between where the trail ended and the narrow, wooden footbridge began, he knew she was right. His mind then turned to the confines of the trail, and while he knew from the nearing noise of the gunfire that he could reach Tick-Tock in seconds, he might end up doing more harm than good once he got to him.

Looking up from checking his watch for the tenth time in three minutes, he felt relief wash through him at the sight of four people breaking from the path into the woods and running across the clearing. He felt a second of fear though when he saw that they were carrying someone, but his attention was drawn off when Tick-Tock and another person quickly followed them, backing up as they shot at something unseen down the trail. He watched as Tick-Tock turned and shouted unheard words at the woman before they both turned and ran.

Seconds later, the dead poured from the opening in the woods to flood onto the clearing.

Steve took in the scene for a split second, and recognizing the person being carried as Denise by her long hair, hoped it was from the effects of the concussion and that she hadn't been bit. Switching his attention to the immediate threat, he fired at two of the Zs in the lead of the pack coming up fast behind Tick-Tock. Relieved when Denise and her bearers raced past him and onto the bridge, he turned and followed them with Tick-Tock and his assistant close behind. Looking back over his shoulder, he knew it was going to be a near thing.

As the six of them raced toward the tree line, Steve turned repeatedly to see where the dead were. A few of the faster ones reached the crossing and were cut down by fire coming from Heather and Brain in the tree line, but it was the main group rushing after him that he was concerned with.

When he saw they were going to reach the bridge before he and the others had reached the safety of the woods, Steve shouted out, "Down, down, everyone down," as he pushed the person next to him flat.

***

Heather fired into the head of what looked to have once been some type of business man by the raggedy suit and tie he still wore before switching her aim to the wad of plastic explosives tied to the rail near the center of the bridge. She had been alternating between shooting the Zs that got too close and aiming at the bomb as she tried to keep the dead back as long as possible while getting ready to blow the bridge at a split second's notice. She could see that the dead had reached the far end of the crossing, and just like the survivors when they reached the trail, the Zs bunched up as they all tried to make their way onto it at once. Unlike the survivors, the dead pushed, shoved and clawed at each other as they forced their way across. Some were forced into the ravine, giving hope to Heather that they landed on their heads. Switching her focus, she saw that the six people racing to the safety of the trees were still too close to the blast for comfort. They needed a few more seconds, but she didn't think they were going to get it.

Hearing Steve call out for everyone to drop down, she watched as they disappeared into the long grass. Glancing to where the first of the herd had made it half-way across the bridge, she knew he had seen them too and had decided to take the risk of being too close to the blast.

Settling in, Heather sighting into the center of the mass of plastic explosives and squeezed the trigger, watching the carnage that followed.

The blast came as a bright flash followed by a dull whump that sent splinters of wood from the bridge high into the air and down into the steep gully it crossed. Along with these, she could see the blown apart pieces of the dead that hadn't been disintegrated by the explosion flying with them for a split second before the area was covered in a cloud of dust. Arms, legs and pieces of dead flesh rose into the air to drop down onto the Zs further out from the immediate blast radius and the six people caught out in the open before the scene was enveloped in a cloud of dust.

***

Easing the door of the storm cellar upward a few inches, she took a quick peek. Letting it down quietly, she returned to her companions and said, "It is mostly clear now, but we must make ourselves presentable first. I refuse to let us go out in the world looking like ragamuffins."

Taking a few minutes, they brushed themselves off from the dust, soot and cobwebs that clung to them from the long crawl between the floorboards, down an old unused chimney, and into the basement.

When she deemed them presentable, she said, "There are a few out there, but nothing we can't handle. We take them out quietly and then move on. Time is of the essence. It's not safe here anymore."

She could see her assistants nod in the dim light of the lantern, so she turned and walked up the steps to the storm doors. Flipping one back to bang against the ground, she stepped up and into the light. Hearing a loud explosion from the direction of the bridge, she smiled as the noise attracted the attention of the few dead still scattered around the lawn. As she watched them turn away, she knew it would be child's play to take them. It was almost poetic how she had done her part in keeping her children occupied before dropping into the escape hatch she had created months ago, and now Steve had done her the same favor in return.

With a smile, Delightfully Grimm unslung her scythe and turned to Thing one and Thing to as she said, "Come, my good friends, there is much reaping to do."

CHAPTER SEVEN

Washington DC:

General Eastridge set his reading glasses down on the report lying on his desk and rubbed his eyes. A dull thud shook the building, letting him know that they had started the airstrikes again. While the dead had initially been pushed back when the Marines retook the capitol, they were drawn in such numbers to the fresh human meat now clustered here that at least once a day, A-10 warthogs had to be called in to bomb the perimeter.

Thinking back to those first days after they had fought their way back into the capitol, he marveled at the speed in which the Seabees had erected a temporary wall that ran from the river straight down K Street, turned on Massachusetts avenue before turning again on fourth street, and then made its way to the 395 freeway before making a left at US One and ending again at the water. Being outside this perimeter, the Pentagon was secured by its own defensive barricade, but was easily accessed by air and subway. While the creators of the DC wall thought that the Potomac would make a natural barricade, they were sorely mistaken, and eventually the wall had to be lengthened to take in the entire shore.

Every time he looked at it, Eastridge was reminded of barricade that circled the green zone in Iraq. The main difference here though, was that the city outside of DC's safe zone had been entirely reduced to rubble as far as the eye could see.

Checking his watch, he saw it was almost time for the daily briefing of the Joint Chiefs of Staff. A wave of anxiety washed over him as he wondered if he had been found out yet. After ignoring the direct orders of the Chairman, he knew it was only a matter of time before A talked to B and B said something to C, and word got back to the Pentagon about what he was up to.

Shaking off his worries, he knew he was doing the right thing. If there was another way to combat the dead that were coming back to life, it needed to be explored. The Malectron was a great weapon in the fight against the living dead, but it was just that, a weapon. Believing that the device would be used for more than herding the dead into remote areas where they could be dealt with, he was risking his life to seek out an alternate solution.

Standing, General Eastridge grabbed his jacket off the coat tree standing near the door and exited his office as the walls shook again.

***

The Chairman of the Joint Chiefs of Staff called the meeting to order. After a quick briefing by the Colonel commanding the city's defenses, he waved the man off and said, "On to new business and its good news gentleman. Just half an hour ago, I spoke with Professor Hawkins and he is ready to move into his new lab." Turning to the naval chief, he asked, "And how is progress on the facility going?"

The Admiral cleared his throat and started to say that it would be ready by the end of the day, but seeing General Eastridge look him straight in the eye and shake his head slightly, he paused. Although they'd had their differences in the past, he knew the Marine Corps general to by a standup guy. He took the head shake as a cue to stall the development of the Malectron, and wondering what was going on, decided to play along for now and see where it went.

Clearing his throat again, he covered his pause by saying, "Excuse me. Must have something caught in my throat."

The Chairman threw up his arms and said in an exasperated tone, "Then take a drink of water and tell me what the fuck is going on with the work on the new facility."

All the men stopped at this sudden outburst and stared at the Chairman. Ignoring this, their commander screwed up his face and asked, "Wellll?"

Sitting straight up in his chair, the Admiral said, "Sorry, sir. The new facility for Professor

Hawkins is coming along well. There are some electrical problems due to the draw required on the generators, but my people should have it worked out within the next three days."

Originally, he was only going to give a one day delay, but with the Chairman acting like he could talk to him like he was some half-assed midshipman at the academy, he'd decided to make it three.

The Chairman paused for a second, his face turning red as he stammered out, "Three days? Three fucking days? I thought your Seabees had their act together. I need that facility to be ready by tomorrow. I have choppers ready to lift Hawkins, his equipment and his people here at 0600 the day after tomorrow. Are we going to drag them all the way here from bumfuck Arkansas to tell them that they don't have power? They're also going to be living in that compound, so how is that going to work? Should I give them your room at the Watergate hotel instead until you get your shit together?" Looking up, he added, "Or maybe move you all out and turn your suites over to Hawkins and his people."

General Eastridge almost laughed out loud at this. He had been to his room once since it had been assigned him, and that was just to get the key card. He rotated its use between his officers on weekends and the enlisted under his command during the week. For himself, he found the couch in his office suited his needs.

Gaining confidence, the Admiral said, "It can't be helped, sir. The requirements on our electrical supply for Hawkins lab will be tremendous. We're already having to reroute power from two different grids in the safe zone, and even that might not be enough."

Pounding his fist down on the table, the Chairman screamed, "Then reroute all the power if you need to. Shit me some power if you need to. Tie a fucking key to a kite string and hope for lightning if you need to, but get that facility ready to run by tomorrow or it's your natural ass."

Standing, the Chairman straightened his jacket. Looking around the table, he made eye contact with each man before saying, "Now onto the matter of our forces still stuck overseas. I know that we've managed to bring some of them home, but we have to focus on getting all of our military personnel back on United States soil. Once they have the Malectron issued them, we can begin our campaign."

Picking up a remote control from the table, he pressed a button. The lights dimmed and a map of the world appeared on the screen behind him.

Pointing to Taiwan, he said, "Once we are done with the United States, this will be our jumping off point in the taking of Asia."

***

On his way to a meeting about the defense of all the safe zones across the country, General Eastridge paused in the hallway when he heard his name called. Turning his head back and forth as he looked through the throng of people moving past him, he searched for a familiar face, but couldn't see who had hailed him.

Shrugging, he started off again, almost walking into a seaman first class. Waiting for the enlisted man to excuse himself, Eastridge was surprised when he said in a low voice, "The Thomas Jefferson Memorial at 2100. It's on your normal route tonight so no one will get suspicious."

Eastridge was about to ask what this was about, but the man had already disappeared into the mob of clerks, enlisted men and officers that streamed past him.

***

General Eastridge waited at the Memorial until 2115 before giving up. Deciding that what he thought he had heard the seaman say was just his mind playing tricks on him, he started walking to where he'd parked his Humvee.

Wishful thinking, he told himself dejectedly as his feet hit the walkway. Despite Admiral Sedlak catching on to my signal to stall for a few days, it would be too farfetched to believe he would set up a clandestine meeting.

A clicking noise made him turn, but seeing nothing except the dark shape of the memorial, he spun back around to continue to his vehicle - and almost walked into the same man that he had almost ran into earlier that day. Seeing him now dressed in tiger stripe fatigues and fully armed, Eastridge guessed he was a Navy Seal. While most of them had been wiped by the president when they were recklessly thrown into combat in the dead cities, Eastridge knew that a few had survived.

The Seal motioned for him to follow and walked off the path between two large clumps of brush.

After looking around to see if anyone was watching, Eastridge followed.

With essential areas receiving electricity first, the only light was that of the moon as the General followed the shadowy figure across a piece of uncut grass and into a small copse of tree. The seal stopped and said quietly, "Here he is, sir."

Thinking the man was talking to him, Eastridge opened his mouth to ask what this was all about, but was silenced when Admiral Sedlak emerged from the shadows to say, "Sorry for all the cloak and dagger stuff, but I had to make sure that you weren't followed."

***

PFC Quintana adjusted the surgical mask over his face to try and block out the rotting, dank stink of the dead. Noticing that his partner's hung around his neck, he asked, "Doesn't the smell bother you?"

"Been doing wall duty for two weeks now," the man replied. "I'm used to it."

Looking over the ruins of Washington DC, Quintana wondered if he would ever be. As far as he could see, the city surrounding the wall had been reduced to a smoldering pile of rubble that still burned in a few places. These hot spots tended to be further away from the wall since most everything close in that could burn had long ago done so due to the constant bombing. The A-10 Warthog's used napalm when they had to work close to the wall, but further out, they used high explosives. Either way, it destroyed the buildings and the dead with equal success, but the napalm left their charred remains behind to create a stink worse than when they were zombified.

Jumping slightly at a small screeching noise that was abruptly cut off, he heard his partner say, "Something got something. At least the food chain is still intact."

"The only problem is that we're at the bottom of it now," he answered quietly.

This got a small laugh.

Turning away from the destruction of what had once been a thriving city, Quintana ran his tongue over his teeth. Grimacing at the buildup in plaque, he asked, "What's up with the toothpaste we were supposed to get on the last resupply?"

His partner shrugged and said in an offhand manner, "Same thing that happened to real toilet paper, tailor made cigarettes and coffee. It's a thing of the past. They're giving out baking soda from the chow hall. You can use that or a pine cone."

"Where in the hell am I going to find a pine cone?" Quintana asked.

After another shrug, his partner said, "You can try around one of the parks or memorials. Not many people know that trick so you should find something." With a snort, he added, "You'll be lucky if you see real toothpaste again in your lifetime."

This suddenly hit home with Quintana. After being stationed in Japan for the last eighteen months, he had been brought back only two days before and was trying to adjust to his surroundings. When the HWNW virus had broken out in Tokyo, the natives had managed to quarantine all of the infected and stop its spread. Japan was one of only two countries completely free of the dead. There, the trains ran on time, the shops were open and it almost seemed like business as usual except for the occasional blackouts and brownouts that plagued the country. The country might only be running at partial capacity, but at least you could still buy toothpaste there.

Looking over the ruins of DC again, Quintana wondered if the U.S. would be able to recover to even half of what the Japanese had accomplished.

***

As his boots thumped on the wooden parapet built along the inside of the wall, General Eastridge's head spun from his encounter with Admiral Sedlak. His mind turned over the possibilities of what he could accomplish now that he had an ally. Wondering if they could get any of the other Joint chiefs to join them, his thoughts were interrupted by a voice that called out, "Halt, who goes there."

Remembering this morning's briefing on passwords, he replied, "Scooby Do."

"Advance and be recognized," called the sentry.

Walking into a small pool of light cast by a flashlight pointing downward, Eastridge asked, "Are you men doing okay?"

"Doing great, sir," the first man said.

Looking to the second sentry, Eastridge only received a nervous nod.

"Any movement tonight?" He asked.

"A few stragglers, sir," the first sentry replied.

"Let's take a quick look then, Corporal," Eastridge told him before climbing onto the top of the wall and leaning over to gaze down at its base.

In the dim light of the moon, he could see more than a dozen dead clustered below him. They looked up with hungry faces, their mouths whining softly as if to say, "Jump."

Turning to the Corporal, Eastridge asked, "This is all of them?"

"Yes, sir," he replied. "There was about two hundred last night, but the airstrikes thinned them out some."

Nodding, Eastridge jumped down onto the parapet and said, "Carry on then," before continuing on his way.

When he was nothing more than a faint shadow, the new sentry asked in awe, "Was that just the fucking Commandant of the Marine Corps?"

"Sure was," replied the Corporal. "He walks a section of the line every night. Usually he comes by a little earlier though."

Shaking off his excitement at his brush with greatness, Quintana cursed at himself as he ran his tongue over his teeth again while thinking, maybe I should have asked the old man if he had any toothpaste.

CHAPTER EIGHT

The John H. Kirby State Park:

Tick-Tock slowly duck-walked through the waist high grass to where Steve knelt at the edge of the firebreak. Stopping next to him, he scanned the area for threats before saying quietly, "I don't know how much longer everyone's going to last if we keep this pace up."

"I know," Steve replied. "Going through the woods has cost us a lot of time and energy. If we hadn't of run into that herd on the path, we'd be a lot further along and in better shape."

Tick-Tock nodded. They had been making good progress until they came across a clearing with a small house in the middle of it. This wasn't the first they had encountered, the two other shacks they had come across had been abandoned, but this one must have still had living people in it since it was swarmed by hundreds of the dead. The group wasn't spotted, but they had to make a big detour to get around it. This shouldn't have been a problem, but when they tried to regain the path, they found it populated by a steady trickle of Zs moving to join their brethren circling the shack. Knowing that a trickle could turn into a flood within minutes of the dead spotting food, they had been forced to go through the woods.

Turning to his friend, Steve asked, "How's Denise?"

Tick-Tock grimaced slightly before saying, "Not good. My guess is that she's got a serious concussion or a skull fracture. She can't even keep water down now and it's gotten so bad that we have to carry her most of the time."

Steve nodded. He had been leading the group, so this was the first he had heard about her worsening condition. Patting his friend on the back, he said, "Then we need to find a place to hole up for a little while."

Tick-Tock shook his head and said, "We can't stop now. We might have kept the Zs at the nuthouse from following us when we blew the bridge, but we can't take the risk of another group getting wind of us if we stop."

Steve shrugged and said, "And it's just as risky if we keep moving. We could run into another herd at any time."

Tick-Tock started to argue, but Steve cut him off by saying, "It's not just for Denise. Like you said, everyone is dead on their feet. We need to stop for a little while and rest up. It's going to be dark soon, and no one's had anything to eat all day, so we need to find a place to make camp."

Seeing his reasoning, Tick-Tock said, "We could go back to that clump of trees we passed about a quarter mile back." Looking at the black stains on his friend's shirt caused by the blood of the dead dropping on him when the bridge was blown, he added, "And there's a stream nearby that you can use to clean up."

Wrinkling his nose at the rank smell of the dead wafting off him, Steve nodded and said, "That's what I was thinking too. It's a good defensive position and we can put sentries out in all four directions to keep a watch for Zs. If the shit hits the fan, we've got plenty of ways to run."

"We also might want to send someone down our back trail a couple miles to make sure nothing is following us," Tick-Tock added.

"Good idea," Steve said. "Once we get everyone settled, I want to scout a little ways down the firebreak too."

Tick-Tock gave Steve a questioning look and asked, "I thought we ruled out using it."

Steve replied, "I know when we first saw it on the map that we thought it would be too risky since we'd be exposed to anything coming at us out of the woods or from the front, but if we send a scout out ahead of us, it might be the safest, easiest way to go. When you think about it, we've been following the trail, and the firebreak is just another trail."

Tick-Tock considered this for a few seconds before saying, "It does head in the general direction we want to go, but is the risk worth it?"

Steve shrugged and said, "It might be less risky going through the woods, but how long is everyone going to last if they have to keep climbing over deadfalls and crawling along old game trails?" Waving his hand to encompass the thick woods on both sides of the firebreak, he added, "And look how hard it is for us to get through this shit. If the Zs try to get through it onto the firebreak, they'll get hung up in it just like we did. On top of that, we'll be able to hear them from a ways off."

Tick-Tock looked at the thick grass covering their intended path and said, "Whoever's on point is going to have to break a trail. We'll have to rotate point every fifteen minutes or so."

Steve looked at him quizzically and asked, "Why every fifteen minutes. I know it's going to be hard on the point man, but the grass doesn't look that thick."

"They're going to have to be twisting their feet outward with every step to break a trail, and I don't want anyone getting too worn out in case we have to run," he replied.

Knowing he was right, Steve felt a sinking feeling in his stomach at the thought that their only defense against the dead now was to run away.

***

Lois crouched at the edge of the stream as she tried to wash the black stains off her face and arms. Shaking her head in disgust, she said to the woman next to her, "This crap is never going to come off."

"Use some sand mixed with water," Connie told her. "It makes an abrasive."

Scraping up some of the creek bed in her hands, Lois rubbed it vigorously over her forearms. It stung a little bit on the scrape she'd picked up when she'd climbed over the porch railing in their escape from the mansion, but she was pleased to see the black stains quickly disappear. Fresh blood seeped from her wound, and knowing it would cleanse it, she nodded in approval.

After the bridge had been blown, she had been worried when the black ochre the dead used for blood and parts of their bodies rained down on her. A hand that had been torn off one of the dead from the blast had landed almost directly on her wound, and she had looked on in shock at the thought that she might turn into one of the Zs. She knew that contact with infected fluids would cause her to become infected, but she quickly reasoned that her scrape had partially scabbed over so she should be safe. Despite this, her mind started playing tricks on her as she fled down the trail and through the woods with the rest of the group. It seemed like every twitch from her overused muscles was the beginning of a seizure. After a few hours though, her fears ebbed when she didn't turn.

Smiling, she said to her companion, "Thanks for the tip, and now it's time for the shirt."

As she started to unbutton it, Connie pointed to where three of the group were cleaning up not far away and whispered, "But there's men here."

Lois laughed and told her, "And if any of them have the strength to do anything about me being topless, I'll be glad to oblige."

Connie blushed as she watched the older lady take off her shirt and bra before scrubbing herself and the garments down. Glancing at the three men a short distance away, she was astonished when none of them even glanced their way. As she watched, one of them even stripped down to his boxers and waded into the shallow creek, crouching down to splash water up onto his chest and face.

Beside her, she heard Lois chuckle and then call out to him, "How are they hanging, Hank?"

The former Congressman from the state of California stopped what he was doing, laughed and replied, "Long loose and full of juice." Leering at her, he added, "Nice boobs. I always wondered what they looked like."

As she took a fresh shirt from her pack and put it on, Lois said mockingly, "And that's the last look you'll get for a while."

Connie's blush deepened at the ribald comments and she turned her attention to wringing out the last of her clothes. Next to her, Lois rose and said, "That's how you deal with men, honey. Give them a taste and keep them coming back for more." Raising her voice to be heard by the three men who had accompanied them, she added, "Now finish up so we can head back. I'm hungry, tired and I the only thing I want to do is eat and go to sleep."

As she headed back to camp with the others in tow, Lois felt clean for the first time in a long time. Not clean like she had taken a shower in her Los Angeles penthouse, but much cleaner than if she had just spent a session in congress. Politics was a dirty business, and she never knew how much she actually hated it was until after the dead came back to life and it was taken away from her.

Looking back at her political career, she felt herself alternately fascinated and appalled by her actions as a politician. She had lobbied for guns to be taken away from everyone, and here she was carrying one. She had lobbied for bigger government and less rights for the common person, and here she was relying on the man and woman standing next to her since government was incapable of helping her. With a chuckle and a shake of her head, she remembered back to when she had stood up in front of Congress and rallied for the rights of the dead after they started coming back to life.

Now she knew they only had the right to a bullet in the head.

Reaching camp as darkness swallowed the woods, she could just make out the shadowy figures of everyone sitting around what would be a fire if they could risk one. Joining them, she was handed a can of cold beef stew. She ate what was offered and was grateful for it.

When everyone was finished with their diner, Steve called for their attention. As she listened to him talk about their plan to use the firebreak the next day, Lois felt complete exhaustion wash over her. She had been tired before, but now that they had stopped and eaten, the day's physical exercise, interspersed with extreme moments of terror, caught up to her. Thinking back, it was hard to believe that they had escaped from Happy Hallows only that morning. Since then, it seemed like she had been in constant motion. She was glad that Steve kept it brief, since all she could think of now was sleep. After he gave out the rotation for the guards around the camp, he told everyone to get some rest.

As she rose, Lois was surprised to find Tick-Tock standing next to her. In the dark, she never saw him approach. In a low voice, she heard him say, "I want to thank you for helping me with Denise today. You saved her life. You're one of the good ones."

Before she could respond, Tick-Tock had vanished into the darkness that had now fully settled over the woods.

Looking to where he had disappeared, Lois felt her chest swell with pride. In a quiet voice, she said, "And it's only because I met up with you and your group. You taught me how to be a human being instead of a human doing."

Content with herself, Lois made her way to where she had spread out her blanket. The night was still fairly warm so she lay on top of it. Lacing her fingers behind her head as she looked up at the stars peeking between the trees, she dreamed of the world she could help create when a cure was found and this was all over. For the first time in her life, she felt like she was actually accomplishing something. Her last thought before drifting off was that the moon should be up when she took her turn at guard. This would make it easier to see any approaching threats.

***

Unable to sleep, Hank looked at the dark forms of the others around him. Due to the chill brought on after the sun set, they were now covered in a variety of sleeping bags and blankets. Some made no sound while a few snored quietly, but everyone was completely out. Although he too was exhausted in both body and soul from the day's exertions, his mind was stuck on the interaction he'd had with Lois earlier at the creek.

Rolling onto his right side, he could just make out where she was laying on her back a few yards away. She had been a colleague of his for many years, but he had never looked at her in the way he did today. Where before, she was nothing more than a vote or someone to sway into his way of thinking, he now saw that she was a very attractive middle-aged woman.

And she noticed me too, he told himself as he thought back to her asking him how they were hanging.

With this in mind, he slowly eased his blanket off and rose to his feet. If he was asked where he was going, he deciding he would play it off that he needed to relieve himself, but there was no need. Everyone was so wiped out that they stayed deep in the arms of Morpheus.

Taking a tentative step forward, he ran a dozen scenarios through his mind on how this could end. Many of the others in the group had hooked up, so why shouldn't he and Lois? There were a dozen good reasons he could put forth on why they should team up in this new land of the living dead, so he knew he had a counter-argument for anything she came up with as to why not.

But, he told himself, if she does end up shunning my advances, I'll simply laugh it off and return to my blanket. If she puts me in the friend zone, I'll chalk it up to one of life's experiences. But, if she welcomes me into her blanket...

Hank smiled and took a confident step forward.

***

Lois's mind swam with a dozen disjointed nightmares. In one of them, she found herself immersed in a cold, black body of water. Because her body really was cold, her conscious mind woke her, and the dream turned into reality as her eyes fluttered open. Realizing where she was and that she was freezing, she tried to reach over to pull her blanket on top of her but found that her limbs were locked in place. Trying to lift her head to see what was holding them, she found her neck was also immobilized.

Having woken from bad dreams like this before, she tried to relax, telling herself that the paralysis would soon pass. Counting slowly to one hundred had always worked in the past, so she tried that. When she was finished, she made to move her arm again but found she was unable to.

Suddenly, fear gripped her at the thought that she had suffered a stroke. Her eyes could still move, so she looked wildly around for someone to help her. Catching some motion, she strained to roll her eyes all the way to the left. Here, they locked onto the dark shape of a man approaching her. Recognizing him, she tried to call out his name.

No sound passed her lips.

Worried that Hank would think she was sleeping and pass by, when he stopped and knelt down, his hand reaching out to wake her, Lois felt relief that someone had found her quickly. If it was a stroke, she knew that she needed to be treated quickly.

With the irrational thought of being taken to a hospital where everything would be made right, Lois closed her eyes. In a delirium, she could feel herself alternately falling and lifting up, as if her body didn't know which way to go. Suddenly, everything went bright white and then dark before turning bright white again. The light turned brighter as she lost all sense of self.

This was when the convulsions struck.

***

Calling Lois's name, Hank reached out to lay a hand on her shoulder. Feeling her body tremble, he smiled in the darkness. A half-second later, when what at first he took to be sexual excitement turned into a full blown seizure, he found himself clutching that same shoulder as he struggled to keep Lois from jackknifing off the ground.

Starting to call out for help, his mind told him not to since how would he explain being here? Decorum dictated that a man did not approach a sleeping woman, and appearances were everything to the one time politician. Looking around to see if anyone had been woken by the disturbance, his mind relaxed when he saw that no one had even stirred.

Looking back down to Lois, he saw that her tremors had subsided and her eyes were open.

Smiling, he said, “Everything’s going to be alright. You’re going to be fine.”

In the darkness, lit only by the moon filtering down through the trees, he couldn’t see the wild feral look in his paramour’s eyes.

Relaxing his grip, but still keeping a hand resting on Lois’s shoulder, Hank started to say, “I didn’t know you were an epileptic.” But the words had barely formed in his mouth when the thing that had once been Lois whipped her head around and sank her teeth into the fleshy part on the inside of his arm.

***

Hank’s piercing screams turned the camp into a sea of bedlam as people jumped up and swung around, pointing guns and flashlights as they sought their source. His pitiful wails and shrieks, acting like a beacon, made it so the guards had no problem finding their way through the woods as they raced toward the commotion.

The first to realize what had happened was Brain. Sleeping only a few feet away, his light revealed the sight of two people rolling around on the ground, one of them with their mouth latched onto the others arm. Thinking that one of the Zs had somehow made their way into camp, he took careful aim at the obvious aggressor and squeezed the trigger of his .45 caliber pistol. The two figures wrestling on the ground moved as the one being bitten tried to break free and his shot was wasted into the ground. Taking this as their cue though, five of the group saw what was going on and also opened up with their weapons. Within a second, others joined in to create a free fire zone of exploding guns and shouts. The two bodies fighting on the forest floor were quickly riddled with bullets and lay still, but, the circular firing squad had created casualties.

***

With Pep at his side, Steve entered the camp to find it a mass of confusion. He could see flashlight beams crisscrossing the area as people swung them around in their search for any new threats, while a few of them pointed downward to where figures writhed on the forest floor or lay still.

Stopping as he tried to analyze what had happened and what needed to be done, the first thing he did was look down to where Pep had halted at his side. In their forced march through the woods, he had wanted to have the dog with him on point to warn him of any imminent threats, but decided against it. If she spotted any of the dead she might give them away with her barking so she was kept near the center with Cindy. With Pep’s senses of smell though, she was perfect for guard duty. Seeing no reaction from the dog, he took this as a sign that the immediate area was free of the dead since she always went wild when any of them were near.

For now.

Realizing that they might only have a few minutes before the gunfire brought the Zs to them, he slung his rifle over his shoulder and moved forward to where a pool of light showed a woman lying motionless on her side.

***

Entering the camp from the opposite side, Tick-Tock left his flashlight off so as to not give himself away. Looking at the chaos that had once been the group sleeping peacefully, he guessed what had happened and moved forward at a run, only making it three strides before tripping over something. Holding his rifle out so he didn’t land on it, his other hand took the full force of the fall as he stopped himself from going face first into the ground.

Wincing at the pain that shot up from his wrist to his elbow, he levered himself up and pulled a mini-mag light from the cargo pocket of his pants. Switching it on to see what he tripped over, he could see a blood wet, tousled mass of blonde hair sticking out from the end of a sleeping bag. Crouching down next to the body, he pushed a glob of wet, stringy hair out of the way and felt for a pulse. Feeling a weak but steady beat, he started pulling more of the wads of stuck together hair apart as he searched for a wound. Finding a large crease in the scalp near the top of the skull, he grabbed a pack that was lying nearby and rummaged through it. Finding a pair of socks, he used them to apply pressure to the wound.

This caused his patient to shudder once and try to get up. Pushing down on his chest, Tick-Tock told him to calm down as he rolled him onto his back and asked, "Are you hit anywhere else?"

"I can't see," the man replied.

"That's because you've got blood in your eyes," Tick-Tock explained. "You got a cut on your scalp, and wounds like that bleed like crazy. Anything else hurt?"

The man thought for a moment before saying, "My ribs hurt something bad."

Recognizing the man as one of the people he had trained, Tick-Tock didn't want to explain how he had run into him by accident, so he laughed and said, "That's because I kicked you for being dumb enough to get shot in your sleep. Now reach up here and hold this tight until the bleeding stops completely. I've got to check on the others."

***

Heather pulled the blanket up over the dead woman's face before turning to Linda and saying, "She never had a chance. Two in the chest, one in the hip." Looking at all the blood sprayed across the area, she added, "The one in the hip must have hit her femoral artery."

Linda nodded and pointed to where Steve crouched over another of the wounded as she said, "I think that's the last of them though."

Looking around, Heather could see that of the six people wounded in the cross-fire, all of them were being treated, or had been covered with a blanket if medical aid was no longer an option.

Rising to her feet, she started to tell Linda that they would make one more circuit of the camp to ensure everyone was accounted for. Before she could start off though, a low whining noise made her freeze. Twisting her head from side to side, she tried to determine from what direction the sound had come. She heard the noise repeated, this time joined by what sounded like a dozen more dead voices calling out for food.

Without hesitation, she echoed the orders already being issued by Steve and Tick-Tock as they alerted to the sound of the dead, "Everyone grab your gear. If the wounded can walk, get them up. If they can't, carry them. Grab all the weapons and ammunition of the three people that died. Move, move, move."

CHAPTER NINE

Russellville, Arkansas:

When Cain brought him the news of their delay in moving the facility to Virginia, Professor Hawkins threw his coffee cup across the room to shatter against the wall.

"What are those idiots in DC doing," he asked venomously as his eyes darted over the shattered porcelain. "They promised that my Malectron would take priority over everything else."

Cain took a deep breath and said, "They told me that it has something to do with the electrical grid and the wiring. They don't have enough power to keep your lab running."

Trying to calm himself, but not having any luck, Hawkins asked through gritted teeth, "So the free world has to wait for the fucking cable guy to show up?"

"It's a little more complex than that," Cain explained.

"Complex my ass," Hawkins retorted. "My Malectron is complex, the double helix is complex, but electrical wiring is simple. If the Joint Chief's had half a brain between them, they would reroute all the power to my new facility and use slave labor to finish my lab so I can move in."

At the words, slave labor, an evil grin crossed Cain's lips. He could think of quite a few people he would like to see breaking rocks until they dropped. He had hitched his wagon to Hawkins's star, and that star was on a steady rise to the top, so it was only a matter of time until he was in a position where he could use his power. With glee, he knew that once there, he would run things the way they were supposed to be. Shaking off these thoughts, he tried to console Hawkins by saying, "It's only a few days, Doctor."

With a deep sigh, Hawkins said, "I know, I know, but with only two working units, and one of them being used to keep the dead away from the camp. We're so close that I worry something will happen. I want you to put someone we trust in the radio room. I want them listening to every incoming and outgoing communication. I also want to know the whereabouts of Cage and his sidekick. I don't need them screwing anything up"

Reaching out to pat Hawkins on the shoulder, Cain said reassuringly, "Don't worry, Doctor. As long as I'm around, you and the Malectron are safe.

***

Major Jedidiah Cage finished reading a copy of the communique Fagan had taken from the radio room and breathed a sigh of relief. He was aware of the imminent departure of the people living in the farmhouse, but now it looked like they had a little time before they moved to Washington DC. Time was what they needed.

Shortly after returning from Mount Nebo, he had gotten word that Hawkins and his people were being ordered to leave immediately for a facility near the capitol. Once there, they could start wholesale construction of the Malectron. His first thought upon hearing this was to order his people to storm the farmhouse to keep them from going, but when this initial flash to use force abated, his rational mind took over as he realized that the only way to do this would be to find someone that was immune. He knew that if he tried to stop the Professor with force that it would be met by force from his guards, so that was out of the question. In addition, since the disappearance of Lieutenant Randal, they were obviously being watched, so sabotage was also out of the question. On top of that, they would be using helicopters from another base to move, so this threw a wrench in any plans of disabling their transport. Their only option was to find an alternative to the weapon that the government thought would be the final solution for the reanimated corpses walking the earth by the hundreds of millions.

With the departure of Hawkins and his people being held up by some kind of electrical glitch, this gave them some time to come up with a plan. There had to work out some way to slow down the doctor for at least a week, since this wasn't the only good news they had received. There had also been word from General Eastridge about intercepted radio traffic between two groups of survivors.

One of them claimed to have a person with them that was immune to the HWNW virus.

The only bad news of the day was that after the last intercept, all contact had been lost. The General had relayed that he had people listening for contact, and that when it was reestablished, he would send two Blackhawk helicopters to bring them directly to the base outside of Russellville. Once here, Doctor Connors could study the patient to help determine a cure. More good news was that the group was located in south-east Texas, a short helicopter flight from their base.

Laying the communique on his desk, Cage said, "This might be the break we've been looking for."

Fagan nodded and said, "It buys us a couple of days, but if we do get someone here that's immune, how long will it take Connors to come up with a vaccine?"

"She told me she can have something in as little as twenty-four hours," Cage replied. "She said that she needs to isolate some kind of enzyme or bacteria or something in there spit, shit or blood that was corrupt in the first test subject."

Fagan raised his eyebrows and asked, "Corrupt?"

Cage nodded and said, "The lady they're working with used to drink heavily. She is immune to the virus, but because of her drinking, they can't find the right thing they need for a fool-proof vaccine."

Fagan looked wistfully at the ceiling as he said, "So if drinking makes you immune, and with as much as I drink..."

Cage laughed and said, "I don't think it works that way."

Snapping to attention, Fagan said in a brisk manner, "To be on the safe side, sir, I think we need to have a few doses of that zombie-bite medicine you keep in your desk."

Cage chuckled as he shook his head. Looking at his friend with an amused expression, after a few seconds, he opened a drawer and extracted a mason jar of clear fluid. Setting it on his desk, he asked with mock sincerity, "Do you really think it will help, Staff Sergeant?"

Coming to parade rest, Fagan replied, "It can't hurt, sir. And besides, we can't do anything except sit here with our thumb up our ass until we hear from the General."

Reaching back into the drawer, Cage retrieved two jelly glasses as he said, "And I hope it's soon."

CHAPTER TEN

The Firebreak:

Steve Wendell crouched in the waist high grass of the firebreak as he watched the first rays of the sun filter through the trees on either side of him. In the gathering daylight, he could now see that the firebreak was also used as a right of way for power lines, the string of power poles holding their useless wires running off into the distance before disappearing into the morning mist. Laying his rifle across his thighs, he cupped his hands behind his ears and slowly twisted his head from side to side, listening for any trace of the group of dead that had been on their trail for most of the night. Hearing nothing, he felt relief that they had finally shook them. They had alternately used the firebreak and cut into the woods in their effort to lose the Zs, and it appeared to have worked. Looking down at himself, he saw he was a mess. Grasping his rifle in one hand, he used the other to try and brush away the chaff and dirt clinging to the front of his pants. With his jeans soaked from the dewy grass he had been wading through for the last few hours, it was hopeless.

Giving up, he checked his watch and saw that the ten minute break he had called was almost up. Now that it was light enough to see, they could send a scout ahead of them to check the area. In their flight from the camp, they'd had to trust in luck that they didn't run into anything, but today it would be different. Today they would move cautiously, since while they could see the dead approaching in the light of day, the dead could also spot them.

Turning, Steve called out softly for Tick-Tock. The grass was so thick that even though his friend was only feet away, he was invisible.

"What's up?" Tick-Tock asked.

"Almost time to move," Steve told him, and then added, "We need to do a quick head count to make sure no one fell asleep and gets left behind."

"I already did it," Tick-Tock answered. "We've got fourteen adults, one child and one dog. All bright-eyed and bushy-tailed."

"You counted yourself as an adult?" Steve asked.

Tick-Tock chuckled and said, "I took some liberty in that."

"How's Denise," he asked.

"Groggy as hell but she's hanging in there," Tick-Tock told him. "We need to find a place to hole up for a little bit."

Pulling out his map, Steve studied it for a moment before saying, "We should be north of the lake by now, so unless the big group from the East radically changed direction, they should miss us. There's another lake a few miles ahead of us and to the north with a small town and a marina on it." Holding the map out so he could read the small print, he said, "Sam Rayburn resort. We could make it in a couple hours."

Seeing him squint and try to focus, Tick-Tock asked, "You getting old? They say the eyes are the first thing to go."

"Getting old doesn't worry me," Steve replied as he folded the map. "My hair starts falling out, they've got a pill for that. My energy gets low, they've got a pill for that. My dick stops working, they've got a pill for that. My worry is getting it bit off if I pop a Viagra."

Tick-Tock laughed softly as Steve readied his M4 and slowly rose until he could just see over the top of the river of grass. Turning in a full circle, he spotted nothing. Dropping down, he said, "We need to send a scout out ahead of us like we planned."

"One of my people already volunteered," Tick-Tock replied.

"Good," Steve said. "Find another one to go with them. I was thinking that it might be a good idea for two people to be out front. That way, if they run into something and one of them gets fucked up, the other one can still come back and warn us. Get them started. We'll give them a five minute head start. As for the main group, I'll take point, you take drag, and

Heather can walk trail."

"Good plan," Tick-Tock said. "I like walking right behind you."

"You checking out my butt or something?" Steve asked with a grin.

"No," Tick-Tock replied in a dead pan voice, "it's because if the shit hits the fan, I'm using you as a meat-shield."

Steve had to cover his mouth to stifle the laughter that poured out of him.

Tick-Tock raised his hand and halted everyone when he saw one of the scouts coming at them in a faltering, loping run. Knowing the woman's gait was due to the grass and not that she had been bitten, he looked down and cursed the thick growth that constantly seemed to tangle around their feet and threaten to trip them.

The group had travelled for three hours without incident, but it was slow going. Even though the grass was brown, brittle and dry from the cooler temperatures of winter, it was still thick. Constant calls of "Wait a minute" came from up and down the line as people stopped to unwrap the long strands from around their legs, feet and ankles. Point was the worst and had to be switched every twenty minutes since whoever walked out front had to break a trail through the virgin waves of weeds. One of Tick-Tock's people had brought along a machete from the mansion, but it was cheaply made and the handle broke off within the first few minutes of use. A rag was wrapped around the tang, but it was still awkward to use.

Not yet knowing what the scout was coming back to tell them, whether it was that a horde of the dead were coming at them at full gallop, or that they had come across some kind of oasis in the middle of the woods complete with blackjack, whiskey and dancing girls, Tick-Tock was grateful for the chance to rest.

Feeling a presence on his right, he turned to find Steve standing next to him. The two of them had alternated with Brain on point, but the grueling labor had taxed all three of them to the point of exhaustion.

"We need to switch this trail blazing crap out with someone else," Tick-Tock told him. "What about Igor?"

Steve shook his head and replied, "He won't leave Cindy's side, and I'm not bringing her up here." Pointing to the scout that was still dozens of yards away as she made her way through the thick grass, he said, "If this is not a dire emergency, we'll get a couple of your people to rotate with us."

Steve and Tick-Tock waited in silence for the woman to reach them. Noise discipline had been drilled into them with such force, that the scout didn't speak until she had stopped two feet in front of them. After catching her breath, she said in a loud whisper, "We've got a whole bunch of dead in front of us."

Steve and Tick-Tock instantly went on the alert, scanning the woods on both sides and their front for sign of any Zs."

Seeing their reaction, the scout said, "Not zombies, but dead zombies." Looking at Tick-Tock, she added, "The good kind. We ran across them a few minutes ago."

"Show me," Steve said as he pointed for her to lead the way.

The stink was one that they had all smelled before, but not to this degree. Hundreds of dead lay scattered across the opening of the firebreak, so many that they flattened the grass for at least two hundred feet in either direction. By the aroma that rose into the air to gag him and the signs of decay on the bodies closest to him, Steve estimated that they had been disposed of days before and then left to rot under the Texas sun. Head wounds and upper body trauma were readily apparent on all of the bodies, with some sporting multiple impacts from what looked like a small caliber weapon on rapid fire.

After reaching the scene of the slaughter of the dead and seeing no threat, Steve had sent the scouts back to bring the main body of the group forward.

When they were gone, he turned to Tick-Tock, he said, "Looks like the military has been through here."

His friend shook his head and replied, "I don't think it was the army."

Curious at his second in command's take on what might have happened, Steve said, "But look at the head shots." Pointing to the torn up foliage on both sides of the firebreak, he added, "It looks like they set up on either side of the way and just waited for the dead to stagger into the kill zone."

Tick-Tock shook his head and replied, "But the woods are torn up directly across on both sides. If it was the military, they would have never fired across the opening and risk hitting each other. If it was an ambush, they would have set up in an L shape so they didn't kill one and other. This was some kind of mechanical ambush." Pointing to the dead lying in the grass, he added, "And whatever happened, it happened in just a few seconds. You can see where none of the dead even made it close to whatever was attacking them. Most of the wound are on the sides of their heads and bodies."

Starting off toward the line of denuded brush to his left, Tick-Tock added, "Let's go see if we can find any sign of what did this."

Using a game trail leading into the forest, the two men only had to follow it a few feet before finding themselves in a clearing. The sun was well up, showing them all they needed to see.

Pointing to two sets of ruts dug into the soft dirt and dead leaves, Tick-Tock said, "Looks like someone moved a couple of mounted weapons in here and set them up side by side. I'd bet my top hat and my house cat that we find the same marks across the way."

"And probably the same thing further down the firebreak," Steve added as he picked up on how so many of the dead had been exterminated in such a short time. "Whatever hit the Zs, hit them at the same time all along their line. Maybe it was the military. Maybe they came up with some type of new weapon that takes out a whole bunch of the dead at the same time."

Walking over to a lone tree standing in the clearing, Tick-Tock reached out and tugged a small, straight object from its trunk. Turning it over in his hand, he said with a smile, "Or maybe an old weapon."

***

Now that the woods on either side of the trail had to be scouted as well as the trail in front of them, the group moved cautiously. With a new, unknown threat lurking in the woods that could be either friend or foe, their progress was slowed down to less than a mile an hour. Coming to an area with overgrown fields on both sides of them, instead of speeding up to minimize their exposure, they slowed even more when they saw that some of the fields had been freshly plowed. Most of them were still fallow, but a few had been cleared for planting. In addition to this, just before coming out of the woods, they had seen where the posts holding the electrical wires above their heads abruptly stopped. The only thing remaining were huge holes in the ground and gouges in the earth where they had been dug up and dragged off.

The signs were obvious that they was a human element nearby, but after their last few interactions with the survivors of the zombie apocalypse, it left the group with an uneasy feeling. Besides Delightfully Grimm and her crew, the few people that they had come across had tried to kill them and take their supplies. With a bad taste in their mouths from what humanity had sunk to, hope that this new group of farmers were friendly was but a fleeting ghost.

The signs of habitation grew as they travelled further along, including more plowed areas as well as a few empty lean-tos. The firebreak gradually rose to a seventy foot wide swath of grass with empty fields on either side, leaving the group on high ground. Feeling exposed despite the cover the waist high grass gave them, Steve was relieved to see where the woods picked up again on either side of the firebreak. Cutting through the woods might give a potential foe the advantage in ambushing them, but the woods also provided cover if they needed to make a break for it. He knew that as long as they were conscious of their surroundings and scouted ahead of them, they should be okay.

Preparing to call a break when they reached the end of the fields, Steve's voice caught in his throat when he saw both of the scouts running toward him at full-tilt boogie. Looking past them down the corridor formed by the woods on either side of the firebreak, he could see what had spooked them even before one of them screamed out, "Zs. A whole shitload of them."

The woman with him called out between gasping for breath, "We saw them from a ways off. Don climbed a tree for a better look. They're stretched out for at least a quarter mile."

Knowing there was no way they could take on so many of the dead, Steve looking around wildly for a place to hide. Seeing only plowed fields on either side of him, he judged the distance to the closest cover. The nearest was a clump of trees a few hundred feet away. It was near the end of the day and the group was already exhausted from the exertions of the day so there was no way they could get there. They wouldn't make it half-way across before the Zs spotted them and gave chase. He could see in his mind's eye as they were picked off one by one as their bodies gave out and they fell behind.

With only the strip of grass on the raised portion of the firebreak to hide in, Steve made a quick decision as he called out, "Everyone down."

The group had seen their predicament and already dropped to the ground so he was the only one to obey his command. The last thing he saw before ducking down was the rustling of the grass as the two scouts scurried through it on hands and knees to join them.

Raising into a half-crouch so he could see the approaching dead, Steve knew in an instant that it was useless. As far down the firebreak as the eye could see, the dead were staggering toward them. They might break left and right when they reached the open fields, but they would still sense or smell the group when they passed. Once that happened, they would fall on them in a wave of dead flesh that would be impossible to repel.

With no choice, Steve called out an order that he dreaded ever having to give. "Everyone circle around Cindy and prepare to be overrun."

Without hesitation, the group crawled through the grass to take up position around the little girl. The stress and strife of travelling through a land populated by the walking dead might have caused distraction, but in the end, they all knew that their only hope lay in the little girl that was immune to the HWNW disease. Past differences in politics, religion and race were forgotten as the group formed up, facing outward from where Igor and Linda crouched next to Cindy, their weapons ready to deal a second and final death to anything that threatened her.

Steve felt a body settle next to him and knew it was Heather. Without turning, he said, "It looks bad, but if the Zs take the easy route through the fields, they might bypass us."

Heather laughed nervously and said, "Don't blow smoke up my ass, babe. I saw what's heading toward us. That and the order to prepare to be overrun kind of gave it away."

Steve grimaced and said, "There's always a chance that they'll bypass us."

Feeling his lovers gaze on him, Steve turned his head to find Heather studying him intently.

Before he could ask what she was looking at, she said, "I love you, but don't bullshit me. If worst comes to worst and the Zs do spot us, do you think we can fight through them and make it to safety?"

Steve started to answer yes, but seeing the look in Heather's eye, he didn't even have to think about it before answering honestly, "No."

Turning her attention toward the thick grass in front of her, Heather said, "Then this is where it will be." Raising her voice, she said just loud enough to be heard by the circle,

"Everyone hold fast. If the Zs spot us, we're finished. The chances of that are pretty good, but don't open fire until you hear the order."

Turning back to Steve, she found him half standing, stooped over as he checking the progress of the dead. Hearing him say, "They're almost to the open area," she felt her heart sink at the thought of losing the man next to her. They had been through so much together, and while they had come very close to death in Galveston bay, once they made it through, she thought they would be home free.

It looked like that was not to be.

Reaching up to pull Steve down next to her so that she could hug him, Heather's hand flinched at a loud thwanging noise followed almost immediately by a series of thumps that echoed across the barren fields around them. She could see Steve start to drop down at the sudden sound, and then raise back up to stare intently across the grass. Within a heartbeat, the loud thwang-thump was repeated again and again too many times to count.

Wanting to see what had happened, but with enough discipline to stay in her position, she called up to Steve, "What the fuck is that?"

By the time she had gotten the sentence out of her mouth, he had already dropped back down and said, "I don't know, but whatever it is, it just about wiped out the Zs. Take a look."

Heather rose into a crouch. The longer blades of grass still blocked her view, so she rose by centimeters until she could see above and between them. Looking toward where the firebreak disappeared into the woods, she could only see a few of the dead staggering around. Gunfire erupted, causing her to drop back down, but not before she saw even these few sacks of dead meat fall to headshots. Voices could now be heard calling out to each other, but the distance distorted their words. Then, the sound of engines starting up completely drowned them out.

Listening intently, Steve heard the engines come to life and then idle. Then they started revving up and then idling, revving up and then idling, as if they were moving back and forth to get in position. Risking another look, he could see eight or nine large trucks had come down the firebreak and were jockeying for position as they backed toward either side of the opening. Men and woman scurried about as they worked to haul some kind of trailers carrying long rectangular objects on them out of the woods to be hitched up. Within minutes, the trailers were attached and the trucks fell into a column. Blue exhaust filled the area between the trees as they sat idling.

The sight was entrancing, and Steve at hoped they were military. Watching them closely, he could see the people moved with discipline and skill, but guessed by the mish-mash of weapons that they carried and their dress that they weren't military. A few wore camouflaged fatigues and carried what looked like M16's, but most were dressed in jeans and work pants and toted a wide variety of automatic weapons.

Despite their apparent skill at killing the dead, he couldn't tell if they were friend or foe.

The mini-army was facing away from his group, and hoping that they would go in that direction when they moved out, Steve felt his stomach drop when he spotted a Jeep Wrangler with a .50 caliber machine gun mounted on its roll cage coming down the column toward them at a high rate of speed. It didn't stop when it reached the end of the woods and kept heading directly at them. As it neared, he could see it was manned by three people. A driver, a passenger, and a gunner. The barrel of the heavy machine gun was pointed upward, but the woman manning it kept her hands on it and could level it at them in less than a second

Calling out for everyone to hold fire, Steve turned and saw that the entire group was watching the Jeep's fast approach with their weapons at the ready. He knew they were well within the range of the .50 caliber, but it hadn't opened up on them. This gave him hope that if these people weren't friendly, that at least they didn't have any interest in killing them.

Despite this, he still called out for everyone to concentrate their fire on the gunner if the shit hit the fan.

The Jeep slowed and the passenger half stood in his seat as he started scanning the tall grass in front of them. They were close enough now for Steve to hear him say to the driver, “Slow down a little more. We don’t want to run anyone over.”

Knowing that they had been spotted, and encouraged by the comment that they not drive over anyone, Steve made a snap decision and stood up. Knowing that the .50 caliber could rip through the grass and decimate his group, he also knew that if they stayed hidden, the Jeep would roll right over them on its current path.

Only twenty feet away, the vehicle slowed. With a clear target, the gunner still didn’t bring her weapon to bear, but Steve swore he could see her hands tightening on the grips.

The passenger started to stand as the Jeep slowed, but as it stopped with a slight jerk, he was thrown against the raised windshield.

Steve suppressed a smile when the man commented, “They used to make it look so easy on The Rat Patrol.”

“The Rat Patrol?” He heard the driver ask.

“Yeah, the Rat Patrol,” the passenger insisted. “It was a TV series starring Robert Conrad as he led his band of merry misfits behind German lines during World War Two. They tore the Nazis a new one.”

Shaking his head, the driver replied, “Never heard of it.”

“Damn kids,” the man muttered as he stood up, turned his attention to Steve, and said. “Looks like we saved your butt, those dead-asses were fixing to roll right over you.”

“Thanks,” Steve replied. “Looks like you have quite a group here. My name is Steve Wendell. We’re trying to get to Fort Polk.”

“Well, you’re in luck,” the man told him. “It’s still there. The Army pulled all its forces back into the base, but they still run some patrols. My name is Rick Styles. I’m the head of the East Texas Zombie Relief Force. We control this area.”

Excited at hearing Fort Polk was still operational, Steve asked, “Are you in contact with Polk?”

Rick Styles shook his head and replied, “We used to talk to them every day, but they cut us off a few weeks ago.”

“So how do you know it’s still there?” Steve asked.

“We hear them broadcasting, they just won’t answer us. On top of that, we took in a couple deserters from there a week ago,” Rick told him. “They said the entire United States military is under orders to cease all contact with civilians. They’re having some major supply issues so they’ve stopped taking in refugees too. All the bases, forts and camps in the US are having trouble keeping their own troops in beans and bullets, so they have to cut back. The military pulled back into all their bases when everything was falling apart, but then they came out swinging. They gained a lot of ground but couldn’t get control of a few key cities. They tried again, but they didn’t have enough supplies to keep them going.”

A million questions ran through Steve’s head, but curious as to how the rest of the world was fairing, he asking, “What happened?”

“Heard they ran out of gas,” Rick said. “We might have oil in Texas, but who’s going to refine it and transport it to the military with all the dead wandering around?” The cities are still thick with Ds, and you just saw firsthand the size of the groups roaming the countryside, so how are they move it?”

Steve grimaced at the thought. Everything needed to sustain an army in the field was either scattered across the United States or imported from overseas. Every supply point, farm or production facility for everything from oil to onions would have to be fortified. Then, you would have to move it across a dead landscape where the inhabitants wanted to eat you. A thought came to him, and eyeing Rick, Steve asked, “I saw what you did to that gang of Zs, but with all the huge herds of dead roaming around, how did you managed to survive so far?”

Rick let out a short bark of laughter before saying, “Survive? Hell, we’re trying to win."

Steve smiled and then laughed out loud. With all the unorganized mobs they had run across, this one seemed to have their shit together and were actually trying to destroy the dead. His immediate reaction was ask to join them, but then he remembered Cindy. She was their main priority.

Sobering, he asked, "So you're part of the military?"

"Militia," Rick corrected.

Steve worried at hearing this at this. For every Militia he had ever heard about that was formed to do good, there were four more formed by crackpots to suit their own needs.

Seeing Steve's eyes narrow, Rick added, "Don't worry, we're the good guys. We keep the peace and kill the dead. The law is pretty simple now. Looters, thieves and brigands are hung and the dead are eradicated. The dead-asses are making it easier since they're running in big packs nowadays."

Steve thought for a moment before asking, "We're heading east, what's it look like in that direction?"

"There are a lot of small packs of dead-asses but there's a few big one's too," Rick replied. "We keep an eye on them so we can set up ambushes like we did here." Eyeing the sky, he added, "Look, Steve, it's getting late and we're heading back to camp. You're welcome to join us if you have a mind to. We can jaw some more once we've eaten."

Steve replied, "There's more than just me. We've got-."

Rick cut him off by saying, "There's fifteen of you and a dog. We've had people watching you since you crossed into our territory yesterday. They reported that you lost a few people last night and have been running all day. Nothing much goes on in this area that we don't know about." He paused and then asked, "So do you want to sleep somewhere safe tonight or not?"

Quickly weighing the options, Steve gratefully accepted the offer.

CHAPTER ELEVEN

Fort Redoubt:

Tick-Tock pointed to the weapon being towed behind the truck and said, "When I pulled that dart out of the tree, I saw about twenty more stuck into the others nearby so I kind of had an idea they were using something like this. I just didn't think it would be so big."

Steve studied the weapon as he tried to remember what they were called. He knew it was used during medieval times, but with modern warfare being what it was, he never would have imagined a resurgence in its use. Fully eight feet wide, it was only twelve inches in height and three feet deep. Numerous holes had been drilled all the way from front to back where a large flat board was strapped to its rear by bungee cords. This board could be retracted along rails and locked into place before the darts were loaded into their holes with about an inch of their tail left exposed. Once triggered, the board slapped forward with tremendous force to launch a spray of small missiles. Mounted with locking handles on its sides so that it could be swiveled up and down, Steve couldn't see anything that would let the weapon be rotated to the left or right. Looking closer, he noted that it was slightly convex in its shape, and realized it didn't need to be. It could easily throw over two hundred darts in a flat arc, decimating anything in their path.

"Kind of like an early claymore mine," Steve commented.

Having decided to ride with the newcomers, Rick said from where he sat next to Tick-Tock, "It's called a porcupine. We've got twenty of them in all with a few more in production. I knew early on that ammunition would be getting scarce, so I went retro. However World war Three is fought, World War Four will be fought with sticks and rocks. I didn't want to go that far back, so we came up with this. We track the larger groups of dead-asses and get in front of them. The firebreak is the best place since we can set up on both sides, but it really doesn't really matter where we do it. The Ds don't know what the hell it is so they walk right up to it. Sometimes we bait them and get a whole bunch staggering right into ground-zero."

"Bait them?" Steve asked.

"We've got some good runners in our crew," Rick answered. "If a group is heading in the wrong direction, they get out in front of them and lead them into the killing zone. We set the porcupines up to fire at between at five feet and six feet high for maximum damage. Anything left standing after that, we clean up with rifle fire."

"What other kinds of weapons do you have?" Tick-Tock asked.

Rick thought for a moment before asking, "New or retro?"

Tick-Tock shrugged and replied, "Both."

"We raided a couple National Guard armories so we've got some mortars and few small field artillery pieces," Rick told him. "All the small arms had already been issued when we got there but they never released the heavy weapons so they were there for the taking. We hit the armories in San Angelos and Lafayette, Louisiana. The others we went to had already been picked clean. Those missions were hairy as shit since they were inside or near towns that had been overrun, but that's probably the only reason they had been left alone. Ammunition is really scarce for the heavy weapons though, so we only use them for perimeter defense. We built a couple of catapults, but we can't seem to get them to work just right. The porcupines are easy to make since you're basically drilling holes in a big block of wood, but we can't quite get the catapults to land their load where we want. For the smaller groups, or single Ds that come around, we use a bow and arrow on them. I've got about twenty people working full time making darts and arrows."

Coughing at the dust kicked up from the dirt road they were on, Rick cleared his throat, turned and spit over the side of the truck before continuing, "We've got plenty of small arms and a good supply of ammo." Pointing to a woman wearing camouflage sitting near the cab, he added, "Those are my officers wearing the cammies, they all carry M16s or M4s. Everyone else carries whatever they're comfortable with or what they've scrounged. When the shit first hit the fan, we we're scrambling to secure all the weapons and ammunition that we could."

Seeing Steve's quizzical look, he explained, "Most of the military grade stuff we picked up was from National Guard units that had been wiped out by the dead. They were exposed to the elements, so we had to move fast before they turned to rusted shit."

"I can relate," Steve told him.

"You stayed alive this long, so I guess you can," Rick said as he eyed the M4 assault rifle in Steve's hands. "I was living in Jasper, Texas when it first started. There were about thirty or forty members of the militia back then. We tried to hold the town but it was useless. Just when you thought you had an area secured, one of the Ds would pop up and infect someone who infected someone else and so on. When I saw it was hopeless, I took what was left of my people and headed for the woods. We built tree houses to live in, but we kind of outgrew them when we took in a couple small groups. We decided that we needed something better, so we pulled out the maps and took a hard look at what was around us. We knew we needed water, so we headed for the lake. It's also got the water treatment plant nearby. That's where we built our main base and fortified it against an attack."

"Main base?" Tick-Tock asked.

Rick nodded and replied, "We've got four other bases. Not as big as Fort Redoubt, but they've all got good defenses with good escape routes in case the shit hits the fan." Continuing with his story, he said, "Pretty soon, word got around about Fort Redoubt and people started coming to us for refuge. No one was turned away except for a few bottom feeders. We took in a couple of big groups of people fleeing Dallas/Fort Worth, so we decided to expand. That's when we set up the first of our other forts."

"Did your people plow the fields that we passed by right before you picked us up?" Steve asked.

Rick nodded and said, "That's one of our spots. We've got a couple closer to the fort, but we need to feed two thousand plus people -."

"Two thousand plus?" Steve asked incredulously, cutting him off.

Rick smiled and said, "Give or take a dozen. Everyone is free to leave if they want, but most stay. Everyone is assigned a job when they get here, and if you don't work, you don't eat. We've pretty much picked the area around us clean of food and supplies, so we have to go back to basics to survive."

Distracted by Tick-Tock as he leaned down to check on Denise, Steve watched as his friend bunched numerous blankets around her to cushion her from the bumpy ride. After they had boarded the truck and started off, she had become sick from the swaying ride and started to vomit. Tick-Tock's people, as Steve called those he used to call the others, had immediately come forward with their sleeping bags and blankets. Since then, she hadn't gotten worse, but she hadn't gotten any better.

Rick looked down at Denise and said, "My guess is a concussion or a skull fracture."

When he saw Denise was doing alright, Tick-Tock asked, "Do you have medical facilities?"

"We've got an infirmary, but our X-ray machine leaves a lot to be desired," Rick told him.

Just the thought of finding out if Denise had a fractured skull made Tick-Tock lean forward and ask excitedly, "You have an X-ray machine?"

Rick nodded and said, "We do, but like I said, it leaves a lot to be desired. We don't have any plates or any way to develop film, so we hooked it up to a screen. It throws off a shitload of radiation, so anytime we have to use it, we make it quick. We have no idea of how many rads it throws off, but the people we've used it on haven't started to glow in the dark, so that's a plus. We know it's dangerous so we only use it when we have to."

The truck started to slow, causing everyone to crane their necks to see what was going on, and that was when the refugees from the insane asylum got their first look at the outer defenses of Fort Redoubt.

The undergrowth and trees had been cut back in a twenty foot wide swath in which triple coils of razor wire had been laid out in a pyramid shape. This fence stretched off from either side of the road as far as the eye could see. A Jeep, similar to the one that Rick had approached them in, was moving away from them at slow speed, the person manning its .50 caliber machine gun slowly swiveling the barrel back and forth as he searched for targets. The vehicle travelled along twin ruts that had been worn down by much use, telling Steve that this was a regularly patrolled area. Looking further down the line, he could make out the top of a watchtower poking out of the fir trees.

"You're not screwing around," he commented.

"This is the first of the outer defenses," Rick told him. There's another line like this a hundred feet further on and then the fort itself."

"Must have been a bitch to cut back all those trees," Tick-Tick said.

"That was the easy part," Rick told him. "We used dynamite and C4 on them. The hard part came when the explosions attracted dead-asses for miles."

The truck started picking up speed after passing through an opening in the wire. As they moved through it, Steve could see two people swing a six foot high wooden gate into place behind them and secure it with chains. Feeling a momentary surge of dread, he studied Rick Styles for any signs that this was a set up. He knew that Style's and his people could have cut them down where they stood when they came across them at the fire break, but maybe the good guy act was just that. An act. Maybe this was how they sucked people in before robbing and killing them. The defenses of Fort Redoubt were meant to keep the dead out, but they would also be more than sufficient to keep anyone from escaping. Looking at Tick-Tock, he could see that his friend was thinking the same thing too.

As if sensing their apprehension, Rick Styles said, "You have nothing to worry about, no one in my group is going to hurt you." He paused before adding, "Unless you try to hurt one of us. We have some rules at the fort, and number one is that you don't kill the living."

Hearing this quelled some of Steve's fears, but he still kept his guard up. Curious, he asked, "What other rules do you have?"

"It's really simple," Rick replied. "No stealing, no cheating and no lying, although that one is hard to enforce. Everyone is expected to pull their weight every day or they don't eat, but the most important rule is, no drama. This isn't an audition for the fucking Jerry Springer show."

From where she was listening nearby, Heather laughed as she remembered the night when the virus hit Clearwater with full force. She had gone to the high school to evacuate some wounded and to get her CAR-15. When she went with one of the local cops to collect her trusted weapon, she saw that they had a bunch of people suspected of being infected were quarantined in the school's gym. She recalled that there was one guy crying and moaning about being able to feel the virus running through his veins. With a second laugh at how he reacted when one of the others in his group turned, she knew that drama queens were something they definitely didn't need.

"So what are the penalties for breaking the rules," she asked.

"Murder is punishable by death by hanging," he replied. "For everything else, we exile you from the forts."

The group took this in as the truck slowed to pass through the second line of defenses. Steve saw that they were constructed the same as the first, but with one small addition. Signs warning that the area was mined were set up every fifty feet. Next to them were similar ones warning that the fence was electrified.

Now we're really screwed if this is a set up, he thought to himself. Expecting that any second they would be ambushed, this thought was abruptly cut off when they reached a clearing and he saw the wall of Fort Redoubt appear.

Softly saying, “Holy shit, now I can see where all the power poles went,” he nudged Tick-Tock and nodded his head toward the defenses Rick Styles and his people had erected.

Set into the ground and pointing outward at a forty-five degree angle, the power poles formed the main part of the wall. Each one of them had been sharpened into a point, but Steve couldn’t see the reasoning behind this since their tops were at least fifteen feet off the ground.

Must be psychological, he guessed.

The trucks broke to their right and parked side by side. In front of them them, Steve could see people hurriedly hooking porcupines up to trailer hitches on a similarly parked line of six-wheeled Army vehicles. A sense of urgency prevailed among them, causing him to turn to their host and ask what was going on.

Seeing he had already jumped over the tailgate of their truck and was a short distance away, Steve filled himself in on what was happening by the barked conversation Rick was having with another man.

“What the fuck is going on, Lieutenant Wilkes?” Rick asked a huge man dressed in camouflage utilities.

“That big gang of dead-asses out of Jasper that were heading west changed their minds and are heading north now,” he answered.

“And you’re doing what?” Rick asked him venomously.

“We were going to lead them off to the West again. You weren’t anywhere to be found, so I took it upon myself to give the orders,” Wilkes told him arrogantly.

In a low, angry voice, Rick asked rapid fire, “And you couldn’t find a radio to call me? The chain of command just gets tossed out the window like a pot full of piss whenever we spot some Ds?”

The two men locked eyes in a hard stare, but Wilkes dropped his after only a second. His shoulders sagged as he said in a soft voice, “I took it upon myself to order out the guard, sir. I saw it as a chance to even the score for Vanessa and the boys.”

Rick’s shoulders slumped too. Speaking sternly but quietly, he said, “I loved them too. It may have been your sister and nephews, but remember, it was my wife and kids that died. Regardless of our personal feeling, we need to make and follow a plan or we’re going to be nothing but a rabble striking out blindly in all directions. We don’t have the people or the resources to be running off every time we see a herd of dead-asses coming our way, and you know how we do it, we plan our strike and then strike on our plan.”

Chastised, Wilkes said, “I’ll order our people to stand down.”

“Not so fast,” Rick told him. “You may have the right plan even though you went about it in the wrong way. Tell me what’s going on.”

Steve, Heather and Tick-Tock had gotten out of the truck and stood a few feet away, listening intently as Wilkes said, “The scouts that were following the herd out of Jasper called in and said that the dead-asses were changing direction.” Pulling out a map, he lay it on the ground and pointed to a yellow line as he said, “They cut north on highway 59. If they keep going in that direction to where it intersects with Highway 63, and if they decide to come back east instead of going north or west, it will bring them real close to us.”

Rick studied the map for a few seconds before saying, “That is a possibility, but not one that requires we go off half-cocked.”

Straightening, Wilkes said, “Since this group has about ten-thousand dead in it, I thought I’d set up some ambushes and whittle their numbers down a little while I try to draw them back to the west.”

Moving closer, Steve asked, “Is that big herd that was west of Jasper?”

Wilkes narrowed his eyes at the intrusion and asked, “And who the hell are you.”

“He’s a refugee,” Rick explained.

"Is he some kind of tactical genius?" Wilkes asked.

"Just a refugee from what I've been able to gather," Rick told him, "but he did manage to lead his group here all the way from Clearwater, Florida so he must have his shit together at least a little bit."

Wilkes gave a grudging nod to this as he checked Steve and his crew out. They looked wild and unkempt from being on the road, but he could see that their weapons were clean and ready to use. He also took in the hard set of their eyes and their defiant posture before saying, "We've got a couple other people here from Clearwater. I'll introduce you to them later."

Steve nodded and said, "Thanks," before pointing down to the map and saying, "The reason I asked about the size of the herd is because I was wondering if it was the same one we were running from. We estimated the one coming toward us to be at least twenty-thousand. If there's another big group of Zs out there roaming around, I'd like to know about it so we can avoid them when we leave."

"Leave," Rick asked in a confused voice. "You've just found the only safe place in a thousand square miles and now you want to go out into the dead lands again."

"We have to get to Fort Polk," Steve told him.

"But like I told you, they're not taking in civilians," Rick said.

"I think they'll accept us," Steve told him.

Skeptical, Wilkes asked, "And why are you so sure of that?"

Steve hesitated as he considered his position. The feeling that they might be walking into a trap had left him, but he wasn't sure how far he could trust these people. After weighing the pros and cons, and knowing it would come out as soon as he could get to Rick's radio and call Fort Polk, he said, "We have someone in our group that's immune to the HWNW virus."

This announcement was met by a skeptical silence. Steve didn't want to add anything else to his simple statement since he could see that neither Rick nor Wilkes believed him. He knew that the harder he tried to convince them, the more likely they would be to doubt him.

Finally, Rick said, "You know you don't have to make things up to convince us to let you stay here. Everyone except bottom feeders are welcome."

"And lying is a punishable offense," Wilkes added. "Telling the truth gets you in, but lying gets you banished."

Steve said simply, "I'm not lying."

"I challenge that," Wilkes said.

Turning his attention to Steve, Rick said, "You have formally been challenged on the charge of lying. This means that you must show proof that you are innocent."

"Or what," Tick-Tock asked from where he stood next to Steve.

Pointing to the gate of Fort Redoubt, he said, "Or you don't get in."

Steve looked to where his group was standing nearby. He could see that they were exhausted from fear and the exertion of their flight from the insane asylum and he knew they needed to rest in a safe place where they weren't under constant threat of being eaten. On top of that, they needed Rick Style's radio to call Fort Polk. They might be able to reach them on the CB radio that they had brought along, but it also might be a day or two before they got into range. Considering the people that they had already lost, he made a decision. Calling out to Linda, he asked her to bring Cindy over. Igor came too and a small circle formed around the little girl.

Feeling like a curiosity in a freak show, Cindy lowered her head in embarrassment as she rolled up the sleeve of her shirt. Looking down at the scars, she could see that they were fading. Linda had assured her that one day they would disappear completely, but for now, you could still see the individual tooth marks. She had avoided looking at the scars because they brought back memories that were hard to bear. Especially the two gaps in the tissue caused by her little brother's missing teeth.

Rick let out a low whistle before saying, "I guess that proves it. Challenge is negated by the truth."

Nodding to where Wilkes stood with a scowl on his face, Tick-Tock asked, "Does that mean he gets exiled?"

Rick laughed and said, "It doesn't quite work that way. We have to try to be as fair as possible to maintain the integrity of our group." Looking down to where Cindy was rolling her shirt back down her arm, he asked, "Where did you find her?"

Steve relayed the story of how they had found her hiding in the building they had took shelter in when the dead rose up and how they were trying to get her to a military base so could be studied and a cure found for the HWNW virus.

When he was finished, Rick said, "It sounds like you found yourself a noble cause in the middle of all this death and destruction. My people and I will help you in any way we can. First of all, I think getting something to eat is in order."

It was then that Steve became aware of an enticing aroma coming from inside the walls of Fort Redoubt. When they had first pulled up, he noticed that the area was slightly hazy and smelled of wood smoke, and now he realized that these must be cooking fires being stoked. His stomach rumbled at the scent of cooked meat as he thought back to when he'd had his last hot meal. Realizing that it had been right before they left the insane asylum, he was shocked that it had only been the day before yesterday. It felt like they had been running and hiding for weeks.

"You said that you had an infirmary?" Tick-Tock asked, interrupting Steve's thoughts of hot food, and making him feel slightly guilty that he had completely forgotten about the wounded.

Rick turned and called out to two of his people to get stretchers for Denise and another woman in the group that had been badly hurt in the crossfire the night before. When they had been carried off, with Tick-Tock and one of his people helping carry them, Rick mentioned food again.

Accepting Rick's offer of dinner, Steve and his people followed him toward the gate and into Fort Redoubt, glancing about as they took in the sights and sounds around them while Rick Styles kept up a running commentary about how they had set up the place.

"When we first got here," Rick told them, "There was less than one-hundred of us. We scouted the area real good and realized that this was the perfect spot with the exception of one problem. Everything we needed was too spread out. At first we wanted to set up to the water treatment plant, but the smell was so bad that it drove us off. Without power, it was pretty useless to us. We needed water, so we cleared out a few of the houses along the shore of the lake and settled in. We weren't as organized back then, but we set up a pretty good defensive position by cutting down trees and using them as a barricade."

"What about the people who lived here?" Steve asked.

"When we got here, the whole place was deserted," Rick told him. "Most of the buildings in this area are rentals, and with the dead coming back to life all around the world, I can say it was definitely off-season for tourists and vacationers. There were still a few of the locals around living at the golf course, but there were only a handful of year-round residents and they didn't show themselves right away. They were probably waiting to see if we were friendly or not."

Putting his hand on Steve's arm to stop him, Rick asked, "Did you get to see how people acted when things started falling apart? I don't know about where you were, but in the cities they were raping, looting and killing each other off in droves. Even out here in the sticks it got pretty bad for a while. We had a lot of people come through here that were fleeing from someplace or running to another, and they were willing to do anything they needed to survive. There were also a couple half-way organized groups that stayed to the secondary roads and looted anything they came across that they thought they might need to survive."

"I saw some of it when everything fell apart," Steve told him as his thoughts wandered to his late night run through Pinellas County to safety. "We locked down right when things started to go bad so we missed the worst of it."

"Then you were lucky," Rick said. "We had barely gotten settled in when a gang of about thirty came through. They saw the barricade we'd put up and must have thought we had a stash of food and supplies we were trying to protect. In fact it was just the opposite. We were well armed, but all were living off fish we took from the lake and some canned goods we scrounged from the houses around us. No matter what it was though, they wanted what we had."

Looking him in the eye, Steve said, "I take it by the fact that you're standing here that you won."

Starting to walk again, Rick said, "Like I said, we were well armed."

As the group moved through the gate and into the fort, Steve was startled by the lack of structures. From where he stood, he could see the far wall.

"You said you had two-thousand people. Where are they all?" He asked.

"Living in the houses all around the fort," Rick explained. "There was no way we could build a wall like this to cover the whole peninsula, so we set up the two outer rings with barbwire and mines and build Fort Redoubt as our fallback position in case everything went to hell. We used the roads and cleared what we had to for the outer fences."

Looking at four separate barracks like buildings surrounding a large open drill field, Steve caught on that the fort was only used for the military arm of Rick Styles organization.

"Everyone from the age of thirteen on up is required to serve in the militia," Rick explained. "We have about one-thousand people living in the area surrounding Fort Redoubt, and they rotate every four weeks for one week of service. At any given time, we have about two hundred men and women on active duty patrolling the wire or going out on ambush. When they are not on duty, they are fishermen, farmers, hunters and scroungers."

"What about the ones that are too old or can't serve," Heather asked.

"Did you see the groups of younger kids and old people outside the gate?" Rick asked.

Heather nodded. She had noticed a group of about a dozen sitting in front of large, stone spinning wheels, but there backs were to her so she couldn't see what they were doing. She remembered one of them was missing a leg, his stump propped out to the side as he bent to whatever task he was performing. There were similar small groups sitting in circles, but their work was obvious as they mended clothes and cleaned weapons.

"Everyone finds a way to serve," Rick told her. "The ones in front of the grinding wheels are making darts and arrows. For the very old, we have a nursing home, but even there, the residents are always volunteering to help in some small way. They are fed and taken care of until they die."

Steve was impressed with the setup. Seeing a long, low building with smoke coming out of chimneys at each end, he asked, "Is that the chow hall?"

Rick laughed and said, "That's our destination. We live on a diet of mostly fish and vegetables, but every once in a while, one of our hunters comes across something that the Ds haven't torn apart and stuffed down their throats. This morning, one of the teams to the north shot a deer so we have venison for dinner."

Rick turned and walked toward the door of the chow hall with Steve and his people in tow. When they entered, they found people eating at dozens of picnic tables with more lined up to pass in front of a stainless steel serving line across the back wall.

"We took that from the local high school along with all the trays and silverware," Rick explained as he stepped behind the last man in line waiting to get fed. For a moment, Steve wondered at this behavior since Rick claimed to be their leader. Considering the man for a moment, he realized that he had enough humility that he wouldn't cut in line or abuse his power. This was indeed a rare find in any individual, much less a leader.

Waiting to move through the line, Steve felt his body relax for what felt like the first time in years. They were alive, safe, and about to settle in for a much needed break. Feeling a hand laid gently on his back as he picked up a tray, at first, he thought it was Heather.

This was until it started patting him as a low voice said, "Oh my god. Are you real."

Recognizing the voice, but not sure if he was dreaming, Steve turned to find Ginny standing in front of him.

CHAPTER TWELVE

Washington DC:

General Eastridge walked the entire length of the Vietnam Veteran's Memorial without being contacted by Admiral Sedlak. When the Admiral had asked in a hushed voice for the clandestine meeting after their daily gathering for the briefing by the Chairman Joint Chiefs, Eastridge had seen the dour look on Sedlak's face and knew it wouldn't be good news. He ran through the possibilities of what Sedlak would tell him, but with so many atrocities happening in the world, and the new ones that the Joint Chief proposed only moments earlier at his briefing, it was a toss-up.

Facing the Washington Monument, Eastridge knew that the first president of the United States had to be rolling over in his grave at what the Chairman of the Joint Chief's had passed into law that afternoon.

First on his agenda was the order for the conscription of all able bodied men and women from the ages of eight to seventy-five. This was met with acceptance from the rest of the Joint Chiefs, as the reality of the situation was that they had no other choice. Even though everyone in the military had been pulled back into base, the losses that they had sustained up until this point had been high. The last surge by the dead, which had caused the order to retreat to be given, had decimated just under ten percent of their available field personnel.

What followed next though, was less than acceptable.

Those under the age of eight and over the age of seventy-five were to be disarmed. Unless you were serving in the military, you were now banned from carrying anything more dangerous than a sling-shot. The Chairman explained that this was a necessary order since lately there had been too many instances of civilians attacking patrols and raiding smaller camps for their supplies.

When asked if the relief camps were to be opened again so that the newly unarmed people could live in safety, The Chairman replied that they would remained closed. This sent a stir around the table that was silenced as the Chairman's brow furrowed and his face turned red. Knowing he was about to erupt, the men fell silent and seemed to find things of interest in the paperwork in front of them and on the far walls where digital readouts scrolled out the latest news from around the world.

The two still working that was.

When the Chairman finally got his temper under control, he explained that the decision to keep the camps closed may seem cold-hearted, but it needed to be done. Nothing had changed in the nation's supply issues, so there was no way they could support the masses that would be left unprotected after they were disarmed. These people were essentially useless in the fight against the dead and would only use up food and water that could be better used taking care of Americas fighting men and women. The older people would naturally be weeded out, and the younger would be strengthened by the trials of survival. When they turned of age, they would be perfect soldiers.

Or feral wolf-children, Eastridge thought.

The next edict handed down from the Chairman was the immediate disbanding of the Supreme Court. Of the original nine justices, only three had survived, so on the outside, it didn't appear to be that large of a usurpation of powers. But if you had been in on the dealings of government from the beginning of the crisis, you knew that no new ones had been appointed for a reason. What was not widely known was that the remaining three had served to make sure that the government didn't overstep its bounds after martial law was declared. In the chaos of the dead coming back to life, they figureheads at best, but they had managed to stop the Chairman from taking complete control of the country after the President was found incompetent to serve.

No mention of where the Justices would now serve was given, and Eastridge shuddered at what their fate would be since they had crossed the Chairman. However, he did know that if there were spikes atop the main gate leading into DC, their heads would adorn them.

The next declaration made by the Chairman was the disbanding of Congress. With their decreased numbers, neither the Senate nor the House of representatives had adjourned in the last two weeks. The last time they has gotten together, they did manage to pass a bill on reopening the relief centers, but it was a moot point. When they were finished, they realized that there was no one to sign it except the man that had shut them down in the first place. The bill was passed to the Chairman who promptly vetoed it. Congress promptly banded together to override the veto, but because of a sudden restriction in movement throughout the capitol ordered by The Chairman, they had been unable to convene. Congress might have been a mere irritant to the Chairman, but they had openly opposed him and had to go.

More heads for the spikes, Eastridge thought.

After all of this, the final order from the Chairman was not surprising. Explaining to the men gathered around the table that since there was no longer an acting legislative or judicial branch looking out for the best interests of the people of the United States, he would take complete control until the crisis had abated and elections could be held.

Acting dictator and chief, Eastridge thought. Now that he has complete control, maybe he *will* install spikes on the gate.

Applause met this announcement. The men around the table knew that as advisors to what was now the most powerful man on the planet, the louder and longer they clapped, the longer they lived. Knowing he had to play along to keep his seat, General Eastridge clapped along with the rest of them.

The meeting finished with the Chairman giving a collection of orders ranging from the honor guard at funerals no longer firing their guns so as to conserve ammunition, to how they would divert some of the small creeks in the area to supply them with water.

Footsteps crunching through the leaves to his left brought him out of his reverie. Expecting to see the Navy Seal again, Eastridge was surprised to see Admiral Sedlak coming toward him through the trees behind the memorial. The area around them was open, causing a bolt of fear to shoot through him. Looking in all directions to see if they had been spotted, he was relieved to see no one.

Holding out his right hand, the Admiral said, "I'm glad you could make. I know it's kind of last minute, but after the events at the briefing today, I don't see that we have a lot of time to waste."

Grasping the outstretched hand and shaking it, Eastridge said, "I kind of expected something like this, only not so soon. I expected The Chairman to strengthen his own position with troops loyal to him before taking over."

"The way I see it, he has more than enough," the Admiral explained. "He's got four battalions of infantry that he's been reinforcing for the last month. They're almost up to full strength with about a thousand men in each. He also has his Green berets and his Rangers. Like my Seals, the green beanie's got chewed up pretty badly, but the Rangers are mostly intact. He's got them billeted in a housing project near the east side of the wall. You have to remember that he also pulled what was left of Delta force from the gulf coast and brought them up here last week for rest."

"That's why there's so much activity in Dog town," Eastridge said aloud, referring to a section of town populated by bars and whorehouses. It was a legendary area that had sprouted up about fifteen minutes after DC had been secured, but was ignored due to the present circumstances. Who was going to order a soldier that was more than likely going to be dead within a few days not to go out to drink rotgut moonshine and get laid?

"Delta's been lying low in Dog town there since they got here," Eastridge told him, "and the Rangers are spitting distance away. I doubt any of these men know exactly what's going on, so they must be getting fed a line about keeping the integrity of the United States intact. Either that, or they think they just got lucky by getting R and R. The one thing I do know is that The Chairman is keeping them isolated so they'll be ready to do his dirty work. He can spin whatever story he wants and they'll jump to do his bidding."

"So, who do we have besides you and me? No one else in the Joint Chiefs stood up to him," Eastridge commented. "He walked into the meeting today and basically took over the United States without firing a shot. What does he need all the troops for?"

"He knows that people will eventually oppose him," Sedlak said. "And he knows that if anyone tries anything that he can send his special forces in. Once they're engaged, he can order his infantry in and they will fight for their own."

Eastridge saw the wisdom of this. In a combat situation, men didn't fight for politics or patriotism, they fought for the guy next to him. Add on top of this that they were facing an opponent that was against God, America, Mom and apple pie, and it was a wrap. Killing other Americans might cause them to hesitate, but they would shoot first and ask questions later if told that they were fighting against someone trying to overthrow the standing government.

"How did you find this all out?" Eastridge asked.

"I might have lost most of my ground combat men in the war against the dead," Sedlak explained, "but my intelligence services stayed mostly intact along with my naval forces. I don't have a whole lot of combat troops to call on, but I know that you have two understrength battalions inside the wall totaling fourteen hundred men, and another two of about the same size at Quantico."

"So you want me to order my people at Quantico to march almost forty miles through a land full of dead things trying to eat them, and then have them assault the DC wall because the Chairman will know that they're coming since they'll be kind of hard to miss as they move through a city that's been bombed flat, and then have them pull off some kind of half-assed coup?" Eastridge asked sarcastically.

"No," Sedlak answered, "getting your men here is where my navy comes in."

Eastridge immediately saw the possibilities. His men guarded the wall along the stretch that faced the Potomac, so it would be easy for them to let his Marines into the city. Getting them out of Quantico and onto boats without being spotted might be a little tricky, but he had an idea on how to get around that. If he played it right, he might even have the Chairman's approval.

Having been trained all his life to plan everything through from beginning to end, a thought came to him. Suddenly finding himself in a Machiavellian plot orchestrated by the Chairman of the Joint Chiefs of Staff, he wondered if he was being drawn into another one. With this in mind, he asked Sedlak the most important question of them all.

"When we pull this off, who takes control?"

Without hesitation, the Admiral said, "We form an ad-hoc committee made up from each of the joint chiefs along with the remaining leaders of the Republican, Democratic and Independent parties. A jury decides on the basis of twelve, so I think that there should eventually be twelve members. To be honest, I haven't figured out who those twelve should be, but if we start with a solid foundation, we can build it from there."

The General watched Sedlak closely as he talked but could see no subterfuge in his answer. He knew he was a good judge of character, and felt that the Admiral had answered honestly.

"And what about the Malectron," he asked.

"We use it in the way it was meant to be used," Sedlak answered, "to push the dead into isolated areas where they can be dealt with."

"You do mean eradicated?" Eastridge asked.

"Completely," Sedlak assured him. "We also need to push forward in finding a cure, but the Malectron will at least give us some breathing room to do that. We need to work together."

After hesitating for a moment, General Eastridge extended his hand to where it was grasped firmly by the Admiral's. The two men looked each other in the eye as they said in unison, "Done."

***

General Eastridge took off his coat as he entered his outer office. Cursing when he saw that his aide was absent from his desk, he made for his own. If they were going to pull this coup off, he needed to get working on his plan. Seeing the door to his office slightly ajar, he called out, "Jim, get your ass out here. Something's come up and we've got a lot of work to do."

Instead of hearing his aide's voice in reply, Eastridge's blood ran cold when he heard the Chairman call out, "Don't worry about him, I told him to take a break. I need to speak to you privately."

Dread flooded through him at hearing this, his first thought being that he had been found out in the plot to depose the Chairman. Jim was probably in custody right now. The man might not have done anything wrong, but guilt by association ran strong in the new head of the United States. After the meeting of the Joint Chiefs, they had been informed that along with the remaining senators and representatives, their staff had also been rounded up for questioning. The excuse was given that they needed to be debriefed, but if it was a simple debriefing, why take them under guard from their homes and offices to an undisclosed location?

Knowing he had no choice but to face his fate, Eastridge made to straighten the blouse of his uniform. What he was really doing though was pulling the back of it down to conceal the .45 caliber pistol in a holster at the small of his back. If given half a chance, he would take out the Chairman. He knew that he would never make it out of the office building alive, but if he was going down, so was the dictator that had seized power. When he felt he was presentable, he strode purposefully into the room.

As soon as he entered his office though, he knew that he didn't have a chance of assassinating the Chairman. While the man made an easy target sitting on the edge of his desk, the two men flanking him with pistols at the ready would cut him down before he got a chance to draw and fire.

Scowling, the Chairman said to the guard on his right, "Search him."

When the man had relieved Eastridge of his pistol, the Chairman said to him, "You've been a very busy boy."

Eastridge felt his heart sink at the thought that they had been found out. If this was it, then at least he would get a chance to tell the Chairman what a scumbag he was.

"I've only been doing my duty, sir," he replied forcefully. "I want you to know-."

Eastridge wanted to say how he was planning the coup because of duty and honor, but the Chairman cut him off by saying, "I really appreciate the extra work you had your men put in at the laboratory so that we can get Doctor Hawkins here as soon as possible. I know that I've been rough on everyone, but getting the Malectron up and running is a priority. I came here for two reasons, the first being to apologize if I stepped on your toes, but it had to be done."

Eastridge was at a loss for words. He remembered how he had reported that he was pulled every third man off guard and sending them on temporary duty to help get the lab up and running, but it was a lie. In reality, these men had been given twelve hour passes to go into dog town.

With a smile, the Chairman added, "And I apologize for cutting you off. Now what were you going to say, General?"

Eastridge fumbled his words for a second and finally picked up where he had started by saying, "I want you to know that it's an honor to serve you, sir."

The words stuck in his throat, but he managed to get them out. If he wasn't being arrested, then it meant he would live to fight another day. If living to fight meant kowtowing to the Chairman, then so be it. If Karma was a train, he wanted to be the engineer when it came around.

The Chairman nodded and smiled as he waved his two bodyguards away. When they were gone, he said, "And that brings me to the second reason for this visit."

Standing, he circled the desk and sat in Eastridge's chair before waving the General into the one that faced it. Eastridge sat heavily, his knees slightly weak from being so close to what he thought was a certain death before dodging it.

Clearing his throat, the Chairman said, "I took absolute power today for a reason. This country needs a strong man to lead it to its destiny of being the one true power on earth. Others have faltered in this time and again, but I plan to succeed. To do that, I made the decision to let the weak fall by the wayside and perish. When you look at history, it is full of stories of great men that tried to help the pathetic masses and paid for it by being pulled down."

Trying to keep the look of utter revulsion off his face, Eastridge could only nod.

"That is why I need strong men like you by my side to help me in my conquest," the Chairman went on. "The Marine Corps built you into the man you are today. They taught you to obey orders and to follow those orders as they are handed down to you by your superiors. The main reason I'm here tonight is to make sure that you are on my side, the side of righteousness."

Knowing that to reply in any other way meant that the two men waiting outside the door would quickly escort him to an undisclosed location from which he would never return, Eastridge said, "I'm with you, sir. The whiners and the crybabies have had it their way for way too long. It's time to get rid of the dead weight and move on."

Although he had a hard time spitting these words out, knowing that Sedlak could do nothing without his Marines made Eastridge utter them.

The Chairman smiled and clapped his hands together. "Good, good. I knew that you were behind me one-hundred percent, but I had to be sure. Now that I know I have your complete loyalty, I can let you in on how things are going to be run in the future. In my experience, the American military machine is the most perfectly functioning entity known to man. We can do everything more efficient than any civilian body. For years, the supply of the armed forces has been left in the hands of private corporations, their contracts going to the lowest bidder. This is part of the reason we are in the mess we're in now. If the oilfields had been run by us, we wouldn't have a shortage of fuel. If the munitions factories were run by us, we wouldn't have a shortage of ammunition. And if the farms, dairies and slaughter-houses were run by us, we wouldn't have a shortage of food. Can you imagine corporations run with the precision that we bring to the battlefield? There has always been talk of unionizing the four branches of the military, and while I vocally opposed it, I was all for it."

Then you can be the one to explain to machine gunners local 513 why they can't go on strike, Eastridge thought.

"Can you imagine a world where the trains run on time and everyone is working toward a purpose?" The Chairman asked.

Thinking of Hitler's Germany and Stalin's Russia, Eastridge bit back his reply and said, "That would be the greatest, sir."

"Yes it would be," The Chairman intoned as he stood up. Stopping half-way, his eyes narrowed and his posture went rigid as he searched Eastridge's face and added, "You know, you can always tell the measure of truth in a man by his eyes."

Eastridge stared back, leaving his expression blank.

After a few seconds, the Chairman smiled and said, "And I can see that you are behind me one-hundred percent."

Eastridge smiled back as he thought, and I can see that you are one-hundred percent drunk on power and a megalomaniac.

"I want you to know that there are going to be a lot of changes around here over the next few days," The Chairman told him. I will be dissolving the positions of the Joint Chiefs and reappointing those that are loyal to me to be the heads of different ministries. I am considering you for the Ministry of deportations. Do you like that?"

"I couldn't think of a better post myself," Eastridge said, and then asked, "But who wouldn't be loyal to you, sir?"

"The Chief of staff of the Air Force for one," the Chairman said venomously. "He is the only one I've had to replace. Everyone else is with me."

Watching as the Chairman headed for the door, General Eastridge was relieved to hear that Admiral Sedlak was still alive and at his post. Deciding that he needed to put the plan they had devised into operation as soon as possible, he said, "Begging your pardon, sir, but something of importance has come to my attention, and since you are here-." He let his voice trail off.

Stopping, the Chairman asked, "Yes, what is it?"

"I have a contingent of men at Quantico that I would like to reassign, sir," Eastridge explained. "Although Quantico is only a forty miles from here-."

"Yes, yes," the Chairman said in an annoyed voice as he cut him off, "I know where Quantico is."

"Yes, sir," Eastridge continued, "then you know that there is no way to transport them here by land, and since fuel is at a premium for air travel, I would like permission for a few of Admiral Sedlak's ships to sail down there to bring them back to help defend Washington DC."

"Are they loyal?" The Chairman asked.

"All my men are loyal to me," Eastridge said truthfully.

"Then go ahead and bring them here," the Chairman ordered. "The chief of the Air Force might not be the only one in the city that is plotting against me, so I'll need good men at my back. Men I can trust. When do you want to do this?"

"Would tomorrow be too soon?" Eastridge asked.

"I'll give the order," the Chairman told him, and then called for his bodyguards as he went out the door.

CHAPTER THIRTEEN

Fort Redoubt:

Steve sat across the picnic table from Ginny in silence. After she had approached him in the chow line, they had hugged briefly, but it was awkward and they broke apart with self-conscious looks at one another and then at their new significant others. Steve to Heather, and Ginny to where Wilkes stood a few feet away. They were served their food, and with no other choice but to be polite, the foursome sat together.

Steve commented about Ginny being in camouflage, and she told him that she the officer was in charge of supplies. A joke about counting trays and beans fell flat, and they lapsed into silence as they ate. None of them knew what to say, and thankfully, it was Wilkes that broke the ice by asking Ginny to tell them how she had ended up at Fort Redoubt.

"Oh, I don't know, honey," Ginny said. "They probably don't want to hear all that."

Wilkes seemed to want something to fill in the awkward silence, so he encouraged her to speak until she agreed.

Turning to Steve, she said, "So like you know, me and Valerie and Keisha went out dancing the night everything fell apart. It was kind of creepy driving through Tampa because there was hardly any traffic, but once we got to Ybor city, it was like everything was normal. Well, almost normal. People were partying and dancing and everything, but they were also talking about the dead coming back to life and what they were going to do when it happened. There was a lot of tough talk and a lot of denial. Most of the guys were all talking about how they would kill a hundred dead with one hand while most of the women were all saying that the disease was never going to make it this far south. No one really knew what was happening though."

She paused for a second and then said, "You know, on an average night, one in four people are carrying a gun in Ybor city, but that night, it seemed like everyone was armed. It was like the end of the world, but no one cared." Turning to Heather, she asked, "Have you ever been to a Hurricane party?"

Realizing that Ginny didn't recognize her from the one time they had met at the bowling alley, she said, "I grew up in Florida."

"Then you get what I mean," Ginny said with a knowing look. "You party like it's the end of the world. You think you know what you're going to do when the shit hits the fan, but you really hope that it misses your fan and just kind of sprays against the wall. Someone else's wall.

"But anyway, I was dancing with Valerie when this one guy shouts out to do the Zombie. Not the old dance, but a new one. It's where everyone stands there all rigid with their hands at their sides and start convulsing more and more before they give a huge shake and then start dancing with their arms out in front of them. I'd never seen anyone do that one so it was kind of cool, but then this one chick drops to the floor and starts shaking all over the place. I thought it was kind of odd since she was wearing a real expensive dress and the floor was all dirty and full of puddles where people had spilled their drinks. I'm laughing though while I'm watching her mess up a Dior original, when all of the sudden she stops and lays still. I expected her to pop up and stick her arms out, but instead, she kind of half sits up and then twists around to bite some guy on the calf.

"There were a lot of people watching, and they all thought it was a new takeoff on the dance, so they start fake biting at each other or sucking on their partner's neck. Everyone floods onto the dance floor to try it, and it was really noisy, so I guess no one heard the guy getting bit as he screamed. The dance floor was really getting packed, so Valerie and I headed for our seats. The table we were at was raised up, so we saw everything that happened next."

Ginny paused as she gathered herself. After a moment, she said, "We could see it start in the middle of this big crowd of people all biting at each other and flailing their arms around. It started with just a few, but then everyone started breaking away from this one spot on the dance floor. It was like a stone dropped into the water of a still pond. The ripples went out in every direction, but it wasn't peaceful or serene. It was a madhouse of people screaming and knocking each other over trying to get away.

"Everyone around us was asking what was going on, and when they saw a couple of people wrestling around on the floor, they all thought it was just a fight and went back to whatever they were doing. I saw a bouncer go over to break it up, but he jumped back holding his arm. Just about this time, the music dropped down as the song changed and you could hear the sound of screams coming from everywhere. The people from the dance floor, the bouncer, and most of all, from the guy that had gotten attacked in the first place. A couple more bouncers jumped in, and finally they got this woman in a headlock. The people at the table next to us thought it was business as usual, but even in the strobe lights, I could see blood all over the place. That was when I knew what was going on."

Turning her attention to Steve, Ginny said, "I'm sorry I didn't listen to you when you tried to explain what was happening."

He nodded and she continued her story. "Like I said, I could see blood all over, so I grabbed Val by the hand and started dragging her toward the front door. There were so many people jammed up there that I knew it would be impossible to get out that way so I led her back to the bar. The bartender was waving people toward an exit door at the back of the club and we followed them out into this alley. There were no lights and everyone was kind of bumping into each other as we tried to figure out which way to go."

Ginny laughed and said, "I remember this one guy kept saying, 'excuse me, excuse me, trying to get through here.' Like that was going to help. A lot of people were using their cell phones for light, but all they showed was that the alley was blocked on both sides. Someone finally found this little narrow passageway between two buildings, but you could only go through it one at a time. I was standing in the back of the group, but I could see light at the end of it. Streetlights.

"Everyone kind of relaxed then and started moving down this narrow passage. When it was our turn, Val was right behind me and there was about five or six people in front of us," Ginny said in a quiet voice. "That was when we heard a bunch of screams coming from the dead end alley. I turned around to look, but it was too dark to see anything except the glow of cell phones. Then one of them flew up in the air like a big lighting bug. The people in front of us stopped to see what was going on, but I knew it was one of those things that had followed us. It must have grabbed the guy holding the cell because you could see other lights going up and down real fast. Whatever had gotten him was being beaten by the people around him. There were a couple gunshots, and one of the bullets must have hit close by because I felt a bunch of brick shards hit my face. I screamed for everyone to run but I could have saved my breath."

Once again, Ginny had to stop to gather herself before speaking. "The little walkway we were moving through was only about shoulder width, and the people in front of us bunched up as they all tried to get through it at once. People were pushing at us from behind too. I felt like my body was getting crushed. I lost hold of Val's hand, but I could feel us moving forward, so I figured I'd just catch her when we were both out. With everyone behind us pushing, we shot out of that passageway and onto the street like a cork from a bottle."

Ginny stopped, and after a few seconds said softly, "But Val never made it through. I waited for her, watching everyone that came out, asking each person if there was anyone else behind them. After a few minutes, no one else came out. I still had my cell phone so I tried to call for help. All I got was this message telling me that due to heavy traffic I had to try later. I had to find out what happened to Val, to make sure she wasn't hurt or anything, so I turned on my light and went back in."

Steve was impressed by her courage.

"The glow from the screen only lit up a few feet in front of me so it was slow going," Ginny explained. "I was really scared of running into one of those dead things, but I had to find Val. I almost tripped over one guy that was kind of half leaning against the wall. He was moaning and kept saying it hurts, so I told him it would hurt a lot more if he didn't get off his ass and get out of there. I helped stand him up and headed him toward the street. I found one of Val's shoes and a lot of blood, but no sign of her. I was near the alley behind the club, and I could hear this whining noise. This really freaked me out because I knew it was human, but at the same time it didn't sound human. I knew right then that wherever Val was that she was dead. All I could think of was her coming toward me all bloody so I turned and ran."

"Wise decision," Steve told her.

"Yeah, maybe so," Ginny agreed, "but when I made it back to the street, I wasn't sure if I would have been safer in the alley. Ybor had turned into a madhouse with everyone running around acting crazy. People were shooting at each other and the only cop in sight was lying dead in on the sidewalk. He must have just gotten killed because he still had his pistol in his hand. I watched some fifteen year old kid grab it and run off. I was standing next to this one lady, and as I turned to ask her if her phone was working, these guys rode by in a pickup truck and just grabbed her right off the street. Just slowed down a little and scooped her up before driving off. She was screaming and they were laughing as they tore her clothes off. Somehow or another I had managed to keep my shoes on, so I kicked them off and started running. I don't even know what direction I was going, I just wanted to get out of there.

"After a while I was so out of breath that I had to stop. I think I puked a little, I'm not sure. I just kept replaying through my head how one second I had Val by the hand and the next she was gone. I had a cramp in my side that was hurting real bad so I focused on the pain. This brought me out of my shock enough that I knew I had to think it through or I'd just be running blind. I was in this area with houses now, and I had to try and get my bearings. Keisha had driven, but I wasn't sure where we had parked. I didn't want to go back into Ybor city, but I didn't have much choice. I had to find out if Keisha had made it out. If she had, I hoped she was waiting for me at the car."

To Steve, she said, "As I was walking, I kept trying to call you, but all I got was that same recording to try back later. I guess everyone in Tampa Bay was trying to use their phone. I looked around for a payphone, but those are almost impossible to find. That was when I realized that I was in a real shitty section of town. There were all these people in the street and they were all really seedy looking. A couple guys called out to me and followed me for a while."

Turning to Heather, she said, "And I don't have to tell you what they were saying. I was worried about getting dragged into one of the houses and getting raped, so I stayed in the center of the street. I think if those guys knew that everything was completely falling apart and that the cops weren't around to bust them, they would have been all over me.

"So I made it almost all the way back to the edge of Ybor when I saw the first National Guard troops. They must have been sent to break up the riot. You could hear the sound of gunshots coming from the city, but you could hear a lot more rifles firing on full automatic. They had set up a roadblock and were letting people out, but they were searching them and taking away any weapons that they found. They had about thirty or forty pistols that they had confiscated sitting in the back of one of their trucks.

"I asked them if they could help me find Keisha, but they said they were too busy. They also wouldn't let me go beyond their roadblock to find her myself. They said that a relief center had been set up in Desoto Park. I told them there was no way I was going to be able to make it all the way to south St. Petersburg, but they explained that it wasn't Fort Desoto Park but a small park a few blocks to the south. That meant that I had to go back the way I'd just come and there was no way I was going to do that alone.

"I went over and stood with a bunch of other people that were in the same boat as I was. They were all trading horror stories about what they had seen, but I kind of tuned them out when I heard that nobody's cell phone was working. I was looking around while I was trying to figure out what I was going to do when I spotted someone I knew."

"Who was it?" Steve asked, hoping it might be one of their few mutual acquaintances. It would be nice to hear news about someone he knew even if it was months old.

Ginny paused and said, "Oh, no one. Just this guy I kind of knew. I think his name was Danny or something."

Steve hid a smile. Ginny never forgot a name of a face, so in other words, it was an old boyfriend and she didn't want to bring him up in front of her new boyfriend.

"But anyway," Ginny continued, "he was looking for his date and was in the same situation I was. They had gotten separated in the riot and he couldn't get back inside Ybor to look for her. He did have his car though. He started talking about sneaking back into the city to look for her, but that ended pretty quick when something near the north of the city blew up. You could see the flames shooting up into the air and all this black smoke."

"I heard about the fire," Steve said. "What started it?"

Ginny shrugged and said, "I don't know. But whatever it was, it almost knocked us off our feet. We stood there watching it for a few minutes trying to figure out what to do now, but then the National Guard guys started yelling at us to get out of the area. They were saying that there was a big fire and the wind was blowing it in our direction. That was enough for us. Danny grabbed me by the hand and took me to his car. When we got in, he opened up the glove compartment and took out a gun.

"Normally, something like this would kind of freak me out, but not that night. The first thing I asked him was if he had another one. He told me he had a rifle and another pistol at his house, so I told him to get us there as fast as he could."

"How far away did he live?" Steve asked, wondering if she had come back across to his side of the bay.

"Right on Davis Island," Ginny told him. "On an average night, you can make it there in about fifteen minutes. Once you get on the expressway, it takes you right to the exit and three minutes later you're at his doorstep. That night, it took us more than an hour. People were flooding the roads trying to get out of town and then jamming up the back roads when they saw the freeways were jammed. I don't know where they all thought they were going. I mean, we were one of the last cities to get hit by the virus. We had to stay on the expressway though because we had to cross the river.

"When we finally made it to the bridge across to the Island, we found it blocked by a couple of pickup trucks. There were a bunch of people with rifles and shotguns hanging around, and they were stopping everyone to make sure they belonged there. One of the guys knew Danny, so we were just waved through. I was never as glad as when we pulled up in front of his house and he shut the engine off. I figured we were safe."

"No one was safe anywhere," Steve said.

"And Danny knew that," Ginny told him. "As soon as we walked through his front door, he told me to start getting ready to leave. I didn't have any clothes or anything, so I borrowed a pair of his pants and a shirt." She laughed and added, "I had to tie a piece of rope around my waist to keep them up since he didn't have a belt that fit my waist. I must have looked like Jethro Bodine."

Steve saw Tick-Tock walk in and waved him over. Wilkes started to rise, but before introductions could be made, Steve asked about Denise.

"She's sleeping now," his friend told him. "They called the doctor and he ran her through the x-ray machine. He said it wasn't a fractured skull but just a real bad concussion. She's on a week's bed rest and then light duty for another week."

Steve's said, "That's great news," but his heart told him it was the last thing he wanted to hear. He knew that they were going to moving again within the next day or two, or even as soon as tonight if Fort Polk sent a helicopter for them. He also knew that Tick-Tock wouldn't leave Denise, so that meant he would be staying here. From the look on his friend's face, he could see that he had already come to that decision.

Not one to beat around the bush, Steve said, "So you won't be coming with us."

Tick-Tock shook his head and said sadly, "I have to stay. I already asked Rick and he said he would love to have another person here with a military background."

Not one to have her limelight stolen, Ginny stood up and said, "It's good to see you again, Tick-Tock. I was just telling everyone about how I got out of Tampa."

Her hair was longer, and she had a few lines on her face that weren't there the last time he had seen her, so it took him a second to recognize her. When he did, his eyes lit up as he threw his arms around her and said, "Holy shit. Ginny."

Although they hadn't been the best of friends when they knew each other at the radio station, the reaction was brought on by seeing that someone was alive that you thought was lost. After a few seconds, they broke apart and Ginny introduced him to Wilkes.

After they had shaken hands, Ginny said, "Why don't you sit down and you can hear of how I got out of Tampa alive." Before waiting for an answer, she started telling them about how Danny had a boat and took her to MacDill Air Force base.

His mind on how he would manage without Tick-Tock's help, Steve barley heard her as she told of being evacuated to a base outside of New Orleans and then sent to a refugee camp. The rest of how she came to be at Fort Redoubt was lost in the pain of knowing that he would soon be separated from his best friend.

***

As soon as they left the chow hall, Tick-Tock said he needed to check on Denise. The camp was nothing but dark shapes as he disappeared around the corner of a building without saying another word. Steve looked on in wonder, thinking that they would at least talk about his friend's decision to stay. He wouldn't try to talk him out of it, but it left a bigger void knowing that Tick-Tock could just cut him off that easily and move on.

Reading his mood, Heather said, "He feels guilty for having to stay here. It probably damn near tore him apart making his mind up."

"He sure doesn't act like it," Steve said in a low voice.

"And how would you deal with the situation if it was me lying in the hospital?" Heather asked.

Steve didn't have to think about it before saying, "The same way."

"Well then, there you go," She said and laughed.

"What's so funny," He asked.

She laughed again and said, "I've always heard the term Bro-mance, but I've never seen one in action."

Steve had to laugh too before saying, "I guess I am acting like he just broke up with me. Now I have to take you to the prom."

Heather's response was interrupted by a young man of about eighteen that walked up to them and said, "My name is Gerald and I have taken the liberty of finding your people somewhere to sleep for tonight, sir. Commander Styles told me to assure you that we would find something more permanent tomorrow if need be. Your temporary quarters are ready if you'll just follow me."

"Commander Styles told me that I would be able to use the radio," Steve told him.

"The generators are shut down for the night, sir," Gerald told him. "We have to ration diesel fuel."

"When will the generators be back up and the radio working?" Steve asked.

"Zero nine-hundred," Gerald replied. "Breakfast is at zero six-hundred and I have orders from the commander to wake you at zero five-thirty. Now if you will follow me?"

***

Linda woke and rolled over in her cot. In the dark, she could barely see the layout of the room she and Cindy had been assigned. They had been billeted in the officer's dormitory, so they had a two person room all to themselves. An officer in the peace-time military might bitch about the accommodations, but she felt like she was staying in the Radisson after all the nights spent sleeping on the ground or in the back of a truck. The enlisted that were on duty lived in one of three one-story barracks like structures, and she was glad she they had room for her in officer's country. She knew she could live with anything that came along and learn to accept it, but she was also grateful for the little things. Like privacy.

Feeling as if her bladder was about to burst, she carefully got up and made her way to the door to use the communal bathroom at the end of the hall. Pep raised her head from where she was curled up at Cindy's feet, so Linda scratched her chin and got a tail wag in response. Giving the pooch a boop on the nose, she went to the door and twisted the knob while pushing. To her surprise, it gave a few centimeters and then shut. Thinking she had been locked in, she felt a twinge of anxiety. Rick had seemed like a decent guy, but maybe that had been an act.

Hearing a familiar voice say, "One second," dispelled her fears.

The door opened outward a few inches and she found Igor peering in at her.

Feeling like a little girl under his unwavering stare, she mustered her dignity and said, "I have to go to the bathroom."

The door opened and she entered the hall. Seeing a chair a few feet away, she pointed to it and asked, "Were you sitting in that and blocking the door? Why aren't you in the barracks?"

"My duty is to protect the chosen one from harm," he answered.

"But we're safe here," Linda told him.

"Are we?" Igor asked.

"Don't you trust Rick and his people?" She questioned.

Without a second's hesitation, he replied, "I trust no one where the girl's safety is concerned."

With a slight smile, Linda asked, "Don't you trust me?"

"No," Igor said in a flat voice.

***

Crammed together onto one of the narrow cots, Brain and Connie had no problem holding each other close. When it was first announced that there was only a few rooms available, they had been worried that they wouldn't be able to spend any time alone together since the barracks were wide open and separated into male and female. It looked like it might be a long, lonely night until one of Tick-Tock's people had spoken up and said that the rooms should go to the original members of the group. He went on to say that they had saved their lives so it was the least that they could do. When it was all worked out, he and Connie had gotten the last room in the officer's quarters. The billet had two cots, but they found they only needed one.

Brushing a stand of Connie's hair from her face, Brain said, "I can't believe we actually made it."

"We're not there yet," Connie said softly.

"But we might as well be," Brain told her. "Tomorrow or the next day, we can be in Fort Polk, safe from any harm. In the meantime though, we're behind four walls with fifty people guarding us. It sure is better than lying in the dirt wondering what's going to come at us out of the woods. And when you think about it, why do we have to go to Polk? I mean, Tick-Tock's not going. We could stay here with him and Denise. Steve doesn't need us to protect him, he'll have the whole Army looking out for him. All we have to do is join up with Rick's people and wait for the doctors to come up with a cure."

"You want to split from Steve?" Connie asked with shock.

Looking into her eyes, he said, "It's the risk I'm thinking about. We're safe here, but if you and I go to Polk, we might end up getting drafted into the Army. Being with Cindy won't mean anything after we get her there. You heard what those people we were sitting with at dinner were saying. Everyone from eight to eighty, blind, crippled or crazy was going into the military whether they wanted to or not. Besides, I know that once I tell Rick about my background, he'll be glad to have us here."

"But you have to serve in the Militia if you stay here," Connie reminded him.

Brain snorted and said, "Only one week out of four. That will be a cakewalk compared to what we've already been through. Besides, with my tech degree, I'll probably never be sent to the field."

"I hear what you're saying," Connie said, "but my mother always told me not to count my chickens before they hatch."

Leaning back to look at her, Brain asked, "Did she really say that?"

Connie laughed lightly and said, "Maybe not exactly, but something like that."

"Well, you can count this chicken, because he's come home to roost," Brain told her as he pulled her close.

CHAPTER FOURTEEN

Fort Redoubt:

Steve woke to a persistent sound of something knocking on wood. At first, his groggy mind thought it was a woodpecker and he reached out for a shoe to throw at it. Feeling something in front of him, he opened his eyes, but all he could see was his hand pressed against a rough framed wall inches from his face. For a few seconds, he wasn't sure where he was, but then it all came flooding back to him.

Rolling over, he saw that Heather had gotten up to answer the door and was having a conversation with Rick. They were keeping their voices down, so he said, "I'm awake."

Rick looked at him and said, "Good deal. Time to get up. I was going to have my aide wake you, but I wanted to talk to you two in private for a few minutes. Get dressed and I'll meet you out front."

When Rick was gone, Steve threw back the blanket covering him and sat up. Looking at where he had thrown his clothes in a pile the night before, he knew that there was no way he was going to wear them again today. He'd had them on since the morning they left Happy Hallow and he could smell them from here.

"I wonder if they have a Laundromat," he asked aloud.

Heather laughed and said, "They just might. I was shocked that they had hot water."

"Yeah," Steve replied while he rubbed his hands over his face to wake up, "Gerald told me that they put a bunch solar heating tubes on the roof. You know, the one's they use to heat pools. He said that as soon as things settle down a little more, they're going to start taking solar panels from houses and wiring them up to provide electricity. A few of the houses already have them, but he said that Rick wants all of them set up by the beginning of next winter."

"I guess that will be the only way to get electricity from a long time," Heather commented.

Pulling on his pants, Steve asked, "Did Rick give you any idea what he wanted?"

Heather shook her head and replied, "He just said he wanted to talk to us. It didn't seem like it was bad news or anything from the way he was acting."

"Well, I could use some good news," Steve told her.

Walking out of the officer's quarters, they found that a heavy fog had rolled in overnight, making it almost impossible to see as far see the walls of the fort. Rick was talking to one of his officers, but he broke off the conversation as soon as he spotted them and motioned for them to follow him. When Steve and Heather had fallen in on either side of him, he said, "I've actually got a couple things to talk to you about. The first is that I want you to know that your friend Tick-Tock made his own decision to join us. I had nothing to do with it. I was almost floored when he came up and asked if he and Denise could stay. I know that he's your right hand man so I didn't want you to think that I talked him into it. I don't want any bad blood between us."

Steve's face hardened at the thought of splitting up with his friend, but it had nothing to do with Rick Styles. He had rolled the situation over in his mind again and again the night before, and while at first he had wanted to blame him, it was obvious he had nothing to do with it. Steve knew that Tick-Tock wouldn't be swayed by any offers from the commander. The only reason he was staying was because Denise couldn't move.

Next, he had blamed Denise, and anger welled up in him at the very idea of her keeping Tick-Tock here while the rest of them moved on. This quickly subsided though when he thought it through. It wasn't her fault, and in fact she had been hurt while blowing up the front doors of the mansion so they could escape.

His thoughts then turned to the dead, the main reason they were all in this situation to begin with. If he was going to play the blame game, this is where the responsibility rested. They were mindless hunks of walking dead flesh, and they were the reason why he and his group had been displaced, on the run, and were now about to split up. He knew that he couldn't kill them all, but he resolved there and then that no matter what, he would get Cindy to a doctor so they could find a cure. Or better yet, a way to eradicate them.

No, Rick Styles wasn't to blame.

Steve stopped, held out his hand and said, "There's no hard feelings. I know why Tick-Tock is staying. You're lucky to have him."

Rick shook the offered hand and said, "I know I'm lucky. Out of my original militia, only about half are left. I need good officers. I have a couple people left that served in the military, but none of them have been through all that you all have."

Steve raised an eyebrow at this, so Rick explained, "Tick-Tock gave me a rundown of what you've been through since the dead started coming back to life. The radio station, the cruise ship, and everything since you all made landfall in Galveston. If I knew I wasn't wasting my breath, I'd try to talk you into staying too."

Steve gave a hard smile and said, "Never happen. I've got more important things to take care of."

"I know," Rick said. "And that brings me to the second thing I wanted to talk to you about. As soon as the generators come on line and the radio room gets fired up, you're going to be calling Fort Polk. They may have orders to ignore civilian radio traffic, but I think they'll listen to what you have to say. Up until about a few weeks ago when they quit talking to everybody except each other, they were asking for anyone that was immune to the disease to contact them."

Steve felt excitement at hearing this. He'd had some doubts that the government would still be interested in Cindy, but those were squashed.

"Once you contact the, the Army will probably be here sometime today or tomorrow," Rick said, "and that's what I wanted to talk to you about."

Steve smiled and said, "Don't worry about the people you took in that are deserters, I won't say anything."

"I appreciate that," Rick said, "but that's only part of it." In a quiet voice he added, "I lost my wife and two boys to the dead. They were in California visiting their grandma when everything went to hell. They tried to get a flight out, but everything was booked up. They tried renting a car, but it was the same thing so they went back to stay with her mom. Vanessa knew what to do, get water and food and fortify the house, but everything happened so fast that she didn't have time. I was on the phone with her when they broke in."

Rick fell silent, so Steve gave him a moment to compose himself.

When he was steady enough to talk, he said, "I also have a daughter. She didn't go to California because she was sick." Waving his hand to take in the fort and the armed guards patrolling its walls, he added, "We take out all of the good sized herds of dead-asses that come our way, but sooner or later we're going to get hit by a group that's so big that it will roll right over us. We've got a good thing going here, but it won't last forever, so I want you to take Stacey with you when you go. I know that it's about as safe here as it is anywhere in the world right now, but I also know that it would be a lot safer for her at Fort Polk. They quit taking in refugees, but if she's with you, they'll let her in. She won't be any trouble and she can pull her own weight. I taught her everything she knows."

Steve knew that he couldn't say no. Rick had saved them from the herd of Zs that were about to overrun them and then took his group in and fed and protected them. And after all, what was one more in the group when all they had to do was take a short chopper flight?

Smiling, Steve said, "No problem."

Heather chimed in, "Of course we'll take her with us."

Surprised that it was that easy, Rick looked shocked. He had been trying to get his last remaining child somewhere safe since all of this began, and in the end, it was this simple.

After shaking hands with Steve and giving Heather a hug, Rick started to lead them to the chow hall. They only made it a few feet though when they were stopped by one of his officers.

"Commander," a pretty, dark haired woman called out as she ran to catch up to them. "I hate to interrupt you, but Z-girl Lisa was spotted outside the fort. You said that you wanted to be informed as soon as she showed up again."

"Shit," Rick said under his breath.

"What's a Z-girl Lisa?" Heather asked.

"One of the dead." Rick explained. "A couple of the officers named her. She's been around since we first set up the camp. I don't know how she's managed to do it, but somehow or another she's avoided getting a bullet in the head. A lot of people say that she's smarter than the other dead."

"Smarter?" Heather asked.

"I'd say its coincidence," Rick told them. "But she only comes out when there's fog, and it's hard to see her because of what she's wearing."

"What's that?" Heather asked.

"She's dressed in a bridal gown," Rick answered. "It's perfect camouflage. Most of the dead we see have lost or worn their clothes off, but somehow or another, she's managed to keep hers intact. I've never seen her, but from what I've heard, she even still has her veil on. It's my guess she's found somewhere to hole up. I remember hearing back when this all this started that a lot of the dead hid in sewers and drainage pipes. We don't have anything like that around here, so we have no idea where she's at. The trees are too thick to search everywhere inside the perimeter, so when we first set up, we just killed the dead when they came at us. As far as we know, we got them all except for Z-girl. That's another reason why a lot of people say that she's smarter than the average dead ass, she never attacks anyone that's armed. It's like she knows she'll get her shit scattered, so she only comes out to grab a chicken or a pig when there's no one around. We've tried tracking her half a dozen times but could never find her. I was planning on settling her account before now, but something more important always keeps coming up."

"And she lives right outside the fort between the wall and the first line of wire?" Steve asked as he eyed the open gate.

"Yeah, Rick replied miserably, "I keep hoping that she'll wander too far and step on a landmine. My biggest fear is that she's going to come across someone that's not paying attention. Then it won't be just a random chicken she's eating." Turning to the officer, he said, "Jennifer, I want you to take five of your people and track this dead bitch down. I want her taken out once and for all."

The woman snapped to attention and barked out, "Yes, sir."

After she was gone, Rick said, "I hope they get her this time. Most of my people can pull off an ambush with no problem, but that's about it. That's one of the reasons I'm looking forward to having Tick-Tock here. I need someone to train them."

Looking at Heather, Steve raised one eyebrow. She smiled back and that was all the answer he needed. Turning to Rick, he said, "Commander Styles, in appreciation for all you've done for us, we are temporarily volunteering our services until the present crisis is over."

Confused, Rick asked, "What crisis?"

Heather said, "We're going to get Z-girl Lisa for you."

***

When the four people from Rick Style's group joined Steve and Heather in the chow hall to go over their plan, Jennifer, the dark haired female officer marched up to them and saluted before barking out, "Jennifer Bosquez-Morales reporting for duty, sir. Commander Styles told me to listen to everything you had to teach us. That way, I can pass it on to others. I will not fail in my duty, sir."

Trying to get her to relax, Steve saluted back and asked, "Where are you from?"

"San Antonio," she replied rigidly.

"So I take it from your last name that you're married," Steve said.

At this, she smiled and pointed to a large, muscular man sitting at a table a short distance away and said, "That's my husband. His name is Javier."

Noticing that she was wearing camouflage while her husband was dressed in work clothes, he asked teasingly, "And he doesn't have any problem taking orders from his superior officer?"

She laughed and said, "He's an officer too. We both served in the ROTC in college. We are on different rotations so one of us is always home with our son. His name is Joaquin. Javier works here in the camp as a blacksmith when he's not serving in the guard."

Seeing that she had relaxed, Steve said, "Alright Jennifer Bosquez-Morales, we're going to keep it as simple as possible. First thing to remember is that the more complex the plan, the more chance there is for a screw up. Did you bring the map?"

She unrolled a hand sketched map of the fort and its defenses on the table, weighing its corners down with salt and pepper shakers before pointing to a spot and saying, "This is where Z-girl was spotted this morning."

"Is this where she's usually seen?" Heather asked.

Jennifer thought about it for a few seconds before answering, "Most of the time. It's at the back left hand corner of the fort where we keep the chicken coups." Pointing to another spot at the far corner, she said, "This is where we keep the pig sties. She also shows up there from time to time. We only keep one person on guard for the pens and the coups now because most of the predators in the area are gone."

"Gone?" Steve asked.

"The dead have either eaten them or ran them off," Jennifer explained. The only predators left are the dead. Even a bear is no match for something that feels no pain and can't be stopped, so it flees. And if there's a group of them going after it..." She let her voice trail off.

Turning to Heather, Steve asked, "So what will it be, chicken or pork?"

After studying the map, Heather asked Jennifer, "What's the area like behind the fort?"

"We cut the trees back thirty feet, so it's wide open," she answered. "Beyond that is a lot of scrub brush and then the forest. The woods are pretty thick directly behind the wall and to the right, but then they thin out as you go to the left."

Heather looked at the map and said, "More than likely, Z-girl is in the woods beyond the chicken coups to the left. When she gets hungry, she tries for some KFC takeout, but if she sees someone, she cuts along the edge of the woods and heads for the pigsty."

"So that's where we'll check first," Steve told them.

***

Wisps of fog drifted across the grass and partially obscured the scrub brush when the hunters reached the back of the fort. Of the trees, nothing could be seen. The mist dampened sound, and occasionally grew so thick that it obscured the rest of the group, leaving them feeling like they had been abandoned. When they spoke to one and other, the sound was muffled despite them being only feet apart.

As he walked along the rear wall of the fort, Steve marveled at its construction. Despite the imposing spikes and sturdy construction, he knew that Rick was right about one thing. If the dead did come at them ten or twenty-thousand strong, even the fortified walls would eventually give.

Smelling the pig sty before he reached it, Steve called for Jennifer to join him at the front of the group. She had been hanging back with her own people, but now it was time for her training to begin.

When she reached him, he said, "You and I are on point. Heather is going to be right behind us in a position called drag. She's there to cover us and set the pace. Get one of your people that can walk backwards without tripping over their own feet and put them at the rear. This position is called trail. That leaves three people. They're to cover our flanks in a staggered position."

When they were sorted out and moving again, Steve called for everyone to stay close because of the fog. To Jennifer, he explained that if they were going after a living target, she should spread her people out with about five yards between them so they couldn't be taken out with a single burst of automatic rifle fire. Ten feet if there was the possibility of mortar or artillery fire.

"But who would use that kind of weaponry against us?" She asked.

"There's still bands of brigands out there," Steve explained, "and they might want to take what you have. Rick told me that you have some heavy firepower to protect the fort, so what makes you think that someone else might not get their hands on some and use it to blow your walls down and take it."

Giving the sty a wide berth because of the smell, they circled around the back of the fort and then moved in close to the wall. When they had only gone a few yard, they heard a voice call out, "Who's there? Who is that? Is that you screwing around with me again, Gene. You think it's funny, but one of these days you're going to get shot playing games like this."

Jennifer said in a voice only loud enough to be heard by the sentry, "its Lieutenant Bosquez-Morales. We're here to try and get Z-girl."

"Well come on then," the disembodied voice called back.

As they moved forward, Steve said, "I want you to set up a daily challenge and reply for the people on guard. One word only for each."

Jennifer grinned sheepishly and said, "We used to do that, but we've kind of slacked off. We haven't had any trouble from any looters in a long time. They see the outer fence and they know that we mean business."

"That doesn't mean you won't have trouble in the future," Steve told her.

"I'll make it a priority," she assured him.

The sentry's shape slowly emerged from the mist as they neared. First as a shapeless blob, then as a blurred human form, and then as a middle aged man standing with a hunting rifle in his hands.

He nodded to them and said, "About time someone took out the Z-girl. She's been a pain in the ass since day one."

"Where did you spot her?" Jennifer asked.

Turning, he motioned with his rifle as he said, "I was checking on the chickens when I saw her. At first I thought it was this damned fog coming off the lake, but then I got a real good look." Turning back to them, he visibly shivered and said, "It was spooky. She was wearing that dress and it was billowing out as she moved. I only saw her for a split second so I didn't get a chance to shoot."

"Which direction was she heading?" Heather asked.

Pointing over his shoulder with his rifle, the sentry said, "Back yonder. I tried to get her to come at me by yelling and making noise so I could get a shot at her, but it didn't work. She's a smart one."

The rest of the group had closed in to try and hear what was going on, so Steve told them to go back to their positions and to face outward. To Jennifer, he said, "You always have to be on your guard. With everyone standing here all bunched up, Z-girl could have come up and bit one of us on the ass before we knew what was happening."

She nodded solemnly and said, "I'll remember that."

Pointing in the direction of the chicken coups, Steve told her, "Move them out. You're on point and I'm on drag."

Surprised that she was being given sole lead of her command so quickly, she smiled as she called, "Move out." After a second, she added, "And keep your interval or you'll be scrubbing pots and pans for the rest of your rotation."

When they reached the chicken coups, they checked to see if there had been any damage to them, showing that Z-girl Lisa had been successful in her raid. Finding none, Steve turned his attention to where the woods were shrouded in mist.

"You said that the trees thin out to the left?" He asked Jennifer.

Studying the area, she replied, "It's a little difficult to tell without any landmarks, but if you go out at a forty-five degree angle from the corner of the fort, you run into the path that leads down to the lake. On the right of it they're thick and on the left of it they start to thin out more and more as you near the lake."

Knowing it would be dangerous to move through the woods in the fog, Steve also knew that they had no choice. If Z-girl only showed when it was foggy, then this was the only chance they had to get her. They would just have to stay extra alert.

Turning to Jennifer, he said in a quiet voice, "Have your people close in until they're almost touching. We don't want anyone getting separated. I want complete noise discipline from here on out. We move as one with everyone facing outward. No one fires a shot unless they're completely sure they have a target."

Jennifer relayed the orders and then made sure everyone was in position.

When she was done, Steve said, "Alright Jennifer Bosquez-Morales, move them out."

It took her longer then she thought it would to find the mouth of the trail, but she knew she couldn't miss it since it lay in the corner where the woods met. When they finally reached it, she was at a loss at what to do next. Stopping the group, she thought for a moment on what to do. She didn't want to ask Steve and Heather because she was the one in command, but if she didn't come up with something quick, she would have to.

Then it dawned on her that Steve was only using common sense in their effort to find Z-girl. He had narrowed down the search area by figuring out what her habits were, and that brought them here. Now she had to narrow it down more.

A plan came to her in a flash, so she said just loud enough to be heard, "Z-girl has got to be holed up somewhere nearby. She can't be breaking through the woods every time she comes to the fort or the sentries would have heard her. We're going to be looking for a small trail or even a hole somewhere in the woods and brush that she uses to get onto the trail. My bet is it's going to be to our right since the trees thin out pretty quick on the left. There's more places to hide on the right. I want every other person facing outward. Keep your eyes open and stop us if you see something. We'll go all the way to the lake, and if we don't find anything, we'll come back and search the edge of the woods behind the fort."

Looking to Steve and Heather to see if they approved, she got a smile and a nod from Steve and a, "Damn good plan, girl," from Heather.

As they moved off, Jennifer noticed that the fog had started to thin a little on the trail, but was still thick in the woods. This made it easier to see what was ahead, but not what might lunge out at them from the side. The trees and brush grew right up to the edge of the path, giving them only a split second to react if something did. Moving her eyes back and forth between both sides of the trail, while also keeping an eye on what was to the front of them, she knew it was more likely that one of the people looking directly into the woods would find the path Z-girl was using. It would probably be a small as a game trail that was mostly overgrown since it was only used once in a while.

Spotting a small creek that cut across their path before empting into the lake, she almost missed its significance when she was distracted by a whispered call from behind her to stop. Turning, she saw that one of her people was pointing his rifle into the woods with one hand while pointing with the other. Easing back to stand next to him, she looked to see what he had spotted.

"What is it?" She asked. "I don't see anything."

Pointing to a break in the thick brush and trees that started waist high, he replied, "Through there."

Confused, she whispered, "But that opening is almost three feet off the ground. Dead-asses can't fly."

Shaking his head, the man replied, "I don't mean she's using it to get on the trail, I saw something through it. I caught it out of the corner of my eye since I was looking for something closer to the ground. There was a break in the mist and I'm sure I saw a figure. It blended in with everything else, but it looked solid."

"Sure you weren't imagining it?" Jennifer asked. "If you look too hard for something, sometimes your mind plays tricks on you."

I'm sure I saw it," the man replied. "It blended in, but one thing stood out. It has something splattered all over it. I'm pretty sure it was dried blood."

The fog shifted in a slight breeze, revealing a small field beyond the line of trees bordering the trail. Looking for a way to get to it without having to break through the wall of scrub and altering their quarry, she could find nothing. Looking through the break again, she saw that the fog had closed back in.

There has to be some way to get from here to there, she thought to herself. Then it came to her. Waving for everyone to follow, she headed for the creek, stopping with her feet in the water as she crouched and looked down its length. The foliage had grown over it to make a four foot high tunnel, making it the perfect path for someone to move through.

Checking her M-16 to make sure a round was chambered, Jennifer thumbed off the safety and carefully moved forward. Her pulse pounding from the adrenalin coursing through her system, this left her focused and aware of everything around her. She could hear the thin trickle of water as it flowed slowly passed her and she could swear that she could even feel the heartbeats of the people behind her.

The light dimmed as she made her way further in, but she didn't stop. Ahead, she could see a brighter area on the right and knew this was her destination. Although she was moving forward at barely the speed a turtle, she slowed even more as she approached the opening. Twisting her body to the right as she took two final steps, she found herself looking through a break in the brush at a small clearing.

Fog still clung to the waist high grass covering it, small tendrils whipping up as a slight breeze came and went. On both sides, the trees were still cloaked in mist but now she could see further into them, telling her that the fog was starting to break up. Spotting something odd at the far end of the clearing, she knew it wasn't right. She had been an art major in college, and one of the things they taught you was there were no straight lines in nature.

Stepping carefully up the bank of the creek, she stopped a few feet into the clearing and motioned for everyone to get in a line abreast. When they were in position, she pointed to what could now clearly be seen as a half collapsed shack.

Overgrown with honeysuckle, it looked like it had been a squatter's shack due to the mishmash of wood used to construct it. Its half caved in roof might have once been made corrugated metal, but it was so rusted and broken up that there was no way to tell. One of its walls was made up from what had once been a sign, its blue and red Pepsi cola logo still faintly visible.

Jennifer looked at her surroundings as she thought it through. The woods made an almost impenetrable wall, telling her that they would have heard her if Z-girl Lisa tried to break through them. The sound might have been muffled by the fog, but she still would have made enough noise to alert them to her presence. The only way between the clearing and the path seemed to be along the creek, and she definitely hadn't come that way.

Looking to the shack, Jennifer said quietly, "She's got to be in there."

"You did really well," Steve congratulated her. "You read the signs and figured it out."

Jennifer nodded and whispered, "But now what?"

"You tell us," Heather whispered back.

Flipping the firing selector on her rifle to three-round burst, she motioned toward the shack and said, "We light it up."

"Good idea," Steve said. "The further away you can stay from the dead when you kill them, the better off you are. If she's in there and we take her out, we win. If we flush her out in the open where we can take her out, we win."

Jennifer waved her hand to get everyone's attention. When she had it, she pointed her rifle and held up one finger before pointing to the shack. She then pointed to her three people and held up two fingers. Then, she pointed to Steve, Heather and herself before holding up three fingers. This told them all to empty the magazine in their weapon in relays, assuring they wouldn't all be reloading at the same time.

When she saw they were ready, she called out, "Fire."

Their bullets tore into the rotten wood of the shack, throwing splinters of wood in all directions. The rest of the roof collapsed with a bang, causing a huge cloud of dust to billow out from its sides. When the firing finally died off, and Steve and Heather had reloaded, they moved forward to check out the rubble.

What was left of the fog helped to dissipate the dust, leaving them a clear view of the destruction they had wrought. Standing in a half-circle around what was left of the make-shift structure, they looked for a sign of anything dead or moving around dead. Nothing stirred in the pile of flattened wood, causing Jason, the man that had first spotted Z-girl, to lean down and grab the edge of a piece of plywood.

Even though Steve thought there nothing hiding in the rubble, he still said, "Be careful."

"Careful of what?" Jason asked with disgust as he flipped the wood over. "She was never fucking here."

Z-girl Lisa was lying in a small depression she had created from hours of pacing back and forth as she fought down the urge to feed. Exposed, she lunged up and forward when Jason uncovered her. Letting out a long whine, she buried her teeth in his forearm and shook her head back and forth as she tried to bite through the denim of his shirt.

The rest of the group jumped back at the unexpected appearance of Z-girl, raising their rifles and trying to get a bead on her wildly shaking head. Blood flew into the air as teeth met flesh, and someone called out that Jason was infected so they should kill them both.

Steve barked out, "No," to this. He had something else in mind. Calling out to Heather, he asked, "Do you have a shot at Z-girl?"

"Now I do," she replied as Z-girl lifted her head to swallow the chunk of meat she had ripped off Jason's arm.

Heather's CAR-15 fired once, the bullet drilling through the zombie's head.

After seeing the spray of black ochre, bone and hair that flew into the air, Jennifer and her two remaining militia members turned their guns on Jason.

Seeing this, Steve again barked out, "No."

"He's infected," Jennifer said. "I've heard you've got someone in your group that might hold the cure for this, but it's too late for him. Standing order number one is that if you get bitten, you get put down."

In what he hoped was a calming voice, Steve pointed to Jason and asked, "But what if he's immune? What if there are a lot of people that are immune and we don't know it because we shoot them when they get bitten?"

This made Jennifer pause for a moment before saying, "Then we wait."

It took five minutes for the first seizure to rack Jason's body. When it did, Jennifer calmly put a bullet through his head before turning to Steve and saying, "He wasn't immune."

CHAPTER FIFTEEN

Washington DC:

From where he stood on the bridge of the LCU carrying two platoons of his Marines, General Eastridge stifled a yawn as he studied the wall surrounding DC. It had been a long sleepless night, but it looked like it was about to pay off. Rising high above the shore, the wall was an imposing barrier, but far from impenetrable. Turning, he counted a total of ten more landing craft carrying the balance of his men. Over six-hundred Marines made up his assault force, the most experienced men and women in his command, each and every one of them ready to do his bidding.

He had arrived at Quantico late the night before and roused the commander of the base, explaining that there was a threat from a rogue group that meant to overthrow the Joint Chief's and take control of DC. Holding out orders signed by the Chairman himself, he commanded that the best of the best of Quantico's combat grunts needed to be formed into a light, motorized battalion and ready to move within the hour.

As Colonel Dennison studied the orders, there was a knock on the door. His aide entered and informed him that a small fleet of Navy ships had shown up at the marina and were requesting permission to dock.

Eastridge informed the Colonel that this was their transport before turning and ordering the aide to have as many of the ships tie up as possible and prepare to load his men. They would be boarding within the hour and leaving shortly after that. Turning to Dennison, he saw that the man was giving him an odd look. After a few seconds, the commander of Marine forces at Quantico asked, "Permission to speak freely, sir?"

Eastridge nodded, so the Colonel asked, "Do we really want to stop someone from overthrowing the Chairman?"

Eastridge knew that news travelled fast even in this world of limited communications. The Chairman might have only taken power hours ago, but he was sure that it was already well known as far away as Guam. Americans may bitch, moan and complain about their elected leaders, but they were elected. On the other hand, the Chairman had seized power and was now the sole leader. To many, this meant that democracy as they knew it was dead.

Giving Colonel Dennison a wink, Eastridge said, "That depends on who's doing the overthrowing."

Instantly understanding, Dennison hurried into his office and started giving orders over the radio. Within fifteen minutes, transport was arraigned, and ten minutes after that, men and women were being ferried by truck to a baseball field near the marina. It took another five minutes for the first of the vehicles they would use in their assault and their crews to arrive, and when they were all present twenty minutes later, Eastridge addressed them.

Knowing that most of the Marines in front of him probably already had a good idea of what was going on because of the ever-present scuttlebutt that plagued every branch of the military, he decided to be truthful. He started out by explaining that a new threat had arisen, one that made the dead pale in comparison. It was the threat of dictators and a loss of freedom. He told them that they would soon be going into battle, and while he didn't go too much into who they would be fighting, he explained that it might mean they would have to fire on fellow Americans. He went on to say that if they won, they could turn their attention destroying the dead, but if they lost, they would be branded traitors and hunted down. When he finished, he told them that he would only take volunteers, and if anyone chose not to go, it wouldn't be held against them.

No one moved for a few seconds, and then an earth shaking, "Oh Rah." Echoed from the buildings surrounding the field. Win or lose, every last one of them was in.

After telling them that they would be briefed further on the short trip to DC, he ordered them to board the boats.

Looking again to the wall around DC, Eastridge tried to find their point of entry. Spotting the opening in the early light, he told the radio operator to call and have the net that protected the tidal pool lowered. This was actually the only way left to get in and out of the city if you weren't coming by air.

When the wall had first been erected, four gates had been built for ground traffic. Convoys coming from Norfolk and Quantico made the hazardous run through the dead three times a week to resupply DC and bring in replacements. With the constant bombing of the city though, the roads were slowly choked off by rubble. The Seabee's tried to keep them cleared, but in the end it was decided to only use helicopters and the Seagate that led into the tidal pool.

Motioning for his radioman, General Eastridge took the handset from him and told his officers to get ready to land. They weren't expecting any resistance, but he told them to be ready for it if there was. They all knew that there was no turning back. If fired upon, they would return fire and switch to their alternate landing spot and continue on with the mission.

As Eastridge's landing craft made its way through the gate, he could see that the tidal basin was mostly dark, the wall leaving it in shadow. There were three docks jutting out on his right that were used for unloading supplies, but for his intents and purposes, they would be too slow in debarking his men.

Instead, the helmsman steered for the far end of the basin.

Leaving the bridge, Eastridge made his way to the lead vehicle, an armored Humvee. Climbing into the rear seat, he monitored the progress of his landing craft as they moved into position. He and Admiral Sedlak might had gotten them this far, but now it was up to the captain of each ship to put them on the shore. He had originally wanted to pass under the Kutz Bridge so they could land right next to Independence Avenue, but the bridge was too low. Instead, they would land to its right and use an access road to reach the main road.

Sitting in the Humvee in the open hull of the slowly rocking landing craft was making Eastridge slightly queasy. Pushing down the urge to vomit, it went away when he heard the engines roar into life and felt himself being pushed back in his seat. They had approached the city in an easy manner, not wanting to alert anyone to their real motive until they absolutely had to, but now all attempts at deception were over.

Within seconds, Eastridge could feel the landing craft suddenly decelerate. This was quickly followed by a jarring thud. Light flooded its interior as the ramp at the front of the boat dropped. The tidal pool was ringed by a retaining wall, so they had planned the landing for high tide. Despite this, the ramp was still tilted slightly upwards. The engine in the Humvee roared to life as the driver sped out of the landing craft and onto dry land. Looking to his left, Eastridge could see the other boats in the small flotilla disgorging men and vehicles.

The driver sped across a small piece of grass and onto a road before stopping. Next to him, the gunner stood in the hatch, slowly swiveling his heavy machine gun as he sought out any threats. Calling down into the cab, he said, "I've got a few people up on the Kutz Bridge looking at us, but nothing else, sir."

Eastridge was pleased. There were so many things that could go wrong with the operation, but at least the worst hadn't been realized. They hadn't been compromised. If the Chairman had somehow found out that they were planning a coup, they would have been met with force as soon as they landed.

The radio crackled to life, letting him know that all of the vehicles were on land and the strike force was ready to move. General Eastridge looked at his watch, noting that it was eight-thirty.

***

Steve checked his watch as he and Heather walked through the gate and said, "We've still got half an hour before they crank the generators and the radio up. Let's go over and check on Denise before we try to get hold of Fort Polk."

Nodding, she said, "With everything that's happened, I haven't gotten a chance to see her."

Turning to Jennifer, Steve said, "you did real good out there this morning."

Tilting her head down and smiling shyly, she replied. "Tracking the dead is actually easy when you take it one step at a time. You just have to use some common sense and be careful."

"Be very careful," Heather stressed. "From our experience, we've found it's the single Zs that come at you out of nowhere that get you instead of the ones that come at you in waves."

After giving her a few more tips, Steve and Heather made their way to the infirmary. Entering its small outer office, they found the remaining six people they had rescued from the Battleship Texas that were still mobile. They were seated in a collection of metal folding and lawn chairs that ringed the walls, but stood when the two of them entered.

Steve noticed right away that none of them would look either Heather or himself in the eye, instead, finding something interesting in the corners or on the ceiling.

Heather noticed too, and fear rushed through her. In a slightly quivering voice, she asked, "Is Denise okay?"

They all started speaking at once, assuring her that she was fine and Tick-Tock was in with her now. Their reassurances died off as one, leaving them looking around again in an uncomfortable silence.

Catching on to what was happening, Steve said, "I already know that Tick-Tock is staying. I'm going to jump out here on a limb here and guess that you're all staying with him."

A woman named Jackie took a hesitant step forward and said, "We're not abandoning you. We talked it over and agreed that if you still need us, we're there for you, but..." Her voice trailed off.

"But you're loyal to Tick-Tock and want to stay with him and Denise," Steve finished.

They looked even more uncomfortable at this.

Steve had a feeling that this was going to happen. These were Tick-Tock's people. Smiling to put them at ease, he said, "I understand. We might still need you, but I'm pretty sure that we won't. More than likely, we'll have Cindy at Fort Polk within the next day or two. You all stepped up in the end and you should be proud of that."

Relieved, Tick-Tock's people visibly relaxed.

Heather asked where Denise was, and six voices spoke at once, quickly directing them to go through a door and down a hall to the open room at its end. Steve knew they were being helpful, but also that they were in a hurry to see the two of them gone. He may have relieved them of their responsibility, but he could see visible signs of guilt in their expressions.

After the door had closed behind them, Heather said softly, "It seems our little group is breaking up."

"It had to happen sooner or later," Steve replied. Mentally shaking off his feeling of loss, it came back in a rush as he reached the end of the hall and spotted his friend sitting next Denise.

***

Tick-Tock saw Denise's eyes flutter and then open wide. Smiling at her, he said, "I have to do all the hard work and you lay around in bed all day."

She smiled and said, "You could always join me?"

Looking around at the other patients in the open room, he said, "The excitement might hinder their healing." Turning back to her, he asked, "How are you feeling?"

"Like I got hit by a truck and then it stopped and backed over me," she told him. "I do feel a little better than yesterday though."

"Probably from not getting bounced around so much," he commented. "The doctor said that you'll start to feel better over the next couple days."

Squinting her eyes slightly, Denise asked, "Is he a real doctor? I mean, he seemed to know what he's doing, but his skin looks all yellow and he's so thin."

"He was a medical examiner in New Orleans," Tick-Tock explained. "I've heard that a lot of people that work with the dead are affected by the chemicals they use on them."

Denise quickly sat up in bed as she said in shock, "He's a mortician."

Tick-Tock laughed as he eased her back down and said, "He's a pathologist, a medical doctor."

Her head spinning from the sudden movement, Denise could only groan in reply.

"Don't worry, babe," Tick-Tock told her, "I won't let him do an autopsy on you until we're sure you're gone."

Sensing someone behind him, Tick-Tock turned to find Steve and Heather standing a few feet away. Heather moved to Denise's bedside and started asking how she was while the two men stared at each other.

Finally, Steve said, "And if Tick-Tock ever dies, don't let them do a toxicology report."

Tick-Tock smiled and said, "They'll find substances not known to mankind."

After a few seconds, Tick-Tock said, "You know that I've got to-."

Raising his hand to cut him off, Steve said, "You don't have to explain. I would do the same thing." Pointing over his shoulder, he added, "I just ran into your people out in the waiting room and they're staying too."

"If you need them..." Tick-Tock started to say.

Steve shook his head and told him, "I won't. I was talking to Rick and he was telling me that right up until the military broke off all communication with civilians that they were asking for people that were immune to contact them. Besides, you might need them here."

Tick-Tock nodded grimly and said, "I just might. I ran into Lieutenant Wilkes on the way over here and he told me they were getting ready to head off that big herd that we dodged at the nut house."

"The one he was talking about last night?" Steve asked.

Tick-Tock nodded and said, "Seems they moved west and merged with another big group before heading north on good old Highway sixty-nine. They're worried that they might come back east, so they're going to try and lure it off toward Lufkin."

Remembering that the town was to their north-west, Steve knew this was their only hope. If the dead came back east toward them on the little two lane road that skirted the lake to its south, they would be truly screwed. Feeling slightly anxious at leaving his friend in what might be a tight spot, he reassured himself that Rick Styles and his people were competent and organized.

Turning his attention to Denise, he asked her, "How do you feel?"

Smiling, she said, "I'll be ready to move in a couple days. Sorry to hold us up when we're so close"

Confused, Steve turned to Tick-Tock who shook his head slightly at him and said, "I need a cigarette. Let's go outside."

Standing outside the front door, Tick-Tock said, "When I first mentioned that we were staying, Denise responded with, 'fuck that' and tried to get out of bed. She said that she was seeing this through no matter what. I finally had to tell her that we were going with you to get her to calm down."

Steve chuckled and said, "She's going to be pissed off when she finds out you lied."

Tick-Tock shrugged and said, "Nothing I can do about it. She's too messed up to walk. The doctor was amazed that she made it this far." Switching subjects, he asked, "What time are you calling the cavalry?"

Looking at his watch, Steve saw it was ten minutes to nine. His stomach did a slight roll when he realized their journey was finally reaching its end. All the names and faces of the people that didn't make it flashed through his head in an instant as he recalled their suffering and sacrifice.

Shaking it off, he answered, “Right now,” and went inside to get Heather.

***

Noting the absence of traffic as his Humvee led the way onto Independence Avenue, General Eastridge was grateful that his operation was being launched on a Sunday morning. Only a few people on the streets stopped to gawk as they passed by, but no one made any attempt to stop them.

And why should they, Eastridge mused. It’s not like we have a hammer and sickle or a red star on the sides of our vehicles. We’re not an invading force, we’re simply United States Marines going someplace or coming from somewhere. The only reason anyone’s even paying us any attention is because most of the combat troops are on the wall, not cruising through the center of town.

To further the illusion, Eastridge radioed that everyone was to keep their weapons out of view and their helmets off. The convoy gained speed as it passed the Smithsonian, but slowed when it reached Maryland Avenue. Here, the lead vehicle veered to the left along with most of the column, while the balance continued straight. Designated as red force, their job was to contain the assets the Chairman kept in Dog town while the main body took control of the capitol building.

As soon as his vehicle turned onto Maryland Avenue, General Eastridge could see his objective ahead. Despite having laid eyes on it hundreds of times, seeing the capitol building always took his breath away. He didn’t want to harm it in his bid to depose the chairman, but he knew that if they barricaded it against him he would order his people to breach its walls. If worse came to worse, they would raze the building, but he hoped it wouldn’t come to that. This wasn’t his main concern though, his biggest worry were the five M1 Abrams tanks ringing its front. They had anti-tank weapons to take them out if need be, but they would still cause some damage before they could be dealt with.

Slowing to a stop in front of a guard post next to the road, Eastridge could see that the four people manning it were more curious at their presence that alerted by it. This was what he had hoped for. After receiving the okay from the Chairman the night before to bring reinforcements into DC, he made sure the news was spread among the defenders of the city. Rumors may travel faster than the truth, but he was sure that by now everyone in the city knew they were arriving today. Since his Marines protected the wall while the Army was charged with guarding the city itself, the plan was to act like they were relieving the soldiers guarding the capitol building. It didn’t seem like that much of a stretch of the truth since the Marines had always been responsible for the security of the President. In this way, they might get around a firefight with the Army. In addition to this, since The Chairman spent all of his time here, they could secure the capitol and take him into custody at the same time.

Stepping from the Humvee, Eastridge returned the salute from the Sergeant of the guard. Noting the man’s nametag, he said, “Good morning Specialist Sepulveda. My name is General Eastridge and I’m here with my men to relieve you.”

“We have no orders regarding that, sir,” Sepulveda answered.

Looking indignant, Eastridge asked, “No one told you we were coming?”

“We heard we were getting reinforcements, sir” Sepulveda told him, “but I have no orders to quit my post. As you know, a sentry’s fifth general order is to only quit his post when properly relieved, sir.”

“And you are being properly relieved,” Eastridge told him in a tight voice. “Now gather your men and proceed to your barracks.”

Sepulveda shook his head and replied, “I have my orders, sir.”

Eastridge was about to argue that he sat on the Joint Chiefs of Staff and that he could order the specialist to go to hell and be obeyed, when he was interrupted by a series of explosions and the sound of small arms fire erupting from the other side of the capitol building. Sepulveda spun as his hand dropped to the pistol holstered at his hip. In the distance, dark smoke rose into the air as the sound of automatic weapons rose and fell. One of the men in the guard shack came to the door and said in a frantic voice, “We just got a report that there’s a firefight going on in Dog town.”

Trying to take advantage of the situation, Eastridge said in a commanding voice, “Specialist, gather your men and proceed to Dog town. My men and I will guard the capitol.”

Sepulveda was about to obey, when the other guard came to the door again and waved him over. He spoke quietly for a few seconds and then disappeared inside. Sepulveda turned slowly as he eyed the General. Slowly, he started pulling his pistol from its holster as he said, “I regret to inform you that I will have to detain you, sir.”

Eastridge cringed inside. The last thing he wanted was to have to kill Americans, but he knew there was no other choice. This was another crime that The Chairman would have to answer for in hell.

Dropping into a crouch, he yelled, “Fire,” as he pulled his pistol.

***

Recalling that it was the same make and model radio they had used at the station, Steve felt a sense of déjà vu wash over him as he took the headset from the operator. Placing it on his head, he adjusted it and nodded to the woman at the control board. She pointed to him, letting him know he was live.

Taking a deep breath, he said, “Attention Fort Polk, my name is Steve Wendell and I am the leader of a small band of survivors out of Clearwater, Florida. We are currently located to the west of you at an encampment named Fort Redoubt. In our group, we have a person that is immune to the HWNW virus. I have been told that you have orders against any contact with civilians, but this girl may hold a cure for the disease. Please advise, over. I will be repeating this message every fifteen seconds.”

***

Lieutenant Dwight listened in disbelief to the radio traffic coming out of Washington DC. Here at Fort Polk, they had gone on full alert when they received the reports of fighting in the capitol, but the question remained; on alert against who. At first, it appeared the Marine Corps and the Army were having it out in the east end of the secure zone, but why? And even then, some of the Army units stationed in the capitol were reporting that they were fighting side by side with the Marines while others were calling out that were neutral. No one seemed to really know what was going on, but this didn’t stop the radio operators from adding to the confusion by reporting whatever rumor they happened to hear.

So far, they had heard that;

The capitol building and the White House were under siege.

The Navy was preparing to shell the city.

It was a coup and the Chairman had been taken into custody trying to flee the capitol.

The Chairman was still in power and had crushed the attackers.

The dead had breached the wall and were pouring into DC.

It was aliens.

It was the Russians.

It was the Chinese.

It was all bullshit, Dwight thought as he took a sip of coffee.

Reaching forward to set his Styrofoam cup on his desk, his hand stopped in midair when he heard one of his radio operators call out that they had civilian radio traffic coming in. Although they received calls for help every day, they were under orders to ignore them.

With the exception of one.

“Put it on speaker,” Dwight told him.

The Lieutenant only caught the end of the message, but it was enough to know that this was the group they were listening for. Picking up his satellite radio, he called the number he had been given by General Eastridge's aide. When the call connected, Dwight thought he would have to try again because of all the interference. Then, he realized that he was hearing the rattle of gunfire. In the background, he could hear someone calling out orders to flank the strong point in the west wing and enter the building.

After a few seconds of this, a voice finally came through the radio saying, "Johnny, I need you to concentrate your fire on the roof. Those snipers are giving us hell."

Not sure who he was talking to, Dwight said, "This is Lieutenant Dwight. I'm trying to reach General Eastridge."

"This is his aide, Captain Moore," came the reply.

Slightly confused, since this wasn't the name of the General's aide, he said, "I need to speak to Major Compton."

"That isn't going to happen, Lieutenant." Moore told him. "He's gone. I'm the General's aide now, so what do you want? In case you can't hear, we've got a few things going on right now."

"I was told to report to the General when we received any radio contact from anyone that's immune to the HWNW virus, sir" Dwight said.

"That isn't going to happen either," Moore said abruptly. "The general took a round to the hip. He's unconscious."

"Then I need further orders," Dwight told him.

The sound of heavy gunfire followed by three loud explosions came through the radio. Moore said, "Wait one."

If it wasn't for the sound of sporadic rifle fire coming through the headset, Dwight would have thought the connection had been broken.

After a few seconds, Moore came back on the line and said, "These are your orders."

***

Steve looked at the radio in disbelief. His body felt weak and his head spun from what he had just been told to do. He barely felt it as Heather laid her hands on his shoulders and he barely heard her say that they would find a way no matter what those scumbags in DC had decided. Visions of a short helicopter ride to safety left him in a rush, replaced by the fear of what they now faced. Trying to shake it off so he could think clearly, he found the idea of having to travel hundreds of miles more through a land populated by the flesh-eating dead too much to comprehend.

Taking off his headset, he spun around in his chair to find Rick Styles looking at him from across the room. The two men made eye contact, and Steve could see that the disappointment on the man's face was obvious. After a few seconds, Rick turned and left the room.

Knowing there was nothing else he could do here, Steve got up to follow him. They had a lot of preparation ahead of them and there was no way they could put everything together by themselves. They might not be able to take the commander's daughter to safety, but they needed Rick's help.

A lot of it.

As he and Heather left the radio room, he heard her say with disgust, "I can't believe they told us that we have to make it all the way to Arkansas on our own," snorting, she continued on in a mimicking voice, "by the best possible means available." Clenching her fists, she went on in with derision dripping from every word as she asked, "And those bastards can't even spare one helicopter?"

Trying to talk it through so he could find some reason, Steve said, "Lieutenant Dwight told us that everything was grounded indefinitely until they resolved a crisis that had arisen in DC."

"Yeah, they're waiting for a loud popping noise," Heather said venomously, "and that would be their heads coming out their asses. And when you asked him how long until the crisis was over, I couldn't believe Lieutenant Whatshisname just kept telling you proceed to a research facility at Russellville by the best possible means available."

Feeling that his growing anger at the situation would spill out if he spoke any more on the subject, Steve decided to remain silent. The last thing he needed right now was to let his rage loose at what was happening.

The primary reason being that he didn't think he would be able to stop it.

When he was told that no help was coming because of some problems in DC, his initial reaction was to change his destination to Washington and grab someone by the throat. The government had been looking for people that were immune to the HWNW virus so they could come up with a cure, and when they were offered one on a silver platter, he and his people were kicked to the curb and told to fend for themselves.

As his disgust rose, Steve reminded himself that anger is only fear coming out sideways. Fear can be dealt with, he told himself, but going off on a tangent will cloud your judgment. Fear will cloud your judgment too, but you've been dealing with the fear of being killed and eaten since day one. Nothing has changed except you. Time to suck it up buttercup, this is where the metal hits the meat. You need to be cool, calm and collected to get through this.

Taking a deep breath to push his feelings of violence away, he still found he could only grunt in reply. As they exited the small administration building, Steve looked around for Rick, surprised that he was nowhere to be seen. They were standing at the end of the open parade ground, and the nearest structure was thirty feet away, so they should be able to spot him. He had only left a few seconds before them.

Thinking that he might have entered one of the offices inside, as he was turning to check, he saw Rick come from around the side of building. With him was a one armed girl that didn't look to be more than twelve years old.

As he and his companion stopped a few feet away, Rick said, "We both have a problem that we thought we had found an easy solution to. The problem is, that solution got pissed away a few minutes ago. What we need to do now is come up with a new solution. You can't take my daughter to safety in Fort Polk, but you can bring her with you to Arkansas. On top of that, you have Cindy, and if she does hold a cure for this disease then you're my best bet."

Steve was relieved that Rick was going to help them. He hadn't doubted that he would, but the amount of help was in question. He knew that if the commander was seeing him as his best bet right now, he would put all his resources behind getting them to Russellville.

Considering the distance they would have to travel, Steve said, "We'll need a couple of armored cars and a shitload of supplies. I might even need some of your people."

"All I can spare you is Stacey," Rick told him.

Looking at the one armed woman in confusion, Steve couldn't see how she could help.

With a short bark of laughter, Rick explained, "She's a pilot."

CHAPTER SIXTEEN

Russellville, Arkansas:

Private First Class Jimmy McPherson watched as the three men from his squad searched for him in the low lying vegetation. His legs ached from straddling a large branch in the tree where he had hidden himself, and his back throbbed from where it was pushed up against a knot on its trunk, but he ignored the pain and stayed perfectly still. Another soldier joined them, causing Jimmy's heart to beat faster. He wanted to close his eyes to hide even further at the sight of Sergeant Fagan but knew that this childhood trick wouldn't save him. Willing himself to become part of the tree, he felt the rapid pulse of blood charging through his system go cold when Fagan turned and looked directly at his hiding spot.

Jimmy felt their eyes lock and he knew his escape was over. He would be dragged from his perch, handcuffed, and brought back to the camp for court martial. He would of course be found guilty, and there was only one punishment for the crime of desertion; death by hanging.

His thoughts surged with resentment that he was only trying to get back to his family, but he knew this was no excuse in the eyes of the Army. As he waited for the sergeant to point him out to the other soldiers, images of his body dangling from a rope ran through his mind. He felt a few drops of urine leak from his penis and soak his pants, knowing that if he wasn't so dehydrated that it would be a flood. Wondering if he could get his rifle un-slung and shoot his way out, he knew his chances were slim to none. It would be him alone against ten men. He might get a couple of them, but in the end they would take him down.

Deciding that dying in this way was preferable to the indignity of a broken neck, or slow strangulation if the rope didn't snap it, Jimmy was slowly reaching for his rifle when he was astonished to see Fagan give him a barely perceptible nod before turning away. Hearing the Sergeant call out to the others that they were returning to camp, he at first thought it was a trick to get him to come down from his perch so they wouldn't have to climb up and drag him from it.

Two voices came to him and he strained his ears to hear what they were saying. They were at first muffled, but came through clearer as the two men approached his hiding spot.

"The Zs must have got him," the first one said.

"Poor bastard," the second replied. "That's a hell of a way to go. He was Sarge's favorite too."

They fell silent and picked up there pace when they heard Fagan's voice call out that they had ten seconds to get their asses in gear or be left behind.

As he watched them disappear into the undergrowth, Jimmy felt a small surge of hope. His rational mind took over a millisecond later as it told him that this was nothing but a trick to get him on the ground but his soul still hung onto the slim chance that he was free.

Seconds ran into minutes and minutes into an hour before Jimmy risked moving. He debated risk versus reward during this time, and finally came to the conclusion that if they were waiting for him, then there was nothing he could do about it. Thinking that at least he could get down from the tree and die on his feet, he almost laughed at himself when he tried to lift his leg over the limb and found it was completely dead. The blood flow had been restricted for so long that both legs were useless.

So much for running, he told himself. You can't even stand.

Shifting position, he propped one leg in front of him on the branch and started massaging his thigh. As blood started flowing again into the knotted muscle, he stifled a cry of pain. Sliding his other leg forward, he worked on that until both felt reasonably steady enough to climb down.

His legs spasmed wildly as he shimmied down the trunk, and when he finally made it to the ground, both collapsed under him. Propping himself against the tree, he readied his rifle and then started rapidly massaging his thighs again as he looked around for the first of his fellow soldiers to emerge from the brush to take him into custody. When he saw no one, his soul surged with hope again, but this was pushed aside by his brain telling his that his captors would wait until he could walk.

That's what I would do, he told himself. I wouldn't want to have to carry anyone.

When the ache in his legs had been replaced by the feeling that a million pins and needles were being poked into them, he knew he was ready. It was time to shit or get off the pot. Using his rifle to lever himself onto his feet, he leaned against the trunk of the tree for support before quickly bringing his M16 up into a firing position.

Slowly scanning the bushes for any sign of life, he saw nothing. Straining his ears for any sound, he heard nothing. Closing his eyes, he sniffed the air, but smelled nothing.

His rifle barrel slowly dropped and relief washed through him as he realized he was all alone. For some bizarre reason, Staff Sergeant Fagan had decided to leave him be. Looking around at the silent woods, his relief was suddenly replaced by fear at this same realization that he was all alone. For months now, he had been surrounded by others who would watch his back against the dead, but now he was on his own.

Hearing a rustling sound coming from a nearby clump of bushes, Jimmy pushed himself off from the tree and staggered off to where he had hidden his pack.

***

Sitting in his office, Major Cage listened to Staff Sergeant Fagan tell him how Jimmy had gone missing from the patrol and how he had let him go before saying, "I know the kid was one of your favorites, but if word gets out that you let him walk away, we're screwed."

"No one saw him except me, sir," Fagan answered. "All of my people were looking for a dead body and didn't think to look up."

Sighing, Cage said, "We're going to have a lot more of our people trying to haul ass before this is over, and we have to keep discipline. The order stands that desertion will be punished by death by hanging, and I need you to enforce it."

Fagan opened his mouth to speak, but Cage lifted a hand to silence him before saying, "And that means everyone. If we don't do it, there's going to be no one left here except you and me."

"And that would be a bad thing, sir?" Fagan asked.

Cage bristled for a second, but then saw the truth in the statement. Looking down at the radio reports on his desk about the battle raging in the Capitol, he felt his heart sink at the thought that even the military was falling apart. If it wasn't bad enough that they were fighting the dead, they were now fighting each other.

Clearing his throat, Cage said, "We need to hang on for as long as possible."

"Or until Professor Hawkins leaves," Fagan suggested. "You know as well as I do that we're on the priority list for supplies because of the good Professor's work here. You also know that even with that, those supplies are few and far in between. We've discussed this before, sir. What do you think is going to happen when he leaves? We've both talked to men and women being rotated in from other camps and forts and we've heard that they don't have a pot to piss in or a window to throw it out. They're all low on food, ammunition and fuel."

Cage started to speak, but Fagan cut him off by saying, "And what happens when Hawkins takes his Malectron with him, sir? From what we've been able to figure out, that's the only thing keeping us from getting overrun."

"But with Washington turned a battle zone, he's not going anywhere soon," Cage countered.

Fagan waved this argument away and said, "They'll have that shit sorted out in a few days. It sounds like they're fighting for control, but it sounds like our ace in the hole there is with us no more. Whoever grabs the brass ring now, they are going to want a weapon like the Malectron."

Looking down at his desk, Cage mentally read through all the radio communiques he had received that morning. From what he had been able to gather, it was some kind of coup, but they still didn't know all the details. General Eastridge had been mentioned early on, giving him hope that the man would seize control, but it had been hours since they had word about who was winning and who was losing. Or about the General. For all they knew, Eastridge was dead and the Chairman of the Joint Chiefs was still in control.

Cage thought about this for a few seconds. He had known all along that once Hawkins left and took the Malectron with him, that they would have a rough time with the dead surrounding the camp. At first, he had almost seen the coup in Washington as a reprieve, but in the end, he knew Fagan was right. If Eastridge was gone, no matter who took power, they would want the weapon in their arsenal.

Looking up at the Staff Sergeant, Cage said, "With everything up in the air, we need to be ready for whatever comes at us. We need to make plans to abandon the camp at a moment's notice." Seeing the smile creep across Fagan's lips, Cage added sternly, "Not preparations, only plans."

Fagan grew serious and said, "Plans only, sir."

"And they're to be kept between me and you," Cage added. "If the troops find out we're getting ready to bug out, there will be panic."

Fagan started to speak, but stopped at the sound of a knock at the door. It opened, and Cage's aide rushed in, saying, "Sorry to interrupt you sir, but I thought you would want to see this right away."

Cage took the slip of paper and dismissed his aide. Reading it through, a smile broke across his face, his first all day.

Holding it out, he said, "Belay any plans to abandon the camp. This is from Fort Polk. It says, 'Group of civilians coming your way by their own means. One immune.' "

***

Steve watched the landscape pass by through the slit cut in the metal plate that had replaced the windshield of the Jeep Commander he rode in. They had passed nothing but trees on the first leg of their journey to the airfield outside of Jasper, but now signs of civilization were becoming more apparent.

First, he saw a long line of abandoned cars long pulled over to the side of the road. Curious as to why they would be out here in the middle of nowhere, he asked Stacey.

"There's a gas station up ahead around the curve," she explained. "We had a lot of people coming here when the dead first rose because the area is so isolated. They thought they could get away from the dead-asses." Pointing to rotting skeletal remains scattered across the road, she added, "They found out real quick that nowhere was safe. My guess is that they must have been all lined up here like a smorgasbord when the dead came out of the woods." Pointing, she said, "You can see they were all bumper to bumper, edging as close to the person in front of them as they could. Like that was going to get them to the pumps faster. Didn't do them any good though since the station had run out of gas two days earlier."

"Then why were they sitting here?" Steve asked.

Stacey shrugged and replied, "Maybe they thought a tanker was going to come. These people must have been on empty to stay around here, since anyone with half a brain would have known everything was falling apart and it was time to head for the hills."

Seeing a gap in the line where the vehicles in front and behind it had been smashed, Steve said, "Looks like someone got away by playing bumper cars when the dead hit."

After steered around the remains of a body in the middle of the road, Stacey pointed to the gas station as it came into view and said, "My guess is it was them."

Steve looked to where she indicated and saw a pickup truck had crashed into the cars sitting next to the pumps. From the amount of damage to the fenders and sides of the vehicles, he guessed the driver of the truck had repeatedly rammed them in his quest to get next to the empty pumps. He had finally gotten stuck when he tried to roll over a small sports car, ending up with his front tires crashing through its roof. Bullet holes riddled the truck and the cars around it, telling a further tale of the gun battle that ensued.

"People were desperate to survive," Stacey commented, "even to the point of stupidity."

Looking at the building, Steve took in the shattered windows and empty shelves. He wasn't sure if it had been raided before or after the demolition derby out front, but his guess was after. He knew that there was a fine line between civilization and anarchy, and the truck trying to smash its way to the pumps had probably made it easy for everyone to step over. Spotting more decaying bodies strewn across the lot, he turned his head.

From where he was sitting in the rear, Rick said, "We didn't have much looting in the town because of the police and militia, but out here it was everyone for themselves. We've been back to Jasper quite a few times to forage what we can and it's pretty much intact."

"Are we going to pass through it?" Heather asked.

Rick shook his head and replied, "The airfield is on the southwest side of town so we'll bypass it. Jasper is outside our secure zone and there is still a lot of dead wandering around."

Looking to where Stacey effortlessly maneuvered their SUV between two wrecked cars, Steve was tempted to ask how she lost her arm. Curious if she had been bitten and they had cut it off to keep the disease from spreading, he wondered if this was the case. He didn't know if amputation would work, but didn't feel comfortable asking.

As if reading his mind, Stacey said, "I lost it when I was ten, not to one of the dead-asses."

Feigning surprise, Steve said, "I wasn't wondering-."

She cut him off by saying, "Everyone wonders. Whenever we get new people at the camp, sooner or later someone asks how I lost it. They're all wondering the same thing, was I bitten and we cut it off."

Rick spoke up, saying, "And we found out that doesn't work. We tried it on a few people and they still turned."

Steve took this in as the realization sunk in deeper that once you were bitten, you were through. He had learned so much about the dead by trial and error, but there was still volumes to know. Like how to eradicate them wholesale. Turning, he looked back to the third row of seats where Cindy sat flanked by Igor and Linda. Hopefully, she held the solution to this.

***

Jimmy McPherson bent at the waist as he vomited up a thin string of bile. Spitting out the taste, he gasped for breath as he straightened. Spinning in a full circle, he looked at the few deserted buildings around him as he sought somewhere to hide. None of them looked secure with their smashed out doors and windows. Another wave of nausea passed through him but he forced it back, telling himself that dying because he was puking from running away from the dead wasn't how he wanted to go out. Steadying himself, he adjusted his pack as he tried to get his bearings.

Not sure where he was, other than somewhere just outside the town of Russellville, he cursed the dead that had made him detour from his route home.

At least they could have chased me in the right direction, he thought ruefully.

Seeing movement ahead of him that disappeared as soon as he focused on it, he wondered if his eyes were playing tricks on him. Deciding that he needed to avoid everyone whether they were real or a figment of his imagination, he knew it was time to get off the main road. When the dead had gotten on his trail, he'd had no choice but to run through the neighboring town of Dardanelle and across the bridge into Russellville, but now he had options. He was in an undeveloped area just outside of town, and to his right was a side road running between fields and small patches of woods. Looking ahead to the buildings that made up the city, he shuddered at the thought of passing through that gauntlet.

Pulling out his map, he studied it for a few seconds before heading off on the road to his right. Knowing that he had to cross the river again to get back on course, he decided to find another spot to the east. He might have lost the group of dead before he reached the bridge, but he wasn't about to turn around and head in their direction again. Even if it meant a detour of twenty miles, he would find somewhere else to cross.

Starting at a slow walk, he picked up speed as the urge to put as much distance as possible between himself and the dead city overwhelmed him. Coming to a spot where the road he was travelling curved to the north, he turned onto a smaller lane that continued to the east. From his previous foraging trips into the city, he knew that if he kept moving in this general direction that he would eventually come to a road leading south that dead-ended at a strip mine. This was one of their staging areas when they went into Russellville because it was always deserted, and this is what he needed. He had been up since 0600, and since then had either been wracked with fear that his escape would be discovered by his own people, or on the run from the dead, so he was exhausted and knew he needed rest.

The mine is the perfect place to set up for the night, he told himself. Tomorrow, I can figure out which way to go. Maybe I can head down to the river and try to find a boat.

Spotting the turn off ahead of him, Jimmy also spotted something else: a huge cloud of dust hanging in the air above the mining site. Stopping as he tried to figure out what was causing it, he knew it could only be one of three things. The dead, his people, or one of the groups of brigands that stayed alive by staying mobile.

Hearing the sound of an engine and spotting more dust being kicked up in a trail that followed the road leading toward him, he didn't wait to find out which one it was. Jumping over a small ditch, he ran ten feet into the woods that lined the right side of the road and dropped down. Gently parting a large growth of honeysuckle, he watched as a two and a half ton truck came into view. At first thinking it was his fellow soldiers because it was a military vehicle, this idea was smashed when he saw the men and women riding in the back.

Dressed in an assortment of bright colored t-shirts, they sported a collection of automatic weapons that would make any dictator from a third-world country proud to have in his arsenal. Besides their personal firearms, the sides of the truck also bristled with three M60 machine guns. On top of this, they were armed with and two fifty caliber heavy machine guns mounted on the front and back of the open bed.

Holding his breath, Jimmy let it out in a rush when the truck roared by him and drove out of sight down the road. In the stillness after the noise of their passing, he could hear the sound of more engines coming from the direction of the mine. They revved up for a few seconds and then fell silent.

I guess that kills that idea, he said to himself.

Without having to pull out his map, he knew of only one other place in his immediate area that always seemed to be free of the dead. It was only a mile more up the road, but there was no way in hell he was going to walk out in the open. Steeling himself to the idea of a cross country trek, he cautiously rose to his feet and started off.

***

Knowing that right now would be a bad time to get attacked, Steve watched for any sign of the dead as they rolled across the airfield toward a hanger in the far rear corner. They had only seen half a dozen Zs since leaving Fort Redoubt, but as soon as the lurching creatures spotted their vehicles, they came straight at them. It had been easy to avoid them by simply driving on, but here on the runway they would be vulnerable.

From behind him, Rick Styles asked tensely, "Anyone see anything?"

This was met by negatives, so he repeated the question into his radio. The other Jeep responded with a no, but this was no cause to relax. With numerous buildings for the dead to hide in, there could be a whole army of them within a hundred yards.

Pointing across the seat, he said to Stacey, "I would say your best bet is the Cessna 414."

She nodded and replied, "That's where I'm heading. We're going to need to fuel it up."

Remembering seeing the patrols going out to check on the location of the huge herd of Zs, a thought occurred to Steve and he asked, "Why don't you use the plane for your reconnaissance? Wouldn't that be an easier way to keep track of the dead?"

"We were doing that for a while but there's not enough fuel," Stacey told him. "In fact, I've only got enough to get you to where you're going. I'm going to take a quick look around the area on my way out, but after we get to Arkansas, I'm grounded for a while."

Rick said, "We've been saving the last of the gas for an emergency."

"And this qualifies," Stacey added.

No one moved for a few minutes after the Jeeps rolled to a stop in front of the hanger, everyone's heads rotating in all directions as they all searched the immediate area around them. Seeing nothing, they cautiously opened their doors and got out.

Rick motioned to the four men that had ridden in the second Jeep with Brain and Connie to cover him as he headed for a small door set in the wall of the hanger. He didn't seem too concerned when he opened a chain lock securing it, letting Steve know that the building had been checked when it was last sealed up. Rick and one of him men disappeared inside, and moments later, the huge hanger doors started rolling apart.

As sunlight filled its darkened interior, Steve could a small helicopter and two single engine planes to one side. Beyond that, he could see the dim shape of another airplane that sported two engines. Although good sized, it didn't appear to be big enough to carry all eight of them.

Seeing his look of concern, Stacey said with a slight laugh, "Don't worry, it's big enough for you and your crew. It's even got a toilet. I would suggest going before we go because it doesn't give you a lot of privacy." Walking into the hanger, she added, "We've got to fuel this baby up, so no smoking for a while."

Walking over to where the rest of his group was clustered around the first Jeep, Steve noticed the hangdog look on Brain's face. He knew that his friend had wanted to stay in Fort Redoubt, but he still might need the technician. He had explained to Brain that he couldn't force him to go, but was asking him to see it all the way through. Brain had reluctantly agreed, but didn't look too happy about it.

Stopping next to Heather, Steve said, "No smoking, they're gassing up the plane."

"So we're going soon," Cindy's small voice asked from the back seat.

"In a few minutes," Linda answered her. "Then it's just a short airplane ride."

"I've never been on a plane," Cindy said.

"It will be fun," Steve told her as he forced a smile. He wasn't sure how fun it would be since he had never flown in something so small, but he had to keep up appearances. He had always hated flying, but he knew that this was the fastest, safest way to get to Russellville. His worst experience flying was when he had crashed in a helicopter back in his Army days, and his best was getting so drunk before a flight to Los Angeles that he passed out and slept the whole way.

Wondering if anyone had any Xanax, he was interrupted by Rick asking him to give them a hand pushing the plane out. When they had wheeled the aircraft into the sun, Steve saw that it was bigger than he thought, but still too small for his comfort. Not that its size mattered. Big or small, sooner or later they all crashed. Fear rose up in him and he started thinking of ways to make it to Arkansas by ground when he heard a whine.

The fear left him in a flash as he whirled around, bringing his rifle off his shoulder and into a firing position in one smooth motion. He stopped when he saw it was only Pep, leaving him wondering how he could be ready in a heart-beat to take on a legion of the dead, but scared shitless to fly.

"I thought we agreed to leave Pepper back at the fort," he said as he lowered his rifle. The dog had been hidden in the back of the second Jeep, but with all the activity, she had stuck her head up to find out what was going on.

"Cindy wouldn't go if she couldn't bring Pep," Linda explained.

From the back of the Jeep, the little girl called out stubbornly, "And I won't. The Pep is my dog. Where I go, she goes."

Not having any experience in dealing with little girls, Steve turned away to gather his thoughts. This brought him into direct view of the plane, causing him to turn back around. His mind spun as to how to deal with the situations as he watched Pepper bound out of the Jeep and look around before spotting him. With tail wagging, she came over to sniff at him before walking over to pee on the side of the hanger. From the back seat of the Jeep, Cindy was crying softly. Everyone was looking at him with accusing eyes, since this was obviously his fault, and just then, Rick called out, asking what they were doing standing around. He followed this up with a terse, "Tighten the hell up, man. You should have your people ready to get onboard already."

Now I'm the bad guy, Steve thought ruefully.

Holding up his hands in surrender, he said, "Pep can go on one condition."

"What's that?" Linda asked.

"Someone needs to give me a Valium."

CHAPTER SEVENTEEN

Washington DC:

Through a fog of pain, General Eastridge listened to Captain Moore's situation report. When he had first been hit in the hip, he had refused morphine since he didn't want the drug to cloud his thoughts but now he was reconsidering his decision. Waves of nausea brought on by his throbbing wound were causing him to black out at times, and when this happened, he was no help to anyone.

"We've taken the eastern section of the city, sir," Moore told him.

"Dog town?" Eastridge rasped out.

"There are still a few hold outs, but we're mopping them up right now," Moore said.

Eastridge cringed inwardly at the phrase, 'mopping up.' These were American troops they were talking about, not some half-assed terrorists.

"How many casualties?" The General asked.

After checking the notes in his hand, Moore said in a quiet voice, "One-hundred and ten dead with almost twice that wounded on our side. Casualties will be forthcoming about The Chairman's people. It was a lot of hit and run fighting in Dog town and we had to level a few buildings."

Eastridge closed his eyes in pain, but it wasn't from his wound. After a few seconds, he asked, "What about the Capitol building?"

"We had to level it, sir," Moore answered. "The Chairman and his people went underground so we're trying to ferret them out. We've secured all the access in and out of the area by blocking the subways and walkways."

"Is he in there?" Eastridge asked.

Moore nodded and replied, "We've intercepted radio traffic going in and out of the command bunker, so this is where he is, sir. The communiques are very disturbing."

Eastridge made a 'come on' gesture, so Moore continued, "He tried to activate the US Strategic Command."

This made Eastridge's blood go cold. These were the men and women in charge of the nation's nuclear weapons.

Having been told only five minutes earlier that he was to brief the General, Moore checked his notes again before continuing, "The good news is that they refused to answer him. The Chairman has all the codes, but I think when he called for a strike against Washington with a low-yield nuke, they saw the insanity of it."

"Does he have the ability to fire them from the command center?" Eastridge asked, knowing that while The Chairman would be safe from a nuclear blast in his bunker, he and his men would be turned into radioactive dust.

"It's possible, sir, but not likely," Moore answered. "We managed to contact Strategic Command ourselves and received this answer." Pulling out a slip of paper, he read, "During this time of upheaval and crisis, the Strategic Command has secured all nuclear weapons until such a time as a stable government is reestablished. All exterior commands have been bypassed, and all orders for the release of any weapons of mass destruction by anyone will be ignored. God bless America."

Well, at least we don't have to worry about being consumed in a fireball, Eastridge told himself. But what about all the other ordnance lying around out there. Even though the United States banned chemical and biological weapons, this didn't mean that they didn't have them. Sooner or later, someone was going to crack open a bunker in East Corn Silo Iowa while they were looking for food or shelter. When that happened, they would either accidentally unleash hell on themselves and the local area, or they would find a Pandora 's Box of death that they could use to carve out a fiefdom through threat of melting everyone's skin from there bodies.

Shaking this thought away, Eastridge said, "What else?"

Captain Moore checked his clipboard again and continued, "The Chairman also called for a nationwide uprising at all military bases across the country. From what we've been able to gather, this order was also ignored. We received a few reports of shootings, but these were isolated. Intel says that it appears everyone is waiting to see what's really going on."

General Eastridge made a huffing noise and said, "They all saw the orders issued by The Chairman and knew what was happening, so it looks like they are on our side."

"Or on their own side, sir," Moore told him. "

Eastridge nodded somberly as he realized that his plan to bring America back under cohesive leadership might have instead fractured it. The Strategic Command had taken control of their own facilities, so how long would it be before more bases, camps and forts did the same? It wasn't like the chain of command had been looking out for their best interests by keeping them supplied with what they needed. And on top of that, their leaders were now going at it like two kids fighting over a shovel in a sandbox.

With determination in his voice, Eastridge proclaimed, "We can bring everyone back together, but first, we need to establish some kind of leadership. To do that, we have to eliminate The Chairman. Once that's been done, we can take control and release the supplies he was holding back for his world domination plans."

"Supplies, sir?" Moore asked.

Eastridge nodded and said, "We have stockpiles of ammunition, food and fuel scattered across the country that we have orders not to release. The Chairman was hoarding them for use in his invasion of the Far East and Russia. They're not huge caches, but they can be used to keep everyone going until we find a way to deal with the dead."

Recalling something, Moore started flipping through the pages of his clipboard. With everything that had been going on at the time, he had mostly forgotten the incident. Stopping, he refreshed his memory as he scanned a sheet of paper for a few seconds before saying, "I remember this coming through. We also received a report from Fort Polk. They were in contact with a group that claims to have someone that is immune to the HWNW virus. I took the call myself."

Excited, Eastridge tried to sit up. Wincing at the pain in his hip, he lowered himself as he grunted out, "What was the outcome?"

"I ordered them to make their way to the research facility in Arkansas by any means possible, sir," Moore told him. Seeing the look of despair on the General's face, he continued in a worried voice, "I didn't know what resources we had under our control and you were unconscious at the time. I took the call when we were storming the Capitol so everything was pretty hectic. Is it important, sir?"

Knowing that the Captain had no idea what was going on, General Eastridge said, "It's very important." Seeing the crestfallen look on his aide's face, he continued quickly, "But it's not your fault, you didn't know what was going on. Now, we'll just have to do the best we can to clean it up. This was the only contact with this group?"

"That was it, sir," Moore said.

Gathering his thoughts, Eastridge said, "I need you to get in contact with Fort Polk. Have them get back in contact with this group and find out exactly where they are. Then, I want you to use every asset at our disposal to get them safely to the research facility in Russellville. I don't give a damn if it's by helicopter, plane or mule train. Just get them there. When they arrive, they are to contact the commander of the base, Major Cage, and only him. I also need you to send a message to Cage to expect them. The Captain knows to pull out all the stops to bring them in."

"Anything else, sir?" Moore asked.

Pointing toward the direction of the Capitol building, General Eastridge answered, "First things first. Before you get on the horn to Polk, I need you to blow that son-of-a-bitch out of his bunker so we can get on with this thing,"

Jasper, Texas:

After handing the last of the backpacks through the hatch to Heather, Steve stuck his head inside and looked with trepidation at interior of the plane. With the sun shining through the windows to light up the earth tone seats and bulkheads, it appeared inviting, but his thoughts were that it looked like a tube shaped coffin. Using any excuse to delay the inevitable, he turned to see if there was anything else that needed to be done before he climbed on board. Noting that their packs had been loaded and everyone else was already seated inside, he realized that the only thing missing from the airplane was him. Spotting Rick Styles coming toward him, he felt relief at the reprieve.

Holding out his hand to the approaching man, Steve said, "I want to thank you for doing this for us. I don't think we could have made it all the way to Arkansas on our own."

"Don't worry about it," Rick replied as he grasped the outstretched hand. "You're helping me out by taking Stacey somewhere safe."

"I still don't understand why you think it will be safer for her at a military base," Steve said. "Fort Redoubt could probably hold off any attack by the Zs as well or even better."

Rick smiled and said, "It's not about what's outside the camp trying to get in, it's about what's inside of Stacey trying to get out. Ever since she lost her arm, she's had to prove that she can do anything that anyone else can do. Back at Redoubt, she's always volunteering for the hardest missions. I don't coddle her, but some of the things she tries to do are beyond her. I can't watch her twenty-four seven, but if she's got her ass planted in an Army base, they'll keep her on a short leash."

Steve nodded in understanding. Trying to stall for time so he didn't have to get on the airplane, he opened his mouth to ask an inane question. He hadn't even gotten the first syllable out of his mouth before he was interrupted by one of Rick's people calling out, "Dead-asses coming out of the woods."

Everyone spun to where the man was pointing.

At first Steve couldn't see anything, but then he spotted half a dozen lurching figures coming out of the brush at the far end of the runway. Not seeing this as a huge threat since they were so far away, he was about to turn back to Rick when a flurry of movement caught his eye. This time, he didn't have to search to see the wave of dead flooding out of the woods. Hundreds of Zs were coming out of the trees to thrash their way across the overgrowth at the end of the landing strip with more flooding onto the tarmac from both sides. Within seconds, the dead covered the south end of the runway.

As he spun and climbed up the steps into the plane, Steve heard Rick order his people to get in their vehicles as he ran for the portable generator used to start the engines. Jumping up the stairs, he spun and grabbed the ropes at either side of the folded down hatch. Heaving with all his might, he called out to Stacey, "Zs on the runway. Get us in the air. Now."

Calling back through the opening leading to the cockpit, she said, "Next stop, Arkansas."

After flipping the top portion of the hatch down and securing it, Steve looked at the open seat next to Heather. Knowing there was no way he was going to just strap himself in without knowing what was going on, he instead ducked into the cockpit and slid into the open chair.

Stacey glanced sideways at him and asked, "Do you know how to fly?"

"No idea," he answered.

"Then get the fuck off my flight deck," she told him.

Ignoring her, he looked out the front windscreen at the wave of approaching dead flesh. In just the short time since they had spotted them, the Zs had made it a quarter of the way down the runway. Worrying that they wouldn't have enough room to take off, he felt relief when he heard the engine on his side of the plane turn over a few times before catching and falling into a steady drone. Looking out the side window, he watched as Rick Styles detached a cable from the engine and hurriedly wheel a small generator away.

Reaching down to buckle his harness, Steve called out excitedly, "let's go."

Stacey only smiled and said, "I thought you didn't like to fly."

"I don't like dying either," Steve shot back. "And if we stay here, that's a sure thing. If we get into the air, I'm guessing my chances of living will improve. Not by mush though."

Motion caught Steve's eye, and he spun his head to see Rick climb into one of the SUVs. Turning to Stacey, he asked, "Where is he going? What about the other engine? He needs to start the other engine."

Twisting a knob and holding it in place, she said, "Settle down, Captain Sky, I can start one with the other once it's running."

With relief, Steve heard the other engine cough to life.

Leaning forward to get a better look at where the dead were, his relief was short lived when he saw that they were halfway down the airstrip and coming fast. Steve thought back to how they had plowed through the dead with trucks, but this was different. He didn't know much about aerodynamics, but he was pretty sure that if they hit one of the Zs on takeoff that it would be a very short flight.

Turning to urge Stacey on, he saw that she was securing a makeshift prosthesis to what remained of her arm. When she was done, she lowered its two-pronged end onto the throttle.

"You couldn't have done that earlier?" He asked.

"I don't like wearing it," she replied, "It chafes like hell."

Looking back to the approaching dead, Steve saw they were close enough now that he could make out individuals in the pack. Dirty and naked, they made a gruesome sight. Some were covered in dried blood, telling him that they had fed on something recently.

Feeling a slight jolt, he looked over to where Stacey was slowly pushing the throttle forward.

At last, his mind screamed as the plane moved forward. Despite not knowing what to do, his hands reached out as if to help. They quickly dropped to his sides though when Stacey swung her arm to the right and held the stainless steel prongs a few inches over his crotch.

In a low growling voice, she said, "If you touch anything, I'll make you a eunuch."

Sweat beaded his brow as Steve said in a calming voice, "No problem, Stacey. See, my hands are nowhere near the controls. You're flying, not me."

Huffing a quick breath from her nose, she said, "As it should be. You're some kind of control freak, you know that."

"Only when my life is in someone else's hands," he answered.

Moving her claw back to the throttle, Stacey nudged it forward. The plane gathered speed and swung slightly to the right to line up with the runway. Sunlight glinted through the cockpit glass, momentarily obscuring the dead. When it faded, they were readily apparent. It seemed like every time he looked, the dead were hundreds of feet closer.

Judging the distance to them, Steve asked, "How much room do we need to take off?"

Stacey didn't answer. Instead, her eyes scanned the dials and gauges on the control panel before saying, "I wish I had more time to let the engines warm up, but, oh well..."

Not liking the sound of her, 'oh well,' Steve closed his eyes. Feeling himself being pushed back in his seat as the plane started to move forward, he opened them a crack to peek. Ahead, he could see the dead slowly coming toward them as the plane picked up speed. His mind flashed to the equations he used to have to solve in high school as he thought, if a plane full of zombie apocalypse survivors are moving down the runway at two-hundred miles an hour, and a group of flesh-eating dead are coming toward them at five miles an hour, what time is lunch served.

Trying to shut his eyes, Steve found he was unable to keep them closed for more than a second. Giving up, he watched the impending collision. His fear rose as they closed with the dead. The engine noise seemed to roar in his ears. The plane seemed to be moving too slow. The dead seemed to be moving too fast. He felt a scream build up. He could now make out individual details of gore on the dead.

Tearing his eyes away, he looked over to where Stacey was sitting cool, calm and collected in her seat. For some reason, this angered him. He was about to scream at her and ask what she thought she was doing, when she said, "Please put your trays in the upright position. The smoking light is off and the bathroom is closed until after takeoff. Thank you for flying Dead Air."

Feeling a slight lurch, Steve whipped his head forward to see the approaching dead drop away as the plane took to the air. They were so close that he was sure that he would feel the jolt of impact with one of them that would send the plane cartwheeling down the runway. The plane's nose rose, and then all he could see was blue sky. They had made it. As his fear of collision with the herd of Zs left him, it was quickly replaced by fear of flying. Gripping the armrest until his knuckles turned white, he shut his eyes.

His mind spun with a thousand thoughts as he wondered if they had remembered to put gas in the plane, would the engines quit, would a wing suddenly fall off, can the dead fly, would they hit a flock of migrating geese...

His fears were not helped when Stacey said out of nowhere, "What are you so freaked out about. That wasn't so close, I missed that first dead-ass by at least ten feet."

Steve's mouth dropped open to reply with a sarcastic comment, but it shut with an audible snap when Stacey banked the plane hard to port, corkscrewing to gain altitude. Despite his fingers already being dug in to the armrest all the way to the metal, his grip tightened.

"Got to make sure that Dad made it out of here," she told him. After looking in his direction, she added, "If you're going to puke, there's bags in the seat pocket on your right."

Steve could only nod.

As she levelled off at three-hundred feet, she said, "Look out your window and tell me what you see."

Whipping his head to the right for a quick glance before looking back at the instrument panel, he gave a strangled, "Trees."

"Come on, you wanted to be up here," she said disdainfully. "If you're going to be up here, I need you to help me out."

Forcing his head to turn, Steve looked out of the side window. The sight of the trees and ground passing by gave him a feeling of vertigo, making it feel like his body was falling back into his seat. Shaking it off, he tried to focus on individual parts of the terrain. Spotting a long line cutting through the woods, he said, "I think I see the road we used to get to the airport."

"Yeah," Stacey replied, "That's it. Do you see their Jeeps though?"

Having something to focus on made it a little easier for Steve to look out of the airplane, but if his eyes strayed to the terrain passing below him, the vertigo came back in a rush. After a few seconds, he spotted what they were looking for.

Leaning forward, he pointed as he said excitedly, "I see them."

"I figured they would have made it further by now," Stacey commented.

The airplane dropped suddenly, causing Steve to whip his head forward and scrunch down in his seat.

Stacey laughed and said, "Don't worry, we're not going down. I'm just going to buzz them."

The plane dropped to fifty feet as she flew over the two Jeeps, wagging her wings in greeting.

Climbing again, she said to Steve, "You can quit worrying, I'm going back up again."

"Up, down, it doesn't matter," he replied miserably. "The only difference is that when the engines quit and we fall from the sky at a greater height, I just have a few more seconds to scream."

After leveling the plane at five-hundred feet, Stacey banked slightly to port as she said, "We're going to check on that herd to the west of Redoubt. I'm going to need you to act as a spotter again when we get close."

Raising a hand in acknowledgement, Steve said, "Just let me know when you need me to help. In the meantime, I'll be over here pretending that I'm really on a train."

The engine's steady drone was interrupted a few minutes later, when Stacey said in a soft voice, "I Guess I won't need your help after all."

Curiosity overcame Steve's fear at her tone. Looking out the window, he saw a ribbon of road leading off to the west. Nothing out of the ordinary, he thought to himself. Then he noticed that the road itself seemed to be moving. Thinking it was the vertigo again, he shook his head and looked again. This time, he realized that for as far as he could see, the road was filled with the dead.

His fear of flying leaving him immediately, Steve leaned forward for a better look as he asked, "Can you tell what direction they're moving?"

"Directly for the fort," Stacey answered as she leaned forward to turn a dial on the control panel to her right. Pulling her boom microphone closer to her mouth, she said, "Fort Redoubt, Fort Redoubt, this is Air One, over."

Steve looked around and found his headset, putting it on in enough time to hear, "Air One, this is Redoubt, over." Even after she cleared her throat, Steve could still hear the tension in it when Stacey said, "You have a large herd of dead-asses numbering in the thousands approaching your location on sixty-three, over."

"We are aware of that, Air One," Redoubt answered.

"I'm coming back. The airfield is overrun so I'm going to land in the open field to the southwest of the water treatment plant. Have someone there to meet me, over," Stacey told him.

"Negative, negative," Redoubt answered. "We have been in contact with Commander Styles and he said to tell you that under no circumstances are you to return. He is aware of the situation and he said to tell you that if you come back, he will duct tape you to your seat and make you fly to Arkansas. What you are doing right now is more important, over."

Steve turned to Stacey, opening his mouth to tell her how imperative it was that they get to the base in Russellville. Seeing the internal battle she was going through written on her face, he chose to remain silent. He knew that since it was her home and what was left of her family were being threatened, nothing he said could change her mind. If anything, his pleas might turn her away from him.

After a moment, she said quietly, "Roger that, Redoubt. Inform the Commander that I am staying on course, but if I can find enough fuel, I'm coming back, over."

"Roger that, Air One," Redoubt replied. "Be informed that we are shutting down the radio. We need all the power from the generators for the fence. If you do make it back, you will be landing on your own. My Guard unit is getting ready to leave for the outer fence, so I have to go. Good luck to you, Air One. Over and out."

Stacey said, "Good luck back at you, Redoubt. This Air One, over and out."

Banking to starboard, she turned the plane on a heading to the east. This brought them within sight of Fort Redoubt, and she and Steve looked at it as they flew over. When it was nothing but a memory, Stacey banked the small airplane north-northeast on a heading toward Arkansas. They had been too high to see the frenzied preparations going on in and around it, but they both knew they had people they loved down there getting ready for the waves of dead flesh coming at them.

CHAPTER EIGHTEEN

Russellville, Arkansas:

Major Jedidiah Cage leaned over his desk as he traced the numerous roads leading into the area. With so many different ways the group coming from Texas could take, he thought to himself that he might as well enlist a psychic to guess which one they would use.

Sitting across from him, Staff Sergeant Fagan said, "Give it a break, sir. Even if they left this morning, they won't be close to us for days."

Without looking up, Cage said, "I feel like I have to do something. Any more word from Polk about them?"

"Negative, sir," Fagan answered. "The last word we received was about half an hour ago. Polk said that they tried to contact them again but they were off the air. Like I told you, after that initial contact, no one has heard from them. They did intercept some secondary radio traffic about a huge group of Zs moving into the area, but that was all."

Almost to himself, Cage said, "Then they're probably already on the move." Motioning for the Staff Sergeant to join him, he asked, "Where did you say they were coming from again?"

Fagan levered himself out of his chair and bent over the map. After studying it for a few seconds, he pointed to a spot on it and said, "The guy at Polk told me they were holed up with a bunch of Militia just south of this lake."

Looking at the possible routes they might take from there, Cage said, "We need to meet them as far out as possible and bring them in. If I were them, I would take the most direct route. They're going to have use secondary roads though because the freeways are one huge traffic jam and they cut through the major cities. That leaves about two dozen dirt roads and two-lane blacktops we'll need to patrol."

"Too many for us to cover," Fagan commented. "We've don't have the manpower or the resources to do any kind of recon in force over that wide an area. On top of that, what if they cut cross-country? The best we can do is wait for them to contact us. I'm sure they'll have a CB radio with them so we just have to wait until they come into range."

Knowing the Staff Sergeant was right, Cage leaned back as he said, "So you're telling me that we put our thumb back up our ass and sit here until we hear from them."

A knock on the door interrupted them.

With a raised eyebrow, Fagan said, "Maybe that's them, sir."

Ignoring him, Major Cage said, "Come in."

The radio operator that had replaced Jimmy McPherson entered and handed Cage a pile of communication slips. The Major dismissed him, but the man stood dancing from foot to foot until Cage gave him a questioning, "Yes?"

Tom thought about whether to answer or to just spin around and leave. He wasn't regular military or even National Guard. In fact, before Z-day, his only job had been working the drive-thru at Taco Bell. He had been conscripted in one of the first manpower drives, and ever since had regretted not finding a better place to hide from the dead and the living.

Half in question, half in statement, he finally said, "You gave orders to let you know about all messages coming in that are from a group heading our way from Texas, sir."

Rifling through the papers in his hand, Cage asked, "Have we heard from them already?"

"We did, sir," the radioman told him, "but the transcript of the conversation isn't in there."

Losing patience, Cage spit out, "Then where the fuck is it and why didn't you call me when they first made contact?"

Cowed by the outburst, Tom took a step backward.

In a calm voice, Fagan said, "Relax and tell me and the Major what's going on."

Tom took a deep breath and said, "I started to contact you right away but one of Sergeant Cain's men was with me. He told me that if I called you or told anyone about what was happening that Hawkins would use me in one of his experiments. That's why I didn't call you, sir. He also took my notes before I could reproduce them, sirs."

Fagan and Cage exchanged a look. Up until now, they had been the ones trying to sabotage the Malectron, but maybe the tables had turned.

"Think back, Tom," Fagan said in an even voice. "What did they say?"

Swallowing hard, Tom said, "I'll tell you, but you have to promise to protect me. I've heard stories about what goes on in the basement of that farmhouse, sirs."

His voice icy, Cage said, "How's this for a deal, if you don't tell me everything they said, what Hawkins does to you will pale in comparison to what I'll do to you."

Feeling trapped, Tom wished he had never heard of the Hawkins, the Army, Arkansas, or Major Cage. Seeing no way out of this, he said, "They contacted us about ten minutes ago. They do have a little girl that was bitten a couple times by one of the dead and never turned, and they said that they're bringing her here."

"Did they say which road they were using?" Cage asked.

Shaking his head, Tom replied, "None of them, sir."

Knowing that time was of the essence and the sooner they knew the route, the faster they could get a squad out to find these people and bring them to safety, Fagan asked abruptly. "Then how are they getting here?"

Imagined scenes of his torture in the cellar of the farmhouse suddenly crept into Tom's mind. Stopping to consider again who really had the power in the camp and who could protect him, he hesitated. In the silence of the office, Fagan's question was answered by the faint sound of aircraft engines.

***

Sitting in his private quarters on the third floor of the farmhouse, Professor Hawkins read through the notes before asking his second in command, "Has anyone else seen these?"

"Only my man and the radio operator," Cain answered.

"The radio operator," Hawkins said with disgust. "So that means that everyone in the camp knows what's going on by now."

"My man couldn't kill him in the comm-shack," Cain explained. "Too many people knew he was in there alone him. He had to settle for threatening him to keep his mouth shut."

"Do you think he'll remain silent?" Hawkins asked.

Cain thought about it for a second before answering, "He's a conscript so he doesn't have any love for the Army. My guess is he'll eventually say something though. My man had the radio guy tell the people on the plane that we would have someone meet them when they landed."

Dropping the notes onto the top of his desk, Hawkins said, "Then we have to move quickly. I want you to get a squad together and head out to the airport as fast as you can. I want the little girl alive if you can manage it since I'd like to eventually examine her. If that proves to be impossible, you may kill her along with her escort. This way, we keep the focus on the Malectron and not a cure to the HWNW virus."

Cain was about to ask a question when the faint sound of aircraft engines caused him move to the window. Joined by Hawkins, the two men watched as a small plane passed by in the distance. Looking down, they saw that this was no cause for interest to any of the men and women in sight. Planes and helicopters occasionally flew by, but the only aircraft that drew there attention was the resupply chopper.

"That's got to be them," Cain pointed out.

"Then you need to get moving," Hawkins ordered him.

As he was about to turn from the window, movement caught Cain's eye. Looking toward Major Cage's office, he could see him standing in front of it with Staff Sergeant Fagan and the radio operator. Fagan pointed toward the airplane and said something to Cage. As he watched, the Major gave orders to three of his men who started double-timing it toward the motor pool.

"Shit," Cain cursed. "Now it's going to be a race to see who can get to the girl first."

As he started to move toward the door, Hawkins halted him by saying, "Don't bother, they've got a head start so here's no way you can beat them. The best you can hope to do is to show up second and try to kill everyone. We both know that there's little chance of that since you will be outgunned. On top of that, the minute they see you getting ready to go out, they'll know something's up."

"So what do we do," Cain almost whined.

Hawkins thought for a moment before asking, "What's the news from Washington DC?"

"Not too good," Cain answered. "It looks like the Chairman is going to lose."

Hawkins waved this off and said, "Then we need to approach whoever ends up in charge. It doesn't matter if they're right wing, left wind or a chicken wing, they will want the Malectron. If they're fighting each other for power, the winner will want the ultimate weapon at their disposal."

"But what about Connors and her anti-virus?" Cain asked. "She can complete it now that she has someone that's immune to the disease. We can't be completely sure the new leaders will choose the Malectron over a way to eradicate the dead, and with no dead to control, we lose our power base."

A sick smile twisted across Hawkins features as he said, "Then we need to keep that from happening. Contact Washington DC on behalf of Doctor Connors and report that the anti-virus is ineffective and all further testing is being suspended. In addition, tell them that foreign troops have been spotted in the area and I request immediate evacuation lest the Malectron fall into enemy hands. This will get them moving since the Malectron will be their only option. Once you have confirmation that we are to be picked up, I want you to destroy the radio. Make it look like an accident, we don't need to tip our hand too soon."

Warily, Cain said, "But Cage and his men control the camp. When the evac team shows up, they'll find out that there is an anti-virus. We don't know who's going to be in charge, and they may decide to go with a way to wipe out the dead rather than control them."

Making a tsking noise, Hawkins shook his head in mock sadness as he said, "Yee of little faith. By the time they arrive there won't be an anti-virus."

Russellville Regional Airport:

Jimmy McPherson came to with a buzzing in his ears. In the fuzzy state between being asleep and awake, he waved his hands at the gnats he imagined flying around them. As he became more aware, he realized that it was still to cool out for flies. Shrugging it off, he didn't care what it was as long as it went away. Pulling his field jacket up over his head to block whatever was annoying him, seconds later he pulled it away when the buzzing grew into a loud drone.

Popping up from the rear seat of the abandoned helicopter, he looked up just in time to see a two-engine plane fly low over the airfield. Watching as it banked gracefully to line up with the end of the runway, he squinted his eyes to see its markings. If they were military, he would run. If they were civilian, he would lay low. The reasoning behind this was that while the military would check out everything in the area while civilians would take one look at the wreck of a helicopter he was hiding in and dismiss it as holding anything useful. With its engine, rotor and fuel tank missing, it was nothing but a shell. And while it would never fly again, with doors that locked from the inside, it suited Jimmy's needs perfectly.

The plane grew in size as it approached, sunlight glinting off its aluminum fuselage. This told Jimmy what he needed to know. From his own personal experience, he knew that anything and everything the Army bought, borrowed, appropriated or stole was immediately blotched with earth tone paint to break up its outline. He could never figure out why they did this with aircraft though since it made them stick out.

The airplane slowly dropped out of the sky to land gracefully on the runway. Ducking down, Jimmy watched as it taxied to the center of a large concrete parking apron a hundred feet away. After rolling to a stop, its engines continued to idle.

Smart move, Jimmy thought to himself. They just dropped into an unknown situation so they're keeping ready to take off at a second's notice.

The hatch dropped from the side of the fuselage and a man jumped down to scan his surroundings. He was followed quickly by a woman and a younger man who spread out to join him in checking the area. Jimmy was pleased in his assessment of his hiding place as none of them paid it any attention beyond an uninterested glance. They weren't the Army, but whenever their gaze did turned in his direction he ducked down. Your average group of looters and brigands didn't usually land in an airplane, but it was better to be safe than sorry.

***

After restraining the urge to kiss the ground when he exited the airplane, Steve focused on the immediate area as he checked for threats coming toward them from the hangers and maintenance buildings that made up the airfield. The nearest structures had their huge sliding doors open revealing a scattering of equipment and aircraft inside, while the buildings that were further away looked like they were closed up tight. He wasn't too concerned about the ones that were further away since if anything came at them from that direction they would have plenty of warning. Switching his attention to a long, low building, he guessed it had once been the main terminal. It was hard to tell though since its floor to ceiling windows had all been smashed out by looters before a fire had gutted its interior. He was relieved that the airfield was too small to have a control tower, knowing it would make the perfect spot for a sniper.

The dead were not the only thing they had to be cautious about.

From his right, Heather called out, "I'm clear all the way out to the woods."

"What about Brain?" Steve asked.

Turning so that she could see him on the other side of the airplane, she got a thumbs up from the tech.

"He's good," she relayed.

Returning to the hatch, Steve called inside, "Shut it down, Stacey but stay at the controls. You can all get out and stretch if you want to. I want everyone to stay close to the plane though."

The engines wound down, making it easier for him to hear as Heather asked, "How long do you think it will take for them to get here?"

Steve shrugged and replied, "I'm guessing an hour tops."

Coming down the stairs with Pep, Cindy said, "But it only took us a few minutes to get here."

Standing next to Igor as they waited for her, Linda laughed and said, "But they have to take the roads, honey." Seeing her disappointment, she added, "Don't worry, we're almost there."

The words, 'almost there' echoed in Steve's head as he scanned the area for threats. It was hard to believe that after making their way out of Clearwater, across the Gulf of Mexico and then through a deserted wasteland where everything wanted to kill them that they were 'almost there'. He wanted to relax and let relief wash over him at making it, but until they were safe inside a secure area, he knew he couldn't.

"Well, I hope they get here soon," Cindy said. "I ate something at breakfast that's giving me a Hasidic stomach."

Everyone laughed while Steve corrected, "That's acidic, kiddo."

"Whatever it is," she continued without missing a beat, "someone needs to give me a Valium."

Their laughter grew louder at her mimicry of Steve.

Connie came down the steps last, her head swiveling as she took in the deserted airfield. After a few seconds, she said, "This place gives me the creeps. Why couldn't we stay in the air until the people from the Army get here?"

"Not enough fuel to keep circling," Steve told her. "Besides, we've got good line of sight at anything coming for us so we're safe until the cavalry arrives."

"And there they are," Linda said with glee as she pointed toward a two and a half-ton military truck turning from the highway onto a frontage road that led to the end of the runway.

"That was fast," Heather commented. She smiled and added in Steve's direction, "And I thought the cavalry was supposed to show up in the nick of time."

"Maybe they were out on patrol and got a call to come pick us up," Steve surmised. "Whatever the case, I don't want to hang around here any longer than we have to." Turning to Connie, he said, "You and Linda grab the packs from the plane."

Her voice rising in excitement as she headed for the hatch of the airplane, Connie said, "Oh my god, I never thought I would live to see this day." After a few seconds, she added, "Literally." Before climbing the stairs, she crouched down and called out to Brain, "They're here to pick us up, babe. We made it."

Brain's reply was lost on Steve as he studied the approaching truck. It was obviously military issue, but there was something wrong with it. As it came closer, he realized that it wasn't the truck itself but the people piled in back of it that had caught his attention. Wearing a collection of colored t-shirts, tank tops or nothing but skin, they looked anything but military. Wondering if discipline had dropped to the point where the officers couldn't even keep their people in uniform, he resolved to keep his weapon with him at all times. Once the little things began to get thrown by the wayside, the bigger things like theft and murder were easier to get away with.

The truck slowed and turned sideways when it was fifty feet from them. This was when Steve saw that everyone in the bed had some kind of weapon pointing at them.

***

Jimmy's fear rose as he watched the truck approach. Now that soldiers from the base were here, he would have to move. He knew they would spread out in a defensive perimeter when they stopped, and this meant they would search any place that might hold a threat. Since the helicopter he was hiding in was only a short distance away, it would definitely get a once over. Looking back over his shoulder, he could see the tree line only a short distance away. He had planned numerous escape routes in his mind, but now he would have to see how they panned out in real life.

"Keep it simple like you planned," he said to himself. "Get out of the far side of this wreck. Start walking backward toward the woods while keeping the chopper between you and them, and if anyone sees you, run like hell."

Calmed by his own voice, he watched the truck as it neared, readying his body to move as soon as he saw he was clear. Recognizing the vehicle as the same one that had passed him yesterday, he reconsidered making a break for it. He knew that the brigands had seen the plane land and had come to investigate, so why would they bother with a broken down wreck of a helicopter when they had what they came for right in front of them?

The truck slewed sideways and came to a halt, finalizing his decision to stay put. With the airplane, helicopter and truck making a large triangle with him at the bottom, either the people from the plane or the brigands would spot him before he was a quarter of the way to the woods.

Having heard stories from the survivors of gang raids, Jimmy knew they stuck to a pretty simple mode of operation. They would steal, rape, kill, and then move on. Knowing that rape wasn't only for women, he slid further down in the foot well of the helicopter and hoped they didn't spot him.

***

Steve started to raise his assault rifle when a voice called out from the cab of the truck, "I wouldn't do that if I were you. Let's keep this a robbery and not a homicide. We've got every one of you in the kill zone and there's nothing you can do about it. All we want is your food, supplies and guns. If you cooperate, we'll be on our way in a few minutes. I want all of you to set your guns on the ground in front of you and back away from them. Don't worry, we got no plans to hurt you."

Laughter from the back of the truck told Steve otherwise. Knowing they weren't in a good position for an all-out firefight, he slowly lowered his M4 but didn't set it down. Wanting the attention on him so he could give Linda and Igor time to get Cindy out of the line of fire, he said, "How can we trust you?"

"You can't," the voice answered. "But if you don't drop your weapons, we'll kill you where you stand."

Eyeing the numerous automatic rifles and three M60 machine guns aimed at them, Steve wondered why they hadn't gone ahead and killed them when they rolled up. With the firepower they had, they could have shredded everyone in his group before any of them had a chance to shoot back. Looking closely at one of the machine guns, his eyes moved to the other two before scanning the heavy machine guns mounted on the front and back of the truck. Now he knew the reason.

Raising his M4 and pointing it directly into the cab of the truck, Steve smiled evilly as he said, "How about this, if *you* don't drop your weapons, we'll cut *you* down."

The voice from the cab asked, "Are you crazy? We've got the drop on you."

Knowing he had called it right by the slight tone of fear in the man's voice, Steve gave a half laugh and said, "Those M60's are belt fed and I don't see any belts in them. The .50 calibers don't even have an ammo box attached to them. If you're going to bluff, at least make it realistic. Some of your guys in the back of the truck might have a few rounds in their magazines, but none of your heavy weapons have any bullets. That evens the odds up enough for me."

Turning his head to the right, Steve could see that Heather had her CAR-15 aimed at the men in the back of the truck. Beyond her, he spotted Brain crouched behind the landing gear of the airplane, his rifle at the ready. Looking up, he saw two shadowy figures in the hatch. He couldn't tell which one was Connie and which one was Stacey, but the outline of their rifles were unmistakable. Slowly spinning his head to his left, he spotted Igor and Linda standing in front of Cindy, their weapons at the ready. Pep crouched next to them, baring her teeth.

The voice from the cab called out angrily, "The heavy guns might be out of ammo, but we have more than enough firepower without them to blow you away. Now drop your weapons."

Steve straightened his posture and said, "I don't believe you. You drop your weapons."

"You drop your guns, I told you first," the voice bullied.

"And I told you second and two's bigger than one," Steve retorted. Wanting to break the impasse he added, "Let's start out like this, you lower your weapons and we'll lower ours. Everyone is nervous and I don't want any accidents."

Exaggerating his movements, Steve slowly moved his M4 from where he had it shouldered to port arms. A few of the men in the truck mimicked him, giving him hope that they could find a peaceful end to this situation. Motioning to Heather, he watched out of the corner of his eye as she lowered her rifle to point at the ground. One by one, everyone on both sides pointed the barrel of their weapon away from human flesh.

Steve knew this was a risk, but he had to defuse the situation. The situation still might turn into the Wild West in half a heartbeat, but he consoled himself with the knowledge that Stacey and Connie were still on target. Hidden in the darkness of the plane, they were practically invisible.

"Now why don't you put your truck and gear and take off," Steve suggested. "No harm, no foul. You go your way and we'll go ours. Just so you know, we were in contact with the Army before we landed and they should be here any minute now to pick us up."

No reply came from the cab and the vehicle stayed where it was. Steve noted that the men in the bed of the truck who had been manning the heavier machine guns had backed away from them and picked up rifles. Not automatic rifles, but hunting rifles. Seeing their bluff had been called, the others in the back had set their automatic rifles down and picked up pistols and small rifles. This told him that they did have some ammunition, just not enough for the rapid fire weapons. The question now was if their leader was crazy enough to put his men up against a well-armed group.

Even though they had the people in the truck outgunned, Steve knew he and his group were vulnerable out in the open. Turning to look, he could see Linda and Igor edging Cindy toward the airplane. Not the best of cover, but it was the only game in town. He knew that no one on his side was going to open fire unless attacked, so it all depended on what the man in the cab of the truck chose to do.

***

Jimmy watched with interest as what had started off as robbery, rape and murder turned into a Mexican standoff. He had felt sorry for the people in the airplane when the truck rolled up and the men in back drew down on them, but now it looked like they were holding their own. They had even gotten the bad guys to lower their guns.

Reconsidering his initial assessment of their character now that he had a chance to compare them side by side with a real gang, he realized that they didn't appear to be the usual sort of riff-raff that roamed the country preying on their fellow man. They were clean looking, well-armed, had women and a little girl with them, and on top of that had arrived in an airplane. Most of the roving gangs on the road today were lucky to find enough fuel to make it from point A to point B and then have enough ammo to raid point B. They were made up mostly of men, and he had never heard of any of them having children with them.

Looking down the length of the truck, Jimmy watched the driver's side door of the cab slowly open and a man cautiously climb out. Reaching inside, he pulled out a scope equipped rifle and crouched down next to gas tank. He could see him clearly from his vantage point, but he knew there was no way the people from the airplane could.

When everyone had put up their guns, Jimmy thought it was over, but it looked like the bad guys were going to try an ambush.

Looking back over his shoulder at the nearby woods, he knew that with everyone's attention on each other that he could easily slip away. His mind screamed out to him that this was someone else's battle and that all he was trying to do was get home to Louisiana and find his family. With this though in his head, he lifted his body to slide backwards and make his escape.

Before his chest lost contact with the metal floor of the cockpit though, his heart took over from his brain and he reached up to unlatch the cockpit door in front of him.

***

Heather caught movement out of the corner of her eye. Turning her head slightly, she could see the door of the abandoned helicopter open slightly and the barrel of a rifle poke out. Her body started to react and bring her CAR-15 up but she stopped when she saw the weapon wasn't pointed at them. Its angle was all wrong. The door would have to be opened fully before it could be brought to bear on them.

Despite catching her reaction in time, she still gave a visible twitch. This motion caused the men in the truck to raise their rifles and pistols before also checking themselves. A ripple went through both sides as they all flinched before slowly moving back to positions of readiness. None of them went as far as to actually point their weapons at anyone, but it was close.

Glancing back toward the helicopter, Heather judged the angle of the rifle barrel and determined it was aimed at the far side of the truck. Wondering who their anonymous ally was, she also wondered what he was aiming at. Looking under the truck, she could see the shadow of someone moving on the other side of it. Shifting her position slightly to the right, she could see a small section of color between the cab and the bed. Squinting, she could see it was faded yellow cloth. Someone wearing a t-shirt.

In a voice only loud enough for Steve to hear, she said, "Get ready, Babe, because it's about to be on like Donkey Kong."

***

Steve felt his body tense at Heather's warning. Although it seemed like the situation was being slowly defused, he trusted her judgment. Not seeing a clear shot at anything in the cab of the truck, he picked out his first two targets from the men in the bed and waited.

***

Jimmy sighted in on the head of the sniper and slowly squeezed the trigger of his rifle, its report almost deafening him in the confines of the cockpit when it fired. With ringing ears, he shifted his aim to the men in the back of the truck and opened up with three round bursts until his magazine ran out of bullets.

***

Despite knowing something was coming, Steve still jumped when the shot rang out. Recovering in milliseconds, he brought his M4 up as his body crouched to present less of a target. Knowing if he sprayed the back of the truck with bullets that his chances of hitting something were greatly reduced, he forced himself to slow down and fire well aimed, three-round bursts into the heads of his enemies.

As he switched from his first target to his second, the thought came to him that he should be aiming for center mass to increase his chances of hitting something. Having dealt with the dead for so long though, his initial reaction was to aim for the head.

Switching to a third target, Steve didn't even get the chance to pull the trigger, watching as the man's chest blossomed red from someone else's bullets. Not seeing any other immediate threats in the bed of the truck, he turned his rifle on its cab. He couldn't see anyone inside, but this didn't stop him from emptying the remains of his magazine into it. After extracting it and inserting a new one, he jumped up into a half crouch and moved forward.

As he approached the truck, he could see that while the brigands appeared ready for a gunfight, they weren't prepared for the automatic weapons fire that tore into them. Hearing screams of, "I give, I give," and, "we surrender," he knew that the fight was over.

Not wanting to lose the shock brought on by their assault, Steve started screaming, "Drop your guns and get out. Put them down and get out now or we'll kill you."

No one moved, so he fired a three-round burst into the air to punctuate his demand.

Two men jumped up and literally threw themselves over the rear gate of the truck before dropping spread eagle on the ground. Heather moved up to cover them while Steve kept an eye out for any kind of ambush. He doubted they were organized enough to plan something complex like drawing their attention by having a couple of them surrender while the rest of them popped up to gun them down, but anyone still alive in the back of the truck might take advantage of the situation.

"Everyone out," Steve screamed as he fired a burst from his M4 into the rear of the cab, shattering the glass in its back window.

One of the men on the ground screamed, "There's no one else. You killed everyone."

Pointing to the abandoned helicopter, Heather said, "That's where the first shot came from."

Steve spun, raising his rifle as Heather said, "They weren't shooting at us, they shot at these scumbags. I don't know who it was but I think they're on our side."

Steve motioned toward the helicopter with his rifle and called out loud enough to be heard by everyone, "Keep the chopper covered, I'm checking the truck." He didn't know if anyone besides Heather was alive to hear him, but it was a moot point to check on them until the area was clear. One of the bandits was in his way, so he stepped over the prone men and cautiously looked in.

Candy wrappers, assorted garbage and sheets of cardboard littered its floor along with seven bodies. Bloody and torn, they gave proof to the accuracy of his group's aim. Hearing a gurgling moan, Steve saw a hand raise up in supplication. Following it down to the body it was attached to, he saw blood pouring from wounds in the man's chest and stomach. Doing the only thing he could for him, he fired once into his head. Moving around to the far side of the truck he saw a body lying on the ground. Keeping it covered as he approached, he nudged it with the toe of his boot, stepping back when the top of its head came off.

No threat there, he told himself as he moved to the cab. The driver's door was ajar so he eased it open with the barrel of his M4 before looking in. Riddled with bullet holes, it was empty.

With the threat gone, Steve quickly rounded the front of the truck and turned his attention to his people.

Fear tore through him when he saw Linda and Igor lying on the ground with Pep running around them in circles. Starting to move forward, he called their names in panic. Not seeing Cindy, his fear turned into a full blown panic. Calling out again, he was relieved when he saw Igor raise a hand and give him a thumbs up. Looking closer, he realized that Cindy's two bodyguards had thrown themselves in front of her to keep her safe.

Looking toward the hatch of the airplane, he saw Connie and Stacey emerge with their weapons at the ready. Connie looked at the bullet riddled truck with wide eyes while Stacey took one look at the bullet holes in her plane and started cursing. From behind the front landing gear, Brain emerged and headed toward the helicopter at a fast trot, his M4 tacking back and forth along its length as he searched for threats. Reaching it, he leaned against the fuselage and sidled up to the now closed door. Bobbing his head forward and back, he took a quick look inside. Turning, he called out, "All clear. Whoever was in it took off."

Searching the tree line for any movement, Steve saw nothing. The phantom sniper was gone. Turning back to survey the area, he noticed that Igor and Linda were still covering Cindy with their bodies. The encounter had been short and murderous but they had all made it through alive. Now it was time to get the hell out of Dodge City.

"It's all clear," he called out to Igor. "You can get up now."

Igor lifted his hand and moved it back and forth.

At first thinking he was giving him an okay, it suddenly dawned on Steve that he was waving him over. Looking closely, he saw two pools of blood coming from where Igor lay in a tangle with Linda. Reaching them in seconds, he saw Igor's leg bent at an unnatural angle. Looking closely, he saw a nasty exit wound in the back of his leg. Calling for the medical bag, he found it being handed to him by Heather.

"Looks like a shattered femur," he told her as she moved to check on Linda. Hearing a gasp, he turned to where she was looking in shock at the shattered remains of the woman's head.

In a strained voice, Igor said, "We both fired as we pulled Cindy down and got in front of her. There were bullets ricocheting everywhere. I laid on my side and kept shooting. Then it felt like someone hit me in the leg with a ball bat. I looked down and saw a bullet had gone through my thigh and hit Linda. Nothing I could do for her so I kept shooting until there was no one left to shoot at."

Pressing a bandage against the leg wound to stem the flow of blood, Steve looked up to check on Cindy, feeling his heart stop when he saw Heather pick up a small, limp, blood splattered form.

Seeing the look of horror on his face, Heather said, “It’s not her blood. She didn’t get hit. It’s Linda’s blood. She’s in shock.” Turning, she yelled, “Someone grab my sleeping bag.”

Laying Cindy down, Heather lifted her legs to elevate them. Connie showed up seconds later and spread the sleeping bag over the little girl before asking what else she could do.

“Talk to her,” Heather said.

Connie’s heart went out to Cindy as she knelt next to her, holding her hands and telling her that everything would be okay. The poor kid had lost so many people that there was no way she would make it through this unscarred.

Steve tightened the bandage on Igor’s leg and leaned back. The man wasn’t going to bleed to death, but there was no way they could move him very far. Looking to where Cindy lay, he times that by two. Knowing the gunfire would attract every Z for miles, he considered the buildings that made up the airport. They needed something they could defend with only a few people.

Finally deciding on what looked like a small maintenance shed, he was about to give the order to move when he heard Brain call out, “Two more trucks coming in.”

Spinning around, Steve studied the approaching vehicles, his mind spinning with how they were going to kill everyone in them. Looking over to where their two prisoners lay spread eagle on the concrete, he considered using them as hostages. Discarding this as the bandits wouldn’t care about their lives, he decided to use them as human shields.

It might be barbaric, he thought, but I was planning on executing them anyway. They might be scumbags in life, but they would prove useful in death.

Scanning the immediate area for cover, he saw there were only two possibilities. Deciding quickly that they would put Cindy inside the plane with Igor and Stacey at the hatch, he looked to where he would position the rest of them in a defensive position behind the truck.

Looking again at the approaching vehicles, he started counting the number of men in the back of the trucks. He had only gotten to three when he suddenly stopped. Dressed in full military regalia, they were the exact opposite of the brigands he and his people had just dealt justice to.

Turning to where Heather stood next to him with her CAR-15 held at the ready, he said, “Relax, Babe. They may be a day late and a dollar short, but the cavalry just showed up.”

***

Jimmy watched from the woods until he saw the two trucks from the base arrive. Turning to look in the direction he planned to travel, he let out a deep sigh at the thought of the distance he needed to cover. It was hundreds of miles across a hostile landscape, but knowing he was heading home made it more than worth the dangers he would face.

Whispering to himself, “Confucius say that the journey of a thousand miles starts with a busted radiator hose,” he took his first step.

CHAPTER NINTEEN

Fort Redoubt:

Exhausted, Tick-Tock slid down from where he had been sitting on the back of the pickup truck before closing the tailgate and leaning against it. Studying the frenzied activity around the front of the fort, he focused on the people making ammunition for the porcupine. Just back from an ambush on the horde of approaching dead, he wanted to call out to them that there weren't enough darts in the world to stem the coming tide of Zs.

Turning his attention to the walls of the fort, he considered whether or not they would hold. He wasn't an engineer but he doubted they would stand for more than a few hours. On his first patrol, they had circled around to the rear of the herd to try and draw them off to the west and he had seen firsthand how different types of structures held up against the dead.

It was simple, he thought, if the Zs wanted to get inside something, they got in. With their crushing weight of numbers, they literally flattened everything in their path. Not everything, he reminded himself. Just the buildings that held the living. It didn't matter if they were made out of poured concrete or steel, after the dead hit them, they looked like someone had run them over with a bulldozer.

Deciding he had just enough time to stop in and visit Denise before he went out again, his plans were interrupted by Rick Styles calling out from the gate, "Hey, Tick-Tock, we just got the latest info from the recon teams so we need all the platoon commanders in the mess hall for a meeting." After waving for him to hurry and calling, "Come on," he disappeared inside the fort.

Running after him, Tick-Tock hoped he could get the low down and skip the meeting so he could visit Denise before going out again. If there was one thing he didn't need right now it was to waste time on a meeting.

Catching the commander halfway across the courtyard, he asked, "How bad is it?"

"Not as bad as it could be," Rick answered. "If aliens landed right now it would really suck."

Tick-Tock smiled and said, "So what you're saying is that we only have to worry about being turned into a meat sandwich instead of being vaporized by a Martian death ray."

"You got it," Rick told him. "Always look on the bright side."

Entering the mess hall, Tick-Tock didn't recognize any of the thirty or forty men and women gathered there. Feeling slightly self-conscious, he wished he were back with his own people. He had been given command of two platoons earlier in the day and he knew this is where he belonged. Meetings and planning sessions were great, but action was better. Of all the briefings he had attended when he was in the Marine Corps, most had been BS sessions with no real aim or purpose other than to tell you things you already knew.

Rick entered after him, causing everyone to come to attention. The Commander waved them to their seats as he said to Tick-Tock in a quiet voice, "Now you get to see my General Patton imitation." After a second, he added, "Or maybe General Custer in this situation."

Tick-Tock smiled, thinking that it might not be that bad. Rick had a no-nonsense style about him that seemed to cut through the bullshit and get right to business.

Walking to a map of the area pinned to the wall, Rick said, "This is a brief overview of our situation. We have our backs to the lake and we have a group of dead-asses coming at us from the southeast and an even larger group coming at us from the west. We've had little to no success drawing them off or wiping them out due to their size. We circle around them and pick at them, but we can't seem to turn them away from us. Our best guess is that the herds are so big that we can't attract enough of them to turn them.

"Our estimates are that the group from the southeast will hit the two, smaller forts in about two hours. There are no ifs, ands, or buts about this. Our recon teams put their numbers at about three to four thousand. We can hold against them with no problem and eventually wipe them out, but the problem is that the herd coming at us from the west has four times that number of dead in it. For those of you that have been on the back side of these dead-asses, you know that nothing can stand in front of them. Their outer edges are estimated to pass within a mile to the south of the fort in four hours. We expect scattered contact with smaller groups ahead of the main herd within an hour."

Pointing to a secondary road on the map that led directly from Jasper to the compound, Rick went on, "What I propose is to draw the group from the southeast in and wipe them out. Right now, they're moving directly at us cross-country. They're pretty spread out, so what I want to do is lure them onto this road where we can deal with them as a whole. We need to do it fast though. We want them gone before the herd coming at us from the west has a chance to join up with them and follow them right to us.

"The second part of the plan will be to lead the bigger herd straight down Highway Sixty-Three. At its closest point, it only comes within four miles of the fort, but like I said, the outer edge of them will come within a mile. We know the dead-asses have some kind of sense that leads them to us, so we have to do whatever it takes to keep them on the road. The hard part will be the timing. We need to draw in and wipe out the herd coming from the southeast while we slow the big herd until we've dealt with the smaller one. Once that's done, we can lure the big group all the way to Louisiana if we want to."

Looking at the men and women in his command, Rick asked, "Any questions?"

Expecting the next thirty minutes to be a waste of time as everyone tried to shine by asking the most intelligent question, Tick-Tock was surprised by the ensuing silence.

"Very well then," Rick said. "I want the commanders of the two smaller forts and their platoon leaders to stay behind along with Tick-Tock. The rest of you know what to do and are dismissed."

As they filed out, Tick-Tock took in the resolve on their faces. These were the men and women that would have the hardest job. They had to be continually moving as they ambushed the dead to slow them down while at the same time trying to attract as many as they could from the flanks of the herd. The range on the porcupines wasn't that great, so they had to shoot and move. If they faltered one little bit, the wave of Zs would roll right over them.

When they were gone, Rick said to those that remained, "We need to figure out how to get the group coming from the southeast out of the woods and onto the road so we can deal with them. They're scattered all over so we've got to lure them in and wipe them out. It's not like the big herd since it stays primarily on the highway. Any ideas on how to draw them in?"

Thinking back to the time at the radio station when Steve attracted the dead while he dropped down onto a MRAP full of supplies and weapons, Tick-Tock asked with a smile, "Have you ever heard of Jap Slap Theater?"

***

After climbing onto the truck, Heather held Cindy against her. She had wiped Linda's blood off the little girl's face but could see where it still stained her clothes. Knowing that shock could kill just as easily as a bullet or a knife, she was relieved when Cindy came out of her catatonic state.

Feeling her stir, Heather said, "It's okay, we're on the truck now. We're almost there."

"It doesn't matter," Cindy mumbled. "Linda is dead. You're all trying to protect me and you'll all be dead. You're just walking around until you get shot or bit."

In a quiet voice, Heather said, "You can't think like that, honey. In just a few minutes, we'll all be safe."

"Nowhere is safe," Cindy mumbled. "The only thing that was safe was my pistol. Linda even gave it to me but it got knocked out of my hand when Igor pushed me down. The gun made me feel safe, like I can take care of myself. It seems like everyone dies when they try to protect me. I need to do it myself."

Surprised, Heather asked, "You had a gun?"

Cindy nodded against her shoulder and said, "Linda taught me how to use it. She said it was for emergencies." Looking up, she asked with wide eyes, "Can I have another gun? If something else happens, I want to be ready. Maybe next time, I'll be able to keep one of you from getting killed."

Heather thought about it for a few seconds before reaching into her pack and extracting a small pistol. Looking Cindy directly in the eye, she said, "This isn't a toy."

"That's the first thing Linda told me," Cindy said. "She taught me everything you taught her."

"Then you need to remember everything she told you and do it," Heather said. Handing the little pistol over, she added, "This was Brain's mother's pistol. He gave it Steve and Steve gave it to me. I've been carrying it around ever since we left the radio station."

Looking at the CAR-15 leaning next to her and the pistol holstered at Heather's hip, Cindy asked, "Why did you carry that little gun all this way when you have all these bigger guns?"

Not wanting to tell the little girl that she kept the pistol in case she needed to use it on herself if she was bitten, she said, "I just put it in my pack and forgot about it."

Satisfied with the answer, Cindy took the small pistol. After looking at it for a few seconds, she extracted the clip and cleared the round in the chamber. Heather had to help her insert the bullet back into the magazine since her fingers weren't strong enough to do it. After putting the weapon back together, she put it in the cargo pocket of her pants.

Looking up at Heather, she said, "Now I feel safe."

***

Leaning in close to the man on his right, Steve asked over the roar of the truck engine, "How far to the base?"

Major Jedidiah Cage looked up from his map and replied, "About twenty minutes. We have to make a detour once we get over the bridge. On the way here, we ran into a roadblock. A building collapsed onto the road." Looking down at the covered body of Linda, he added, "That's why we couldn't get to the airport sooner. I'm sorry you lost one of your people."

Reminding himself that the dead were the ultimate cause of all this death and destruction, Steve didn't blame Cage for being late. In fact, while he had only met the Major a few minutes ago, he felt comfortable in the man's presence. When the officer and his soldiers had arrived, he had been the first person to get out and ask if they were all right. When Steve explained what had happened, Cage took charge of the situation, ordering his medic to take care of Igor and his men to take the two bandits into custody. Within minutes, he had situation completely under control and everyone loaded into the trucks.

Looking over to where Cindy and Heather were having a quiet conversation near the cab, Cage asked, "Is that the little girl that's immune?"

Steve nodded and said, "She was bitten a couple times and never turned. We found her in Clearwater."

Cage gave a low whistle and said, "You've brought her a long way, my friend."

"And not just in miles," Steve answered quietly. "She's had a rough time of it so make sure your doctors take it easy on her."

"Don't worry about that," Cage told him. "We've been searching for anyone that's resistant to the HWNW virus since this all started. With everyone shooting the people that got infected, we don't know how many of the immune got killed off. What you have here is one of the rarest commodities on the face of the earth so the doctor in charge is going to treat her like the crown jewels."

"Is there a cure to the virus?" Steve asked.

"Doctor Connors told me that she's close," Cage told him. "She needs one more test subject."

"Will the anti-virus kill the dead?" Steve asked.

"Yes," Cage answered. "We all call it an anti-virus but it's more of an eradicator."

Excited by the news, Steve asked, "How long will it take to create?"

Cage thought about it for a minute before saying, "I'm not a virologist so I can't say for sure but I would guess a few days at the very least. Maybe weeks though, I really don't know."

Thinking of Tick-Tock and Denise back at Fort Redoubt, he knew they didn't have days. He had witnessed firsthand how close the Zs were to the fort and guessed they only had a matter of hours before the huge herd of dead reached its walls.

With concern in his voice, Steve said, "I've got some friends back in Texas that are in a tough spot and don't have much time. Is there some way we can evacuate them?"

Cage briefly explained what was going on in Washington DC and finished with, "As far as I know, everything is grounded until the situation is resolved. The only thing we had orders to do was to locate and pick you and your group up." Seeing Steve's crestfallen expression, he added, "When we get back to base, I'll contact DC and see what we can do. How many people do we need to pick up?"

Thinking of all the men and women at Fort Redoubt, Steve answered, "A few thousand."

Leaning back slightly, Cage said, "You have a lot of friends. You must have been a terror on Facebook."

Steve chuckled at the joke and then explained about Fort Redoubt, finishing by saying, "There's really only eight people that were in my group but we can't leave the rest of them to die."

Shaking his head, Cage replied, "I might be able to swing a couple of choppers, but that's about it."

Hoping that the helicopters got to the fort before the dead overran it, Steve said, "Do whatever you can to do to get my people out, Major. If you can pull everyone out, that would be even better. They're the only reason we made it here."

Cage nodded solemnly and said, "I'll do what I can."

The truck engine revved, causing Cage to stand up and look over the cab. After briefly scanning the area, he ordered, "Everyone get ready to run the gauntlet. Doesn't look too bad today, but it's still going to be bumpy."

"The gauntlet?" Steve asked the Major as he sat down.

"There's a ring of dead surrounding the camp," Cage explained. "We have to bust through them to get in and out."

Worried that the safe haven they were going to was about to be overrun, Steve asked, "Is your fence secure?"

"The dead aren't at the fence," Cage answered. "One of the eggheads invented something that keeps them back a ways."

Steve began to ask what it was, but the whining of the dead quickly grew too loud to continue. Seconds later, he could feel the truck start to shudder and bounce in a familiar way as it struck down and rolled over the first of the Zs. Looking around at the soldiers accompanying them, he was reassured that they didn't appear worried. After a full minute of being bounced back and forth and up and down, the ride steadied and the truck slowed considerably.

Curious, Steve half-stood and looked over the tailgate. The second truck, its front grill and bumper splattered with body parts and black blood was just clearing the ring of dead. Expecting the Zs to follow the vehicle in a loping run, he was shocked that they stayed where they were. Looking to his right and left, he saw thousands of the dead standing just inside the trees and brush that ringed the camp. Now that they were away from the whining of the reanimated corpses, he could hear a new sound coming from the Zs. It was a moaning, painful sound.

Turning to face the camp, Steve could see it was ringed with concertina wire and a tall chain-link fence. Seeing the insulators spaced equally across it, he guessed it was electrified. Looking back at the horde of dead, he also knew that it would be no barrier if they came at it in a rush.

Rubbing his arms, Steve suddenly realized that the hair on them was standing up. Reaching up to run his fingers through his hair, he could feel it prickle.

Seeing him doing this, Cage explained, "You'll get used to it. It's one of the side effects to the Malectron."

In awe, Steve asked, "Is that what's keeping the dead back?"

Cage nodded and said, "It's the only thing between us and them."

Sitting back down, an idea started to form in Steve's mind. Seeing they were approaching the gate, he tabled it for later. First they would get Cindy to Doctor Connors and then he would find out if he could pull his plan off.

When they were safely behind the wire, Steve studied the camp as they drove through it. A majority of the structures were tents or shipping containers with signs in front of them touting their use. Looking down a side road as they passed, he saw the camp had a barbershop, a quartermaster and a mess hall along with a hospital. It all looked hastily put together and like it had been here for years rather than months. Ahead of them on a slight rise, he spotted the only permanent structure.

Seeing where he was looking, Cage said, "That's where we're taking Cindy. The farmhouse is where they set up the lab. We can turn her over to Doctor Connors and then I'll find some quarters for you and your people. I'll make sure that Doctor Connors keep you updated on her progress."

Hearing this, Heather half stood and said defiantly, "One of us is going with her, Major. We're not leaving her alone for a second."

Holding up his hands in a placating gesture, Cage said, "Calm down. I'm sure that won't be a problem. We want Cindy to be as comfortable as possible."

Satisfied, Heather said to him, "Good, I'll stay with her first."

Cage nodded, his attention drawn away by the squawking of his radio. Picking it up, he hit the transmit button and said, "Major Cage here, over."

Loud enough for everyone to hear, a tinny voice came through the speaker saying, "Major, it's Fagan. We've got a fire in the radio room, over."

"How bad, over?" Cage asked.

"We can't tell yet, sir," Fagan answered. "They just finished putting it out when I got here. There's still a lot of smoke, over."

Looking at the men in the back of the truck, Cage regretted having left Fagan behind. He needed someone he could trust to finish escorting the civilians to the farmhouse but his first priority was seeing how bad the damage at the radio room was. He doubted Hawkins would try anything, but you never knew. Not having time to explain everything that was going on with the doctor, he called for the truck to stop and pointed to a Second Lieutenant and said, "Perry, I want you the deliver the little girl to Doctor Connors. No one else but Connors. Once you've done that, I want you to bring the rest of these people to my office."

"Yes, sir," Perry acknowledged.

Nodding once to Steve, Cage said, "The Lieutenant will take care of you." The truck had barely rolled to a stop before he climbed over the rear gate of the truck and started running in the direction of a small plume of black smoke rising from the far side of the camp.

As the truck started off again, a feeling of unease washed through Steve at the thought of Heather escorting Cindy. He knew it wasn't the little girl's fault, but it seemed like everyone that chaperoned her ended up dead. Correcting himself, he looked to where Igor lay on the floor and thought, five dead and one wounded.

Shaking the feeling off as they pulled up in front of the farmhouse and got out, he told himself that they were probably in one of the safest places in the world right now. Looking up to the porch to where a man in a white lab coat was introducing himself as Doctor Hawkins, the personal assistant to Doctor Connors, he felt reassured. Hawkins looked and sounded very professional as he explained that Doctor Connors was in the middle of some tests and had sent him to greet them. Hawkins had no problem with Heather escorting Cindy and even seemed to welcome the idea, putting them all at ease with an ongoing banter about how happy he was that they had made it here safe.

One by one, the remains of the group hugged Cindy and told her everything would be okay. The little girl made Steve promise that he would take care of Pep and made everyone else promise to look out for each other. When they were finished with their goodbyes, Heather kissed Steve, took the little girl's hand and followed Hawkins and another man toward the front door.

As they drove away, Steve thought to himself: what could go wrong?

***

After entering the farmhouse, Hawkins turned to the right and stopped in front of an empty desk as he said, "Like I told you earlier, Doctor Connors is in the middle of some tests right now so you can wait for her in the parlor." Nodding to the man that had accompanied him, he added, "I have my own duties to attend to so I want to introduce you to Sergeant Cain. He will be in charge of your security while you're here."

Heather turned around and nodded at Cain who had taken up a position of parade rest behind her. Spinning back to address Hawkins, she felt the cold metal of a pistol barrel pressed against the base of her skull.

In a low voice, Cain started to say, "Don't do anything stupid," but barely got the words out of his mouth before Heather sprang into action.

Dropping Cindy's hand, she raised her left arm in an upright 'L' and spun at the waist, knocking Cain's pistol out of his hand. Letting her momentum continue to spin her around, she followed up with a fist to the man's jaw. Dropping her hand to her pistol as she spun back, she stopped when she saw Hawkins already had his out, its barrel pointed directly to where Cindy stood frozen in shock.

"Don't do it," Hawkins warned. "I will kill the child if you so much as twitch."

Despite being confused at the sudden assault, Heather recovered quickly. She didn't know what was going on, but she also knew that it didn't matter. Her first priority was taking out the threat in front of her. Watching Hawkins' eyes, she waited for him to take them off her for as much as a second. She had been a cop once and was trained to draw her weapon and put three in the black in less than two seconds.

From behind her, Heather heard a groan and rustling as Cain got to his feet. Knowing she didn't have much time, she waited for Hawkins to give her an opening. Instead, he stood unmoving, staring at her like some type of unblinking predatory lizard.

Feeling a tug at her waist as Cain took her pistol, Heather didn't give up, knowing that he also had to take the CAR-15 slung over her shoulder. All she had to do was wait for him to try and take it and she would show him and Hawkins another trick in hand-to-hand combat.

Seeing Hawkins nod for Cain to proceed, she got ready to attack. She would take control of the rifle and disable the man behind her with two moves and put three bullets in the doctor's head before he knew what was happening.

Expecting to feel Cain's hands on her, she instead heard him say, "Fucking bitch, I should have done this coming through the front door."

Heather's world went black as his fist smashed into the soft spot behind her ear.

Outside of Jasper, Texas:

Tick-Tock banged a crowbar in a steady beat against the tire rim hanging from the roll bar of the Jeep Wrangler as he yelled, "All-e-all-e-in-come-free. Come out, come out wherever you are."

The Jeep bounced heavily, almost throwing him over the side.

Angrily, he called to the driver, "Take it easy. You almost tossed me to the wolves."

"Sorry, sir," the woman replied. "Some of these holes are so overgrown that I can't see them until I hit them. Are we close enough yet?"

Looking at the mob of dead following them and then at the road only a hundred feet to their front, Tick-Tock slid into the passenger seat and said, "Yeah, we're close enough. Even the dead-asses can't miss us. Get us onto the blacktop."

The Jeep accelerated, bouncing so hard that Tick-Tock told the driver to slow down.

"Sorry, sir," she replied. "I just hate being this close to those things."

"Well, this is the last of them so you can relax for a little while," Tick-Tock told her. "There are going to be a few stragglers here and there but the guys from the smaller forts can deal with them." Seeing relief on the woman's face, Tick-Tock added, "My guess is that we'll move to the west after this so don't relax too much."

The Jeep bounced onto the road, its ride smoothing out enough for Tick-Tock to climb in the back again. This was his second trip into the boonies to draw in the dead and his arm felt like lead from swinging the crowbar. Despite this, he started rhythmically striking the tire rim again.

Judging the distance between the dead and their Jeep, he called out for the driver to slow down, explaining that they wanted to draw the Zs in, not outrun them. Looking ahead, he saw where the trees started on either side of the road to create a thick barrier on either side of it. These would act as a funnel to keep the dead bunched up. Fifty feet further on, he spotted a red line spray painted from one side to the other on the asphalt.

"We're almost in the zone," he yelled to be heard above the whining of the dead. "Slow down just a little. We want to make sure we get as many as we can. Try to keep us about ten or fifteen feet in front of the fastest ones."

The driver nodded, switching her fearful gaze between the rearview mirror and the road in front of her.

Tick-Tock looked at the trailing mass of dead, their bodies torn and twisted as the loped, scurried and scampered after the food that stayed just out of reach. Most of them were completely nude, showing a variety of gruesome wounds that leaked black fluid, but a few were dressed. Looking closer at these Zs, Tick-Tock could see dried blood staining their clothes to mingle with the black ochre leaking out of their bodies. Glancing to the south, he guessed that a stronghold somewhere had recently been overrun and its occupant's zombified.

Thinking of Steve and hoping that he and the others had made it safely to Arkansas, he wondered how long it would be until the doctors in Russellville came up with a way to eradicate the dead. A few days? A few weeks? Looking to the north, a feeling suddenly washed over him. Not knowing why, he was suddenly sure that his friends were safe and a cure would be coming out soon.

Shaking his head as he looked at the freshly made dead, he whispered, "Poor bastards. If you could have only hung on for a little longer."

His driver interrupted his thoughts by calling out, "We just crossed the first line."

Turning his attention to a second one painted further down the road, he said, "Keep it steady, we're almost there."

Looking to the right, Tick-Tock could see the first of the porcupines tucked back in the brush. They had set up ten in total, staggering them on either side of the road. Gauging the size of the group they had trailing behind them, he guessed they would have to fire six of them. The first group he had led into the kill zone had been bigger, spreading outside of the ambush to its front and rear by fifty feet. The dead-asses the ambush missed were easily taken care of with small arms fire, but it had been a big waste of ammunition. More darts could be made, but there was no one manufacturing bullets anymore.

When he saw they were three-quarters of the way through the kill zone, Tick-Tock told the driver to speed up. She wasted no time in mashing the accelerator and speeding over the second red line. Stopping a hundred feet past it, she turned in her seat to watch the slaughter.

The dead came on in a relentless wave, pushing each other out of the way in their eagerness to be the first to dig into the food that had stopped only a short distance away. Tick-Tock almost laughed out loud when it appeared that one of them was actually sticking its foot out to trip the others next to it. Looking closer, he saw that half of the Z's leg had been chewed off, causing it to swing out sideways with each step. Those that fell were trampled by the mass of reanimated flesh coming up behind them, some to rise again after they passed, but some suffering crushed skulls by the tromping feet of their brethren.

Seeing that the herd was completely in the kill zone, Tick-Tock lifted his radio and pushed the transmit button. Holding it close to his mouth, he said, "Let her rip."

Hidden in trees, the 'triggers' and they were called, yanked on lanyards attached to retaining pins. These released the boards that slapped forward against the darts sticking out from the back of the porcupine.

With the now familiar sound of a loud twang followed almost immediately by a thump ringing in his ears, Tick-Tock watched the devastation wrought on the dead. Black ochre flew in all directions as the darts made contact with dead flesh, boring through the skulls and into the brains of the Zs. A few fell immediately, but most stood for a second before dropping en masse to the blacktop. It almost reminded him of a game of ring-around-the-rosy when they all fall down.

Lifting his M4, he ordered his driver to turn around. Proceeding slowly back to the kill zone, he watched the triggers come out of the brush and start dispatching the crawlers, children, and anything else that was below the flat arc of darts thrown at them. Using a variety of bows and arrows and spears, they were done with the cleanup in minutes.

When he saw the trucks coming down the road to pick up the porcupines and their crew, Tick-Tock ordered his driver to head for Fort Redoubt. Their work here might be done, but there was still plenty to do to the west.

Leaning back in his seat, Tick-Tock let the wind blow over him as he relaxed for what felt like the first time in days. Part one of their plan had gone off without a hitch and now it was time to finish off part two. If it looked like plan two was going to fail, he had his own personal plan three.

Switching on his hand-held radio, he turned it to the frequency being used by the units out of Fort Redoubt before pushing the transmit button and saying, "Mobile twelve to Mobile one, Commander Styles come back, over."

The reply was almost instant. "This is Styles, over."

"We're finished down here and I'm on our way back to fort number two to link up with the rest of my people and head back to Redoubt, over," Tick-Tock told him.

"Negative, Mobile twelve," Rick said forcefully. "You are to proceed up Highway sixty-three as fast as you can and link up with the other units from Redoubt. I've already recalled your people and they will meet you on the road, over."

"What's going on, over?" Tick-Tock asked.

After a few seconds, Rick replied, "We had the herd bottlenecked about ten miles from Redoubt where the Highway comes closest to the lake but part of the main group split off to the north. They're heading along the shore directly for the fort. I've diverted some of the units on the highway to deal with them so I need you and your people to take their place, over."

Tick-Tock was about to reply when someone cut in on the frequency and said urgently, "This is Jackson at fort number one. We just got a report that a huge group of dead are coming at us from the south. Request orders, over."

Pressing the transmit button, Tick-Tock said, "This is mobile twelve, Jackson. Be informed that we just finished up with the last of them, over."

"This is a new herd," the woman replied. "One of our mobile units was out looking for stragglers and ran into them a few minutes ago. They've already made it through Jasper and are heading north-northeast, over."

"What's their size, over?" Rick asked.

"Between four and five thousand," Jackson replied. "Our guys estimated their numbers when they crossed the open area to the north of town, over."

Another voice suddenly broke in saying, "This is mobile five and we have reports from Fort Redoubt that they have dead-asses coming at them from the direction of the lake. They were stopped at the outer fence but more keep showing up. We're on our way to reinforce them, over."

Before anyone could reply, the radio erupted more reports from units scattered all over the area of the dead coming at them from different directions. None of the herds of Zs were large, but no one seemed to know where they were coming from.

Finally breaking in through the chatter, Rick ordered everyone to regroup at their nearest rally point and await further orders.

Hearing on the radio that the dead were popping up all over the place, the Jeep's driver slowed and started pulling over to the side of the road so she could listen.

Noticing this, Tick-Tock ordered, "Get this thing in gear and get us moving."

Sitting up straight in her seat at his commanding tone, she replied crisply, "Yes, sir. I'm heading for Highway Sixty-three right now, sir."

"Belay that," Tick-Tock told her. "I want you to head for Fort Redoubt as fast as you can."

She nodded and floored the accelerator, making the rear end of the Jeep slew back and forth until she got it under control. Cringing slightly, she waited for a reprimand.

Deep in thought, Tick-Tock's only thoughts were on Denise and plan three.

CHAPTER TWENTY

Russellville, Arkansas:

Major Cage could barely contain his fury as he looked at the scorched interior of the radio room. Turning to Staff Sergeant Fagan, he asked, "What in the hell happened here?"

"They think it was an electrical fire, Major" Fagan answered. "The operator left the room to go to the latrine and when she came back and opened the door, the rush of air fed the flames and blew her back against the far wall."

Concerned about the operator, the anger left Cage's voice as he asked, "How is she?"

"She's got second and third degree burns over the front of her body. The medic said that he doubted she would make it through the night, sir."

"Call for a medevac," Cage ordered, the words barely out of his mouth when he realized the folly in his statement. Looking down at the charred remains of the operator's chair, he added, "As you were."

"No calls going in or out for a while, sir," Fagan commented on the state of the room. "The next contact we'll have with the outside world is tomorrow morning when the resupply chopper gets here. They can bring us back a new radio on their next run."

Looking closely at the mess around him, Cage realized that while everything was scorched by flames and blackened by smoke, none of the equipment seemed to be completely gutted by the fire.

"Do we have someone who can fix this?" he asked.

"Specialist Canady was the only one with the technical knowledge, sir," Fagan informed him.

"Was?" Cage asked. After a second he understood and added, "And she's got second and third degree burns."

Fagan nodded and said, "The rest of the men and women that worked in here were just operators. Canady was the only one with any technical knowledge, sir."

"I don't like being out of contact but it looks like we have no choice but to wait for the resupply chopper tomorrow," Cage said. Shifting position, he could feel the grit from the fire grind under his boots so he added, "What we need to do first is to get a couple of people to clean up in here. When they come to replace the radio, I don't want anything holding them up. Once you've got that underway, I want you to come to the office. The people that brought the little girl in are waiting for us and I want you to be there when I debrief them."

"Do you really think this might all be over soon, sir?" Fagan asked.

"From what Connors told me, she's close to the anti-virus," Cage answered.

Fagan waved the remark away and said, "I know that, sir, but it just seems unreal that with everything going on that a ten-year old girl holds the key to end it all. It's kind of hard to believe."

"It's easy enough to have hope and belief," Cage told him. "All you have to do is make a decision to do it. You have to remember though that once the dead are gone, it won't be the end." Seeing Fagan didn't understand this, he added, "We've still got to rebuild everything."

Seeing Major Cage's conviction was enough for Fagan. He decided that he would believe that the Major believed until he could believe it himself. Calling through the door, he said in his best parade ground voice, "Tully and Whitmore, I want you to get some brooms, mops, rags and water and clean this mess up." Turning back to Cage, he said, "Let's go debrief the civilians, sir."

***

Cain entered Professor Hawkins office and snapped to attention before saying crisply, "My men have taken up defensive positions inside the farmhouse, sir." With a wink, he added in a dry voice, "And they're ready to fight to the death to protect you and the Malectron from the dirty seditionists trying to steal it."

Hawkins smiled and asked, "So they bought the story about Cage and his men trying to take it?"

"Hook line and sinker," Cain answered as he dropped into a chair. "I even threw in that the Major might be working for the Russians. I got the idea from what you had me tell Fort Polk about foreign troops being in the area."

Hawkins laughed and said, "Good, good. Now if Cage tries anything, we'll be able to hold him off until the helicopters get here. Did you check if my assistant is finished with the preparations for my test?"

"I just came from the basement and everything is almost ready," Cain answered. "Jim, said we would be good to go in about an hour."

Checking his watch, Hawkins frowned and said, "That will cut it a little close. The choppers are going to be here in two hours."

"But you're using fourth generation dead in the test," Cain told him. "The time from infection to reanimation shortens the further down the line you go."

Hawkins sighed and said, "I guess it will have to do. I just wanted the chance to study the effects or lack of effects for a little longer."

"Once you're set up in DC, you can do all the testing you want, Professor," Cain told him.

Waving him off, Hawkins said, "I'll be too busy working on the Malectron. The little girl and the rest of them are disposable."

Rubbing his sore jaw, Cain said, "I wish you would let me dispose of them now."

With a wry grin, Hawkins asked, "A little miffed that a mere woman got the drop on you?"

"I'm just curious why we've let them live so long," Cain grumbled, not wanting to let his boss know the truth.

"We need the little girl for now," Hawkins explained. "As for Connors and the woman, I'm keeping them alive in case we need hostages."

"Hostages," Cain said in a curious voice. "But my men can defend us if Cage and his people try anything. We'll cut them down before they can get within a dozen feet of the front door."

"And what about the back door?" Cain asked.

Cain snorted in derision and said, "They have to approach from the front to get around to the rear and we've got a clear view all across the camp. Besides, the only way into the house from the back is the coal chute, and god help anyone that drops in there."

Hawkins countered by saying, "But you must remember that the greatest victory is when nary a shot is fired. When the helicopters get here, I want to get on them free and clear, not running through the middle of a firefight. I want you to bring Connors and the woman down to the lab for now, but if Cage and his people try anything, we'll bring them onto the porch and put guns to their heads and threaten to kill them. You have to remember that the Major is a civilized man and won't risk harming the hostages. When the helicopters get here, we can use the women as shields to get to the landing pad. Once we're off the ground, I don't care what you do with them. Keep them as play toys or get rid of them at your leisure, it makes no difference to me. Just keep them out of my hair."

"They won't be a bother for too long," Cain said quietly, a smile breaking out on his face at the thought of pushing the woman named Heather out of a chopper at three-thousand feet.

Fort Redoubt:

Tick-Tock heard the sound gunfire grow in volume as they neared the fort. Trying to pinpoint its source, he realized after a few seconds that it seemed to come from everywhere.

He tried the radio again to let them know he was coming in but gave up in frustration. It seemed like everyone was breaking in at the same time, clogging the channel with a lot of useless information.

He had listened to their chatter on the short drive to the fort and wasn't surprised to hear the gradual breakdown of discipline. No one was giving their position or what they were up against so there was no way to put together any kind of successful counterattack. Then it got worse. With the dead coming at the fort from three directions, most of the troops were breaking ranks and heading for the hills or hightailing it to their loved ones.

This helped to relieve the guilt he was feeling at what he was about to do.

Rounding a bend in the road, Tick-Tock spotted the outer fence. Relief washed through him when he saw that the gate was still manned. With everyone running blind and the dead coming at them fast, he figured it would be abandoned or overrun. He was also relieved to see armed men and women spread out along the length of the fence, telling him that not everyone had run.

Pulling up to the opening, he called out to the guard, "What's going on. I can't get anyone on the radio."

"Standard operating procedure," she replied. "If the channel you're using is jammed with traffic, move up two channels. Commander Styles is the only one allowed to transmit on three and he's organizing our defenses right now. If you need to call something in, move down to channel two."

Turning to his driver, he asked with exasperation, "Why didn't you tell me that?"

"I've never heard it before," she replied.

The guard broke in, saying, "Only platoon and squad leaders have radios so she probably didn't know."

"So what's happening?" Tick-Tock asked her. "Where are the dead?"

Waving her hand to encompass the forest all around them, she replied, "From what I've heard, they're everywhere. The dead that split off from the main group coming at us from the west are hitting the outer fence along the lake right now. There were more of them than we thought and they've moved along it all the way to the east of the fort. We have a big herd coming from the southwest and the main group from the west left the road and is coming at us cross-country now."

"How bad is it to the east?" Tick-Tock asked.

"There aren't many dead-asses in that direction yet," the guard told him. "Right now we're pulling troops from over there to reinforce some of the other sections of the fence. We're keeping the gates open until the last minute to take in stragglers and the recon teams that are still out. You're probably the last of the stragglers though because we just got a report that the Ds have made it to this road. If anyone else id out there, they're cut off or dead."

Knowing that he still had a chance to get Denise and run, Tick-Tock told his driver, "Get to the fort as fast as you can."

Having heard that the dead were right behind her, she wasted no time in getting him there.

As the Jeep skidded to a stop near the main gate, Tick-Tock jumped out and ran for the gate, slowing as he joined the steady flow of people going into Fort Redoubt. These were the very old, the infirm and young children. Outside of the fort, troops were preparing to board the last of the trucks and Jeeps that would take them to the perimeter. Watching as one by one they loaded up and pulled away, he looked around for his Jeep and driver. Seeing that it too was being piled with ammunition and readied to go out, he resolved that they would have to walk.

Hearing gunfire from the far side of the fort, he was reassured that the defenses along the lake were still intact. Once he got Denise out of the fort, they could head to the east and make their breakout from there. He would deal with the landmines by lobbing heavy rocks onto them to set them off and the wire could be cut with his K-bar knife after he disabled the electricity flowing through it.

Thinking it through, he decided that if the guards were still there that more than likely they would join him in his escape. Everything was going to hell fast and the Zs were on their way so they probably didn't want to hang around to be a main entrée. Who knows, he thought, maybe one of them even has a layout of the mines?

Deep in the flow of refugees, Tick-Tock was carried into the chaos of the courtyard. In the waning light of the sun, hundreds of people crowded around, yelling to one and other as they searched for loved ones or asking a million questions of the few troops stationed there. Moving slowly through the dense crowd toward the hospital, he stopped when he heard someone call his name. Turning in a circle, he finally spotted one of his people wending her way toward him through the swarm of people.

"You saved me a trip coming to find you," Tick-Tock called to her over the din. "I'm going to get Denise out of the hospital. I need you to get everyone else together and meet me outside the gate. One of you bring some wire cutters if you can find them."

Not wanting to be mobbed by people begging to go with them, he didn't add that they were getting the hell out of Dodge.

As he turned to go, she stopped him by saying, "Denise isn't in the hospital. She checked herself out."

"Where is she?" Tick-Tock asked.

Pointing to where the parapets on the inside of the walls were being hastily manned, the woman said, "She's up there somewhere."

"I'll find her, you go get the rest of the group," Tick-Tock told her as he headed for the nearest ladder.

Russellville, Arkansas:

As Cage and an NCO passed him in the Major's outer office, Steve could smell a burnt odor coming off them. Expecting to be kept waiting since they had the fire to deal with, he was surprised when Cage waved to him and said, "Come with me."

Although the couch he was half lounging on was the most comfortable thing he had sat in for days, Steve wasted no time in jumping up and following the two men. Once inside Cage's office, the Major waved him toward the chair in front of his desk and said, "Sorry about keeping you waiting. We've had a few problems."

"Fire in the radio room," Steve commented as he sat down. Both men appeared grim so he asked, "How bad was it?"

"We won't be ordering pizza anytime soon," the NCO said.

Cage gave the Staff Sergeant a dirty look as he said, "I'd like to introduce the newly demoted Private Fagan, my straight man."

After exchanging greetings, Steve said, "If there's anything we can do to help while we're staying here, just let us know."

Fagan gave a half laugh and asked, "Can you fix a radio."

Steve smiled and said, "I can't, but I have someone in my group that can."

Both men looked at him skeptically so Steve told them about how he and Brain had been working at the radio station when the HWNW virus broke out, and then gave them a synopsis of how his group had only managed to make it this far because of the technician's knowledge.

When he was finished, Cage looked at Fagan and said with raised eyebrows, "It won't hurt to give him a shot at it."

Fagan shrugged and said, "I don't see how he could do anymore damage. It looked like everything was pretty much fried, sir. And if he does get it to work..." Fagan shrugged.

This was enough for Cage. It would take two days to get a replacement radio to the base and that was far too long to be out of contact. Standing, he said, "Then let's do it."

Fort Redoubt:

With her long brown hair tucked up in a black bandana and her face turned toward the rapidly darkening forest, Tick-Tock almost didn't recognize Denise as he approached her. Stopping only because the woman seemed unsteady on her feet and was leaning too far backward, he reached out to keep her from falling off the parapet. When she turned at his touch, his heart leapt with joy when he saw her face. Changed his reach from a steadying hand to enveloping her in a hug, he said, "It's me, Babe."

In disbelief, Denise said, "Tick-Tock?"

"I just got back," he explained. "What in the hell are you doing up here?"

Clutching him tightly, she said, "They had so many people coming into the hospital that were so badly wounded that I felt guilty for being there just because I was a little dizzy. Rick came through looking for volunteers to man the walls so I got up, got dressed and came out here."

Loosening his grip on her, Tick-Tock quickly grabbed her again when she started to fall over.

"You shouldn't be out here," he told her sternly, his thoughts on how he would get them away from the fort.

"I can stand if I lean against something," she explained.

"Can you walk?" he asked, his heart dropping at the reality of the situation.

"I made it this far," she told him.

And it looks like just doing that wiped you out, Tick-Tock thought to himself.

Trying to think of another way out of the fort besides on foot, he came up blank. There was no way Denise could make it as far as the gate much less away from the dead that were swarming the area. Even with the help of his people, it would be impossible.

His thoughts were interrupted as Denise reached out to caress his shoulder and ask, "What are you doing back here, Honey? I thought you were out with the patrols."

Not wanting to tell her the about their now aborted escape, Tick-Tock smiled and said, "I came here to be with you, Babe."

***

His shoulder aching, Lieutenant Wilkes pulled the string on the bow back and let his arrow fly. Seeing it pierce the eye of one of the dead, he didn't stop to congratulate himself on his aim as he drew another from his quiver. Feeling only three left, he pulled one out and nocked it as he looked around at the men and women in his command to assess how many arrows they had left. With an audible grunt of displeasure, he saw that most had the same or even less than he did. They had each started off with thirty apiece, but the dead coming at them down the road were so numerous that they had almost used them up in the first five minutes of contact.

Not wanting anyone to use their firearms and attract more dead toward them, he called out, "Fall back to the outer wire. Fall back to the outer wire. We'll rearm at the gate."

Pleased to see his men and women retreating in an orderly manner as they fired their remaining bolts before turning and running for the safety of the wire, Wilkes made sure that everyone was past him before he followed. Fatigued and winded from the ongoing battle he had been fighting for the past three hours, his feet felt like lead as he picked them up and dropped them in a faltering jog. Behind him, the mob of dead, indifferent to the feeling of being tired or the need to breath only took seconds to cover the fifty feet to where he and his command had taken their stand.

Looking ahead, Wilkes noticed that the men and women who had already made it to safety were taking up position behind the razor wire on either side of the gate and were switching from bows and arrows to automatic weapons. Seeing that their numbers were bolstered by two jeeps with machine guns mounted on them, he started waving and shouting, "No gunfire, no gunfire."

In reply, they screamed for him to get down.

Fear shot through Wilkes when he realized what was happening. The hours of listening to the constant whining of the dead had made him inured to their noise. This coupled with his own labored breathing and the blood pounding in his ears made him deaf to the sound of the dead only feet behind him.

Turning his head slightly, Wilkes could see dirty hands reaching out to him from at least a dozen reanimated corpses. Feeling a surge of adrenalin, it lasted for only a second before turning into a sick feeling in his stomach. Fearing that he would be ripped apart by the dead before they were gunned down if he dropped to the ground, he also knew he would never make it the last twenty feet to the gate before the dead caught him.

Opting for the long-shot, he dropped down.

Dozens of automatic rifles and two .50 caliber machine guns opened up, their bullets tearing into the wall of dead flesh surging down the road. Thick, black ochre sprayed out as the rounds impacted the reanimated corpses, covering the ground in a sheet. Those hit by the heavy machine guns literally flew apart while the rounds from the automatic weapons punched neat entry holes and ragged exit wounds through the bodies of the dead. Dancing and shuddering from bullets that hit their extremities and torsos, only the Zs hit in the brain or the spinal column fell in the first salvo.

Seeing that they had literally obliterated the dead closing on Lieutenant Wilkes, the defenders of Fort Redoubt reloaded and switched from a firing on full automatic to squeezing off short bursts into the craniums of their attackers. While most of them were more than proficient with the bow and arrow due to long hours spent practicing, the rationing of ammunition for their firearms showed in their marksmanship. By the time the last zombie dropped to the ground in a spray of bone, brain and black blood, they had fired off half their ammunition.

Even after the firing stopped, it still took Wilkes a full minute to realize that the one-sided firefight was over. Lifting his head, he looked at the haze of gunpowder hanging in the air to his front before looking back at the lifeless bodies of the dead. From beyond the wire, a cheer rose up and calls of, "We won," and, "We beat them back," came to his ears.

Standing, he looked down as he brushed the dirt and mud off his clothes so his people wouldn't see the rage etched on his face. Trying to contain himself, he forced himself to be grateful that they had saved his life while at the same time choking back a tirade at how badly they had fucked up.

Don't you see that this is only the tip of the iceberg, his mind screamed at them? You dumbasses blew your load for a few hundred dead. Now what the fuck happens when the rest of them come rolling toward us? That's why we've been using the bows and arrows and spears. We need to save our ammunition for the main body and we've got to maintain noise discipline.

Finally getting control of himself, he raised his head and called for his radioman to report that the dead-asses had reached the outer fence on the south side of the fort.

"But we wiped them out," the man called back.

Completely exhausted from his close call, Wilkes didn't have the strength to put him in his place. In a quiet voice, he said, "Just call in the report."

Making his way through the gate, Wilkes heard the whine coming from behind him. From a distance, it sounded to him like a car with bad breaks coming to a long stop. The sound gradually rose in a crescendo until the first of the Ds appeared, staggering wildly down the road as they fought to move faster toward the food. The two-lane blacktop was quickly packed from one side to the other with the hungry dead as the trees on either side waved crazily with their passing.

Attracted by the gunfire, they were coming at a run.

As the dead rushed toward them, Wilkes found the strength to scream, "Prepare to be overrun."

Russellville, Arkansas:

Brain took a long look at the burned out interior of the radio room to get his bearings and then got to work. Pulling out a screwdriver, he took the front panel off the main receiver and studied it. After removing two more and peering at their interior, he said, "I know what the problem is. If you have an electrician, you need to get him in here."

Not entirely trusting the young technician, Fagan asked, "You figured out what's wrong with it that fast?"

Annoyed at his skills being questioned, Brain told him, "Yeah, you need a new Flux capacitor."

Seeing the Staff Sergeant ball his fists, Cage intervened by stepping in front of him and asking, "So you think you can fix it?"

Brain gave him a withering look and said, "I don't *think* I can fix it, I *know* I can fix it. It's going to take a little while though."

Slightly annoyed at the Brain's arrogant manner, Major Cage asked, "How long is a little while?"

Feeling like he had asserted his dominance enough, Brain told him, "If you can get your electrician in here to restring the burned out crap, I should have you up and running in about thirty minutes or so." Patting the side of the receiver, he added, "This is the military version of the same stuff I used to put together from kits when I was a kid. Being the military version, its casing is built to be resistant to water, shock and fire. It doesn't look like any of the insides were damaged but I won't know for sure until I power them up. Even if some of the electronics got fried, I should be able to cannibalize the other equipment for parts."

Having surveyed the damage for themselves, Cage and Fagan looked at him in shock that it would be so easy.

Seeing their hesitation, Brain raised one eyebrow and gestured toward the door as he said in a trying voice, "An electrician please."

Annoyed by the insolence in Brain's tone, Fagan let it out as he called through the door, "I need the electrician on duty in here A.S.A.P. If he's eating, I want you to wipe his mouth and drag him in here. If he's on the shitter, I want you to wipe his ass, pull his pants up and drag him in here. If he's fucking someone, I want you to pull him out, pull his pants up and drag him in here."

His command was met by a flurry of movement in the outer office as the men and women on duty scurried to do the Staff Sergeant's bidding.

Satisfied, Fagan turned to Brain and said, "I'm going to station a runner outside the door. If you need anything, you tell them to get it. As soon as you have the radio fixed, I want you to send them to get us."

Brain gave a half salute and said, "Aye, aye, Captain."

Reminding himself that the technician was a civilian, Fagan held his temper at the man's disrespect as he led Cage and Steve through the door. When they were outside the building, he said, "He's an arrogant little fucker, isn't he."

Steve laughed and said, "You should have met him before all this."

Seeing the Staff Sergeants face grow red as he dwelled on Brain, Cage changed the subject by saying, "We should go up to the farmhouse and see how Doctor Connors is doing."

"If she's available," Steve said. "She was deep in some test or something when we dropped Cindy and Heather off."

Cage stopped in his tracks, looking worriedly at Steve, he asked, "You didn't turn the girl over to Connors?"

Anxious at the Major's reaction, Steve hesitantly said, "She was busy so her assistant met us. He and a Sergeant took them into the house."

From behind him, Fagan said ominously, "Connors doesn't have an assistant."

Leaning forward, Cage asked, "What was the name of the man that met you up at the farmhouse."

"Some guy named Hawkins," Steve told him, his blood running cold with fear at the reaction this brought from Cage and Fagan.

Both men said, "Shit," at the same time and started running for the farmhouse.

Not knowing what was going on but deciding it wasn't good, Steve followed right behind them, quickly catching up with Cage.

Men and women stopped to stare at their commanding officer, his chief NCO and a civilian racing through the camp. Those in their path found they had to jump out of the way or get forced out of the way by Fagan who had taken the lead. He was going from point A to point B and anything in front of him moved to the side or got bowled over. As they ran, Cage filled Steve in on the basics of Hawkins and the Malectron. He got as far as telling him about the strange disappearance of Lieutenant Randal when he noticed that Fagan had stopped by the side of a shipping container and was peeking around its corner.

Sliding to a halt next to him, Cage asked, "What is it?"

Fagan said, "Take a look, sir," and moved out of the way. Cage took his place and cautiously leaned out. At first, nothing seemed out of the ordinary, but then he noticed the windows. Every single one of them on the second and third floor were wide open. Looking closer, he noticed that their curtains had been drawn back and someone was visible just inside. The windows on the first floor were closed, but on closer inspection, he could see that they were boarded up on the inside.

Leaning back, Cage said, "It looks like Hawkins has got his men watching for us. He's got the first floor barricaded too."

"But what in the hell is he doing?" Fagan asked. "He can't stay in there forever. He'll need food and -," his voice cut off as he thought of the fire. In a flash it all made sense.

Cage came to the same conclusion and said, "He's pulling out, that's what he's doing. He got hold of someone to come pick his scumbag ass up and then had the radio room torched so no one would find out."

Anxious to move forward, Steve said, "So let's take them out and move in. That bastard's got Heather in there."

"And he'll shoot her as soon as we attack," Fagan told him.

"If she's even still alive," Cage said. Instantly regretting this, he added, "My bet is he'll use her as a hostage."

Fagan moved forward and took a look around the corner. After a few seconds, he leaned back and said, "The only way would be a frontal assault across open ground and that's out."

"Why not," Steve asked. "You've got armored Humvees with heavy machine guns. We can get close and then rush them."

"We've also got rocket launchers and grenades to blow the windows open on the first floor," Fagan told him, "but none of that will do us any good. We'd have to use small arms only or risk torching the building. That farmhouse must be about a hundred years old and it'll go up like a roman candle when the first tracer from one of the .50 calibers or a rocket hits it. On top of that, Hawkins has your woman and the little girl as well as however many of the scientists he'll grab to use as hostages. My guess is he'll bring them out and use them as shields the minute we start to roll up on them."

"So a frontal assault is out," Steve said. "What else can we do?"

With a sigh, Cage said, "There is another way in but it won't be pretty."

***

Swallowing hard, Second Lieutenant Perry's mind raced as he thought of all the ways that the Major's plan could go wrong. At first when he and Fagan approached him and explained that they needed him to create a diversion, his mind had been full of heroic images of nighttime infiltrations and remote detonated explosives. Ready to do just about anything to make up for handing the little girl over to Hawkins, he never expected this.

Awkwardly holding a spray of flowers as he walked through the foyer of the farmhouse and stopped in front of the guard sitting behind a desk, Perry said, "I'm here to pick up Doctor Connors for our date."

Having been told to expect some kind of assault on the farmhouse to steal the Malectron, the guard had pulled a .45 caliber pistol and held it underneath his desk when the lookouts on the second floor reported that someone was approaching the front door. They had been vague about who it was, saying only that it was a surprise. Expecting Rambo to burst in armed with everything that could kill, he looked in disbelief at the Second Lieutenant in full, dress uniform holding a bouquet of flowers and asked, "Are you fucking kidding me?"

Perry shook his head and replied, "It's our first date."

"Isn't she a little old for you?" The guard asked.

Saying the first thing that came to mind, Perry blurted out, "Age means nothing. Don't you know that love is blind?"

The guard chuckled as he said, "And that's definitely what I'd have to be to date that."

Before he could pick up his phone to page Connors, it buzzed with an incoming call. Picking the handset up, he said, "Front desk."

"Are those flowers for you?" A voice asked, followed by laughter in the background.

"Fuck you, Stiller," the guard said.

"Make sure he buys you dinner before you put your ass in the air," Stiller said. This was followed by more laughter. "Just to let you know, we're all glued to the close-circuit TV. We want to watch when you and your boyfriend walk off hand-in-hand into the sunset."

Slamming the receiver down, the guard stared at it malevolently.

In an exasperated tone, Perry said, "Now that you and your buddies are done screwing around, could you call and tell Miss Connors that I'm here."

Wanting to get the Second Lieutenant out of there as fast as he could and get everyone's attention off him, the guard picked up the phone and hit the page button. After a second he said, "Doctor Connors, please call or come to the foyer." Hanging up the receiver, he turned to the camera mounted on the wall and flipped it the bird.

***

After radioing Second Lieutenant Perry to start walking toward the front of the farmhouse, Major Cage, Staff Sergeant Fagan and Steve covered the last fifty feet to the back of it. It had taken them half an hour to get into position, since to avoid being seen by the spotters on the upper floors, they had gone out through the fence by the helicopter pad before circling around and coming in through it behind the farmhouse. With their night vision goggles, they could see the dead clustered in the woods. Their whining and moaning increased at the appearance of food but the Malectron kept them at bay. Having to stay as close to the trees as possible to avoid being spotted, occasionally one of the dead would stagger toward them before reeling back into the woods, making it a harrowing trek.

Leaning against the back wall of the farmhouse, Major Cage looked for the coal chute. Shuddering when he finally spotted it, he steadied his breathing and tried to clear his mind for the task ahead. The forty inch square flap of metal looked innocuous but he knew it was the door to hell.

Pointing it out to the others, he said quietly, "We go in one at a time just like we planned. I'm first followed by Staff Sergeant Fagan and then Steve. Kill everything that you see because there are no friendlies down there. Once we've cleared the area, we need to find the door that leads into the labs."

Fingering the silencer attached to the M16 Fagan had given him, Steve said, "I want to go first."

"Not happening," Cage told him. "You're a civilian and you're personally involved with the hostages so you're lucky I even brought you along."

Moving to the coal chute, Cage reached down and unlatched its metal cover. Lifting it up, he stepped back at the smell wafting out of the opening. Along with the expected moldy odor of the dead was the stink of putrefying flesh. Pulling a bandana out of his pocket, he tied it around his face and looked in.

After a few seconds, he said, "The chute is about fifteen feet long and the slope isn't too bad. I can see the bottom where it ends, but that's it. No dead around."

"Can we bang on something and try to attract them?" Fagan asked.

Pointing up at the house, Cage shook his head and replied, "Might attract the wrong kind of attention. There's only one way to do this."

Taking a deep breath and holding it, Cage sat down and stuck his feet in the hole, preparing to slide into hell.

CHAPTER TWENTY-ONE

Fort Redoubt:

After spending some time with Denise, Tick-Tock went in search of Rick Styles. The now constant sound of gunfire was distant so he felt safe enough in leaving her alone for a few minutes. The lights that normally illuminated the camp were off, the electricity used to power them having been diverted to the electrified fence, so he had to shuffle his feet to make sure he didn't step on anyone. Many of the people that sought sanctuary in the fort had found places along the wall to set up small camps, but there were so many that they spilled into the main courtyard. Quiet conversations filled the air, everyone speculating on the imminent arrival of the dead. A few cooking fires burned, giving him just enough light to weave his way through the mass of refugees.

Entering the building that housed the communication center, Tick-Tock spotted Rick sitting in a chair outside the door of the radio room with head propped up on fists, staring at the far wall as if in a trance.

Commenting on this, Tick-Tock said, "From your expression, I take it the aliens have landed."

Looking up, Rick seemed surprised to see him as he said, "I thought you would be half way to Louisiana by now."

Tick-Tock laughed as he said, "And miss all the fun."

Rick's reply was interrupted by one of him men coming to the door and saying, "The inner barrier has been breached in three locations, sir. There's too many Ds coming in for our people to hold them anymore."

Sighing, Rick said, "Order everyone inside the fort and have the electricity switched from the fences back to the compound. They're probably so broken up by now that they're not doing any good anyway. Turn on the floodlights so the troops fighting out in the boonies can find their way in."

"But won't that also lead the dead-asses straight to us?" The man asked.

Rick laughed and said, "I'm pretty sure they know where we are."

As the man turned to go, Tick-Tock asked, "Any word from fort one and two?"

"One is still off the air," the man told him. "Fort two called in a few minutes ago and reported that they're planning to break out to the east."

Standing, Rick waved for Tick-Tock to follow him as he entered the radio room. Leading him to a map of the area, the commander studied it for a few seconds before saying, "I told them to give it a shot. They might have a chance if they take off now. They're the furthest fort to the east so they probably aren't completely surrounded by the Ds coming in from the southeast."

Wishing he was at the fort two, Tick-Tock asked, "So where does that leave us?"

"Surrounded," Rick answered. "When the main herd split and a bunch of them came along the lake it really screwed us. They circled around the entire camp. On top of that, we haven't gotten any transmissions from fort one for almost half an hour so my guess is they got overrun. They were directly in line with the group coming out of the southwest. That's what cut us off from fort two. By now that group has probably joined up with the main herd to our east."

"And the aliens," Tick-Tock asked.

Rick laughed and said, "They're not here yet, but when they do land, I hope they eat the dead and piss gasoline because we've got too many of one and not enough of the other."

Tick-Tock laughed and then turned serious as he asked, "How long do you think we can last?"

Rick thought about it and said, "If the walls hold, I'd say we have enough food and water for two weeks. Fuel is our biggest problem since it was already getting scarce before all this. Running the lights is eating up our power but we need them right now. It figures the Ds would hit us at night."

Thinking about the fortifications, Tick-Tock said, "The walls are all angled out so we should be able to reinforce them with the weight of the refugees in the fort. The dead will be pushing in and up so all they have to do is climb on them to counter the force with their weight."

Rick smiled and asked an officer standing nearby, "Did you hear that?" The man nodded so Rick said, "Then get the people in the courtyard organized."

As the man went out the door, Rick turned to Tick-Tock and asked, "By the way, how's Denise?"

"She's up on the parapets," he answered.

Concerned, Rick asked, "Is she well enough for that?"

"No," Tick-Tock answered, "but I'm not going to try and convince her to go back to the hospital. She's a very willful woman."

"Maybe I can talk to her," Rick told him. "Besides, I want to be out there when the dead hit so I can try to keep everyone organized."

As the two men moved through the courtyard, they could see a dozen of Rick's men getting the refugees in place along the west side of the fort. With the lights now on inside the camp, it was easy for them to make their way through the throngs of people milling around as they waited to be sorted into groups of ten and moved into position. Conversations were hushed and hurried, everyone thinking that if they kept their voice down that they wouldn't attract the attention of the dead.

Using two inch square pieces of wood nailed into the telephone poles, Rick and Tick-Tock climbed the angled wall and onto the narrow parapet. Sidestepping around the defenders, the two men found Denise twenty feet further on. Noticing that she was no longer leaning against the wall with her head down, Tick-Tock thought she was feeling better.

He started to comment on this, but she quieted him with a quick, "Shhh."

Realizing that she had only perked up because she had heard something, Tick-Tock tuned out the noise coming from inside the fort and focused on the woods. Faintly at first, he could hear the whining of the dead. The noise grew in volume, reminding him of the Doppler effect of a speeding car coming toward him. He noticed that the sound didn't grow in volume as fast as a Formula One race car on the track, but it was rising quick enough.

The next sign Tick-Tock had of the approaching dead were the tops of the trees moving. Starting as far out as he could see, the entire forest seemed to come alive as the dead passed through it. Like a groundswell forty feet in the air, the shuddering of the foliage showed their progress as they neared the camp. Watching the surge until it reached the clearing between the woods and the fort, he looked down when he saw the dead break out of the woods.

The first of the reanimated corpses came forward in ones and twos, bringing gasps from some of the defenders on the parapets. This trickle quickly turned into a raggedy wave as more and more of the dead broke through the brush into the clearing. Within seconds, the field was packed with bodies moving in a rush toward their food. Dead feet trampled over each other, breaking bones, but the mob was so densely packed that it carried the debilitated Zs along with them. Out in front of them, the leading edge of the horde hit the wall, their impact not even making the telephone poles buried deep in the ground shudder.

Knowing better than to think this would be the same case with the main body of dead, Tick-Tock called out for everyone to brace themselves. Reaching out to Denise, he put one arm around her while the other hand clenched the top of the wall in a death grip.

Heedless of injury, the main body of the horde smacked into Fort Redoubt with a dull thump, the impact causing the telephone poles to shudder and dust to rise off them in a sudden cloud. Being angled outward, hundreds of dead were pushed into the base of the wall and crushed by the weight of the others piling in behind them. The lights along the entire west side of the fort flickered for a few seconds but stayed on.

Half expecting the wall to collapse when the dead hit it, Tick-Tock was amazed when he found himself still alive. Outside of the fort he could hear the screeching whine of the dead and inside he could hear screams and calls from the courtyard, but the sound that overrode them all was the creaking of the wall as the dead pushed against it by the thousands.

Looking both ways down the length of the parapets, he could see at least five different places where it was starting to buckle. This was the first sign that their fortifications were starting to fail. Only two or three of the less secure telephone poles were being pushed in at each location, but if they were separated from the others the whole wall would start to crumble.

Moving down the parapet toward the nearest breach, Tick-Tock and Rick stopped when they saw dozens of people scurry up the angled barrier to jump up and down on the bulging posts. Seeing this, others ran forward to repack the small amount of dirt displaced at their base as they were slowly realigned. All along the barrier, men and women worked to keep the wall intact, knowing if there was even a small breakthrough by the dead that it would cause a flood of them to pour into the compound.

After checking to make sure that Denise was okay, Tick-Tock joined Rick as he inspected each repair on the west wall. Reaching the last one and finding boards being nailed across it for reinforcement, Rick called out over the deafening whine of the dead, "Holy shit, it held."

Listening to the increasing creaking noise coming from the overstressed telephone poles, Tick-Tock replied, "Yeah, but for how long?"

Russellville, Arkansas:

Doctor Hawkins opened the door to his lab and smiled at his three hostages tied and gagged at the far side of the room. Nodding to his where Cain was seated in the corner, he said, "They look comfy. Have they given you any trouble?"

"Connors has been as quiet as a church mouse and the little girl is no trouble," Cain told him. "The other one is a handful though."

Hawkins looked at Heather with mock disgust as he shook his head in disapproval. As if speaking to a child, he said, "Now you behave young lady." Turning his attention to his assistant, he said, "Time is getting short so we should begin?"

Jim moved toward Cindy and picked her up, sending Heather into a flurry of short kicks as she fought against her bonds. Whipping her head back and forth as she writhed on the floor, she tried to shake off her gag while struggling against the zip ties that held her hands and feet.

Frowning at this, Hawkins walked over and grabbed her by the hair. Raising her face up so they could see eye to eye, he said, "If you continue with this disgusting display of futility, I will stick *your* arm into the cage."

Despite this threat, Heather still did her best to head-butt him.

Reeling away to avoid the blow and shoving her back, Hawkins stood and looked down at her. After a few seconds, he said, "Your usefulness is limited to how well we get along. My suggestion to you is to remain passive. The less trouble you are to me, the longer you live."

Turning his attention to the twenty-foot square, glass testing area, he watched with satisfaction as the girl was strapped into a wheeled office chair. When Jim released her arms, she swung one up to strike him, but he easily avoided the clumsy blow.

Turning toward where Cain was seated, he said, "Although Jim seems a little more adept at dodging female fists than you, please give him a hand."

Cain scowled at the crack as he stood and walked over to the girl. Grabbing her left wrist in an iron grip, he easily forced her hand down to the arm of the chair and zip-tied it in place.

Moving to the other side, he helped Jim secure her right arm to a piece of metal welded to the chair at shoulder height.

When they were done, Hawkins took in the sight of the little girl strapped to the chair with her right arm sticking straight out to her side and said, "Looks like half a crucifixion."

Cain was the only one who laughed at the joke.

Hawkins turned to where Doctor Connors lay on the floor and said, "Bet you didn't think of this little experiment, did you?"

Her eyes wide with shock, Connors could only stare in disbelief.

Smirking, Hawkins said, "That's what I thought. You always did sit on your moral high-horse when it came to field experimentation. Now we get to see if the little girl is really immune to the HWNW virus. We will let one or two of the specimens into the testing chamber where they are free to take a few bites of her proffered arm and then wait and see what happens." Turning to his assistant, he said, "Move her into position, Jim."

Watching as the chair rolled across the floor, Hawkins had a moment of doubt when it looked like the little girl's arm was too low and would hit the shatter-proof glass. He breathed a sigh of relief though when it slid all the way in to her shoulder.

When Jim was done securing the chair in place, Hawkins asked him, "How many dead do we have in the containment room?"

Checking a clipboard hanging from the front of the control panel. He answered, "Sixteen. Eleven men and five woman."

Looking at the testing chamber, Hawkins said, "We really only need a couple so don't leave the door open for more than a few seconds. I don't want too much damage done to our subject and have her bleed out." Pointing to the Malectron, he added, "As soon as she's been bitten twice, I want you to repel the dead and bring her arm out."

Jim nodded and moved his hand to the switch that controlled the door on the far side of the chamber as he said, "Let me know when you're ready, Professor."

Hawkins was about to give the order to proceed when someone started paging Doctor Connors on the intercom system.

Hawkins turned to Cain and asked angrily, "What in the hell are your idiot people paging Connors for."

"They don't know we have her down here," Cain explained. "As far as they're concerned, she's still working."

"Who in the hell would be looking for her?" Hawkins asked.

Holding up his hands, Cain said, "How should I know?"

"Whoever it is, go upstairs and get rid of them," Hawkins ordered. Turning to Jim, he said, "Open the door."

***

After climbing into the coal chute, Major Cage braced his knees against its metal sides, releasing the pressure to slide a few feet before halting himself. After scanned the opening with his rifle and seeing nothing, he repeated the maneuver. When he was only three feet from where the chute opened into the basement, he took a deep breath and let himself slide all the way in.

Dropping down the three feet to the dirt floor, he raised his M16 as he whipped his head back and forth in search of the dead. Seeing only the half-rotted wooden walls on either side of him that made up the coal bin, he cautiously moved toward its opening ten feet in front of him. Not hearing any of the dead whine at his presence, he wondered if there were any left. From behind him, he heard a soft thud followed seconds later by another. Without having to turn around, he knew it was Fagan and Steve joining him.

Peeking around the corner, Cage could see a scattering of broken furniture and old tools in the green glow of the night-vision goggles. A soft series of whines came to him, making him look closer at the clutter to find its source. Feeling a presence behind him, he motioned for

Fagan and Steve to join him. The coal bin was only six feet wide, causing the three men to stand sideways as they half-crouched in its opening.

In a whispered voice, Cage said, "I can hear them but I can't spot them."

Motioning toward the wall to their right, Fagan whispered back, "It looks like the basement is L shaped. They must be around the corner."

After scanning the numerous places where the dead could jump out at them as they made their way to the far end of the cellar, Cage ordered, "We'll move forward in a triangle formation. I'll take point and you two cover me. I'll watch where the basement turns the corner so you two concentrate on our rear and our flanks."

Taking a step forward, Cage froze in place as a blinding flash of light whited out his night-vision goggles. Before they went blank, he caught a glimpse of writhing shadows cast across the floor and walls at the far side of the basement. The whining voices of the dead started up, echoing against the block walls. His blood ran cold at the sound, but at least it told him that the dead were congregated around the corner. Whipping off his goggles, he could see the vertical band of light narrow and disappear, leaving him completely blind.

Realizing that the light had come from a door opening and closing, he put his goggles back on and waited impatiently for them to adjust. The noise of scratching and scraping on metal joined in with the whine of the walking corpses, letting him know that the dead were pawing at the door. Being completely blind, this did little to appease his terror that they were creeping up on him in the dark

His fear ebbing in direct proportion to the green glow of the basement coming back into focus, Cage stepped forward when his vision was completely clear. Although careful to give any obstacles a wide berth, he quickly made his way to the corner. Looking around it, he spotted over a dozen dead pawing and clawing at the far wall. Looking closer, he could see that he had been right, they were clustered in front of a door.

***

Hawkins watched with clinical interest as the two reanimated corpses entered the glass enclosed room. Heedless of the screams coming from Cindy, and the barely audible curses coming from Heather and Doctor Connors, he said to the dead, "Come along, my little creatures. Come and get a quick treat."

Dressed in rags, the two zombies swayed back and forth for a few seconds. Black blood seeped from scratches and bites running down the first one's arm, while the second showed no sign of injury. The only way anyone could tell it was dead was by its bluish-grey skin color. Hawkins was pleased with this, having insisted on having only the best specimens to experiment on. This group in particular he had actually cultivated by letting the dead infect healthy humans without letting the victim be too badly damaged.

After having spent days locked in the dark, the two zombies recovered quickly from the burst of light, looking around for only a few seconds before spotting Cindy's arm sticking through the glass. Like the others back in the holding chamber, they had sensed living flesh on the other side of the door and had clustered in front of it, waiting for it to open. Creatures of habit and instinct, they knew that when the door opened, they would receive some type of food. Whether it was raccoon, deer or human, they didn't discriminate.

Focused completely on the very reason for their existence, they let out loud whines and lurched toward Cindy's arm. Reaching it at the same time, the two creatures lunged forward and sank their teeth into the proffered meat. Ignoring their prey's pitiful screams, they simultaneously bit into the soft flesh of her inside forearm and upper bicep.

Cindy's cries of terror became shrieks of pain as she fought to break loose from the chair holding her in place. Hawkins ignored this as he leaned in close to watch the initial flow of blood from her wounds. Not wanting the dead to do too much damage, when he saw the skin break and the teeth of the dead sink all of the way in, he called for Jim to turn the Malectron on.

Everyone in the observation area felt their hair stand on end as the device was activated. Its effects were swift, causing the whines of the dead to turn into moans of pain as they were repelled across the room. Pawing at the air, they stood with their backs to the wall as they tried to force themselves toward the food still struggling against its bindings.

Never tiring of this reaction, Hawkins stood watching them with glee until he was interrupted by Jim saying, "Doctor, one of the specimens took a good chunk of flesh out of the test subject's bicep. She's bleeding quite profusely."

Turning his attention to where Cindy had passed out in the chair, Hawkins could see blood running from her upper arm to soak her shirt in a growing stain of red. Frowning, he tried to gauge whether or not she would bleed out before his experiment was complete. After a few seconds of watching the heavy flow, he gave a huff of displeasure and said, "Pull her out and put a compress on the wound. The one on her forearm doesn't look that bad, so leave it open where I can observe it. Keep it wiped clean so I can watch for the first signs of her blood blackening if she turns. When you're done, turn up the power on the Malectron. I want to see its full affects one more time."

Jim nodded and unfastened the chair from the brackets securing it to the floor. Rolling it a safe distance from the hole in the safety glass, he retrieved a compress from his medical kit and tried to wrap it around the little girl's bicep. Finding himself restricted by the straps securing her arm to the cross brace on the chair, he released the three holding her right arm. Cindy moaned as she regained consciousness, rolling her head up to look at him as he finished tightening the bandage.

Avoiding her eyes, Jim said, "Suck it up, kid. If you live through this, you'll be a part of medical history."

"It hurts." Cindy rasped as her body tightened in agony from her wounds.

In a stern voice, Jim said, "Like I said, you need to suck it up. I can't give you anything for the pain until the experiment is complete. Now keep your arm elevated until I get back."

With her pain channeling into anger at how she was being hurt and abused, Cindy glared at Jim as he walked over to a black box sitting on the control panel. Despite the thickness of the glass in the testing chamber, she could hear the moaning of the dead grow louder as they shrank even further into the corner when he adjusted a knob on it. Looking down to where her fellow captives lay bound on the floor, she locked eyes with Heather. Cindy didn't comprehend why the woman kept looking down at her right leg and then back up to her and nodding, but then she understood.

***

With the amount of noise the dead were making, Major Cage had to draw back from the corner and raise his voice as he said, "I want Staff Sergeant Fagan on my right and Steve on my left. Double tap every target. Steve, I also need you keep an eye on our six in case we did pass any of the shitheads and they come up behind us. We go on the count of three."

Looking back around the corner as he prepared to say, 'one,' Cage saw that his voice had attracted half a dozen of the dead. Only feet away, they were coming toward him at a full run. Without hesitation, he jumped into the twelve foot opening while shouting, "Three."

Fagan and Steve rounded the corner and took in the situation in a millisecond. Not having time to get into position, both men raised their rifles and opened fire at the oncoming Zs. Brains, pieces of skull and black ochre flew into the air as the dead danced a final jig of death. With this immediate threat eliminated, it gave the three men free reign to deal with the dead clustered around the door. Their noise suppressors coughed out a deadly rain of lead that quickly dropped the reanimated corpses clustered at the far end of the basement.

Cautiously moving forward as their night-vision goggles adjusted from the muzzle-flash of their weapons, they stopped and kicked each corpse to make sure it was dead before moving on to the next. Only once did they have to fire into the skull of any of the Zs, a woman that had been hit twice in the lower face and knocked down before being pinned by the bodies falling around her. As Steve approached, she lunged toward him and worked her shattered jaw in a gnashing motion until he ended her suffering with a well-placed shot. When they were sure they had exterminated all the dead, they reloaded in preparation to storm the rest of the basement.

Reaching the door first, Cage laid his hand on it and said, "Its metal but I think it's only wood core with some sheet metal laid over it for reinforcing." Pointing toward the top of the jamb, he added, "They've also got a big-ass bolt securing it up at the top and an operating arm to open and close it."

"How do you want to proceed, Major?" Fagan asked.

Anxious to get to Heather, Steve replied, "Like this," and emptied the magazine into the bolt securing the door and the motor that controlled the arm.

The bullets ripped through the metal and pushed the door open a few inches, letting in bright light. All three of the men whipped off their goggles and blinked rapidly to adjust their eyes. Still seeing white spots, Steve nudged the door with the toe of his boot and looked through the opening, not noticing how every hair on his body stood almost straight up. The first thing visible was a glass wall with a man standing on the other side of it. To his right he could see through another wall where someone bent over Cindy as he tied a bandage around her arm. Not sure who they were, he raised his rifle but held fire.

And then he spotted Heather.

CHAPTER TWENTY-TWO

Fort Redoubt:

Tick-Tock looked out over the sea of dead pushing against the walls of the fort. Glancing down the length of the wall, he could actually see it move in and out like some kind of breathing animal. In the illumination thrown by the lights circling the perimeter, he could see where the telephone poles buried in the ground were being slowly worked loose faster than the defenders could reinforce them. So far, there had only been a few minor breaches in their main line of defense, but there was no way it could hold forever.

Knowing that it was only a matter of time before the reanimated corpses broke through, Tick-Tock's mind raced with ways to escape the coming carnage. Neither he nor Denise could fly, so that was out. A tunnel might work, but he didn't think they had the time to dig one before the dead broke through. Looking at the three catapults in the courtyard, he knew they didn't have the range to throw them over the dead to safety, and on top of that, even if they wrapped themselves in mattresses, the landing would probably kill them.

As he wracked his brain, he suddenly remembered overhearing Rick tell Steve that all the forts had pre-set escape routes. After looking down to where Denise napped with her back against the wall, and wondering how she could sleep with the constant screeching of the dead, he asked the two women next to him to keep an eye on her. Hefting his rifle as he gave one last look at the thousands of dead outside the wall, he went in search of the commander.

Checking the radio room first, Tick-Tock wasn't surprised when he didn't find Rick. The man was a hands-on leader, so he knew he would find him working with his people in the defense of the fort. Circling the inside perimeter of the encampment, he saw hundreds of people frantically working to keep the walls intact. Some were nailing whatever wood they could find across the poles to reinforce them, while those that were unable to do physical labor, used their body weight to counteract the push of the dead.

A crashing noise made his blood freeze, and he looked around wildly for where the dead had breached their defenses. Relaxing slightly when he saw it was only some workers dismantling the chow hall, Tick-Tock scanned the other buildings and saw they were also being stripped of all usable material. Nails were pulled from boards that would be used again to secure them to the wall in an ongoing battle to reinforce the only thing standing between them and a horrible death.

Spotting a familiar figure ahead, Tick-Tock tried to recall her name. She had joined them from the Battleship Texas, but had kept such a low profile that there was nothing she'd said or done to stand out and remember her by. Not wanting to call out, 'Hey you,' he approached her and asked, "How are you doing?"

Looking up from where she was concentrating on pulling nails from a board, shock crossed the woman's face when she saw who had addressed her. Jumping to her feet, she stammered out, "I'm fine, sir."

Tick-Tock smiled to put her at ease and said, "I'm looking for Commander Styles."

"I haven't seen him, sir," she told him. "The rest of your people and I joined the demolition teams after we couldn't find you at the gate."

Tick-Tock cringed. He had been so distracted by other events that he had completely forgotten about telling his people to meet him out front. As he was about to apologize, a loud crack broke the silence. At first thinking it was another section being pulled away from one of buildings, he tensed when he heard screaming. Seeing people running for the east wall, he joined them.

As he raced to where a group was clustered near the northeast corner, Tick-Tock knew two things. One, that the dead either had or were about to break through the wall, and two, that he would find Rick in the middle of whatever chaos was about to ensue.

Reaching the edge of the crowd, Tick-Tock could see where three of the huge telephone poles were starting to be pushed in. The parapets had buckled and fallen from the force, hitting those that had been using their weight to push back against the dead. Numerous people were climbing over the wreckage to lay flat on the wall or bounce up and down to push it back into place, while others tended to the wounded. Despite this effort, the split widened as two poles parted, showing the snarling faces of the dead in half-shadow as they tried to move from the darkness outside the wall into the light.

Orders had been given to use their ammunition only if the walls were breached, so Tick-Tock unslung his M4 and sighted in on a dead face pushing its way between the gap. Flesh peeled away from its cheeks as twisted its head to force its way in, letting out a high-pitched whine as it saw food almost within its grasp. Before Tick-Tock could get his first shot off, numerous pistols, rifles and a shotguns from the nearest defenders rang out. As the dead thing and its fellows fell away under the hail of bullets and buckshot, more of the living moved in to throw their weight against the poles, slowly easing them back into place. Workers with boards and nails swarmed forward, hammering makeshift braces in place to reinforce the wall.

When the barricade was secure, Tick-Tock noticed that no cheer went up from the defenders at their success. Drained, they dragged their tools and planks to the center of the fort to wait for the next crack in their defenses. Watching them, Tick-Tock knew that sooner or later they would collapse from exhaustion, while the dead needed no rest in their relentless push to get inside the fort. This had been the fifth breakthrough so far, telling him that the walls were slowly being weakened.

Spotting Rick standing near Ginny as he directed the last of the crews tending to the wounded, Tick-Tock walked up to him and said bluntly, "You told Steve that you had an escape plan."

Slightly annoyed at the interruption, Rick said brusquely, "Yeah, we did."

"You *did*?" Tick-Tock asked, his hope flying away.

Ignoring the question, Rick waved a stretcher crew in to collect a man with a broken leg. When they had him loaded and were on the way to the infirmary, the Commander turned to Tick-Tock and pointed up to the radio tower as he said, "We planned to use zip lines to get over any big herd of dead-asses that surrounded the fort. We could also use them to get behind any living attackers."

Not seeing anyone sliding to safety, Tick-Tock asked, "So what gives? Why aren't we using them?"

With a futile shake of his head, Rick told him, "They only go as far as the tree line."

Understanding struck Tick-Tock as he realized that the wires didn't go out far enough.

"We weren't expecting a herd this big to hit us," Rick explained. "You can still use the lines, but you'll end up stuck in a tree with a couple thousand Ds around you. I prefer to take my chances here."

"So what else can we do to get the hell out of here?" Tick-Tock asked.

"I've had the radio room calling for help for the last hour," Rick told him. "Fort Polk finally answered, but they have everything grounded. They put in a request for an airlift and are waiting for a reply. I spoke to the Lieutenant on duty and he told me about some internal strife in Washington DC. They've almost got it sorted out, but it's going to be a while before they can get permission for a rescue."

"What do we do until then?" Tick-Tock asked.

A loud crack split the air, letting them know that another part of the wall was starting to cave in.

Turning to run toward the latest breach, Rick said, "Keep patching holes."

Russellville, Arkansas:

With the rage of seeing Heather trussed up on the floor surging through him, Steve was about to let loose on the man in front of him when a whining noise to his right caught his attention. Swinging his rifle in that direction, he spotted two of the dead with fresh blood smeared across their faces, pushed back against the wall like they were plastered to it. Focusing on the immediate threat, he shot each of them in the head before moving his sights back to the man directly across from him.

The fluorescent lights threw a brilliant glare over the lab as he squeezed the trigger, sending half a dozen rounds into the glass. Expecting it to shatter and the man beyond it to go down, Steve was surprised when his bullets only left blackened, saucer sized marks in its surface. The man in the lab coat looked surprised too, cringing back as the first rounds hit, and then looking down at himself in shock that he wasn't spouting blood from numerous holes.

Trying to adjust to the situation, Steve looked for a door leading out of the testing chamber. Spotting a glass pane with hinges set into it, he quickly realized that there was no doorknob and the hinges were on the other side. In frustration, he fired off the rest of the bullets in his magazine at his initial target. Once again, they thudded into the shatter-proof wall, sending up tiny shards of glass but not punching through.

As he was changing magazines to try again, Steve felt Major Cage lay a hand on his shoulder and say, "Don't bother. You'd need a fifty caliber to punch through that."

Shaking the restraining hand off, Steve reloaded his M16 and raised it to his shoulder, swinging the muzzle back and forth as he searched for some weakness in the barrier in front of him. His eyes coming to rest on the second man, now hiding behind Cindy, he screamed, "Open this mother-fucker up."

This only caused him to cower even further behind the little girl.

Turning his sights back to his first target, Steve yelled at him, "If I hit it enough in the same spot, the bullets are eventually going to punch through."

Seeing the situation, Hawkins replied with a laugh as he stepped to the right, "And I will simply move." Spotting Cage and Fagan, he added, "I see the Major and his sidekick have arrived. Good to see you again, gentlemen." Nodding to Steve as he gestured to himself and the second man, he said, "My name is Doctor Hawkins and this is my assistant, Jim. But I haven't had the pleasure of making your acquaintance."

Ignoring this, Steve glanced down to make sure Heather was still alive. Seeing her struggling as she tried to free her arms and legs, his heart filled with fury at what had been done to her. This, combined with the pompous tone Hawkins used caused his anger to pass the boiling point. Even though he knew it was fruitless, he still sent ten rounds smashing into the glass.

Hawkins flinched but stood his ground, the bullets striking only feet from his face. Taking a step forward, he studied the impact points as he said in a mocking tone, "Like they say on the firing range, nice grouping."

Realizing the doctor was baiting him, Steve pushed his anger down. Instead of feeding into the man's banter, he started searching for some way through the glass. Spotting a blood splattered hole, he knew there was no way he could hit the doctor from that angle. He might be able to get a clean shot at the second man, but by the time he reached the hole and took aim through it, Jim would be gone around the corner. Looking to Cindy, he saw her staring at Heather. The little girl was bloodied but alive, giving him hope.

From behind him, Fagan asked in a low voice, "Where's Cain?"

"Who's Cain?" Steve asked, his eyes scanning the surface of the glass for some weakness.

"Hawkins' do-boy," Fagan answered in disgust.

As if hearing his name, Cain walked through a door at the far side of the lab, shock registering on his face as he took in the scene. Seeing Cage, Fagan and another man inside the testing chamber, he pulled his pistol and raised it to fire at them.

Hawkins stopped him by saying, “Don’t waste your bullets, Mister Cain. They can’t get at us and you can’t get at them. It appears we are at an impasse.”

Understanding the situation, Cain’s mind spun as he tried to figure out what to do next. He could see by the marks on the glass that numerous shots had been fired, but he hadn’t heard anything until he walked through the door. Glancing at the noise suppressors on the invaders rifles, he understood why, while at the same time registering that his men hadn’t heard anything either and weren’t coming to the rescue. He thought of firing a few bullets to alert them, but realized that with the sound-proofing done to the entire lab area that it was unlikely they would hear the gunfire.

Doctor Hawkins was one step ahead of him though, as he said, “I however, have analyzed the situation and come up with a solution.” Pointing to Steve, he said, “By the way this one keeps looking at the woman that knocked you down, I would guess he’s got some kind of connection to her. Lover? Sister? Fuckbuddy? Who cares? I want you to set an example, Mister Cain. I want you to put a bullet through her heart. After that, if Cage and his fellow cretins do not make their way back the way they came, I want you to hold Doctor Connors head against the glass and spray her brains all over it. This way, they will know we are serious. I don’t want any problems when we make our way to the helicopters.”

Looking down at Heather and then up at Cain, Hawkins said, “Whenever you’re ready, Mister Cain.”

***

Cindy understood what Heather was trying to communicate to her just as the Steve broke into the observation area. Thinking that they were saved, her heart fell when she saw his bullets bounce harmlessly off the shatter-proof glass. Hoping he would find a way to save them, she watched with dread as the man named Cain came through the door of the lab. In horror, she listened to the doctor’s orders to kill Heather.

Thoughts of how Ginny, Susan, Mary, Sheila and Linda had all died trying to protect her tore through Cindy’s heart. Remembering her vow that it wouldn’t happen again, she steeled herself. Her right side was almost immobile from pain, but she knew what she had to do.

Her arm screamed in agony as she moved it, causing sweat to pop out on her face and her breathing to turn shallow and labored. Forcing her hand down to her right side, she pulled up on the flap of material covering the cargo pocket of her pants. Digging inside, she felt the object she was looking for. With a rush of adrenalin at the ignorance of Hawkins and Cain, she rejoiced in the thought that while Heather had been searched and disarmed after she was knocked out, they hadn’t bothered to do the same to a ten-year old girl.

Pulling the pistol out of her pocket, Cindy dragged back on the slide and chambered a round. Lifting it, she sought out Cain. Seeing him smiling evilly as he lifted his own pistol and waved it mockingly at Steve, she thought she might be too late as he lowered it to point at Heather’s chest.

Not hesitating, Cindy lined up the sights on her little pistol with the center of Cain’s body and squeezed the trigger twice. Expecting the loud boom of Dirty Harry’s .44 magnum, the sharp cracks of the small caliber rounds took her by surprise. Also expecting Cain to be flung back by the bullets just like the people in the movies did, she thought she missed when all he did was let out a grunt and stiffen. Preparing to fire again, she saw two spots of blood on the side of his chest, merging into one as they grew. Knowing she had hit him, but ready to fire again if she needed to, she tracked Cain in her sights as he swayed for a second before collapsing to the ground.

Feeling hands grab her arm, she saw Jim was trying to wrestle the pistol from her grip. Twisting it in her hand, Cindy pulled the trigger again. The bullet went wild, but it was enough to make Hawkins’ assistant jump back and scurry away backward on all fours to pin himself against the wall.

Spinning in her chair, she leveled the barrel of her weapon at his chest and said in a strained voice, “Untie Heather.”

Jim stayed frozen against the wall.

Having seen how he had moved the last time she fired her pistol, Cindy pulled the trigger again. Only meaning to put a bullet into the wall to the side of him, she was shocked to see it clip the outside of his left shoulder. Tears sprung to her eyes and she started to beg his forgiveness, stopping when she saw him leap to his feet and run over to where Heather lay on the floor.

Turning her attention to Doctor Hawkins, Cindy saw that he was rigid with shock. White faced, his mouth opened and closed as he tried to form words. Seconds ago, he might have been in control, but now he was at her mercy.

Using a scalpel from a nearby tray, Jim cut Heather loose. Numb from being restrained for the past few hours, she rubbed her wrist and ankles for a few seconds before standing. As circulation restored feeling to her body, she gauged the distance to Hawkins. When she felt she was ready for any counter-attack, she jabbed out with her right fist, hitting him square in the jaw. Thrown back by the punch, the doctor dropped to the floor.

Turning a steely gaze on Jim, she said, “You have ten seconds to open the door to that fucking rat cage and let my boyfriend in or I'll rip your balls off and feed them to you.”

It only took him three.

With a target to vent anger on, Steve stepped through the opening in the glass wall and slammed the butt of his rifle into Jim's face. As the man fell to floor with blood spurting out of his nose, Steve turned and fired three times into the lifeless body of Cain. The man didn't even flinch, telling him Cain was dead, so he turned his attention to Hawkins. Advancing on the doctor, he raised his rifle to smash it into the top of his head, but stopped when Heather screamed, “No.”

With his M16 raised over his shoulder, he looked between her and where Hawkins crouched down, cowering as he whimpered for mercy. With a snarl, Steve said, “This piece of shit was ready to have you killed, so I'm going to fuck him up.” To punctuate his statement, he reared back to bring the butt of his rifle down with as much force as he could.

From behind him, Cage shouted, “Don't do it, Steve. Hawkins is a douche-nugget, but we need him.”

Stopping again, Steve asked, “For what? Target practice. Z bait?”

“We need him to get out of here,” Cage explained.

Gesturing toward the door leading to the coal chute, Steve said, “We can go back out the way we came. We left a rope to climb out.”

“But how are we going to get Cindy up it, out through the wire, along the woods and back into the camp?” Fagan asked.

Looking to where the little girl sat strapped in the chair with a torn arm and blood staining her shirt, Steve felt his anger leave him in a rush. Lowering his rifle, he went to her and started loosening her bindings as he talked softly to her about what a good job she had done protecting Heather. Thinking by her lack of reply that she was in shock, he was relieved when she said in a calm tone, “I didn't want to shoot him, but he left me no choice. He was going to hurt Heather. He was a bad man.”

Heather had joined him in freeing her, and in a calming voice said, “You did real good, Cindy. You saved me. Now we have to get out of here. Do you think you can walk?”

As they were about to lift her from the chair, Hawkins said. “She's been bitten. You need to leave her tied up until we know if she turns.” Having regained some of his arrogance when he saw that he wasn't going to be beaten, he added in a haughty tone, “You people are so ignorant. I'm surprised you've lasted this long.”

Everything that she had experienced since she entered the farmhouse came back to

Heather in a rush. Being knocked out and held hostage by the doctor and Cain, watching Cindy being strapped into a chair and used as a human guinea pig, and then almost being shot flowed through her mind at once. Although she had tried to stay calm and keep Steve from killing Hawkins, she reached where the doctor was being held by Fagan in two steps. Watching as his eyes went wide, she gave him three quick jabs in the stomach, listening in satisfaction as the breath whooshed out of him.

As Fagan started to drop the gasping man, Heather told him, "Hold the son-of-a-bitch up. It makes it hurts worse."

Fagan laughed as he hoisted the doctor upright and asked, "You military?"

"I used to be a cop," Heather replied. "We had to deal with a lot of scumbags like him."

Turning to tend to Cindy, she heard the man named Cage say to Hawkins, "You have two choices now, Herr Doktor. You can get on the intercom and have your people stand down, or I'm going to lock you in the testing chamber with a couple of the dead we bypassed in the coal bin."

Hawkins' eyes went wide and he wheezed out that Cain's men would never take orders from him.

With an evil smile, Fagan squeezed a pressure point on the inside of Hawkins' elbow and said, "Then tell them an airborne strain of the HWNW virus was accidentally released."

Still defiant, in a strained voice, Hawkins said, "You idiot. For that, all you have to do is set off the biohazard alarm."

Irritated that he had forgotten about the alarm, Staff Sergeant Fagan nonetheless gave Hawkins' a good squeeze on the pressure point that brought him to his knees.

Looking toward a red box mounted on the wall with a biohazard sticker next to it, Cage turned to Steve and said, "Get everyone ready to move." Pulling a two-way radio from his pocket, he adjusted the channel to contact the entire compound and pushed the transmit button before saying in a calm voice, "Attention, attention. This is Major Cage. We will be conducting a biohazard drill at the farmhouse in five minutes. Don't be alarmed and pass this down the line so we don't have a panic. I say again, this is only a drill."

After repeating the message twice, he switched channels to contact the men and women he had quickly assembled into a reaction squad in case their mission went south. Hitting the transmit button again, he said, "This is Major Cage. The biohazard alarm is going to be set off in a few minutes to clear the farmhouse. I want all personnel exiting the building to be detained, over."

"Detained by what means, sir, over?" A voice questioned.

Without hesitation, Cage replied, "By whatever means available, just be on the lookout for Lieutenant Perry. We're going to give it two minutes after the alarm goes off before we come out. There will be eight of us, over."

Freed from her restraints, Doctor Connors said, "I will stay behind with the girl. Every second we waste in developing the anti-virus means that more people are infected. The sooner we start, the more people we will be able to save." Seeing Cage hesitate, she added, "The farmhouse will be deserted except for us, and you will have total control of the base, Major. We will be in no danger. If I can start working right away in locating the strand of DNA that was missing from the other woman, I can possible have the anti-virus ready in two to three days."

"I'll stay with her," Heather chimed in as she retrieved Cain's pistol. Looking down at the dead man, she added, "Besides, this piece of shit took my rifle and I want it back."

Seeing the logic of plan, Cage pushed the transmit button and said, "Correction, there will be five of us exiting the farmhouse. The two in lab coats are our prisoners. I want you and your men to provide a security perimeter. Doctor Connors, her new assistant and one other will remain behind. If they need anything, I want you to move heaven and earth to get it for them, over."

"Acknowledged, sir," The voice replied.

Hearing yelling in the background as the man transmitted, Cage asked, "What's going on, over."

In a reluctant voice, the man said, "We have someone here calling himself Brain that keeps screaming about saving someone named Tick-Tock. He showed up a few minutes ago telling us that he fixed the radio and was getting distress calls from Fort Polk about this place named Fort Redoubt that was about to be overrun. I was going to have the medics sedate him, but he had a communique from Polk asking for anyone in the vicinity to help the civilians trapped there, sir. DC still has all air traffic grounded, but I guess it's not all air traffic though because we have three Blackhawks inbound, over."

Perking up at hearing this, Hawkins said, "Those are for me and my people. The joint Chiefs sent them to take me and the Malectron to Washington. Your best course of action would be to release me immediately."

Steve ignored him, motioning frantically for the handset as Major Cage told the radioman to put Brain on. Seconds later, the tech's voice came over the speaker saying, "I got the radio working and heard that Tick-Tock's in trouble. Fort Redoubt got hit by a couple big herds of Zs and they're about to be wiped out. We have to help him and Denise, over."

His mind spinning on how to save his friend, Steve flashed back to the plan he had concocted on the ride from the airfield. Turning to look at Hawkins, he felt an instant distrust for the weasel. Seeing where Jim was slowly sitting up and shaking his head to clear it of the blow he had received, Steve strode over to him and asked harshly, "Where's the Malectron."

Pointing with a shaking hand at a box strapped to the top of the control panel, he replied, "That's it. Please don't kill me. I was only following orders."

"Just like the Nazis and the Liberals," Heather commented with disgust in her voice.

Ignoring this, Steve asked, "Do you know how to operate it?"

Nodding, Jim said, "I do."

Turning to Major Cage, Steve said, "I need that box, my new buddy, Jim, and one of those helicopters." Looking at Hawkins with disgust, he added, "And I might as well take this asshole along for the ride. I have plans for him."

Not used to taking orders from a civilian, Cage balked for a second until he realized what Steve wanted to do. Glancing at where Heather and Doctor Connors were checking Cindy's wounds, he knew that they would have had little chance in coming up with a way to kill the dead if it wasn't for Steve and his people.

Making his decision, he walked over to the biohazard alarm and pulled the handle.

CHAPTER TWENTY-THREE

Fort Redoubt:

Seeing one of the dead make it through the wall and past the spearmen, Tick-Tock fired twice into its snarling face as he wondered how long his ammunition would last. With fifteen major breaches in the past two hours, it was taking every bit of effort from those inside the fort to keep the dead from flooding into the compound.

Watching as a dozen creatures from hell squirmed through another gap where two telephone poles had been pushed in, he raised his rifle, but held fire when five men rushed in with long spears. With short thrusts used to punch holes in the craniums of the dead, they quickly eliminated them. More walking corpses moved forward to be dispatched by the spearmen, causing a logjam of lifeless flesh to stack up in the gap. Tick-Tock noticed that while the dead were plugging the hole with their bodies as they fell, the reanimated corpses behind them were clawing them out of the way just as fast in their quest to get in. Anxiously, he looked around for the men and women in the patching crew, but saw they were already busy on two other breaks.

Turning his attention back to the wall, Tick-Tock watched as one of the spearmen missed his mark, hitting his target in the shoulder when it moved at the last second. Trying to retract his spear from the creature, the man screamed when the dead thing lunged forward, pushing the shaft of the weapon through its own body as it sought to get closer to the food. In an attempt to kick it off, the spearman raised his foot just as three more of the dead squirmed their way through the gap, grabbing his leg and sinking their teeth into it.

Seeing he was a goner, Tick-Tock shot him once in the back of the head.

With only four spearmen to resist them, the dead slowly forced the living back.

Sighting in on the reanimated corpses tearing at the fallen spearman, Tick-Tock squeezed the trigger of his M4, firing off three rounds and downing all three of the dead. Reaching for his final magazine, fear ripped through him when he realized it was gone. Darting his eyes back and forth as he searched the ground, he spotted it lying near the breach in the wall where he had been standing when the dead started pushing their way in. Looking around for help, he saw that the other armed men and women had their hands full as they shot down the Zs that were on the verge of pouring into the compound. From all around the fort, he could hear the steady sound of gunfire, telling him that the dead were breaking in all over the compound.

With anger brought on by fear at what seemed to be a hopeless situation, Tick-Tock let out a bellow of rage before rushing forward. Twisting out of the grasp of one of the dead that had made it through the gap, he reached down and ripped the spear from the body of the creature he had shot and started punching holes in the skulls of the dead. Crazed by rage, his vision went red as he thrust forward again and again with the spear. As he reached the hole in the wall, he had the presence of mind to pick up the loaded magazine for his rifle before returning to his slaughter of the walking corpses.

The light around him dimmed as he advanced. He could hear nothing, but took no notice. Focused only on killing the dead, he lost sense of time and space, concentrating only on the twisted face in front of him before shoving the point of the spear through it and moved on to the next. His combat training took over, naturally directing him to climb atop the piles of dead bodies to keep the high ground as he advanced. His adrenalin pumping, he felt like he could go on forever, wiping out all the dead-asses by himself.

Suddenly feeling himself being grabbed and pulled rearward, he twisted his body and fought against the creatures that had gotten behind him. Thrusting backward with his spear, he felt himself immobilized as more hands grabbed it while also latching onto his arms and legs. With a bellow of rage that he couldn't hear, his right hand slipped down to the pocket where he had secured his last magazine of ammunition, struggling against the buttons securing the flap over the cargo pocket. With his only thought being that if he was going down that he would take as many of them with him as he could, Tick-Tock hoped that the dead would first tear into his chainmail shirt before finding flesh. This would give him enough time to clear them off him. As he was pulled to the ground and dragged rearward, a face appeared directly above his, causing him to relax. In an instant, he knew it was over.

His hearing coming back as the killing fury left him, he could barely make out Rick Styles yelling, "You crazy son-of-a-bitch, you were almost ten feet outside the wall. What the fuck do you think you're doing?"

Smiling at what he took as a compliment, Tick-Tock let his fellow defenders pull him into the fort. Even when he was safely inside, they still restrained him, worried that his berserker rage hadn't been spent. Knowing he had to get his head and his ass wired together, Tick-Tock tried to get his mind to shed the dregs of the insanity that had possessed him by focusing on the men and women hammering a patch in the hole they had just pulled him through.

The sight of dead arms and legs thrusting through the openings between the boards disturbed him for some reason, so he turned his attention to the sound of gunfire coming from around the compound. Noticing that it seemed to be diminishing, he worried that everyone was on their last rounds or were fighting with sharpened sticks like himself.

When his hearing was fully back and his mind clear, Tick-Tock felt he had returned to reality enough to be released. Croaking out something that even he didn't understand, he swallowed a few times to wet his throat and managed to say, "I'm fine, you can let me up."

The people restraining him looked skeptical, but Rick stepped forward and said, "Turn that crazy bastard loose. We might need him again."

Feeling his limbs freed, Tick-Tock rolled onto his hands and knees before slowly rising to his feet. While he was examining himself for wounds, Rick told him, "We already checked. I don't know how you did it, but you didn't get bit. You got a few tears in your shirt, but I think that armor you wear stopped you from getting infected." Looking at where his people were securing the last board over the gap in the telephone poles, he added in a quiet voice, "I have to thank you though. From what the people here told me, they were about to be overrun when you went full Viking and pushed the dead-asses back so they could close the gap."

After considering Tick-Tock for a moment, Rick asked in a slightly awed voice, "What came over you. I only got here in enough time to catch the last of it, but you were like some kind of crazed beast."

Exhausted, Tick-Tock pulled the magazine of ammunition from his pocket, held it up and said, "I dropped my last clip and was trying to get it back from the dead-asses."

Rick laughed and said, "Well, I'm glad you got it because you're going to need it." Handing him his spear, he added, "You also might need this. Whatever ammunition you have on you is your last. Do what you can with it, but use it only as a last resort. We've managed to stop all the breakthroughs, but it's only a matter of time before we have more."

As if in response, a large crack came from the far side of the fort. Tick-Tock only needed a split-second to realize which direction it had come from before he was off and running. Not feeling the pain in his back, arms and shoulders from wielding the spear, his only thought was where the latest breakthrough was happening.

Exactly where he had left Denise.

Reaching the parapets where Denise had been sleeping, and seeing it had collapsed to lie in a jumble at the base of the wall, Tick-Tock's felt his stomach drop before it leapt back into his throat to almost choke him. Looking frantically through the wreckage, he was surprised when he couldn't find any bodies. Spinning around at the sound of her voice, he found his love directing the crews rushing forward to close the gap in the wall.

Running up to her and grabbing her in his arms, Tick-Tock said with relief, "You're safe."

Looking at him like he was crazy, she replied, "Of course I am. We heard the wall start to break long before it caved in so we got the hell out of the way."

Turning his attention to the split in their defenses, Tick-Tock saw that it was a major one, probably the worst since the dead first surrounded them. Seven of the telephone poles had been pushed in, one so far that it was almost standing straight up. When the dead had first hit the wall, hundreds of them had been crushed into the wedge at its base, and these now made a step that others crawled up to push their weight against the upper part of the barrier where it was weakest and they had more leverage. Although he knew if they had built the wall straight up and down that it would never have withstood the initial assault, he wished they had used something heavier.

Like steel beams.

Knowing this was fantasy, Tick-Tock reacted by rushing forward. Before he had taken two steps, he saw another 20 inch wide telephone pole being levered out of position by the dead as they forced their way in. With the constant sound of gunfire, the whining of the dead, and the screams of the defenders almost deafening him, he couldn't make out any orders coming from the officers. Not slowing, he started slapping people on the back to get their attention as he passed them, calling out, "Follow me," as he ran into the middle of the fray.

A few of the defenders he tagged followed him immediately, but most stayed frozen in place at the thought of rushing toward the dead now pouring through the wall. By the time Tick-Tock and his recruits reached the few defenders trying to hold the savage horde back, they numbered only ten. Without thought for their own lives, they used whatever was at hand to stop the flow of corpses coming at them. Clubs were raised and lowered onto dead skulls too many times to count as spears were thrust forward, twisted, and quickly retracted to be pushed in again to skewer the corrupt brains of the dead. Occasionally, one of the Zs would slip by them, only to be promptly shot down by one of the rifle men that covered them.

Tick-Tock looked neither left nor right as he repeatedly shoved the point of his spear into the craniums of the dead. Aiming for an eye, or the dripping, black orb where it had been torn out, he found this was the fastest way to drill into what was left of their brain and eliminate the dead. He could see that while he and his small group weren't pushing the dead back, at the same time they were keeping them from flooding into the compound. Hope surged through him that with a few reinforcements, they would be able to push the Zs back. Realizing that he could see his targets better, he blinked his eyes rapidly in the first light of the rising sun.

Looking around wildly for more people to help them, Tick-Tock stopped when he saw the beginning of the end of Fort Redoubt.

With the dead scrambling over those crushed against the base of the wall in the initial assault, and with the thousands behind them clambering over each other in their unrelenting urge to feed, the dead had managed to build a bridge of dead flesh high enough to cross the top of the wall. At first visible in ones and two across a fifty foot wide swath, in the dim illumination of the light, Tick-Tock watched in horror as they became a flood of bodies scrambling between the wooden spikes to slide down the inner face of the wall and attack across a wide span.

Looking around for Denise, he spied her thirty feet behind him, frantically motioning to him to run. Glancing to his left and right, he noticed that everyone else was turning to flee the dead. Disgusted at their cowardice, Tick-Tock joined them, knowing that he couldn't stand against the hordes alone. With the dead close behind him as he fled, his mind spun as he tried to think of a place where he and Denise would be safe. Coming up blank, he knew it would only be a matter of minutes before the Zs rolled over everyone in the camp and the feasting began. If they only had a few more people to defend this section, they might have been able to hold the dead off.

Out of breath as he neared where Denise was waving for him to hurry, Tick-Tock was about to vent his anger at the others giving up, when she cut him off by screaming, "It's too late. Get down," as she dropped flat on the ground.

Peering through the haze of gun smoke and dust kicked up by the defenders, Tick-Tock saw why everyone had abandoned their positions. They weren't fleeing the dead, they were getting the hell out of the way. Lunging forward, he threw his body across Denise as the twang-thump of the porcupines filled the air.

As soon as the whistle of darts flying over his head dissipated, Tick-Tock jumped to his feet and hoisted Denise to hers. Keeping her hand clenched in his, he pulled her along as he ran toward the semi-circle of defenders that had set up around the breakthrough to push the dead back.

Reaching safety, Tick-Tock turned to see that while the dead who had made it over their defenses had been wiped out, more were pouring over the wall. As he heard calls of, "Fall back," and, "Retreat," mixed with the screaming of people running one way and then the other as they found the barricades of Fort Redoubt being breached in this manner all around the perimeter, he knew this was the end.

An aching in his left hand made him look down, and seeing the rifle still clenched in it, he turned to Denise and said, "Whatever happens, don't leave my side."

Tick-Tock's heart dropped as he said this. He knew it wasn't because he felt he could save his love, but when there was nowhere left to run or back up to, he would finish them both.

Using the bodies of their brethren as a walkway, the dead poured over the wall into the fort from all directions. With so much fresh meat close to their grasp, they rushed forward as one to claim it. In their mindless haste, they ran into a phalanx of desperate, spear and club wielding humans to fall by the hundreds. Despite this, the unending wave of dead swarmed forward as they were pushed by the thousands behind them.

At first bolstered by the porcupines, the living defenders quickly found the archaic weapons too slow to reload. One by one, the strongpoint set up around them fell to the onslaught of rushing dead, leaving the living to destroy them with spears, clubs, and stones. As they were backed into a slowly shrinking perimeter at the center of the compound, the living found their only respite when one of their own fell to the dead. When someone was dragged down, it caused a swarm of reanimated corpses to fall on the spot, fighting each other for a mouthful of meat and giving the living a brief respite.

The bodies of the living and the dead that had been destroyed quickly piled up, pushing the humans into a steadily decreasing circle as more reanimated corpses crawled over the top of the gruesome heap and leapt at them in their attempt to feed. Old men and women rushed forward as the more able bodied fell, only to find themselves quickly exhausted by the fight and taken down.

When the man next to him was pulled into the mass of ragging dead, Tick-Tock used the pause to take a quick look around. After turning one way and then the other, he estimated that there were less than three hundred living being forced into a slowly shrinking ring. On his left, he locked eyes with Denise.

As he was trying to come up with something reassuring to say, she cut him off by shouting over the whining of the dead and the screaming of the defenders, "You're going to have to do it for me. I won't be able to do it myself."

Relieved and horrified that she understood how desperate their situation was, he yelled, "Now?"

Shaking her head, she replied, "At the last second, I want you to put a bullet through my brain. Until then, we fight."

Turning his attention back to the dead, Tick-Tock saw that his brief reprieve was over as three whining, naked creatures from hell lunged toward him. Blocking one with his chainmail coated arm, he jabbed forward with his spear to dispatch the second. The third was taken out by Denise as she connected with its head with a club she had taken from one of the fallen.

Seeing a dozen more dead take their place, Tick-Tock looked to the never-ending wall of walking corpses pushing forward over the mounds of bodies. He knew it was a hopeless situation, but his mind still raced as he tried to find some way out of the slaughter. Even though he had been given the okay to kill both Denise and himself before the dead infected them, he kept hope that he wouldn't have to resort to this dire finish.

His mind flashed to the radio and generator rooms, but after looking in that direction, he dismissed the idea. These were the two most secure buildings in the compound and were being used to house the children. Only twenty feet away from the advancing dead, Tick-Tock knew it wouldn't matter if he and Denise did manage to squeeze in, since the structures would only stand against the dead for a short while before being crushed and their inhabitants dragged out and torn apart.

The thought of this angered him, but it wasn't enough to overcome the exhaustion racking his body. As he tried to tap into his earlier berserker strength, he knew it wouldn't come. His body, mind and soul had reached their limits. Looking over to Denise swinging her club in slower and slower arcs, he knew it was almost time. He would rather it came quick and painless for her, so he dropped his spear and unslung his rifle.

Reaching down to pull the charging handle back, Tick-Tock heard an unusual noise as he sighted in on the side of his love's head. Over the whining of the dead and the screams of the last few defenders, he heard something that he hadn't heard in what seemed like years. Looking up, he saw a dim shape coming over the trees in the distance before slowing to hover over the center of their steadily shrinking perimeter. Recognizing it instantly, he screamed at the top of his lungs in triumph as he turned his M4 away from Denise and toward the onrushing dead.

***

Taking in the situation on the ground at a glance, Steve pulled the boom microphone of his headset away from his mouth and yelled at Jim, "Turn that thing on."

Holding his hands up in futility, he replied, "I need a power source. I need at least five thousand watts powering two-hundred and twenty volts."

Knowing by the lights visible atop the half demolished wall that the compound still had electricity, Steve leaned out of the side door and scanned the few remaining buildings in the slowly shrinking circle of the living. As he spotted a low block structure with dozens of cables stretching out of it, he leaned between the seats of the pilot and copilot and yelled, "I need you to set us down there."

After quickly checking the situation, the pilot started giving orders to his crew to prep the area so they could land.

***

Firing off the last of the bullets in his magazine at the wall of advancing dead, Tick-Tock dropped his M4 as he searched for another weapon. Spotting a table leg that someone had been using as a club, he snatched it up and jumped into the steadily diminishing line next to Denise. His energy renewed at the sight of the reinforcements, he dispatched two of the advancing corpses before glancing back at the helicopter.

Seeing it still hovering over the center of their perimeter, he regretted not saving two rounds for Denise and himself as he screamed at it, "Did you just come to fucking watch, or are you going to do something?"

In answer, the mini-guns in the side doors of the helicopter opened up, spraying a wall of 7.62 bullets into the dead at almost five-thousand rounds per minute. The two door gunner's aim was true, cutting into the heads and shoulders of the living dead not three feet in front of the defenders, mowing down the attacking cadavers and sending up a shower of black ochre along with chunks of brains, skulls and flesh. The whine of the Gatling guns quickly overpowered the whine of the dead as they swept back and forth across the horde like a fire hose.

At the first sound of firing, Tick-Tock grabbed Denise and pulled her back as he continued to swing his club at the dead coming toward them. Although stunned as he watched the sudden onslaught of death from above, he only staggered a few feet backward before stopping and moving forward and destroy the few dead still standing. As he cut into the remaining thin line of reanimated corpses, he heard the guns stop and the pitch of the rotors change as the helicopter landed.

After spearing the last of the dead that had been too close to be destroyed by the mini-guns, Tick-Tock looked at the mobs of dead further out, climbing across the shattered bodies of their brethren in their quest to eat. While thousands had been cut down, the thousands that remained in the herd were still advancing on them. Judging the distance, he guessed they had a few minutes before the wall of corpulent flesh reached them.

Turning to the helicopter, Tick-Tock could see it was already being mobbed as the survivors of Fort Redoubt tried to climb aboard. Through the chaos, he saw three figures trying to fight their way through them. Spotting two familiar faces, Tick-Tock felt a grin cross his face as he yelled at Denise, "Come on, they need our help."

***

Jim cowered behind Steve and Brain as they pushed people aside, screaming at the mob to get out of the way. In a frenzy, the people trying to get on the Blackhawk screamed back at the two men to save them. A million thoughts flashed through Steve's mind, including using his M16 to clear the way. Instead, he raised it into the air and fired off a burst. When this barely fazed the frenzied crowd, he lifted the butt of his rifle to knock them aside. As he was about to come down on the head of a younger man clawing at his shirt, he saw him grabbed from behind and jerked out of the way.

Thinking by the way he had been snatched backward that one of the dead had gotten him, Steve spun his rifle around and lowered its barrel into the first face that came into view. As his finger started to squeeze the last half ounce of pressure on the trigger, he stopped in shock at who he was aiming at.

"Tick-Tock," he yelled in joy at the sight of his friend.

"Where are the evacuation choppers?" Tick-Tock asked without preamble.

"Glad to see you too," Steve said with a laugh. "It was a battle, but Washington released ten choppers out of Fort Polk to pull everyone out. They're about a twenty minutes behind us."

Pointing to the dead advancing across a field of bodies, Tick-Tock said, "We don't have an hour. Unless you've got a couple more gunships hidden up your ass, we've got about five minutes."

Lifting up the Malectron, Steve said, "I don't have any gunships, I've got something better."

***

Watching Tick-Tock disappear into the generator building with Steve, Brain and another man, Denise turned her attention to the oncoming wave of dead. Hefting her club, she heard a familiar voice call her name. As she turned, she found Rick Styles coming toward her.

"What's going on?" He asked. "I saw Steve and Brain running like hell for the generators, but when I tried to ask Steve, he told me he didn't have time to explain." Pointing to the Blackhawk, he added, "And where's the evacuation helicopters? That thing won't hold more than ten or twelve people."

Glancing around to gauge the distance to the oncoming dead, Denise saw she had enough time to tell Rick what she knew. "The choppers are about twenty minutes out," she told him. Seeing Rick's face fall as he looked at the solid wall of dead-asses coming toward them, she added, "But Steve has some kind of plan to hold off the dead until they get here."

Confused, Rick asked, "What kind of plan? If he wants to help us hold off the dead, he needs to get his ass out here."

Shaking her head, Denise replied, "I don't know what he's doing. I don't know anything more than what I just told you." The conversation over, she turned to face the dead.

Her head spinning as she crushed the skull of a straggler that had survived the helicopter's staffing raid, Denise didn't think she would last long. While she had faith in Tick-Tock, she wasn't sure how much more she could take due to her concussion. Her head felt like it had swelled up to twice its normal size and she felt herself swaying back and forth as she tried not to throw up.

Looking at the wall of dead coming toward her, she took a deep breath and prepared to meet them. As she tried to pick out her first target, she saw it was useless. Packed shoulder to shoulder, the dead were so thick, and coming so fast, that she would be lucky to take out any of them before being taken down. Glancing back at the generator room, she wanted to call out for Tick-Tock, but knew he wouldn't hear her. Shifting her body as she turned to meet the onrushing wave of resurrected corpses, she lifted her club as she watched their advance.

When they were twenty feet away, she saw them stagger and lurch over the bodies piled in heaps on the ground. At fifteen feet, she saw them gain momentum as they reached the relatively flat section of bodies mowed down by the mini-guns. As they sped up, she could hear sporadic rifle fire as some of the defenders tried to stop the assault, while others used their weapons to take their own lives. From the beginning, she knew she couldn't kill herself, so she glanced one more time in the direction of the generator building, praying that Tick-Tock would show up and end her life for her.

Not seeing anything except the wall of advancing dead coming at her from that direction, she turned to face her fate with the hope she would be torn apart so badly that she couldn't come back. Raising her club at the onrushing dead only feet away, she suddenly felt as if her body was being electrified. All of the hair on her arms, legs and head stood on end, reminding her of when she had taken speed in college. Wondering if this was how everyone felt when they died, she swung her club in a wide arc at the closest zombie.

And missed.

Stunned that she didn't connect with the head of the Z, Denise twisted her body and tried to connect on the backswing.

And missed again.

Not understanding, she stopped and took aim at the first head she could distinguish in writhing mob of dead only feet away. Swinging down with deadly force, she felt anger rush through her when the dead thing lurched backward, making her miss for the third time.

Frustrated, she took a step forward, but was restrained by Rick.

"Something's stopping them," The Commander yelled.

Pausing, Denise could see that what he was saying was true. The whining of the dead had turned into a moaning as they looked around wildly, frozen in place only feet away. Their arms still reached out at the fresh meat in front of them, but their bodies seemed to be held back by some invisible force. Then she noticed a shift. In tiny increments, they were backing away. She observed that they weren't moving to the rear as fast as they had come at them, but as she watched, the entire mob of dead started inching backward.

Her shoulders slumping in exhaustion, Denise let her arms drop to her sides and the club slip from her fingers. The intensity of the moment, combined with nausea from her concussion, hit her at once and she bent over to throw up. When she recovered, she looked around in wonder at the expanding circle of dead. Now almost climbing over each other in their haste to get away, they moved past the destroyed walls of Fort Redoubt and into the field beyond before they stopped. Swaying slightly as she felt herself start to slip away into unconsciousness, she felt two arms steady her. Turning, she saw it was Tick-Tock.

Letting herself lean against him as her vision shrank to a pinpoint, Denise could only ask, "What?"

"It's something Steve brought along," he explained. "It pushes the dead back."

As the darkness closed in, joy swept through her at the knowledge that she and her love had lived through hell.

***

With so few left to rescue, the airlift went quickly. As Steve, Tick-Tock, Denise, Rick Styles and Ginny climbed onto the last helicopter, they paused to look back across the destruction of Fort Redoubt. Lost in thought at how many had been killed, their eyes scanned the area until settling, with some satisfaction, on one particular sight.

When the pilot called for them that it was time to go, Steve pulled a two-way radio from his pocket and pushed the transmit button before saying, "Unplug it, Brain and then get your ass on the chopper." Donning a flight helmet, he adjusted it as he made sure he was connected to the pilot and co-pilot.

From across the compound, Brain came out of the generator room at a full sprint with Tick-Tock laughing at him and yelling, "Run, Pork chop. Run. They're right behind you."

From the thousands of dead circling their position, the moans of the reanimated corpses returned to whines as the repellant power of the Malectron stopped. Now, with nothing to hold them back, they rushed forward as one.

The helicopter left the ground as soon as Brain was aboard, and as it powered into the air, Steve said into the intercom, "Captain, please do me a favor and hover at a hundred feet. There's something we want to make sure of."

"We only have enough fuel to stay on station for about five minutes," he replied.

Judging the distance between the onrushing dead, and where Hawkins and Jim were running in one direction and then another atop the chow hall as they sought an escape route from the quickly tightening circle of ravenous zombies, he replied, "Don't worry, Captain. It won't take more than a few seconds."

The dead hit the building, collapsing what was left of it and falling on both men at the same time. With so many carnivores, and so little meat, they were quickly covered by clawing hands and teeth that ripped them apart.

Regardless of what Hawkins and Jim had done, Ginny had been against leaving them on the ground. Steve looked to where she had her arm wrapped around Rick Styles' shoulder and thought back to when Heather had explained to him in Clearwater how she gravitated to whoever was in charge. Ginny glared at him and then said something into Rick's ear.

Seeing Rick look at him, wink and smile, Steve knew that this man wasn't about to fall for any of Ginny's shit-talking. She might try to stir something up, but Rick would keep her in line. He knew the secret to surviving in this world.

Leaning back in his seat, Steve closed his eyes as he thought; never take yourself too seriously.

CHAPTER TWENTY-FOUR

Fort Polk, Louisiana

Hundreds of people watched from nearby helicopters, and through video feed, as the bi-plane dropped out of the sky. After wagging its wings once, the crop duster started spraying a yellowish mist from its vents, coating the hundreds of dead staggering down Highway 171. For some time, nothing happened, causing many to think that the test was a failure. As General Eastridge was about to call for the pilot to make another pass, the first walking corpse dropped to the ground. One of the observation aircraft zoomed in with its camera, showing a black, puss-like substance leaking from its nose, mouth and eyes.

Holding their breath, the observers watched in amazement as more of the living dead dropped to lay on the ground, their life's blood seeping from every orifice in their body.

From his hospital bed in Washington DC, General Eastridge turned to Admiral Sedlak and commented, "As my son likes to say, 'That's a wrap.' "

Owens Grove, Louisiana:

Jimmy McPherson carefully made his way over and around the rotting bodies of the dead, wrinkling his nose in disgust at their smell. Glancing down, he saw what was left of their shirts and chests soaked in the black goo they used for blood, seemingly having come from their nose, mouth and ears in a torrent. He didn't know what was wiping these creatures out, but whatever it was, he was grateful. He still occasionally came across an active biter, but for the last few days, these were few and far in between.

His first sign that something was killing the dead was when he had been forced to cut through a small town in southern Arkansas. He had watched for two hours before approaching its outskirts, but had seen none of the walking corpses until he reached the center of town. Here, he found a small square loaded with corpses, but they weren't walking around. Hundreds of bodies lay scattered across the road, covered in black goo that ran from their decaying carcasses into pools before flowing in small rivulets between the cobblestones.

At first worried that the Army had exterminated the Zs, and that they still might be around, Jimmy ran down a side street to find somewhere to hide. Coming across more bodies, he noticed that their faces, chests and crotches were soaked with the black ochre they used for blood. Looking closer, he noticed that besides the ravages of being bitten and torn when they were alive, and then walking around dead for a few months, none of them had a head wound that would account for their demise.

Cautiously, he made his way back to the town square to look around. Not finding any ejected shell casings, he knew gunfire hadn't taken down the dead. Pausing to try and make sense of it, he only considered the situation for a second before accepting it for what it was and moving on.

With the absence of the dead, Jimmy noticed more and more signs of the living over the next days, but these had been mostly eyes in windows, peering with fear through slits in barricades as they watched his passing. He had come across a farmer two days ago that had been suspicious but friendly, telling him that he was on the right road to Owens Grove, but it was still a ways off. He also warned him of the Army setting up roadblocks, and advised him to make a detour so he would come at the town from the south.

Now stepping over another body sinking into the dirt as it rotted away to become one with the earth, he looked around to get his bearings, quickening his pace to get away from the stink of the dead. He knew he was close to home but he wasn't exactly sure how close. With no one to tend them, the fields had grown wild to spill onto the road, narrowing it down to no more than a wide trail and obliterating any landmarks. A hundred feet ahead, he spotted where it had been cut back, telling him that someone was alive and farming. If they were friendly, he would ask for directions. If not, he would move along. He was close enough to home that he might know who it was, and his spirits rose at the thought of seeing a familiar face again. Who knew, he thought, they might even have information on his brothers and sisters.

Closing on the opening to his left, something familiar along the edge of the road caught Jimmy's eye. It had been months since he'd seen it, so it took him a moment to understand why it jogged his memory. When it all came together though, his heart leapt and he let out a whoop of Joy.

Tilted slightly back from thousands of deliveries being stuffed into it, and with its white paint faded from the sun, the mailbox stood where it had for decades. Knowing that when he got closer he would see an equally faded red 'McPherson' painted on its side, Jimmy felt tears squeeze their way from the corners of his eyes. Not believing it was real, he stretched his hand out as he hurried forward to touch it.

His attention was drawn by movement on his left, and when he turned, he saw a woman approached him across the clearing with an M16 held at the ready. He had come too far to be shot down now, so he stopped and held his hands out from his body. Beyond her, he could see the ruins of the farmhouse he had grown up in had been arraigned into a fort of sorts, where two other figures aimed rifles at him from the rubble. Not recognizing the dirty bedraggled people, he wondered if squatters had taken over their land. If that was the case, he would leave peacefully and come back later. This meant war.

Focusing on the immediate threat, he was trying to decide how to deal with the woman coming toward him when he saw her suddenly stop and let her rifle drop to her side. With her head tilted in disbelief and her eyes wide, her mouth moved, but no sound came out as she tried to form his name.

Dirty and looking like she had aged ten years, Jimmy barely recognized Jo-Jo. Swallowing the lump in his throat, he choked out his sister's name. From behind her, he could see his other sister Jackie emerge from the wreckage that had once been their home, coming toward him in a rush with his brother Jessie in tow, both of them calling his name.

Falling to his knees, Jimmy let his body slump in relief as tears rolled down his face.

He couldn't believe it.

He had made it.

He was home...

Fort Polk, Louisiana:

Connie and Brain were the first to leave. Wanting to see if their friends and relatives were still alive, they decided to embark on a cross country search for their loved ones. As they drove away from Fort Polk, they looked in amazement at the steady stream of small to gigantic crop dusters and water dropping planes flying in and out of the airfield.

Turning to Connie, Brain said, "They told me this morning that this is going on all over the country. Now that most of the big herds of dead have been pushed together by the Malectron and wiped out, they're doing search and destroy missions on any small ones that get reported. If they see so much as a single Z staggering along a back country road, they wash it down."

Watching a low flying DC-10 go over them, Connie asked, "Is it safe though? I mean, they're spraying so much of that stuff around, and they don't even know what the effects are on humans. They're so hot to wipe out the dead that they never really tested it."

Shaking off thoughts of Agent Orange, Brain reached over and grabbed his love's hand. Giving it a squeeze, he said, "I used to have hope, but now I have faith. It will all work out, Honey."

***

Out of the corner of his eye, Tick-Tock watched with suspicion as Steve and Heather made their way through the motor pool toward him. Ignoring them as he loaded a case of MRE's into the back of the Humvee and reached for another, he dreaded the coming scene.

When Steve started to raise his arms as he neared, Tick-Tock said, "If you try to hug me, I'm going to knee you in the balls." Turning his attention to Heather, he added, "You, on the other hand, are more than welcome to come and get a piece of me."

Heather laughed and stepped forward, embracing Tick-Tock like she would never let go. When he started squirming like a little kid being kissed by his great aunt, she turned to Denise and the two women fell into each other's arms, tears rolled from their eyes as they went back and forth about how much they would miss each other.

Turning away from the emotional scene before it got him going too, Steve said, "This kind of sucks. We had to find out from Rick and Stacey that that you were taking off. You couldn't even say goodbye?"

Securing a backpack into the Humvee with a bungee cord, Tick-Tock replied, "I was going to swing by on my way out of Dodge."

Knowing that his friend wasn't big on emotional goodbyes, Steve changed the subject by asking, "Where are you heading?"

Tilting his head to one side, Tick-Tock replied, "I'm not exactly sure. Wherever we end up, we're going by sailboat. Denise wants to go to Europe, but I want to see Australia. I decided that we're going to flip a coin. Heads, we go east, and tails we go west."

"Very scientific," Steve said sardonically.

Tick-Tock grinned and replied, "That's what Denise said." In a lower voice he added, "And if she doesn't win, I'll let her go two out of three, or three out of five until she does. She deserves it after everything she's been through. I've heard Europe is almost done clearing out the dead, but some of the more remote places are still having problems with them, so that kind of swayed my decision too."

Steve nodded and said, "The anti-virus that Doctor Connors cooked up is being mass produced and distributed worldwide, but after dead-day, a lot of little crackpot governments and fiefdoms popped up. We even have a few communities scattered around the states that don't want the government stepping in. President Eastridge and the other eleven on the committee are trying to contact all of them, but some of them don't want their help. There's still a lot of chaos out there."

Tick-Tock shrugged and said, "Then fuck them. Let them be overrun by the dead-asses if they don't want help." Nodding to where his people were loading another Humvee, he added, "And besides, look at how great those committees work. We started off with a shitload of live committee members and now we're down to two."

Steve smiled at his friend's comment and pointed out, "And I see you're taking them with you, so that's got to say something on how people learn. Besides, the new government doesn't work like they did. They're not trying to alienate people, they're trying their best to wipe out the dead and get everything up and running again."

Fastening the cover on the back of the Humvee, Tick-Tock said, "Then I guess I'll get to see it when I come back to the States." Calling for Denise and his people to load up, Tick-Tock looked across the motor pool at the flurry of activity and said in a quiet voice, "Doesn't look like that will be anytime soon though. To tell you the truth, there's too much organization and too many rules for me. Even though that buddy of yours, Cage, got command of Polk, it's getting a little rare around here. We might still get treated like the saviors of the free world as we know it, but I know that's wearing off when I get yelled at for throwing a cigarette butt on the ground. Denise and I decided that we're going to explore the new world out there, and if anyone comes along and tries to tell us how to live our lives, we'll just move on. Europe got hit harder than most continents because of their strict gun laws, so there's probably entire towns with only a few living people in them. You should think about coming along. We can hang out in Paris, London and the French Riviera."

Steve laughed and replied, "Cindy, Heather and I are leaving for North Carolina in a few days. Heather has got family there that she wants to check up on. The military didn't want to give Cindy up, but there are no more tests left to be done to her. Besides, she..." Steve paused before continuing, "*We*...all need time to heal. Beyond North Carolina, who knows? After the Usual Suspects, I'm not too hot on going anywhere by sailboat, so I think we'll stick to the Americas and dry land."

Tick-Tock reached out with his right hand and said. "One thing I do know is how much you like plans, so let's make one. In one year, we meet in Key Largo for the first annual Zombie Annihilation Squad of America reunion. We can talk about how wide everyone's ass has gotten and laugh at how insane we were."

Steve smiled as he stretched out his own hand to grasp Tick-Tock's and said, "It's a deal. But how do we let Brain and Connie know."

Tick-Tock laughed and said, "I already did. I told them before they took off."

The two men shook hands, but it only lasted a second before turning into a hug.

As they broke away from each other, Tick-Tock said, "Be careful."

Steve nodded as he replied, "And you do the same."

Watching his best friend drive off, Steve felt Heather slide her arm around his waist. They stood silently for a few minutes until the two Humvee's disappeared into the confusion of the motor pool.

When they were gone from sight, Steve looked around at the mass of activity and said, "I know we talked about leaving in a few days, but how about we go tomorrow? This place is getting a little crowded."

Wrapping him in a hug, Heather gave him a kiss and said, "I'm with you, Babe. I'll get Cindy ready to leave tonight. Let's go see what's out there."

As they walked hand in hand back to their quarters, Steve thought of all the good men and women that had given their lives in the quest. Their names and faces would forever be burned into his memory, just as they were engraved in a monument at the entrance to Fort Polk.

At the bottom of the memorial was something he had insisted be added.

"They never lost their humanity."

Finis

August 29, 2014
Naples, Florida

AFTERWORD

Let's just keep it short and simple:
I hope you've enjoyed reading The Dead Series even half as much as I enjoyed writing it.

Godspeed...

Jon Schafer

Made in United States
Orlando, FL
10 December 2022

26086793R00095